TARZAN AND THE VALLEY OF GOLD

EDGAR RICE BURROUGHS UNIVERSE™

The Edgar Rice Burroughs Universe is the interconnected and cohesive literary cosmos created by the Master of Adventure and continued in new canonical works authorized by Edgar Rice Burroughs, Inc., the corporation based in Tarzana, California, that was founded by Burroughs in 1923. Unravel the mysteries and explore the wonders of the Edgar Rice Burroughs Universe alongside the pantheon of heroes and heroines that inhabit it in both classic tales of adventure penned by Burroughs and brand-new epics from today's talented authors.

*This was not only one of the strangest jungle trips he had ever taken,
but also one of the strangest jungles he had ever traversed.*

TARZAN AND THE VALLEY OF GOLD

By

FRITZ LEIBER

Cover art by
RICHARD HESCOX

Interior illustrations by
DOUGLAS KLAUBA

EDGAR RICE BURROUGHS, Inc.
Publishers
TARZANA   CALIFORNIA

Tarzan and the Valley of Gold
© 1966, 2019 by Edgar Rice Burroughs, Inc.

Trademarks including Edgar Rice Burroughs®; Edgar Rice Burroughs Universe™; Enter the Edgar Rice Burroughs Universe™; ERB Universe™; the Wild Adventures of Edgar Rice Burroughs™; Tarzan®; Tarzan of the Apes®; Lord of the Jungle®; Tarzan and Jane®; The Tarzan Twins™; Barsoom®; John Carter®; John Carter of Mars®; Dejah Thoris®; A Princess of Mars®; The Gods of Mars®; The Warlord of Mars®; Pellucidar®; David Innes™; Amtor™; Carson of Venus®; Caspak™; The Land That Time Forgot™; Va-nah™; The Moon Maid™; The Moon Men™; The Mucker™; The Custers™; The Eternal Savage™; The Mad King™; The War Chief™; The Apache Devil™; The Cave Girl™; The Girl from Farris's™; The Girl from Hollywood™; I Am a Barbarian™; The Lad and the Lion™; The Man-Eater™; The Monster Men™; The Outlaw of Torn™; and Pirate Blood™ owned by Edgar Rice Burroughs, Inc. The Doodad symbol; the Edgar Rice Burroughs Universe™ logo; the Enter the Edgar Rice Burroughs Universe™ logo; the ERB Universe™ logo; the ERB, Inc. solar system colophon; and the Since 1912 Tarzan® logo are trademarks of Edgar Rice Burroughs, Inc.

Cover art by Richard Hescox and interior illustrations by Douglas Klauba © 2019 Edgar Rice Burroughs, Inc.

Special thanks to Christopher Paul Carey, Scott Tracy Griffin, Janet Mann, Cathy Wilbanks, Tyler Wilbanks, and Mike Wolfer for their valuable assistance in producing this novel.

First hardcover edition

ISBN-13:
978-1-945462-20-7
- 9 8 7 6 5 4 3 2 1 -

Dedicated to the Memories of
Edgar Rice Burroughs
A. Conan Doyle
Talbot Mundy
and
Ian Fleming

and also to the Living Persons of
Hugh Walpole, semanticist
Clair Huffaker, script writer
and The Brazilian SPI

Morrer se preciso for, matar nunca!

The author wishes to acknowledge his indebtedness to Senhor Castro of the Los Angeles Brazilian Consulate for information about his country, and to Bob Foster and, in particular, to Andrew Kempner for information and visualizations graciously furnished about karate and ákido. However, none of these gentlemen should be held responsible for any improbabilities and unlikelihoods in this book.

TABLE OF CONTENTS

FOREWORD

S y Weintraub was ready to take Tarzan into the swingin' sixties. And he wasn't shy about telling the world.

"Tarzan is no longer the monosyllabic ape-man but the embodiment of culture, suavity and style," shared the filmmaker in "Tarzan: Still a Swinger but Suave," a July 1965 interview with the *London Sunday Times*. "He's equally at home in a posh nightclub or the densest jungle."

Weintraub, a hotshot young television producer from New York, had recently taken over the Tarzan film franchise in a metaphorical passing of the vine from veteran movie mogul Sol Lesser. Lesser had produced 16 Tarzan films in 25 years, and the time had come to step back. Weintraub and Lesser came to terms during an April 2, 1958, lunch meeting, with the latter selling his ape-man cinema stakes for $3 million.

Though Tarzan remained a financial juggernaut in the motion picture jungle, Lesser's traditional ape-man formula—including Tarzan's mate Jane, their adopted son Boy, Cheeta the chimp, and their treehouse accommodations—was waning with post–World War II audiences, which had grown increasingly sophisticated as the world shrank and radio, television, and theatrical newsreels brought exotic foreign lands into their consciousness.

Weintraub's vision was to update Tarzan, bringing the ape-man into the modern world with more mature plotlines and characterizations. Lesser's discovery Gordon Scott returned to the role in *Tarzan's Greatest Adventure* and *Tarzan the Magnificent*, a pair of films shot partially on location in East Africa and patterned after the popular Westerns of the day, with a lone Tarzan doggedly hunting down a band of criminals to bring them to rough jungle justice. Two more Tarzan films starring Jock Mahoney followed, set in India and Thailand, to take advantage of economical location shoots and enhance Tarzan's appeal to global audiences.

With each Tarzan film more profitable than the last, Weintraub was ready for the final phase in his plan—a trio of films shot in Latin America, starring Mike Henry, a handsome professional football player and former linebacker for the Pittsburgh Steelers and Los Angeles Rams, chosen from a pool of 400 candidates. At 6'3" and 220 pounds, (Tarzan film historian Gabe Essoe dubbed him "Tarzan by Michelangelo"), Henry seemed the ideal candidate to play this iteration of Tarzan, with which Weintraub would capitalize on the latest media fad—international intrigue investigated by spies like James Bond.

The first film on the slate, with the working title of *Tarzan '65*, saw the ape-man arriving in Mexico to stop scheming supercriminal Augustus Vinaro (David Opatoshu) from looting the lost civilization of Tucumai, aided by his hulking henchman Mr. Train (Don Megowan, like Mike Henry, an alumnus of the University of Southern California football team).

Starlet Sharon Tate was announced as Henry's female costar, but her manager Marty Ransohoff removed her from the picture before it began shooting, hoping to cast her in higher-profile fare. She was replaced by Nancy Kovack as Sophia, Vinaro's expendable moll who later casts her lot with the ape-man. The pair must also steward Ramel, the lost princeling of Tucumai (Manuel Padilla, Jr., in his first appearance in the franchise), back to his homeland, further complicating their journey. Beastly support came in the form of Major the lion, Dinky the chimp, and Bianco the leopard (changed to an indigenous jaguar in the novel).

Filmed entirely in Mexico on a budget of $1.25 million, production began on January 25, 1965, with locations including the Plaza de Toro arena, Chapultepec Castle, the Cacahuamilpa

Cave, and the Teotihuacán ruins, with interiors shot at Estudios Churubusco.

Retitled *Tarzan and the Valley of Gold* for theatrical release, the film was helmed by Robert Day, who would return for the succeeding Henry outing, *Tarzan and the Great River*—his fourth and final Tarzan feature as director. Cinematography was by Irving "Lippy" Lippman, whose 60-year career encompassed Roscoe "Fatty" Abuckle silents and television's *The Love Boat*. An upbeat title sequence crafted by Phill Norman garnered several industry awards. *Valley of Gold* was scripted by Clair Huffaker, a Western novelist and screenwriter, whose work here was rendered into a prose novelization by Hugo Award–winning fantasy author Fritz Leiber.

Leiber won the assignment from Edgar Rice Burroughs, Inc., Vice President Hulbert Burroughs after submitting the first chapter as a sample of his approach to the material, at the behest of publisher Ian Ballantine. The author included several details from Huffaker's script that did not make the big screen, including the battle at the car-wash, the use of machine-gun bolas to down the helicopter, the attempted overland assault on Tucumai, the prison stockade, and the tank trap. Leiber further embellished the storyline, adding color, exposition and details about Brazilian culture, politics, and geography not included in the film's brisk 90-minute run time. Among Leiber's additions were relocating the setting to the Amazon jungle and providing the lost tribe of Tucumai a mystical means of hiding their Incan civilization.

Tarzan and the Valley of Gold received only one paperback printing in 1966, falling out of print in the ensuing half century. Edgar Rice Burroughs, Inc., is pleased to rerelease this novel for a new generation in the first hardback edition.

Scott Tracy Griffin
Director of Special Projects
Edgar Rice Burroughs, Inc.

PREFACE

When Ian Ballantine of Ballantine Books, Inc., suggested the possibility of a book based on the Tarzan motion picture *Tarzan and the Valley of Gold*, featuring former Ram Football star Mike Henry as Tarzan, I was skeptical to say the least. Who was there, after all, who could even approximate the magic and style of Tarzan's creator, the late Edgar Rice Burroughs?

Mr. Ballantine then persuaded Hugo Award winner Fritz Leiber to write a trial chapter for a Tarzan yarn. When I read the piece, titled "Tarzan in the Bullring," I was very pleased and excited by Leiber's command of action and suspense. I immediately gave Mr. Ballantine our approval to proceed.

Fritz Leiber, an accomplished and successful author himself, has been an Edgar Rice Burroughs admirer for many years, and his novelization of the Clair Huffaker motion-picture script is a fast-moving and exciting Tarzan adventure that reflects his affectionate understanding for the character of Tarzan as created by Edgar Rice Burroughs.

I am certain that if Edgar Rice Burroughs were alive today he would very much enjoy reading *Tarzan and the Valley of Gold*.

> Hulbert Burroughs, Vice President,
> Edgar Rice Burroughs, Inc.
> Tarzana, Calif.
> April 25, 1966

EXIT FROM CAVES →

Elevation 3,000 ft.

TERRACES OF MAIZE

CIDADE DE TUCUMAI

Peccaries

WATER QUARRIES

QUINOA, MANIOC, ETC.

PASTURE FOR VICUNAS & LLAMAS

Elevation 1,000 ft.

Hardwoods →

Fruit trees

Great Temple of Sun

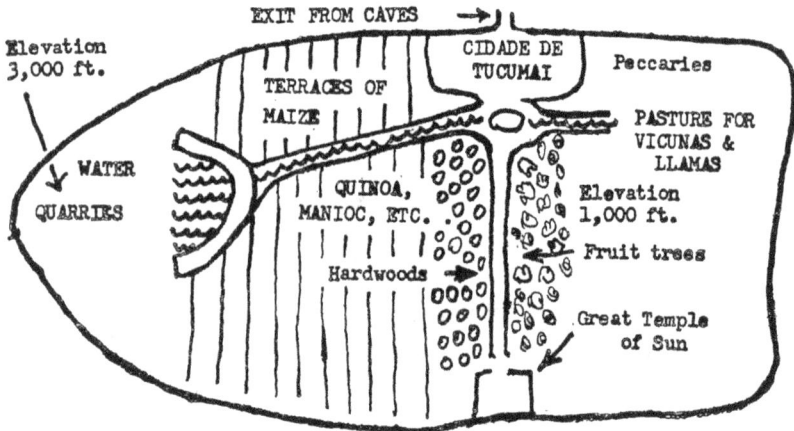

VALE DE TUCUMAI

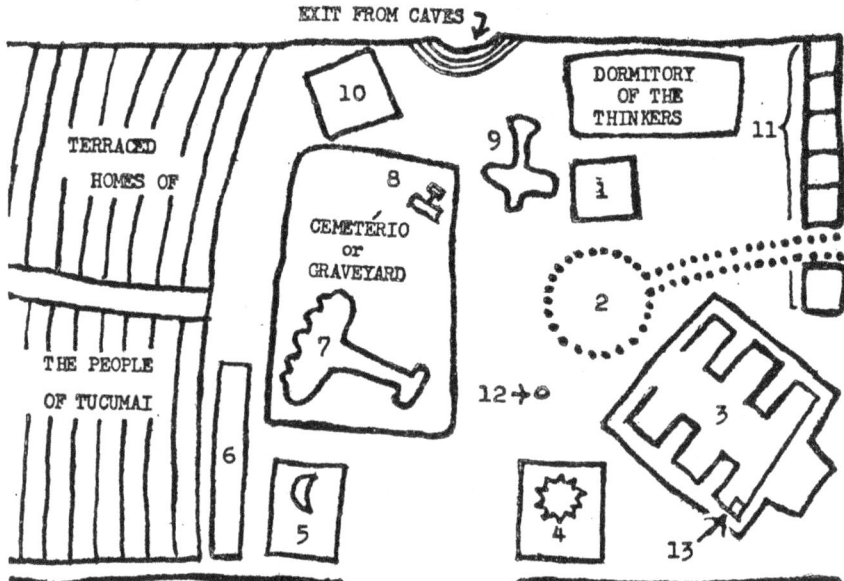

EXIT FROM CAVES

DORMITORY OF THE THINKERS

10

9

11

TERRACED HOMES OF

8

1

CEMETÉRIO or GRAVEYARD

2

THE PEOPLE OF TUCUMAI

7

12 →

6

3

5

4

13

1. PRISON
2. STOCKADE
3. TESOURARIA, or TREASURY
4. SMALL TEMPLE of SUN
5. TEMPLE OF MOON
6. HOUSE OF MAIDS

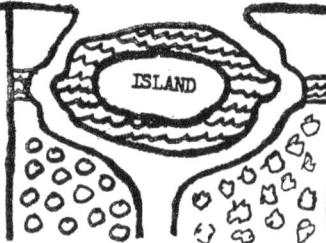

ISLAND

7. A-20
8. DEMOISELLE
9. CONDOR
10. TEMPLE CUPAY
11. WORKSHOPS
12. WELL CUPAY
13. WELL CUPAY

CIDADE DE TUCUMAI

DRAWN BY LIEUTENANT FONTOURA, CHECKED BY TARZAN AND
COLONEL JUAREZ, AND ENGLISHED BY PROFESSOR TALMADGE

CHAPTER 1

The Gate of Fright

A narrow shaft of sunlight, bringing its message of the hell of afternoon heat outside, lanced down the lofty stuccoed corridor of the hotel El Meseta in Central Mexico. It struck a golden burst from the tight-fitting, gold-sequined, pink-stockinged suit of the big, muscular Englishman standing in front of a door that had noise behind it. There was a square white cardboard box under his left arm.

The door opened eight inches. The noise redoubled, and there was a gush of the smoke of harsh black tobacco and the fumes of brandy and the reek of human sweat—all odors which the Englishman had noted halfway down the corridor. He could even have told you the exact number of men and women in the room—nine and two—and their approximate ages and states of health.

A dark face with a trace of awe in it looked up at him from under a mop of coarse black hair slicked back with gardenia-scented pomade.

"Señor Milord," the small man said, bowing slightly. He pointed toward the next door. "*There* my patron rests alone, in preparation for the dangers and exertions that come at four o'clock. *You* he will see."

"*Gracias,*" the Englishman thanked him softly and turned away in the direction indicated.

The small man watched, vaguely wondering what was in the white box. *El Inglés loco!*—he thought. *But within the hour the Englishman's madness will have been cured by the horns.*

1

He meant the horns of the bulls which are bred solely for fighting—and dying bravely—in the ring. In this case Miuras, the best, flown by jet at great expense from their home ranch near Seville in Spain.

The big Englishman tested the second door, found it unlocked, then silently opened it and stood framed there, his head brushing the lintel.

Inside, a man knelt in prayer before a dresser on which had been set a silver crucifix and a small picture of the Holy Virgin flanked by two tiny candles that flamed unwaveringly.

The man was as tall as the silent one in the doorway, but thin as a lath. Two pale scars on forehead and jaw added distinction to his long, melancholy face. He wore dark slippers and pink stockings that went almost to the knee. The rest of him was clad in the tight-fitting Suit of Lights that is the uniform of the matador—in this case green, ornamented with green sequins and gilt braid.

The Englishman waited with the natural reverent consider- ation he had for all honest believers in any worthy religion.

The other crossed himself a last time, stood up, turned, then— "Juan—I mean John—Clayton!" he said, his long face breaking into a pleasant smile. "I'm glad you came early."

"Manolecito, my friend," the other replied simply, gripping the proffered hand with warmth.

The one in green stepped back and critically surveyed him up and down.

"What's wrong?" the Englishman asked. "Haven't I my Suit of Lights properly on?"

"No, no, all perfect," the other assured him, "and quite worthy of a Lord Greystoke. Though I must confess that you look more like a somewhat lean bull—Señor Toro!—than a bullfighter. You will excuse me for mentioning such matters, but there is a lot of muscle on you for the horns to hook into." Then the long, scarred face grew very solemn. "I beg of you, Juan—John—to reconsider this exploit once more. I know the placards are up: 'TODAY!

TWO GREAT TOREROS: The formidable MANOLECITO! JOHN CLAYTON, who battles *without cuadrilla!! A mano a mano* (hand-to-hand)! Four bulls of the Miuras'!

"I know, too, how strangely eager you are for this meeting, so uncharacteristic of your reputed beliefs, and all you have done to arrange it."

John Clayton made as if to comment, but Manolecito held up a hand and continued, "I also know of your vast skill with the beasts of the jungle—it is even rumored that you speak with them—but let me tell you this: The fighting bulls are another matter entirely. They are strong and swift beyond belief, their actions unpredictable even to the lifelong expert. For generations they have been bred in isolation for fighting spirit alone, for courage to charge the lance or cape or red muleta and *espada*—sword—until they die. They have lost the sense of self-preservation natural to other animals. They have had no opportunity whatever to learn the language of beasts, if—pardon me—there be one."

The big Englishman smiled. "What would you say, Manuel," he asked quietly, "if I told you that last midnight, none knowing, I stole to the corral in the Plaza de Toros and there in the darkness spoke long and seriously with Solitario and Tren? They had trouble understanding me at first, but finally they began to remember the age-old language, in which bull is not bull, but *gorgo*." The last was more growl or rumble than word.

Manolecito shook his head uncomprehendingly. "I know you are no liar, John Clayton," he said at last with conviction. "Still, there comes a day in any man's life when he may be honestly mistaken…" Then suddenly he asked, "How did you know that Solitario and Tren would be your bulls? The pairing and drawing were not done until noon today."

"That's easy," the man in the golden Suit of Lights grinned. "I didn't know. I simply talked to all four animals. Your first bull, El Rey Negro, is a proud one—he promises to kill his matador, the Black King does, but also to fight fearlessly and fairly."

The other's eyebrows rose, and again he shook his head

puzzledly. There was something comic about his long-faced, incredulous bafflement, but the big Englishman completely suppressed any impulse to smile.

Finally Manolecito gave a great shrug of his strong, narrow shoulders and said, "These matters I do not understand at all. As one who has fought the brave bulls all his man's life, I am confused. But let me tell you this, *hombre*—whatever they said, or you truly believe they said, *the bulls are dangerous*—more dangerous than the lion or tiger, which they have fought and conquered in the arena. Also, you'll have no jungle and vines to help you, only the wall and sand-floored ring. I know you have planned for your handling of the bulls certain tactics on which you rely and which you have not even told me about.

"But be advised by an old hand, *amigo*—do not attempt to go it alone. Borrow some of my *cuadrilla*—my picadors and banderilleros—to help you cut Solitario and Tren down to size before you tackle them."

The big Englishman shook his head.

Manolecito gave another shrug, a little one. "I thought that would be your answer, John Clayton. One last word, however: I am called Manolecito—little *little* Manuel—from my resemblance to Manolete, the greatest and wisest matador of them all. Yet on August 28, 1947, at Linares, Spain, Manolete was gored to death by Islero, another bull of the fatal Miura breed which you and I will fight in a few minutes. Hundreds of my colleagues of lesser note have also met their death on the horns. It is a very great risk you take."

"Thank you, *amigo bueno*," the other replied. "In turn I should remind you that the special tactics I intend to use may not please the audience or even you. The crowd may become angry, and your own reputation may suffer. I wanted to repeat to you this warning."

Manolecito answered with one of his infrequent grins. "I am sure you have some rare surprises in store for us. But I know you are a brave man and one of honor. I believe I guess your motive for this uncharacteristic thing that you, a declared friend of animals, are doing—and I shall hold my tongue about that now. But whatever you do, John Clayton, our friendship remains firm.

"By the by," he added more casually, "I am curious about one thing. What have you in that box under your arm?"

"Eight small wreaths of roses," the other replied without expression.

Manolecito shook his head with more wry incomprehension. "For our funerals?" he asked with a jesting, bitter smile.

Before answer could be made, there was a discreet knocking at the door.

"It is the time," Manolecito said, his eyes sobering.

"*Vámanos!*" said John Clayton.

They went.

Tiers of concrete seats, jostlingly full, looked down on the circle of sand that was the bullring of Meseta. On the side called *Sol*, where the tickets were cheaper and you looked the low sun in the face, there was noisy horseplay, and many men drank beer from cans and cheered *"Ole! Ole!"* at any pretty girl. There was a little more dignity on the shady side, where there were well-dressed businessmen, leather-cheeked *rancheros*, the officers of the local soldiery come on their free passes, and many a pretty señorita with colorful mantilla. Here and there in the boxes were sharply tailored *aficionados* of the bullring who had flown up from Mexico City—Meseta lay almost on the Tropic of Cancer, east of Durango and south of Monterrey—and also a sprinkling of American tourists and other foreigners.

Among these last and occupying all of a front-row box was one group of three which stood out by contrast. First of these to catch the eye was a beautiful blond girl looking European and very bored, as cosmopolitan in her appearance as the other women in the stands were provincial or merely chic. Beside her, a well-dressed man, equally cosmopolitan, gazed brood-ingly down on the ring; you would have imagined he looked bored, too, unless you had got very close to him—then you would have noted the dark, frightening glow in his hooded eyes. Behind these sat a huge brute of a man with a black patch over an eye, but equally well-dressed and reading with quiet absorption the first page of the latest edition of the *Los Angeles Times* which was headlined: HUNT WIDENS FOR TREASURE JET.

But everywhere else in the stands was the hum of excited speculation. Manolecito—incomparable on his good days! Yet he had bad ones. And this unheard-of Clayton—doubtless one more mad foreigner who fancied he could equal the matadors of Mexico and Spain with their years of practice and their inborn understanding of the great traditions of the bullring. To fight without *cuadrilla*—what insane courage! But also improper, an insult to tradition, smelling—how would you say it?—more of the circus than the bullring. But soon the truth would be known, if only the lazy officials would give order—

The centralmost of the three judges stood up in a large box high in the stands. There was wild cheering. The brass band struck up "La Virgen de la Macarena," the eerie march which begins many bullfights. One of the four gates in the wall of the bullring opened wide, and there strode in, side by side, a man in glittering green and a man in glittering gold, one with a pink cape, the other with a yellow one.

Behind the man in green there came in file two men on unhappy-looking horses armored with thick quilted padding— the picadors with their stubby lances—then two lightly stepping banderilleros and three *peòns* with their capes, lowest members of Manolecito's *cuadrilla.*

Behind the man in gold marched no one.

As they circled the ring and saluted the judges, their reception was mixed. There were cheers and handclapping but also some boos. Someone yelled, "Hi, Golden Boy! You think you're so beautiful the bull will fall in love with you?" There were other impudent calls: "You think you're a human medal?" "Hey, Montezuma!" "*Ole*! Atahualpa!"

Then someone threw an empty beer can of a golden tint.

It missed John Clayton by yards. Police with pistols at their belts made a show of converging lazily toward the point where the thrower had disappeared in the seething mass, but the crowd caught the joke of the colors and laughed its appreciation.

The man with the darkly glowing eyes in the front box on the shady side leaned forward an inch and said softly, "A golden man! That is a good omen for us—though this 'fighting without *cuadrilla*' stinks."

"Dear Augustus, you never fail to find your omens, do you?" the beautiful blond beside him laughed—with perhaps a faint note of nervousness or fear.

Behind them, the man with the eye patch methodically folded his newspaper and clamped it under his left elbow, while his huge chest shuddered with a vast, silent yawn.

All the brightly clad men had now retired behind the chest-high red-painted stout wooden wall of the *barrera*, which encircled the ring a few feet in front of the higher wall of the stands, except for the four short stretches where the four gates were.

Barrenderos—sweepers—quickly smoothed the sand. The crowd grew quiet with tension. A large sign that read: "13 EL REY NEGRO," appeared over the Gate of the Bulls, the only red one.

The sweepers retreated. The red gate flew open. Out slammed a red-eyed half ton of black-hided destruction with great sharp horns of the forward-pointing sort called *cornibacho*. It charged across the ring with astonishing speed, snorting its challenge.

Standing grim-faced behind the *barrera*, John Clayton watched Manolecito kill El Rey Negro. He stoically forced himself to observe every detail: the first "working" of the bull with capes by the *peons* and green-clad matador; the stabbing of its neck and shoulders with the short-headed spears of the mounted picadors—one horse was overturned and its belly gashed open by the horns of the enraged bull—the planting in its now blood-streaming shoulders of the gaily ribboned, barbed steel daggers called banderillas—here El Rey screamed horribly and John Clayton thought, *This is one thing they never report in the newspapers or even mention in the books.* Next the "working" of the still murderous but badly injured animal, its hide now more red than black, by Manolecito, who caused the bull to charge time after time at the small red cloth of the muleta, the horns missing only by inches the firm-standing, glittering green, insolent, lean figure, now blood-splashed, of the matador. Finally the killing of the bull by a single thrust which Manolecito delivered on the run straight over the horns, so that the curve-tipped sword plunged its full length into the bull's body, piercing El Rey's heart, who after five seconds fell down dead.

The crowd momentarily redoubled its cheers. Mostly for his fine kill, Manolecito was awarded the two ears, which were duly cut off the dead beast and presented to him, while harnessed mules pulled the huge body through the Drag Gate and fresh sand was generously strewn over the great red splotches.

John Clayton's reactions were of two sorts. Though rating it stupid, he admired the bull's great courage, which had kept the animal returning to the attack after such hideous punishments as would have sent many a wiser jungle beast racing off in retreat to plot vengeance another day. He also admired the courage and skill of Manolecito, the way he held his body straight without flinching back as the horns almost brushed his chest or thigh, confident in his judgment that this time the beast would not suddenly hook his horns sideways, away from the muleta and into the man. And like the judges, John Clayton respected the cleanness of the matador's kill, no matter how dirty the work that had gone before.

But far more deeply and strongly, the big Englishman was revolted and angered by the bloody spectacle. His deepest and earliest sympathies had been with beasts rather than men, whom he had long known to be the cruelest beings in the world—though on occasion also the kindest. There were moments when the torturing and baiting of El Rey Negro had awakened in him the killing madness. He had had to use iron restraint to keep himself from vaulting the *barrera* and ranging himself on the bull's side against all his tormentors—yes, even Manolecito, his friend—and especially against the cheering, stamping, and screaming crowd sitting safe in the stands.

For it was in the audience that John Clayton saw the most damnable and dangerous effects of the brutal show. Here men cruel already—and women, too, even girls—were being further trained to find delight in death, to enjoy without risking their own skins the sight of torture and cunningly delayed killing. And not only the death of animals but of men, too—their own tribe—for John Clayton knew that the crowd would gladly have watched Manolecito tossed and gored again and again. More gladly, for that matter—to see a man die would have been the greater thrill. And all this in a world now threatened by an atomic death that might poison even the jungles and the seas, as well as wipe out mankind, a world that could no longer afford to nourish any cruelty or the least callousness toward the prospect of mass death.

The man called Augustus murmured to the blond girl beside him, "A kill of some beauty, *chérie*, though not worth two ears. Now we shall watch the golden man—or clown. It is at least a way to pass the brief time in this abysmal town while Romulo makes the *Conquistador*'s engines smooth as silk. He has his deadline."

"A misfortune that a motor should have failed now," the girl whispered back nervously, though her face was as cool as ever. "I will not feel safe until we are south of the Equator."

"I never have a misfortune," the man with the darkly glowing eyes asserted sternly, "except such as I have anticipated and allowed for."

There were as many cheers as jeers as the gold-clad matador slipped through the narrow opening in the *barrera* and lightly ran out onto the newly smoothed sand. This *Inglés* was a rare one! Did he think he was the bull, to make his entrance first? A comedian perhaps?—but the posters should have warned of that. (Comic bullfighters were not unknown. The great Manolete himself briefly belonged to such a troupe in Spain during his earliest years.)

The sign over the red rectangle of the Gate of Fright, as bullfighters call it, now read: "14 SOLITARIO."

John Clayton looked around, grim-faced, in a full circle at the crowd. Then lifting his hands to his throat, he ripped off his 12-pound coat with its sequins and braid, careless that both sleeves were torn to the elbows in the process. He tossed it to the nearest point of the *barrera*, where it hung glittering against the red paint like a great twisted nugget of real gold.

There was an audible gasp of shock from the crowd. Then began the cries of protest.

Ignoring them, John Clayton swiftly ripped off the rest of his gaudy clothing, tossed it after the jacket, and stood barefoot on the burning sand in a leather loincloth alone.

In his hands he held two objects which had been concealed under his tight shirt and glittering tight trousers or *taleguilla*: a long hunting knife and a lasso coiled in a tight ring.

He stood at his tallest, and he was as motionless as a palely bronze statue of a Greek athlete, indifferent to the angry shouts that beat upon him.

Then someone high in the crowd recognized him and screeched over the shouting, *"Tarzan! Tarzan de los Monos!"*

Soon the rest of the stands took up the excited cry. Some, for varying reasons both simpleminded and sophisticated, believed the truth—that Tarzan was a real man; others thought of him as a character in the films, or as a particular film star—but unquestioningly all of them knew Tarzan of the Apes and were delighted that he should appear in person in Meseta.

Tarzan commandingly lifted a hand. The cheering swiftly sank to a whispering murmur. He faced around toward the farthest stretch of *barrera*. Then the hand with the knife went back, there was a blur of bronzed arm, a long flash of steel in the sunlight, and with a loud *thunk!* the knife was deeply embedded in the red-painted wood.

Without an instant lost, Tarzan repoised himself and swung his other arm in a long, graceful arc. The tightly coiled lasso sailed in a high parabola through the quiet air and landed like a rope quoit on the handle of the knife and hung there.

Then Tarzan strode to the exact center of the ring and faced the Gate of Fright.

Cheers had rewarded the feats with knife and lasso, but now the voice of the crowd took on a different note, a questioning and somewhat hostile one. It was all very wonderful that the world-famed Tarzan should appear in Meseta, but that he should meddle in their revered national sport of the *tauromachia* was another matter. He didn't dress properly, was practically naked—wasn't that an insult? Why, he hadn't even a cape—and how in the name of the Devil could a *torero* work a bull without a cape? Also he stood insanely in the very center of what is the bull's *querencia*, or territory, during *Primer tercio*—the first third of the fight. He couldn't possibly escape from there, unless… Surely this one must be carefully watched and strongly rebuked at the first impropriety of action!

Some of the young men in the stands and many of the señoritas, watching the tanned figure that stood like a youthful god defying outworn customs, felt a sympathetic thrill, but few of them dared speak or show it.

Tarzan himself, standing in the burning sun, his sensitive nostrils assaulted by the reek of the crowd and the dark stench of old blood, was thinking of very different matters. He was wondering whether, in the yellow glare and great noise, Solitario would remember the sympathies engendered and the simple words spoken last midnight and, after a long wait in the dark, understood. He must put his faith in the integrity of the brave, if stupid bulls. At a moment like this confidence was everything.

He recalled how he had twice wrestled a bull by its horns to a fall in the proud stronghold of Alemtejo,* but this was a different and more difficult contest.

---

* *Tarzan and the Madman* (Tarzan 23)

The red gates opened wide, there was a shout from the crowd, Solitario came charging in, and then, unlike the first bull, he skidded to a halt and stamped the sand and tossed his widespread *capacho* horns and snorted in challenge.

Hide and horns were dark yellow, almost the color of gold, a most unusual rarity in a Miura.

Tarzan lifted high one hand, palm forward, and cried sharply, "*Toro*! Hey, *toro*!"

The huge golden bull lowered his head and charged straight at the bronzed figure. Faster and faster the golden hooves drummed the arena. Here was truly a *locomotora*, a veritable railroad locomotive of an animal!

Tarzan stood motionless until the bull was no more than 20 feet away and a thin scream had begun to issue from the throats of the female members of the audience. Then, as if the palm of his hand were a tiny muleta, Tarzan drew it abruptly down and two feet to the right.

Solitario altered his charge by just that distance. For a moment the two figures seemed to merge, then Solitario had pounded by and there was a red streak on Tarzan's rib cage, where the near horn had brushed him.

The crowd rose to its feet and shouted a great, "*Ole!*"

Tarzan turned. Solitario reversed direction in a cloud of sand. The unheard-of Pass of Death was repeated, this time to the left and without blood drawn, although the distance between horn tip and skin was only two or three finger widths. Again came the deafening, "*Ole!*"

Ten times Tarzan, using his palm alone, compelled the bull to repeat that astounding Pass. And very swiftly, too, for a fresh unwounded bull is speedier than an injured animal. Sometimes the horn of the bull slashed past high and sometimes low, according to where Tarzan held his hand. The great "*Ole!*"s rebounded without cease between the circular concrete stands.

Meanwhile an action of a different sort was going on in one part of the shady side of the stands, as Tarzan noted in swift sidewise glances. Messengers were speeding between the judges' box and the officials and military officers below.

Tarzan did not, however, note the man named Augustus lean from his box and lightly slap on the side of the head the soldier slouched beneath it. This one looked up angrily—to receive a handful of silver American dollars and the command, *"Help get the pics in the ring, por favor!"* The soldier grinned.

Two picadors—not Manolecito's—had mounted their horses and were moving, their nags prodded by a soldier's rifle butt, into the ring through the door marked "PICADORS."

With an abrupt downward sweep of his hand to the sand, Tarzan brought Solitario to a sudden halt and stood beside the proud, panting animal with one hand lightly touching a golden horn tip and the other held high. Then before the cheering slackened, he took two quick steps backward and lightly vaulted astride the bull's back.

Solitario reared then, bucked, kicked out with his mighty hind hooves. With each flashing movement it seemed the man must be thrown off. But the grip of Tarzan's heels and knees to the rib-slatted golden sides was like iron, and his fingers laced about the horns as tightly as talons. And all the while he leaned forward and spoke gruffly yet softly into the bull's right ear words only a Neanderthal would have known among men.

The words were, *"Gorgo! Vando gorgo! Tand gom! Tand-panda! Tand bundolo!"* meaning roughly, "Buffalo! Good buffalo! No run! Quietness! No fight-to-kill!"

Of a sudden Solitario quieted and, as Tarzan tapped with his heels, began to circle the ring, stepping briskly and proudly.

Tarzan decided that the stupidity of the brave bulls had its good side. Once their trust was won, they were blindly obedient.

The fickle crowd had become uncertain again. This was beginning to look too much like the low stunts of a rodeo. Catcalls and rooster crowings mixed with the cheers. A few seat cushions and some more beer cans came pattering down on the sand.

The two picadors appeared on their padded nags in Solitario's

path. The great golden beast halted, all aquiver with the urge
to charge his traditional foes. It took all of Tarzan's mastery and
more strange, harshly whispered words to hold him in check.

Just then Tarzan saw green shoulders and a long scarred face
grinning widely at him over the *barrera*. There was high mischief
in the usually melancholy eyes.

"Hey, Tarzan!" Manolecito called. "Catch!" And with that he
tossed lightly and casually but with great accuracy a picador's
lance, which Tarzan caught as easily.

The Lord of the Jungle (*and now of the bullring also*, he thought
with a chuckle) instantly saw the same humorous possibility
that Manolecito had divined. He made Solitario advance step
by quick step, while he pointed his lance not at the heavily
padded old horses but at the picadors themselves.

The picadors began to back away, but not quickly enough.
One halfheartedly attempted to pic Tarzan's bull and had his
lance knocked out of his grip by a smart sidewise swipe of
Tarzan's own weapon. The other, urged on by a shrill call from
one of the lower boxes, tried desperately to spear Tarzan, who
knocked the weapon aside at the last instant with his fist and
then thrust sharply with his own lance. The point stopped a
fractional inch short of the man's chest, but by that time the
fellow had fallen in terror backwards out of the saddle.

That finished the picadors. Horses and men raced ignomini-
ously out of the arena, while the crowd happily booed and jeered
them.

Tarzan wasted not a moment, now that the audience was
once more—at least momentarily—on his side. He called to
Manolecito, who quickly handed him across the *barrera* four
small wreaths of roses. Then Tarzan ordered Solitario to the
opposite end of the ring and commanded him with a "Hey,
toro!" to charge, at the same time sprinting toward the bull
himself.

Just as it seemed they must meet head-on, Tarzan slipped
aside, and when the bull came clear, there was a wreath of red
roses on its near horn.

The crowd quickly got the point that the wreaths were to take the place of the barbed banderillas in this strange show. Once more there were booings—it occurred to Tarzan that many segments of the human race were worse than the little chattering monkeys in their changeability of mind. Perhaps some of them had recalled—and thought it a shameful fantasy—the American cartoon of Ferdinand, the bull who loved flowers.

But this time at least the cheers conquered the booings. When Solitario's horns were doubly rose-ringed, Tarzan repeated the first series of passes, ending with two in which he turned his back on the bull as it charged, judging the bull's distance and his speed and direction of movement by keen hearing alone.

Then he mounted Solitario once more and rode him, not to the Drag Gate but to the red Gate of the Bulls. There he sprang erect—golden man on shoulders of golden bull—and looked around grimly at the crowd, then gave utterance with deliberation and challenging fierceness to the shuddering victory cry of the bull ape.

It quieted the crowd as nothing else that afternoon had. Indeed it cowed them. Each had a fleeting glimpse of the ragingly fierce heart there can be in one who fights for gentleness and peace among man and beast. Each had a fleeting awareness, too, of the meanness of his own hatreds and hidden blood lusts.

The red doors opened. In the semidarkness the scampering bull-handlers looked to Tarzan like astonished gnomes as he rode Solitario back to the corral.

The rest of the *corrida* seemed like a breeze to the two matadors, although as a matter of truth they each took greater risks than they had done in the first half.

Perhaps it was because the crowd now seemed wholly with them. Indeed, there was an uncustomary note of respect, even of awe, in the cheering—as if for once they realized that, if they behaved themselves badly, something unpleasant might conceivably happen to *them*. The victory cry of the bull ape has a long echo.

Manolecito worked his bull in the customary fashion, yet insisting on a minimum of savagery. There was only the lightest piccing and he placed the banderillas himself—only two of them, barely driven in, with the addition of a rose wreath over a horn in honor of Tarzan. In caping the bull, he worked within inches of the animal, while with the muleta he reduced inches to their fractions. Twice he was knocked down and once shallowly gouged across the chest, but he never moved his feet after he planted them or stood one inch shorter than his full height—his body was straight as a post. When at the end he stood beside the gasping, momentarily subdued bull with the blood trickling down its black shoulders and, his green Suit of Lights ripped and darkened by red, raised his hand to the judges, there was no question but that handkerchiefs should be waved by such of the crowd as carried them, and that the centralmost judge should at last wave a handkerchief, too, making it official that this brave animal be spared and sent back to pasture to breed brave daughters and sons.

Tarzan worked Tren at first somewhat as he had Solitario, but then added variations which he had learned from a careful study of the murals and other paintings of ancient Crete, where more than 3,000 years ago youths and athletic maidens had worked the bulls without injuring them. (It was strange, with hot sand underfoot and dark animal rushing by, still to have flashes of memory of the quiet hours he had spent poring over musty manuscripts in his cool, lofty study in England.) He commanded Tren to charge him and at the last instant seized the bull's horns and somersaulted—first entirely over him, another time onto his back, where he landed facing the bull's tail, but keeping his footing.

In the box the golden-haired girl said coolly over her shoulder, "Do you find it amusing, Mr. Train, that this bull bears your name—meaning the same in Spanish and pronounced the same?"

"No, Miss Sophia, I do not find it amusing," the huge man with the black eye patch said.

There he sprang erect—golden man on shoulders of golden bull…

"But the man is putting on quite a show," she said with a touch of animation and malice, "while Tren is taking a tremendous beating."

"The man has not yet delivered a single hurt to either of the animals, Miss Sophia," Mr. Train replied woodenly.

"But that's just the point—" the girl protested.

"It is not the point," the man beside her said harshly. The dark frightening glow in his eyes was now clearly one of rage. "The sole point of any bullfight, good or bad, is the great Ritual of Death, which this ape defiles! He even tempted Manolecito into following his filthy lead—I thought the Swordsman of Guadalajara had more integrity. And I thought you had better taste, Sophia."

"I was only joking, *chéri*."

"It is not a matter to joke about! Mr. Train, what is your opinion of this clown?"

The man with the eye patch seemed to consider that for a short moment, then replied softly, "He has speed and cunning, Mr. Vinaro, but he lacks weight and the will to kill."

"Exactly! What do you say to that, Sophia? Or have you fallen for this glorified beach boy?"

"Augustus, I told you once I was joking," she replied sharply, yet with a twinge of terror she could not quite conceal.

Meanwhile Tarzan had done a handstand on Tren's horns while the bull reared. There were other tricks. Finally he dived under Tren as the animal galloped over him.

Once more there was no question but that this bull be spared. And when the *corrida* was all over and night had begun to fall, many members of the audience, instead of hurrying noisily from the stands, sat for a while as if entranced. Then, rousing, they shook their heads and talked together in low voices and with halting phrases, as if recovering from the spells of a master magician—or perhaps two.

Among the delaying ones were the three in the front box. They sat silently in the gathering shadows. Then Augustus Vinaro looked at his heavy gold wristwatch.

"The deadline I gave Romulo draws near. Yet I would not leave this afternoon's crudities altogether unpunished." From an inner pocket he carefully withdrew a dully gleaming black sphere the size of a child's marble. He reached it slowly to Mr. Train. The big man's huge, horny-edged hand closed about it very slowly, as if it were a moth.

Then Vinaro said, "Mr. Train, find a small boy with a marksman's eyes and a wiry throwing arm. Persuade him to…you know. If Manolecito is still with Tarzan, it doesn't matter. Give the boy a peso or two, tell him a suitable story, and also threaten him suitably."

"Yes, Mr. Vinaro. But could not I myself deliver this?" The softly clenched hand moved a fraction. "Or take other measures?"

"Out of the question! We must adhere to schedule. This other is only my whim. Sophia, don't shrink from Mr. Train or from me. Even that hairless ape showed some courage. Go ahead of us, Mr. Train—you have your errand."

CHAPTER 2

Aeródromo Meseta

T hat night at the Meseta airport Tarzan and Manolecito
stood alone on the edge of darkness under the props
of an ancient Fokker trimotor, waiting for their different planes. They were midway between the main building,
which streamed light, and a high wire fence beyond which
children played who were little more than racing voices in the
dark, and taller figures of gloom passed slowly in twos and
threes, and an occasional firecracker went off with a healthy
snap and flash. The two *toreros'* reputations had given them
freedom of the field and escape from the stuffy odorous waiting
room. Tarzan wore light gray tweeds and had a single suitcase
beside him, while the matador, slumped forward now from the
taping of his chest, was adorned in a conservative tropical
worsted of the sharpest cut.

The *aficionados* with their pleas and their autograph books,
their wine bottles and fruit and chatter, had at last fallen by the
wayside or had been firmly snubbed into retreat—unless some
of the lingerers beyond the fence were their rear guard.
Manolecito had directed his *cuadrilla* to go off and buy drinks.

The lanky matador now took his nose out of a newspaper
he'd been scanning by the light from the waiting room, crumpled
it in a loose ball, and tossed it away as he stepped back beside
Tarzan in the dark.

"Pepe Bello and Chamaco II cut themselves some ears in
Mexico City," he said. "Also, the burned wreck of that passenger
jet carrying bullion and jewels has been discovered in the Mojave

20

Desert of the U.S.A. No survivors—and no treasure. Someone claims he saw a swift red plane following the jet past Phoenix. Pirates of the Air?—the demented gringo newsman asks."

Tarzan said, "Red would be the worst color for such a plane, unless—"

A volley of firecrackers and happy yells beyond the fence cut him short.

Tarzan suppressed a snarl. All his life he had carried the animal's hatred of sudden, loud noises. Even these, harmless and trivial as they were, made him feel uneasy.

Manolecito said, "My countrymen! By day they scream insults at *toreros* in the ring, by night they salute them with firecrackers! Or perhaps it is the eve of some admired saint I have forgotten. A vociferous people. Soon an ancient and rickety DC-3 will bear me to Chihuahua to face more such noisemakers. While for you, *amigo*, a grand jet of the V.A.R.I.G. will soon dip down. They're strange birds on this Meseta field, the jets are, though it's big and strong enough for them. But for the world-renowned Lord Greystoke one of them will come bowing down to bear him off to some new, rare adventure in South America." There was a hint of a wistful question about the last phrase.

"It's no secret, Manuel, at least to you," Tarzan said easily. "This morning there was forwarded to me from London a cable from a Professor Lionel Talmadge, who lives at Cuiabá, in the Mato Grosso state of Southwestern Brazil. It said only, 'Our friend Ruiz has discovered a mystery.'"

"And on this slender summons you fly a fifth of the way around the world," Manolecito replied humorously, yet with a touch of envy.

"Because I know the men involved," Tarzan explained. "Professor Talmadge is a distinguished British anthropologist, while João Ruiz—" he gave the Portuguese *John* something of the sound of *Zhoun*—"is a rare student of animals, who also collects them for zoos—a man long my friend."

"Ah, the animals," Manolecito remarked. "Wherever you go, they soon come in. For you understand animals...and you also understand men." The matador's voice grew serious. He coughed, lit a harsh black cigarette of the sort called in Latin America "chest-breakers," and went on, "Yes, you know men. Today, *hombre*, you made me take the most ridiculous risks I ever have in my much-overrated life." He waited, then added, "And perhaps fight the best *corrida* of my career, too, no matter how sardonically they will report it in the Federal District and in Madrid."

Tarzan said, "You made me take some needless chances, too. Diving under the bull—that was foolish of me. Poor Tren didn't know where he was putting his hooves—I had to wriggle like Histah, the snake." He added, "You're certain our three bulls will be put to pasture and stud, not routed back somehow to the ring?"

Manolecito said, "*Hombre*, besides the other measures we took, I told the impresario here that if I ever heard rumor of such an unworthy business, I would tell such tales of his cheating and miserliness to other *toreros* that all would shun Meseta. It's not gentlemanly to threaten in such fashion—a Greystoke wouldn't do it—but I'm cynical, I'm no idealist, my heart is hard. You know that, don't you?"

Tarzan said, "Certainly, Manuel," but there was humor in his voice. "I'm sure it was purely by chance that your second bull this afternoon was spared. You wished to kill it, but the crowd thwarted you."

"This afternoon was a miracle, a grand exception." Manolecito went on harshly, "But if you truly know men, you will also realize that now that the miracle afternoon is over, I'll go on killing bulls as I always have. Oh, perhaps a touch more honor, a bit less cruelty here and there, but essentially I'll go on being the same old fancy butcher in gilt, until a bull, or the crowd and a bull, or—for a great wonder—old age finally gets me. I will always remember the dream of kindliness and of life thrilling and merry without bloodshed that you gave me this afternoon, yet I will go on being a bull-slayer. It is my livelihood—and my life."

"I understand," Tarzan said after a pause.

Another volley of firecrackers went off, this time with a couple exploding inside the fence. Tarzan's irrational uneasiness increased. The flashes showed several small figures running away.

Manolecito spat out, "My countrymen! It is a scandal that the police do not prevent such dangerous antics. They will wait until a firecracker explodes by the tank of a fueling plane and then they will strut about the blackened wreckage, seeking culprits." He went on, "You also understand about the crowd, don't you? Today they, too, glimpsed your dream, but next week they'll be screaming for blood—bull's or matador's—and more loudly, to drown out the memory of today. Yes…there'll be that little memory in them all, frightening them, maybe softening their flinty hearts the barest trifle. And in a few of them perhaps the memory will be more than a little."

Tarzan nodded moodily, his face unreadable in the gloom. He was scanning the dim silvery fence. It seemed to him that now only one small figure lingered there, some distance beyond it.

Manolecito said, "This dream of yours, *amigo*—it is like a very tiny seed you plant, eh?"

"Something like that," said Tarzan.

Manolecito sighed the sigh of a man who has said all he can on a difficult topic. Then he spoke up in his normal voice. "Do this one's ears deceive him, or is that the sound of a jet warming up?"

"You're right," Tarzan agreed, listening to the muted banshee wail from beyond the waiting room. "I make out two engines only. Yet we saw no jets on the field earlier."

"Perhaps it was in the hangar, undergoing repairs," Manolecito suggested. "Come, *hombre*, let us investigate this rarity."

He started out briskly in a course that would take him in front of and around the brightly lit main building, to the edge of the great dark concrete ribbon of the main runway.

Tarzan hesitated a few moments. His uneasiness was reaching a peak. Yet he could not decide from which direction danger threatened. A jet warming across the field? A small boy beyond the fence? These were hardly menaces. Suddenly he snatched his suitcase with his left hand and started out after Manolecito, striding swiftly.

He had not taken a dozen paces when he whirled around and almost instantly threw himself flat on the ground, shielding his face and head with his right arm.

At the spot where he and Manolecito had been standing there was a blinding flash and the CRAAACK! of a fierce blast, followed by the faintest *pittering*, felt as much as heard, against the tweed sleeve of his bent arm. An acrid vapor tickled his nostrils.

"By the Devil's horns, that was the grandsire of all firecrackers!" he heard Manolecito call. "*Amigo*, are you hurt?"

"Not at all," Tarzan called back, springing up and striding toward him. "A six-inch salute, I'd judge."

In his mind he doubted this very much. He would surely have seen the sputtering fuse and looming shape of any such toy as it fell.

"Ah, the malefactor!" Manolecito cried. "Is pursuit in order?"

"No, I doubt we'd catch anyone," Tarzan answered cheerfully.

In his mind he was not so sure of this, either. Just after the blast, along with the strange *pittering*, he had heard two other faint sounds—a sobbing of fright and then small bare feet pounding across hard adobe earth.

A few persons had come out of the waiting room, but seeing no flames or other excitement, they went back. Tarzan and Manolecito continued toward the runway. Suddenly the droning banshee wail multiplied in volume, and a dark sleek shape was surging toward them along the runway, faster and faster.

"No lights on it, or along the runway, either," Manolecito observed. "More scandal!"

As the jet approached, they noted another reason why it had been hard to see at first. It was painted dead black, though with thin lines of silver trim. It had a high tail and most graceful overall shape.

It was a slim, beautiful fish, created to haunt tropical deeps and speed on silent kills.

Suddenly it veered toward them, its landing wheels almost leaving the runway.

They darted back. A black wing tip lashed by. Then the black, silver-edged jet swung back toward the center of the runway. For a long, dreadful instant the great twin daggers of flame pointed at them, and they felt searing heat on their skins and saw the greenish-yellow glare through their shut eyelids as they staggered in the mighty double thrust of scorching air.

"*Ai! Ai caramba!*" Manolecito yelled. "What a scandal of bribery and incompetence was mounted for that take-off! I am singed! My suit and hair smoke!—no, not quite that," he added, feeling the areas.

"Almost a scandal of death," Tarzan said grimly, watching the speeding plane. It swerved twice more, slightly, then steadied and climbed sharply into the sky.

"Tell me, *amigo*," Manolecito said, grasping Tarzan's shoulder, "what murderous black hawk of night was that?"

"A Junkers Geschäfts-Meister—meaning Executive—jet," Tarzan replied. "About the finest plane Germany has built since she was permitted to manufacture civilian aircraft again. Not the usual paint job, of course. Should be Geschäfts-Führer—but they're still leery of the sales power of that word, remembering Hitler. More than that I can't tell you."

"Ah! One of those insolent Prussians then. I know the breed. They cannot observe a man without trying to stamp on him."

"The Geschäfts-Meister has been purchased by wealthy companies and men—and nations—throughout the world," Tarzan objected mildly. "Manuel, you're right, there must have been bribery involved. Do you suppose that if we went to the hangar and questioned the mechanics—"

"We would only find mouths stuffed with silver—with perhaps an extra wadding of fear," Manolecito said. "But let us get off the field, comrade, at all events. It appears that you and I are far safer in the bullring. Perhaps from the waiting room we can speak to the control tower and—"

The lights along the runway flashed on, another faint throbbing made itself heard in the air, and the tannoy cried out grandly in Spanish, as if announcing the approach of a queen, "Flight 17 special! A Boeing 707 jet of the Brazilian line, *Emprêsa de Viação Aérea Dio Grandense!* Passengers for Rio de Janeiro only!"

"One passenger," Manolecito corrected softly.

"Too late for any investigations now," Tarzan said. "That'll be mine." He recovered his suitcase, and as they walked together toward the waiting room, he added, "Manuel, *mi amigo*, guard yourself from the bulls and from all other manner of animals, including men—and not forgetting small boys."

Manolecito looked at him thoughtfully. "The same advice to you, Tarzan. I have a feeling you will need it."

CHAPTER 3

South by V.A.R.I.G.

Tarzan unbuckled his seat belt and smiled at the air hostess. She was a willowy girl dressed in a long-skirted deep scarlet uniform with very narrow gold piping. Her shoulder-length dark hair almost made a carnival thing of her jaunty scarlet cap. She was clearly curious about the handsome passenger who had been able to summon the great jet off its normal course, but clearly also reserved in her curiosity. She held a small tray with a tall purplish drink.

"*Um refresco*, sir? It is a beverage of fruit juices, which some find pleasant."

"Thank you." Tarzan sipped, recognizing lime, orange, plum, grape, pineapple, and papaya. He drank off half and smacked his lips appreciatively. Then, "I would be grateful if you would find me a newspaper."

"Certainly, sir. Which one?"

"It doesn't matter."

She hid her slight puzzlement well and swayed down the aisle toward her alcove by the door to the piloting compartment. Her uniform matched the velvet seat covers, the tiny curtains, the touches of aluminum anodized a golden shade, and the deep yellow-and-scarlet checkerboard carpeting—new old-fashioned, regal touches which Tarzan enjoyed. It matched the queenly sound of *Emprêsa de Viação Aérea Rio Grandense*, even though *emprêsa* meant enterprise, not empress. V.A.R.I.G. Why not V.A.R.G.?—he asked himself. Perhaps because those letters would suggest Getúlio Vargas, the great Brazilian leader who

27

had shot himself in 1954 rather than relinquish power, and about whom feelings were mixed. Yet where but in Brazil could you have had a man like Vargas, alternately dictator and elected president—a hero of the people, yet hated for the "muddy sea of corruption" about him?

The beautifully upholstered jet was less than half full. Tarzan's purchase of two seats had been unnecessary, except as an honorable bribe. He wondered if the crash of the "treasure jet" might have caused some cancellations. Odd that bullion and jewels should be transported together and with passengers too—some great jewelry house's shipment, possibly.

Midway in her return journey, the hostess was stopped by a fat jeweled hand and by a female voice, which enunciated laboriously, *"Señorita, que hora es?"*

"It is midnight, madam. We have just left your Rocky Mountain time zone."

"Gracias, señorita." Then, breaking into English, "You're really a very sweet girl."

"Obrigado, senhora," the hostess replied a bit stiffly, preparing to move on.

"Wait a minute—what does that mean? I don't think it's in my phrase book." The woman sat up straighter. "Aren't you supposed to say *'gracias,'* too?"

"No, madam. *Gracias* means 'thank you' in Spanish. *Obrigado* means the same in Portuguese, which we speak in Brazil."

"But *obrigado* sounds Japanese. How strange! George," the woman complained to the bald head beside her, "I've bought the wrong phrase book."

"Don't worry, Winnie," the man assured her. "Spanish and Portuguese are exactly alike except they're spelled differently."

"I am sorry, sir, but they are very different languages," the hostess insisted.

"While *obrigado*," she added, "is in no way Japanese. Nor is it *gracias* spelled differently."

She hurried on to Tarzan and laid on his knees a copy of the New Orleans *Times-Picayune.*

"*Obrigado,*" he said solemnly, but with a wink.

She wrinkled her nose at him and showed her white teeth in a little grin. She seemed inclined to linger.

"It might be possible to find the lady a Portuguese phrase book," he suggested, "or at least a *refresco.*"

She left with half-concealed reluctance. Tarzan spread the newspaper to its center pages, carefully removed his coat, held the right sleeve over the paper and shook it. He frowned, not hearing the sound he'd hoped for. He took out his comb and began to comb the tweed at the elbow. Ah, there it was—a tiny *pit.* And now again—*pit-pit.* He methodically continued the combing until all *pittering* had ceased. Then, draping his coat over the empty seat ahead, he carefully shook the material he'd gathered to the center of the spread newsprint and felt it with a finger tip. Tiny rough grains, as he'd expected. He funneled them into a white envelope, stared at them closely, then took a small pocket magnifier from a vest pocket and inspected them again.

They were tiny irregular black grains with sharp corners—a gleaming, fine black sand. Certainly not the material of a fire-cracker or of Meseta's adobe soil.

On an impulse he wet a thumb, picked up a few of the grains on it, and rubbed them briskly against the window beside him, which was now looking down from a great height on moonlit water, the Gulf of Campeche. He returned the grains to the envelope, then inspected the reinforced glass closely. Eyes and fingernails both told him that now there were several tiny scratches in it.

He leaned back thoughtfully. A high explosive with a casing of black industrial diamond—or any rate some material harder than glass. And thrown by a Mexican street urchin. Now what could that signify?

After a while he shrugged his shoulders, drew from an inner pocket a cablegram, and read again: "Our friend Ruiz has discovered a mystery. Lionel Talmadge." He smiled moodily. He had already discovered one himself. There were mysteries everywhere, if you only observed. Just now the big Boeing was nearing Yucatán, home of the mysterious Mayan culture, of which Tarzan had once encountered a weird offshoot on an island in the Pacific.*

A middle-aged, kindly, weather-toughened face grew in his mind's eye. It was that of his friend João Ruiz, who understood animals—not as Tarzan did, from the inside, yet very well, using all a civilized man's imagination. It would be good to talk with Ruiz, preferably outdoors by a camp fire. Ruiz had snared and studied very many of the animals of the great continent, still less explored than Africa, that soon would be hurtling northward beneath this Boeing 707: the jaguar, the armadillo, the peccary, the holy quetzal bird, the gigantic condor, the deadly snake fer-de-lance, the bone-crushing anaconda, the river-dwelling caiman with its great reptilian jaws, the dagger-toothed piranha fish, the bird-catching spiders with diamond eyes, the sloth—evolutionary relic—and many more...

Sleep crept upon him. He switched off his reading light, lowered the arm between his seats, and slipped off his shoes. The thoughts of jungle animals and the lingering fruit tastes of his *refresco* took his mind back to his boyhood. Almost asleep now, he pictured himself as a reckless and boastful young tar-mangani climbing to the top of a swaying tree five miles high, quite beyond the anxious calling of Kala, his ape foster-mother. His fingers and toes half curved around gilded holds in the seats beneath and before him as his eyes fell shut.

One hundred miles ahead of the V.A.R.I.G. jet and at a half mile greater altitude, the *Conquistador* split the starry night above Yucatán. The Caribbean already gleamed ahead.

The commodious cabin of the Junkers Geschäfts-Meister was decorated in dull black trimmed with silver, as was the jet's exterior. In a wide bunk and under black silk sheets and a black vicuña blanket, Sophia Renault lay with her slender body straight and her eyes closed. Her breathing was slow and even. Her face

---

* *Tarzan and the Castaways* (Tarzan 24)

held an expression of cold disdain. Her hair spread across the black silk pillow like golden spider webs.

Mr. Train, erect and impassive, his visible eye closed, was sitting in an extra-wide black upholstered seat to the rear. His great bulk of solid muscle made it seem like a child's barber chair.

Augustus Vinaro lounged in a black, silver-worked dressing robe at a big radio panel forward. Through the door to the piloting compartment he could watch the harsh, low-browed, three-quarters-rear profile of Romulo at the controls. The savage, impassive face of the pilot was bathed in moonlight greenish from the wind screen. Beside Vinaro was a glass jar of gleaming hard candies.

A tuned-down loudspeaker was saying, "…estimate the total value of the gems and the jewelers' metal, still unlocated at this moment, at between seven and eight million dollars—"

With a sharp twist Vinaro cut off the newscast. "Four million at the most—and that at the best open market prices!" he snarled. "Typical American salesman's brag—or else an attempt to shake down the insurers. Well, at least my goldsmiths will add another million to the four by their artistry, while this piddling operation feeds an incomparably greater one."

"Still, it was a beautiful coup on your part, if I may say so, sir," Mr. Train commented quietly, his unpatched eye half opening. "The strip-away red enamel on this ship—a stroke of genius."

Vinaro permitted himself a sardonic chuckle. "The Germans are still the world's finest chemists and mechanics when they're allowed to be," he remarked. "Workmen worthy of their hire, though too tactless and overbearing and—yes, too hysteric—to be trusted in the crucial stages of an operation. Worse even than Slavs. While all Orientals are hysteria squared and cubed. Give me the cold-blooded Latin or Anglo-Saxon always."

"Of all your great competencies, sir, I believe I admire most, by a hair, your scheduling of operations running concurrently."

Vinaro grimaced pleasantly. "That indeed is the master art," he admitted. "To initiate an operation, let it mature without my presence—which, for one thing, is apt to make my men a little *too* nervous. Then to arrive from another corner of the world just as the curtain rises and the master touch is needed. The analogy of a surgeon in his operating theater springs to mind. Then back around the curve of the earth to where another operation has been ripening. Which reminds me that we should now be able to raise Cuiabá."

He tuned the radio dials with the patient precision of a concert violinist, clapped on a pair of earphones, touched a button marked SCRAMBLE, and spoke into a microphone, softly yet most distinctly.

"Arrow One to RZ Two."

After two repetitions of that call, he listened for a moment and said, "Who was asleep down there? Thank you, your name is noted in my memory. Report!" After a long pause he said, "Very well. Mount at once the action against the RZ in the opposing camp—the one with the shorter name. Repeat!... That is satisfactory. Close."

He brushed a hand across the dials, tossed aside the earphones, and gazed solemnly at Mr. Train.

"I should have granted your request of six hours back," he said softly. "Rodriguez has the copy of a cable Talmadge sent yesterday to a man he thought was in England. The cable read: 'Our friend Ruiz has discovered a mystery.'"

He paused. "The man to whom the cable was sent was one John Clayton, Lord Greystoke—in brief, Tarzan, the clown of the bullring, yet a master of jungle fighting who might annoy us in the Mato Grosso. He clearly means to answer the cable in person—it puzzled me that a V.A.R.I.G. jet should be diverted to Meseta. Now the operation against Ruiz and the boy Ramel must be mounted at once—I've given Rodriguez orders—and Tarzan must be eliminated. I missed a golden opportunity for the latter. If I had sent *you*, Mr. Train, you would not have failed, as the boy did, or as I did, for that matter, when we took off."

"You thought the matter of no great import then," the huge

man interposed soothingly. "Your whim, you said. You could not have anticipated—"

"Mr. Train," Vinaro said sharply, "I enjoy your well-phrased flattery, but I never permit it to cloud my judgment. I *could* have anticipated—and if a like occasion ever arises, I *will.* There were omens enough: the gold-suited man, the golden bull, the golden sun, the jacket a-dangle from the *barrera* like a great nugget—always remembering that gold is the heart and key of this operation. Also the coincidence of your name with that of the fourth bull, plus the outraging of my aesthetic values in the matter of the Ritual of Death, and above all the coincidence of Tarzan's presence at Meseta. Clearly my insight into the collective unconsciousness of humanity is not perfect—with all those omens I *should* have anticipated."

He scowled around the cabin. His gaze stopped at Sophia Renault. "This Tarzan is now a problem," he said loudly. Her expression did not alter, her shut eyes flicker, or the rhythm of her breathing change an iota. Smiling, he silently selected a licorice ball from the glass jar and tossed it so that it lit on the black blanket exactly over her waist.

The upper half of her body, clad in black nightdress and bed jacket, jackknifed erect in an instant. The black sphere was rolling off the bunk. She caught it with a desperate snatch. Her fist, holding it, shook. She grasped at her wrist with her other hand to stop the shaking. It didn't, much. The muscles of her beautiful face were jerking, as if she had a tic.

"Taste it," Vinaro suggested softly. "Go ahead, Sophia, taste it."

She looked toward him with doubtful, wild, white-rimmed eyes. Then very slowly she drew her fist to her lips and pressed her tongue between fingernails and palm. She withdrew her tongue and sucked it.

"Sweet, isn't it?" Vinaro observed. "Yet with a touch of the bitter."

She looked at him and at the candy jar. *"Cochon! Cochon!"* she screeched suddenly. *"Chien!"* She made as if to throw the licorice ball at him, but placed it instead in a silver ashtray. Her hand was still shaking, though not much.

"Girls who pretend to sleep while they listen must be taught lessons," Vinaro said gently. "Whether I be a pig or a dog, it remains possible that you are fickle enough to be interested in this Tarzan. Just as you may have been interested in the boy Ramel—in a somewhat different way, perhaps—and aided his escape from me to Ruiz. If you were one of my men, I would kill you, simply as a safety measure, without inquiring further into your guilt. But since you are what you are, the problem is more complex: how long beauty can weigh down the scale against suspected treason to my person—and how long beauty itself can survive in such a balance."

Sophia sat back in the bed, piling the gleaming black pillows behind her and spreading her golden hair across them. She did not deign to look at Vinaro, but he saw that she held her shoulders back and her head high and had, by an effort, composed her lovely features.

He laughed softly.

Tarzan dreamed that wicked tarmangani, dressed in jungle garb and aided by gold-decked priests of Opar,* were cutting down his five-mile-high tree. He prepared to leap to Goro, the moon, before the tree fell.

He awoke with all senses alert, as a jungle animal does, yet with the dream still as real for a moment as the scarlet-draped, gold-appointed cabin around him. For another instant he wondered if the jet was crashing—the Boeing 707s had their troubles, as had the Constellations and Comets and Viscounts— one Boeing 707 of this same airline had crashed in 1962 near Lima, Peru, with 97 dead.

The ceiling lights were out in the luxurious, long cabin. Small glows made weird shadows, to which the heavy and light breathings of sleeping passengers were an eerie accompaniment.

But then he reminded himself with a smile that the improved

---

* *Tarzan and the Jewels of Opar* (Tarzan 5)

Boeing 707s were as safe as huge jets could be. Also, what was he doing worrying about death by air crash when he had just risked his life over and over in the bullring—and might risk it again, for all he knew, in the Mato Grosso? How Manolecito would grin!

Of course, there was the inevitability of mass death in an air crash—still Tarzan at heart did not believe that. A doubled lifetime of youthful experience and the hyper-swift instincts and movements of the jungle-nurtured would lead him to survival; it was his faith.

Perhaps he should fear death the more because his full youth had been prolonged beyond the total lifetime of most men. Yet somehow Tarzan did not. He knew he had always possessed—and at this moment still possessed—the feelings and appearance and powers of robust youth, despite his mature judgment and his vast store of experience and learning. He had never been able to decide whether his prolonged youthfulness was due to an unknown ingredient in a witch doctor's blood and herbs and molds, with which he had once been treated,* or to his having lived all his life, unique among men, on the thin borderline between the animal and the human, gifted with the natural instincts of the former and the wisdom of the latter—or to some other, unsuspected cause altogether. Sometimes he imagined his youth would last forever. At other times he fancied it might vanish in an instant and he become an aged dodderer overnight, somewhat like the wonderful one-horse shay. But what would happen would happen—he had learned that much from the fatalistic Arabs who threaded the dangerous trails of his home continent, Africa. Meanwhile he would live his youth to the full, using its every moment.

These thoughts did not altogether dispel his dream-induced uneasiness. Moreover, having slept, he was restless. After slipping on his shoes and coat, he trod silently forward. The couple who had been misinformed about the language of Brazil snored gently side by side, like two fish making bubbles. The air hostess,

---

* *Tarzan and "The Foreign Legion"* (Tarzan 22)

asleep in her small seat, her trim cap slid forward a little, looked like a tired, tall child. He moved back and bumped his feet a bit as he once more advanced. She was awake now, adjusting her cap, and she greeted him with a smile.

"*Desculpe, senhorita,*" he excused himself, "but I wish to speak to the copilot."

She looked unsure; he smiled encouragingly; she stood up and said, "I will seek to bring him to you, *senhor.* If you have the goodness to wait…" and went through the door forward.

In a few moments she was back with a maroon-uniformed, pale, plumpish man of stern expression, which turned to smiling respect as Tarzan drew a large, slim leather case from his breast pocket and showed him, behind the plastic cover, two notes on thick paper, the one signed with an undecipherable flourish above the words, "Secretary, Organization of American States," the other with a simple, "Elizabeth, Regina," in very black ink written with a broad-nibbed pen.

"I would like to sit forward with you for a time," Tarzan said graciously.

"It would give us the greatest pleasure," the other assured him, bowing.

There were times in civilization, the ape-man told himself, when it was as well to have the friendship of the great as it was in the jungle to be able to boast the protection of Tantor, the elephant, or Numa, the lion—or rather, in this case, Sabor, the lioness.

The nose of the great Boeing was full of starlight. Tarzan felt as if he had climbed to the very top of the rain forest of his childhood, far, far above the middle world of leaves and lianas, and still farther above the humus-floored ferny underworld where beasts and gomangani—the black man—prowled.

The stars were as bright as they were said to look from the moon. Achernar, forever below the horizon in northern latitudes, shone like a beacon ahead, flanked by the pale puffs of the Small and Large Magellanic Clouds, lesser Milky Ways. Yet someday man would reach those incredibly distant islands of stars. Tarzan wondered if he would live that long.

He sat relaxed in the copilot's chair. Beyond a simple greeting, the dark, hawk-faced pilot had not spoken to him. Naturally impassive, Tarzan thought, or more likely he sensed that his aristocratic British passenger desired silence.

A snowy floor of cloud a mile below hid the dark waters of the Caribbean, or rather Colombia by now.

The world seemed a small place from here. East—to his left—across the South Atlantic lay his beloved Africa, today split into a welter of new nations, ruled for the most part by the once-despised gomangani, sometimes listening but more often not to their good and bad tarmangani and even now malmangani (yellow man) counselors. Africa had sprung into the future. In a way the South American continent below him was now the older one, less explored. Soon the jet would be passing across the great Amazonian basin and then the vast, thinly populated jungles and plateaus of his ultimate destination, the Mato Grosso, altogether lacking jet airfields. *I should have brought a parachute,* Tarzan thought humorously—*I may pass straight over Lionel Talmadge's and João Ruiz's heads.*

Yes, it was a small world indeed—and unfortunately a world riven by hatreds. Tarzan wondered where his loyalties lay. To England first, no doubt of that, and to her lioness queen. Then to the great white race of the tarmangani ruling Europe, the Americas, Australia, New Zealand, a few other outposts. Then, in a diluted way, to all the sections of the human race—tarmangani, gomangani, malmangani—though indeed some individuals among all three of these were very difficult to love, or even like at all. The ones who threw bombs at you, for instance, or caused small boys to throw them, or slashed at you with their swift vehicles.

But deeper in a way than all these loyalties, Tarzan realized, was his devotion to the still greater race of the mangani, the great apes who had kindly reared him—yes, his devotion to *all* the mangani, whether human or brute, civilized or savage, speaking a language of science and subtlety, or one too primitive for civilized ears ever to tune in. For what was mankind but great apes groping toward the stars?

And it was a much-changed world from that of Tarzan's young manhood. Two suicidal wars had altered it almost beyond recognition. Atomic power, rockets, computers, wonder drugs, "firesticks" beyond any ape's dream of weapons, freedom or the hope of it burning like fire in all men's veins, new bright national prides that were in some instances a sickly phosphorescent leprosy. He thought of the very few places and persons that seemed still unchanged to him—tiny islands in a sea of chaos. First always among these was his wife Jane, Lady Greystoke, now managing their great estate of Chamston-Hedding, once chiefly a preserve for wildfowl, now half farm, half scientifically thinned forest—food and wood for England. Some hinted she was growing old, and it was true that she shunned the bright lights these days, but to Tarzan at least she was still the lovely and resourceful Jane Porter whom he had carried off into the jungle in 1909 and married in the cabin where his father and mother had died, Jane's own father Professor Archimedes Q. Porter conducting the ceremony.*

Now Tarzan thought wistfully of Jane and, smilingly, of himself. For all his wealth and maturity and powerful friends, he was essentially still a young man seeking adventure and trying to make realities of wildly idealistic dreams, as he had in the bullring at Meseta.

And forever discovering danger! Once again he puzzled over the attacks on him in Meseta. Or had they been attacks on Manolecito? The incident of the weird black-diamond bomb argued against that—it had not been thrown until Manolecito had walked away.

He asked the pilot, "Have you seen anything this trip of a Junkers Geschäfts-Meister jet, black with silver trim?"

---

* *Tarzan of the Apes* and *The Return of Tarzan* (Tarzan 1 and 2); for further data on his and Jane's longevity, see *Tarzan's Quest* (Tarzan 19).

The pilot shook his head, frowning.

"They're sweet ships," Tarzan said.

"Yes, too sweet. Meaning too swift and too easily converted into military jets capable of carrying anything from a recoilless eighty-eight cannon to a hydrogen bomb."

Clearly this man did not trust the Germans—and perhaps reflected the prejudice of the Brazilians against any but defensive warfare.

Copilot relieved pilot as the hours ticked off. The air hostess brought snacks and coffee and maté—Paraguay tea. Tarzan dozed pleasantly. The moon sank in the west. The cloud cover became streaky, vanished. The landscape ahead was a vast semicircle of darkness. Only twice did Tarzan note a tiny cluster of a half dozen lights.

Finally the sky paled ahead and a faintly gleaming streak slowly widened at the horizon—the Atlantic at last. The pilot replaced the copilot. Tarzan let himself be persuaded to stay in the inspector's chair.

Unhurried messages began to pass between the pilot and the control tower of Galeão airfield on *Ilha do Governador*, used by all the big intercontinental jets. Governor's Island informed them that the northwest wind which had helped them all night was still blowing there. They would approach from the sea.

Dawn came along. The sea was distinguishably blue as they swung over it in a wide semicircle and headed up Guanabara Bay. Tarzan caught a glimpse of a curving broad beach assaulted by long ocean rollers and backed by lines of white hotels and apartments now bright pink in the dawn—the famous Copacabana. It slipped behind the gleaming height of the fantastic pale granite Sugarloaf, or Pão de Açúcar.

Beyond that vast gleaming blunt-topped rock rose the greater height of Corcovado, dominated by its huge stone crucifix. All around, Rio de Janeiro lay like a winding lake of buildings, from which rose great steep-sided islands covered by greenery and shacks—for here, by a Brazilian paradox, the homes of the poorest occupied all the "view lots," as Americans might describe them, and looked down on the homes of the wealthy and the better-paid workers. Soon they were swiftly passing the city's docks and proud center and crossing a last blue stretch of Guanabara Bay, busy with shipping. Then, after the familiar moments of tension, they had touched down, braked, and taxied in.

"Muito obrigado," Tarzan thanked the pilot.

"De nada," the other answered with a smile and shrug—"For nothing,"—the so typical mixture of amiability and mild hauteur.

The air hostess' good-bye was faintly wistful.

Tarzan and his one suitcase—and the all-helpful case of letters in his breast pocket—went swiftly through customs. He changed 100 pounds into Brazilian currency and snagged a taxi without difficulty.

"Aeropôrto Santos Dumont," he directed the driver. Once again he must double back in his journey, this time to a smaller airport jutting out from the center of Rio into the Bay.

He took no special notice of a sleepy-eyed, unshaven man in a rumpled linen suit and a panama hat that had seen better days—a man who seemed not to look at Tarzan or hear his words. Yet when Tarzan's taxi was gone, the sleepy-eyed one suddenly scurried to the nearest phone booth.

CHAPTER 4

West by Cruzeiro

Augustus Vinaro and Sophia Renault sat at a bounteously laden breakfast table at the street edge of the terrace of a penthouse apartment atop the newly rebuilt Aeropôrto Hotel, which stands between President Roosevelt Avenue and the fabulous Avenida Beira Mar overlooking both Guanabara Bay and the Santos Dumont Airport of downtown Rio de Janeiro. The newly risen sun bathed them with golden light and made perfect a morning still cool.

They tinklingly touched together highball glasses filled with dark *refrescos* laced with rum, or *cachaça*, as it is called.

"To a golden city!" the man toasted.

"With golden subways and newsstands!" she replied.

"You're not being serious," he criticized.

"But I am, *chéri*," she defended herself laughingly. "Serious to the point where I even dare joke. And when one dares that with the formidable Augustus Vinaro…"

There had been no sound, but suddenly Mr. Train towered above them.

"Henrique phoned from Galeão," he said. "Tarzan has arrived by V.A.R.I.G. and taken a cab to Santos Dumont."

For an instant the girl's eyes looked troubled. Then she was once more all charm and flattery.

"You are the clever one, Augustus," she said. "The rest of us wondered, 'Where will Tarzan go?' You said *here*—and behold!"

"It was very simple," Vinaro said. "The man moves with speed. He wants west. He is a Britisher, and Cruzeiro has just purchased

41

twenty English planes. Mr. Train, station yourself with the binoculars. Inform me when you have spotted Tarzan."

As the huge man moved toward the other end of the terrace, Vinaro continued, "Mr. Train's one eye sees more than the two of most of humanity."

"He is your golem, your great zombi," the girl chattered on with a gaiety that held a note of hysteria, "while you are the black magician, the black golden-eyed spider. You sit quiet at the center of your web. This Tarzan's foot touches an outmost strand. At once you know, you take measures—"

"While you, Sophia," Vinaro interrupted, "do a poor job of concealing your interest in the same man. Nor do I much prefer being compared to a spider than to a pig or dog. You're thrilled by big muscles and brutal strength, aren't you? If I were not utterly certain of Mr. Train's loyalty to me…"

"Oh, really, you're impossible this morning," the girl snapped. "I cannot please you in any way." She began to eat, in tiny but rapidly chopped forkfuls, the hot golden breakfast pastries on her plate.

"Your slender beauty pleases me, Sophia. Your orange-yellow frock sets it off well, while honoring my golden purpose," Vinaro said rather solemnly. "Those *empadinhas de camerão* look good. What's in them?"

"Shrimp, finely sliced heart of palm, olives. A bit like Japanese *tempura*. They *are* good."

"And fattening," Vinaro observed.

"What is that with your steak?" she asked. Her fork had slowed.

"Roast manioc flour. That with a tender grilled fillet is called *churrasco*. Fattening, too, except that I shall only taste the manioc. The psychologists—those fools who pilfer the wisdom of artists and men of the world and call it a science—say that overeating is an expression of fear. The woman seeks unconsciously to protect herself from what she dreads, with a wall of fat."

Sophia pushed her plate aside with only one patty half consumed. She took up her *refresco*.

"All fruit has a sugar in it called fructose, assimilated into the blood without digestive change, like the glucose of corn syrup," Vinaro lectured casually. "While rum, especially the dark, contains more sugar than any other hard liquor."

Sophia put down her *refresco* and lit a cigarette. Vinaro forked off a mouthful of beef, dipped it in the dark roasted manioc, and chewed reflectively. Then he reached down beside his chair and laid on the snowy tablecloth a long-barreled Smith and Wesson .38.

Tarzan's taxi sped down the great modern bridge which links *Ilha do Governador* with the mainland. It reached the highway which joins Rio to Petrópolis, now a mountain resort for the wealthier tourists, but once summer residence of those long-reigning genial emperors, the Dom Pedroes, father and son, who were not overthrown until the Revolution of 1889, long after Spanish South America had thrown off the cruel iron yoke of Spain. Here the taxi turned left toward the big city and soon was traveling down the fabulously beautiful Avenida Rio Branco. Relatively few *Cariocas*, as the inhabitants of Rio are called, were abroad so early, yet of these most wore fantastic colorful costumes of all historical periods. Some reeled a bit.

The street was thick with multicolored confetti; there were white splashes on the splendid walls where bags of flour had burst, while Tarzan's keen nostrils caught the sweet scent of many perfumes and, under it, the still sweeter scent of ether.

Before his driver told him so, Tarzan remembered that this was the last day of Rio's world-famous pre-Lenten carnival. During the noisy, laughing, samba-ing nights, many of the throng would be equipped with "perfume-shooters"—flasks of perfume-scented ether which produced a freezing cold sensation on the skins of those hit with the fine spray.

He found himself thinking how easy it would be to make way with or kidnap a man or woman during the carnival. The anesthetic ether available everywhere—the victims merrily lured into a dark area—an ether-drenched handkerchief clamped to the nostrils and mouth...

Yet at the same time Tarzan found himself admiring the childlike gaiety of these people of the Occidental South. They had discovered how to retain something of the natural joy of primitive tropical man while remaining highly civilized.

These reflections were interrupted by the cabdriver remarking, "It's lucky for you you're only passing through, *senhor*. The city is packed to bursting for the carnival. You couldn't conceivably get a place to sleep for any amount of money, though *you* might"—he glanced at Tarzan in the rearview mirror—"for love."

"What of the *very* rich?" Tarzan asked.

"Oh, they live in a stratosphere of their own," the driver replied with a shrug.

Then suddenly he was cranking up the window beside him. "Close yours, *senhor*," he called. "Swiftly!"

"Why?" Tarzan asked as he complied.

"A flight of those new bees," the driver called back. "Some imbecile scientist imported fierce, honey-rich queens from Africa, hoping cross-breeding would make their progeny mild—but it made them fiercer! The new breed is being stamped out, but it still turns up, even in Rio."

For a moment there were *pingings* against the windshield and other panes. Then the swarm was past. Tarzan reflected on how, even today, Nature can strike at a great city.

The taxi passed the great Monroe Palace of the Senate, crossed President Wilson Avenue, and swung left into Avenida Beira Mar. Soon they were passing the Aeropôrto Hotel, had turned left into Santos Dumont Airport, and drawn up at the yellow-fronted facade of *Serviços Aéreos Cruzeiro do Sul*, the airline named after Brazil's monetary unit, the cruzeiro.

Tarzan paid off the driver with a few notes and several aluminum-bronze five-cruzeiro pieces. Brazil had discontinued silver coins long before the United States.

He stretched hugely and yawned, realizing that in one night

he had crossed almost the entire tropical zone, from just south of the Tropic of Cancer to just north of the Tropic of Capricorn.

He bought from a barefoot boy two newspapers—the *Brazil Herald*, printed in English, and *Diário de Noticias*—tossing the grinning lad several copper-nickel centavo pieces.

He had the feeling that he was under hostile observation. He looked around casually. Something flashed for an instant on the roof of the Aeropôrto Hotel, then winked out.

Mr. Train strode like a huge swift cat—a battered tom with only one eye—along the terrace edge, the binoculars in one of his huge paws.

"Tarzan has arrived at Santos Dumont, sir," he informed Vinaro, "and entered the waiting room of Cruzeiro."

Vinaro smiled. "Good. Send a telegram to the organization in Cuiabá: 'Our English customer arrives by eight-fifty plane. Spare neither expense nor care to ensure a memorable welcome.' Also a telegram in similar language to our Brasília representative, so that we will be informed if Tarzan stops over at the Capital or, though most unlikely, shifts to another route at that point. Likewise to our Goiânia man. Meanwhile phone Romulo to have the *Conquistador* ready for take-off in two hours."

"It would be possible to radio from the plane, sir," Mr. Train suggested respectfully. "Telegrams are uncertain in this land, even to Brasília."

"On your errands!" Vinaro rapped out, rising from the table. "I have no mind to chance giving the authorities in this area any hint that we possess such a powerful sender as the *Conquistador*'s."

Mr. Train vanished. Sophia Renault rose, too. She patted her flat stomach complacently, then tightened her wide belt of golden-colored leather another notch.

"I am losing weight," she announced. "Will you love me, *chéri*, when I am only a skeleton?"

Vinaro paused for a moment. Then, "Yes, I believe I will," he answered, grinning like a skull. "It may be possible I will build a chapel for your adoration. My Religion of Death, you know.

But while a girl is still alive, it is best that she cover her skeleton with just the right amount of flesh, neither a pound more nor less." As Sophia lit another cigarette, her hands shaking very slightly, he went on, "You thought I planned to shoot Tarzan from this terrace, didn't you?"

"Don't be a fool, Augustus!" she snapped. "Anyone knows you are far too prudent, too discreet, to make such an open, reckless—yes, courageous!—attempt on a man's life. Because for you to shoot from ambush in a city would be courage!"

Vinaro smiled. "Your *intellect* told you I would never attempt to assassinate Tarzan here in Rio. But your *feelings* argued to you that I might. It was to check on your feelings that I laid the revolver on the table. Clearly you have a feeling for Tarzan."

"Then shoot me and get it over! Or stir a little cyanide into my next cup of black coffee!"

Smiling more broadly, Vinaro shook his head. "Any woman has feelings for a strong, handsome, sun-bronzed man. They are untrustworthy, the whole female sex. It is a question of the depth of those feelings, and in the case of yours for Tarzan, I am not yet sure of that. Besides, you forget my methods. To her with whom I am truly angry, I give a jewel—not the dull black buttons I keep for men, but a lovely, glittering, unique gem of my own devising."

"Brasília, Goiânia, Cuiabá, Corumbá!" the tannoy summoned importantly. Tarzan was pleased when he saw that the plane was one of the new four-engine British Herons, shining with Cruzeiro's yellow-and-white and bearing its golden monetary emblem. The Dollar Airline, this would be called in the U.S.A. Tarzan preferred prop planes when he had time for them, and Lionel Talmadge's cable had given him no sense of urgency.

Unlike the V.A.R.I.G. jet, this plane was crowded, chiefly by soberly clad bureaucrats bound for Brasília, which replaced Rio as Brazil's capital city in 1960. Tarzan had heard that a few top government officials daily commuted by jet the 875 miles! But the jets did not go on to Cuiabá, lazy capital of the Mato Grosso.

Unlike the V.A.R.I.G. hostess, too, this girl was energetic and tiny, wore her hair in short bangs, and looked part Indian, very attractive in her dark yellow uniform. Tarzan immediately won her friendship by telling her that his trip was connected with *Serviço de Protecão aos Indio*—the Indian Protective Service—for indeed João Ruiz had ties with that worthy and widely admired agency. When they took off, he was seated in her alcove, where he could get the best view of the entire field.

Almost hidden in a cluster of private planes there was, Tarzan thrilled to note, a Junkers Geschäfts-Meister finished in dull black. So those who by intention or, less likely, by accident, had almost killed him and Manolecito had come as far as Rio!

Were some old ill-wishers on his trail?—he wondered. Or had his performance in Meseta angered some wealthy mad *aficionado* of the bulls so much as to make him want to hunt Tarzan down? Or was the mystery Ruiz had discovered a dangerous one—to such a degree that Tarzan had been marked down for death as soon as he received the cable—in which case Ruiz, and Talmadge, too, must be in even greater danger?

Tarzan dismissed the two last possibilities as overly fantastic, at least on present evidence.

He did ask the tiny vivacious air hostess, whose name was Jovanna, about the black jet. She smiled eagerly.

"I saw its travelers alight, *senhor*—although, alas, their names I do not know. Three men, one woman. Of the men, one like myself a *mameluco*—Indian blood with Portuguese. A very hard man, I judged. The second, a great pirate of a man with only one eye! He very hard, too, to be sure. *Inglês*, I thought, like yourself, though not so gracious. Or are you from the Colossus of the North?"

"No, your first guess was right. I'm English, not American," Tarzan told her. "What about the third man and the woman?"

"Both gentlefolk, dressed with much style and expense. He, a master, with the eyes of command! She—" Jovanna shrugged and gave Tarzan a wry grin. "She—I must confess it—blond, slim, most beautiful, like a European film star."

"You have not much to envy her for, Jovanna, I'm sure," Tarzan said.

She looked at him gratefully. "She and the masterful man seemed *amasiando*—how do you say it?" She blushed a little under her dark skin. "She his paid friend—not wife."

"How could you tell that about them?"

"She had not the submissiveness and helplessness of a wife," Jovanna said carefully, frowning past Tarzan in thought. "Yet she seemed to fear him and court his favor, as by trying to amuse him. Also she dressed"—she hesitated—"too rich for a wife."

"That's very clever of you," Tarzan said. The group sounded like none of his past enemies, though Jovanna's description teased his memory.

A little later he returned to his seat. The Heron had left Guanabara Bay behind and soon was climbing the mile-to-two-mile heights of the Serra da Mantiqueira. On the lower slopes Tarzan noted broad plantations of tobacco and of coffee trees in their trim green rows. Then he caused himself to sleep. Like soldiers, the beasts of the jungle sleep when they can—and jungle beasts had been Tarzan's tutors.

He did not wake until the Heron began its descent toward the great flat plateau where Brasília lies near the headwaters of rivers draining into the Amazon, the Paraná, and the Sao Francisco—Brazil's three largest drainage systems—with the heights of Chapada dos Pireneos in the hazy distance. Before landing, the Heron circled the city, which looked indeed, as it had been designed to, like a bird in flight or an aircraft with swept-back wings.

There was much flashing glass and metal to be seen, for Brasília is the newest great capital in the world, built between 1956 and 1961 by the ambitious President Juscelino Kubitschek at the expense of more than a half billion dollars, a good deal of the construction material brought in by airlift. At the head of the strange bird-of-the-ground it was easy to make out the twin 30-story, glass-walled congressional office towers, the truly fantastic "flying saucers" of the Chamber of Deputies and the

Senate—one turned up, the other down—many modernistic flying buttresses, and a huge hemispherical glass cathedral supported by great curving beams like the legs of a golden spider. White and golden-yellow apartment buildings were the wings, while the body and tail consisted of stores, theaters, and parks.

When the plane landed, Tarzan got out, but chiefly to stretch his legs, for the stop was a short one and the airport at some distance from the center of Brasília. However, he found himself looking with a new respect at the Brazilian flag flying above the airport buildings. That green, golden, and blue banner with 22 white stars forming the great heavenly constellation of the Southern Cross was truly the emblem of a people who were not merely genial and humorous, but also lived up in action to the motto written across their flag: "Order and Progress."

While he looked aloft, musing on the flag and its meanings, he lost any chance of noticing the man in a gray flannel suit who discreetly from the shadows observed Tarzan with binoculars until the ape-man climbed back into the plane and it taxied off. Then he hurried to a black Volvo parked on the other side of the airport buildings and drove off with great speed.

An hour later there was a longer stop at the older city of Goiânia. In the new airport restaurant Tarzan made a hearty meal of *feijoada completa*—black beans, rice, cooked jerked beef, and vegetables. He sprinkled it thickly with a course light flour, which stood in bowls on the tables like grated Parmesan cheese in an Italian restaurant, but was in truth manioc flour, known to the Northern Hemisphere only in the large-grained form of tapioca.

He recalled that the manioc or cassava root must be first roasted to drive off the deadly prussic acid which it contains, but this did not spoil his appetite. In fact the good food made him somewhat less sensitive than usual, so that he missed the cautious peerings of a distant waiter and did not sense the growing acids of suspicion in the man.

In the kitchen the waiter whispered to a cook's helper, who in turn spoke in low tones to a crippled *cafuso* outside. This poorly clad person of Indian-Negro descent limped off rapidly toward the telegraph station.

When the Cruzeiro Heron took off from Goiânia in midaft-ernoon for the long flight west to Cuiabá, the plane was not so crowded—Tarzan had two seats to himself. He also noted that the types aboard the plane had changed. The bureaucrats with their conservative modern suits and smaller hats were all gone. There were more men in boots, more sun-browned types with the look of the rancher or river man or jungle traverser. The city types were older and wore more old-fashioned clothes—well-worn linen suits with wide lapels, and wide-brimmed panama hats. There were a few more mulattoes and *mamelucos*. There were no women except for a wrinkle-skinned ancient with a doctor's bag, and, of course, Jovanna.

She paused by Tarzan's seat now and said quietly in English, "After this morning's conversation and compliments, you have hardly spoken to me—though you have been in no way dis-courteous," she hastened to add. She rested a dark, finely formed hand on the edge of Tarzan's seat, so that it touched his shoulder. "From this," she said, "I think two things. First, that you are a good man."

Now it was Tarzan's turn to blush a little. "I try to be, Jovanna," he said. "I have a wife in England."

"So," she said with a small grin and a wrinkle of her charming nose. "So that is that. Besides, you leave the plane at Cuiabá while I continue with it to Corumbá, a small city of many mosquitoes, an end to all romance. The second thing I think," she went on quickly, "is that you are a man whose mind is filled with a problem, and, like most such men, a man with enemies. I noted that at both Brasília and Goiânia you inquired if the black jet had arrived ahead of us—which it might well have done, with its great speed."

Tarzan almost started. He had, in truth, done exactly that. He'd told the girl she was observant, but he hadn't realized to what a degree. Well, at any rate the reply at both airports had been negative, while Cuiabá lacked a jet airstrip. He could put the Geschäfts-Meister out of his mind.

Jovanna said, "I have kept talking to our pilots. Now one of them clearly remembers that your black mystery plane was equipped with rocket brakes."

So the black jet *could* land at Cuiabá! While it certainly would hold enough petrol to make the Rio-Cuiabá trip direct, since it had last night crossed the entire Amazon Basin, where there was only one jet field—at Manaus, which was more distant from Brasília than Rio was from Cuiabá. He must revise his thinking.

"I'm very grateful to you, Jovanna," Tarzan said. "I don't know how I'd ever get along without you."

"Ha! With that surely most beautiful *Inglés* wife of yours, of course. But I have now more things to tell you—things of a less certain nature. No, thank you, but I may not sit beside you. The grandpapas round about us would whisper—la, but you are the one for creating the appearance of an intrigue while shunning the same! But I forgive it—you are *estrangeiro*. Now listen."

The pert face grew grave. "Two of the men on the black jet were hard types and the third a master of hard types, clearly. Now in the last weeks I have noted a gathering of hard types near Cuiabá. Oh, nothing obvious! For example, on my sixth flight before this one, there were several hard types in a bar at Corumbá. They were crew of a large barge carrying three great agricultural machines, they said they were, closely covered with canvases. The barge was headed up the Paraguai—toward Cuiabá. Their leader, a man named Voss, tried drunkenly to make friends with me."

"I bet you slapped his face for him," Tarzan said.

"Ha! You think I beat off all men, except perhaps you with the beauteous wife? A *mameluca* must take thought for her future. This Voss was not altogether a beast, though I will tell you I was not charmed with him—if it makes you happier to hear that. But to return to this matter of the hard types.

There must be almost a hundred who have journeyed to Cuiabá of late. Some by this air route and others. Some by automobile from Porto Velho in Rondonia. Some by slow train—pity them!—from São Paulo by way of Campo Grande. Some up the Paraguai. But all assembling in Cuiabá or rather somewhere nearby in the jungle of the Mato Grosso.

"Now you may think," Jovanna went on, "that this matter of hard types is all the imagination of a small, easily terrified, most imaginative woman. But no. We have *rough* types enough in Mato Grosso—even my Indian people can be killers—but the *hard* type, the type of the hired gunman, no. Their gathering is ominous."

"I don't know how I can repay you, Jovanna," Tarzan began.

"You cannot," she told him simply. "I must go now—that old one wants his *refresco*."

Tarzan thought, this girl has a head on her shoulders; she speaks the truth. There must be money somewhere in this mystery Ruiz has discovered. Big money—and a gathering of vultures. But why, if there were dangers, hadn't Talmadge warned him? Perhaps Talmadge simply didn't know—he was a scholar and not very heedful of the practical world around him. Tarzan was possessed of the desire to get to him—and to Ruiz, too—as soon as possible. Well, at least he had cabled Talmadge yesterday morning, the day of the bullfight, now seeming long ago. The man should be expecting him, perhaps would be at Cuiabá airport.

He moved to the window, and soon something else had possessed him. Below were no towns, no fields, no roads, but only unending forest—broadleaf evergreens, he judged, tropical hardwoods such as the *pau-amarelo*, with here and there stands of great palms. Somewhere he had heard that Brazil held one tenth of the forests of the whole world and was, after centuries of slash-cuttings and burnings, still more than half forest. But something deeper than this rehearsal of information was taking hold of his mind and feelings as he watched the unbroken green acres coming and passing by in long, gentle waves.

This was none of your safe British or American flying, Tarzan told himself, with a landing spot always within gliding distance. This was adventuring at risk across the nearly unknown.

They crossed a dark, steamy river that must be the Araguaia, Tarzan decided. Then more leagues of unbroken forest with a still more tropical look. He could almost see the lianas and vines, the blotched orchids and great ferns that must lie below. What he saw now, he knew, was only a roof, the gently waving green roof of the silent, mysterious, shadowy, humus-carpeted world of the jungle a hundred or more feet below the treetops. Tarzan's own world, though in another continent than Africa— that was what gripped his being.

From dead ahead the setting sun lanced the long cabin with gold.

Green flames blossomed from the silvery leading-edges of the *Conquistador's* short black wings, cutting in half its airspeed as, skimming low, it touched down on the Cuiabá airfield.

A minute earlier a six-passenger Messerschmitt helicopter had taken off from the section of the field reserved for private planes and hangars, despite an admonitory hooting from the skeletal control tower. Now it touched down beside the *Conquistador* at the instant the latter came to a full stop at the end of the airstrip.

Two men looking hard both in body and soul piled out of the helicopter. A silver ladder descended from the jet. The *mameluco* Romulo came tumbling down it like a monkey. The other three travelers descended with more dignity, though rapidly. Mr. Train carried in one hand two suitcases which looked the size of dispatch cases in his big, hard paw.

"Wilson, taxi the *Conquistador* to the hangar," Augustus Vinaro ordered one of the men from the German-built heli. "Then hangar doors closed and stand guard. Cabral," he addressed the other, "after helping Wilson, report at once to Portinari. He may have work for you. The rest of you, into the heli!"

A few seconds later they were drumming west with Romulo at the controls. The sun, half set, was straight ahead. The tilted vanes as they dipped cast strange whirling shadows into the cabin.

Vinaro said in Sophia Renault's ear, "The stage is set, my dear, for Tarzan when he arrives in two hours—and the stage director, knowing all is perfectly rehearsed, takes a walk. Or, in this case a heli flight. And *this* director has two shows opening the same night—for in a matter of hours Rodriguez will be moving against Ruiz."

"You are incomparable, *chéri*," Sophia told him, her lovely mouth close to his lobeless ear with its slight satyr tip. Her coral lips were emphasized by the pallor of her face, just as her smiles were made exotic by the terror lines around her eyes. "We are flying to the Castle?"

"Yes, to the Castle!" Vinaro replied vivaciously. "The Castle that is only a way station to the City of Gold!"

In that instant the vanishing sun flared, the high clouds turned bright yellow, yellow flooded the cabin, and for the moment its occupants—Vinaro in his white linen suit, the pale Sophia in her creamy frock, even the genteel, brutal Mr. Train—all seemed people of gold. While the beat of the vanes was like the drums of a conquering expedition, and the whirling black shadows its tossing plumes.

With great casualness Sophia asked, "I suppose Tarzan will be brought to the Castle for questioning?"

Vinaro smiled and consulted his large gold wristwatch. "My dear," he said, "in exactly two hours and twenty minutes, if that Cruzeiro flight arrives on time, Tarzan will be dead."

CHAPTER 5

"An Indolent People..."

Cuiabá, capital of the Mato Grosso, lying on the Cuiabá River at the headwaters of the Paraguay drainage system, almost on the dividing line between the jungle and hills of the north and the swamps and subtropical forest of the south, is a city of contrasts. It is a lazy, locked-off place, yet its population is sprinting toward the 100,000 mark. Indians, some of them among the most primitive in the world, wander there from the north, leaving their deadly blowpipes outside town. There also come suave political refugees from Argentina and nearby Bolivia. Trucks and carts bring in great bags of ipecac, the root which doctors use to make men vomit and also employ in the treatment of amoebic dysentery. In smaller bags come gold and diamonds won from the rich surrounding sands. There are old mansions of the successful planters. There is also a noisy though limited night life. There are fine civic and cultural buildings, and there are shacks.

There is even a great gas station with—wonder of wonders—a completely modern car-wash, strongly and elaborately fenced and nicknamed "The Watery Colossus of the North," although its owner is a good Brazilian. Tourists from *los Estados Unidos*, having traveled the long twisting highway from Pôrto Velho across the wilds of Rondônia, greet it with cries of amazement and have their dusty, mud-splashed Cadillacs and Chryslers washed shining bright. It is also reported on the best authority that a large Indian family once brought their ancient Buick there for cleansing and insisted on marching in single file behind their car, so that they might share the pleasures of their vehicle's bath. Although warned against the strength of the detergents and the heat of the water, they persisted in their decision and emerged smiling, shining bright and wholly uninjured, down to the last two-year-old.

There is a modern airport, yet its parking area for automobiles lacks lights, like the parking areas in many suburban railway stations in North America.

This balmy evening the parking area was empty until a black Morris sedan drew in beside some tiny-leafed pepper trees. A man with a chauffeur's cap stepped out of it and came around the hood.

There were lights—red, green, and white—in the starry sky to the east, coming in fast. The airport tannoy called in Portuguese, "Cruzeiro Flight Number One from Rio, Brasília, and Goiània, arriving eight-fifty, on time."

A black Lincoln came ghosting up beside the Morris. In it were three big men whose harsh, deadly, north-of-the-Equator faces contrasted sadly with the mild Capricornian night.

Fifty yards back, the motor of the Lincoln had been switched off and its rear doors quietly opened. The tannoy covered up the slight sounds of its coasting. It was moving at barely a footpace when it reached the Morris.

The first noise the man with the chauffeur's cap heard was heels striking hard earth and a voice that softly called his name, "Antonio!"

He turned swiftly, his right hand snaking to the grip of his belt-holstered Colt Cobra .38.

Pale flames and thudding sounds came from in front of the dead-white right hands of the two men who had sprung from the back of the Lincoln. Their right arms jerked with the recoil of their weapons.

The man named Antonio stopped reaching for his gun and instead merely touched his belly lightly, as if he had mild indigestion. There were dark eruptions from the back of his spine, neck, and head.

Before he hit the ground, hands in white canvas gloves grabbed him and bore him into the grove of pepper trees. One of the three informal pallbearers snatched off the chauffeur's cap and used his white gloves to wipe it carefully clean of blood and brains before he tossed his gloves onto the corpse beside the two other bloodied pairs.

"A black mark against you, Luigi," he said softly. "We were not to aim at the head." Then he placed his revolver with its silencer-swollen barrel under the driver's seat of the Morris and put on the hurriedly cleansed chauffeur's cap and loped toward the runway where the Cruzeiro Heron, white and yellow in the airport lights, had just taxied to a stop.

Tarzan let the seven other passengers for Cuiabá go ahead of him. He stopped at the head of the aluminum stairway. Looking up from a level just above his elbow, Jovanna said smilingly, "I hope we'll make another trip together."

"I hope so, too," Tarzan answered.

"Do you have any suggestions as to how our flight could be improved?" the little *mameluca* inquired briskly.

Tarzan grinned. "Yes. Next time let's not allow any other passengers."

"Ha! Once again the gallant compliments—when it is safe for you to make them. But watch out—I may be your hostess on your return trip!" Suddenly her grinning little face grew grave. "Also, watch out for the hard ones."

"I will," Tarzan assured her. "And thanks a lot, Jovanna. *Muito obrigado.*"

"*De nada.*" The little face was now a mask.

Tarzan walked down the aluminum steps feeling oddly happy. Jane, he thought, would like Jovanna with her good-humored teasing. He remembered something he had once read about Brazilians being "an indolent people...softened by tropical breezes, lazy servants, and their vast country's natural wealth…" Well, they certainly were an amiable people, though some of them were energetic enough, like Jovanna— or, for that matter, this dark, smiling fellow with the chauffeur's cap who had suddenly appeared at the foot of the aluminum stairs.

"Sir?" this one called up at him eagerly. "Are you the man they call Tarzán? Senhor Tarzán?"

"Yes," Tarzan answered, "though we might try 'Lord Greystoke,' don't you think?"

"Yes, indeed, milord. I am called Antonio. Humble Antonio only. I am to take you to the residence of Professor Lionel Talmadge. May I carry your suitcase?"

"Certainly," Tarzan assured him, handing it over. Relieved of the small burden, he quietly flexed his muscles, slightly cramped from long sitting, and hurried after Antonio, who was certainly setting a brisk pace for one of "…an indolent people." Good of Talmadge to have sent the man!

His nostrils thrilled to the spicy, perfumy, resinous scents of the warm night—and under them, very faint but most exciting of all, the dark, moist aroma of tropical jungle.

Then suddenly all his nerves were a-quiver, for now he was getting another scent, one that must have a nearby source, since it strengthened so swiftly—the thick sweetish scent one gets when one nears a spot where Numa, the lion, has just made a kill.

Or rather not Numa, but a *mangani* of one of the civilized breeds, for now there was the reek of cordite in addition to the scent of blood.

There was no transition a man might have noticed, but now Tarzan was all alertness, his very skin more sensitive under the light gray tweeds—a swift creature of the jungle beneath his civilized trappings.

He was in a dark parking area. Antonio had put his suitcase into the back of a black Morris and was obsequiously holding open that door for him. Fifty yards off upwind a black Lincoln stood with motor idling. It seemed unoccupied, yet with the petrol fumes was intermixed the acid stench of several tar-mangani excited by fear, hate, or the drive to kill.

Tarzan made his decision. Watching Antonio's every move-ment now, he stepped into the car and seated himself to the left, out of view of the driver's rear-view mirror. It was stuffy—the windows were all closed. Antonio climbed into the driver's seat and, after one failure, set the motor going. The Morris swung around in a wide circle and headed down a street of warehouses. Behind them, Tarzan heard the sudden growl of another car. He leaned forward behind Antonio and again got the scent of death, very strong. It was coming from the cap the man was wearing. While in the rear-view mirror he could see the black Lincoln coming on with only parking lights, gradually narrowing the gap between the two cars.

Tarzan leaned back and said, "Don't you like air?" casually.

Antonio replied, "The night sort carries miasma and bats and other noxious fliers."

Tarzan remarked, "At the airport, Antonio—was anyone hurt near this car within the last few minutes?"

The driver's shoulder muscles stiffened. "No, *senhor*...I mean, Lord Greystoke." He leaned forward and drove for a moment with one hand. Then, "Why do you ask, milord?"

Tarzan said mildly, "There was the smell of blood near the car. That usually means someone's been hurt."

Antonio had something on his lap now, Tarzan knew, some-thing he had taken from under the seat. The man said, "Perhaps someone cut himself, milord. Most people wouldn't notice such a thing."

Tarzan countered with, "Do you think most people would notice that we're being followed? By a black Lincoln with half lights."

"We are, milord?" Antonio asked blankly. "Then let's just turn in here and see what they do."

Tires squealing, the Morris swerved into a large dark service station. Speeding between four locked pumps and a barred-off service area, it entered a large, flat, asphalted circular space entirely surrounded by a high fence of heavy woven wire. A gate of the same material stood wide open where they had entered. A cut length of chain dangled from it.

Tarzan thought—irrationally perhaps—*arena!*

Curving across the circular area, almost from end to end, yet leaving some space all around it everywhere, was a strange irregular tunnel which at some points could be seen through and at some points not. On the other side of the tunnel from the gate, and up against the fence, was scaffolding of some sort.

This much Tarzan saw as Antonio turned sharply right and then instantly left again, into the tunnel.

Other tires were squealing, too. Only a few yards behind them came the black Lincoln, but instead of turning into the tunnel, it braked with a surge and squeal just beyond the tunnel. Three men piled out, two carrying Schmeisser submachine guns. Antonio braked viciously. As the Morris rocked to a halt, its windows were deluged with soap and water. Tarzan felt—again he did not know why—as if *he* were an animal being blinded. Instantly Antonio turned in his seat, raising his revolver with swollen barrel.

But another man's "instantly" is Tarzan's "slowly." He let the forward surge of the braking carry his body into what is some-times called "the death seat," beside the driver, but which in this case would be "the life seat," he knew. Before his shoulders struck the glove compartment and braced themselves there, his hands had grasped Antonio's gun arm at wrist and elbow, and now he heaved.

Antonio's rising swing-around, which he had started himself, became a surge that tumbled him into the back seat. His gun was jerked from his hand.

Tarzan, rising swiftly, his back pressed to the windshield all bubbly white outside, thought, *Now I am the animal's head and Antonio his belly and chest and heart. Most hunters try for the heart shot.*

He had a dim glimpse of Antonio's horrified face as the

man sought to lift himself from his sprawl in the back seat. Antonio's hand, shooting out, pulled down the lever of the right rear door.

Then with a crashing and cracking that seemed thunderous in the confined space of the sedan, two dozen jets of flame lanced through the right rear windows. Glass spattered; Antonio's body jerked and danced as bullets pierced it in two crisscross lines, like the plungings of two great sewing machine needles.

While the sudden brief fusillade was still resounding, Tarzan slipped behind the wheel, touched the windshield wipers into action, shifted into first, and sent the Morris surging forward.

As the Morris hurtled down the tunnel of the car-wash which Tarzan saw through the large triangular eyes created in the soapsuds by the wipers, the Lord of the Jungle appraised the whole situation in an instantaneous and utterly uncivilized fashion—for ever since the first shot came shattering, the beast half of his brain, startled and furious, had taken control of him.

He had often driven cars before, even in British and European road races, but never as now. He was not Tarzan driving a black Morris. No, he and the car had been transformed into a single creature of vast power—*buto*, the rhinoceros!—a strangely compounded *buto* of steel and flesh, but *buto*, nonetheless.

And to what was *buto* opposed this time? Simply to another larger *buto*—or, no, rather to a *tantor*, the elephant, a stupid though swift *tantor* with three tarmangani hunters in a howdah on his back.

The Morris-and-Tarzan *buto* would know how to deal with *them*!

He was almost at the tunnel's end. The Schmeisser men, with infuriating swiftness, had piled back into the Lincoln, which was racing him around the perimeter, outside the car-wash and to his right. They were well behind him, but he would lose time making the sharp left turn out of the tunnel.

He made it with a short skid, merely hoping that any soap had been burned off his tires by now. The right rear door swung wide open, and he felt weight leave the car—Antonio's riddled body. In a screaming second gear now, he spurted forward. He grunted with animal satisfaction as he heard the Lincoln bump on Antonio's body and saw its headlights, on high-bright now, jump up and down. Then he snarled like a beast as the Lincoln still came on after him—the idiot tarmangani mahout should have lost control of his *tantor* at that point!

Now a choice ahead. He could race almost straight out of the wire arena by the door where he had entered, or he could swing back of the car-wash, following the Lincoln's tracks. If he made the first choice, they would have straight shooting at him as he fled between the pumps and the service area.

He made the second choice—and had the satisfaction of hearing a fusillade *whirrr* off through the empty gateway he had just bypassed.

Now he was on the perimeter, just like the Lincoln, and they were swinging around the car-wash after him—a circular chase. He dodged the scaffolding, which was of four-by-fours, noting that they carried at a height of 15 feet several stout wide planks, bent by a great solid mass of piled red bricks. The *buto* or Tarzan-Morris section of his brain went red with rage at this typical tarmangani trap barely evaded, but the Tarzan-alone section docketed the information.

Another Schmeisser fusillade went ricocheting off the metal of the car-wash as he darted behind its farther end, but now the *tantor-Lincoln* was gaining, just as *tantor* would in a real race with *buto*. And this time the tarmangani in the howdah would *expect* him to dash again behind the car-wash and have their guns aimed for that—yet still have him at their mercy (hate!) if he did dart out of the arena down the straight.

The cruel, blinding headlights swung at him from behind. He braked fiercely, as if intending the sharp right-hand turn out of the arena—then stamped the accelerator to the floor as he once more swung behind the car-wash.

There were two fusillades this time. The first missed him entirely to the front as he braked. The other mostly missed him to the rear as he accelerated, though two bullets *whanged* against the metal of the Morris.

The circular race continued. The *tantor*-Lincoln was still gaining. The scaffolding loomed ahead. But by now the Tarzan-alone brain sector had managed to communicate its plot to the *buto* brain sector. The Tarzan-Morris beast craftily slowed a little, risking the chance of an early fusillade. It came, and one bullet holed the windshield over the wheel from behind, but Tarzan had ducked his head into "the life seat." From there he guided the Morris so that it smashed successively through the three four-by-fours supporting the bricks on the inside.

They rained down like millstones on the Lincoln, a massive red hail even *tantor* could not withstand. Jolting with the blows and still seeking to evade them, the Lincoln swerved too fast, rolled over, and crashed, upright again, against the car-wash.

Tarzan snorted in triumph. The Tarzan-Morris creature slowed still more, became sluggish in victory, as it swung around the end of the car-wash, missing Antonio's mangled remains (a sign that the basically gentle Tarzan-alone brain was regaining control) and heading toward the open gate.

Buto had slowed too much. One of the Schmeisser-bearing tarmangani, surviving the Lincoln's roll and thrown into the car-wash, sprang up, burly and shock-resistant as a great ape, dashed into the Morris's path, and aimed his bloody face and his Schmeisser at the oncoming Morris.

Tarzan, feeling a *buto* rage at the vile tarmangani's powers of survival, ducked again into "the life seat" and stamped the accelerator. Six bullets riddled the windshield, and then there was a bump-and-crash as the submachine gun man got it.

Tarzan swung erect and recorrected the Morris's course the shade necessary to send it out of the wire-fenced arena.

By the time he was passing between the gas pumps and the service area, the *buto* brain had dissociated itself enough for Tarzan to be thinking, quite prosaically, that most automobile drivers on the Great West Road out of London, or on the

Berlin-Hamburg *autobahn*, or the Pennsylvania Turnpike were only *buto* brains operating subconsciously.

By the time he turned into the street again, he was reviewing in his mind the map of Cuiabá which Jovanna had given him and which he had memorized, and deciding on the shortest route to Professor Talmadge's residence.

He was also feeling some amazement that the motor, gas tank, and apparently all four tires of the Morris had survived the duel in the arena of the car-wash. Also amazement that the street was still dark and empty, not filled with a gathering crowd and curious cars. How long *had* the duel taken—30 seconds, 40 seconds, a minute even? *Buto's* brain does not record time as a tarmangani's.

The route decided on, Tarzan was wondering about the brain that had devised the insane outrage back in the car-wash. It was not the brain of the men in the Lincoln, he decided. They were simple, brave, brutal, *hard* types who, if given their choice, would have gunned him down on the airport parking lot, very possibly with success.

By contrast, the car-wash attempt on his life was monstrously oversubtle, grotesque, baroque. A man surrounded by unexpected soapsuds from which erupted death!

No, he was up against and from now on would have as his chief opposition—in whatever insane war this was—a brain that wanted to kill in such fantastic, cryptic, startling ways as to cause his victims to die in a state of utter terror, astonishment, and *even admiration of their murderer.*

CHAPTER 6

The Ticking of a Wristwatch

P rofessor Lionel Talmadge's oak-paneled study held clues
to his interests and to his character, too, though it would
have taken an astute mind to deduce much of the latter.
One wall was covered with great maps of the Brazilian states
of the Mato Grosso and Rondônia, and the countries of Bolivia
and Peru. These held many extra names penciled in, routes
pencil-traced and sometimes erased and retraced. Stuck here
and there were many pins of various colors, including silver and
gold. At the window end of this wall was a large stone fireplace.

The opposite wall held mostly works of art: bold black-and-
white block prints by Maria Bonomi; flaringly colorful abstrac-
tions by the Japanese-Brazilian Manabu Mabe; Indian bracelets
and necklaces and pectorals of copper, silver, rock, and bone;
statuettes of strangely garbed saints from the *macumba* cult,
which has distant links with voodooism; weird masks, ghostly
and animal; and towering headdresses of long feathers, brilliant
and colorful as jewels.

The third wall, in which was the door, was racked with
weapons, from a wooden sword set with flakes of obsidian and
a long blowpipe with its tufted poisoned missile (like a powder
puff or a thick feather duster for a doll's house with a darning
needle for handle) to certain unimpressive fountain-pen-looking
objects which only the expert in terrorism and assassination
would have recognized as being projectors for fluid nerve poison,
cyanide, and the like. Between those strangely similar extremes
were many knives and guns, including a jet-and-silver inlaid

percussion-cap revolver and a gold-finished Beretta .25. There were louvers in the top of this wall.

The fourth wall was all leaded windows, open now so that the fine copper screening glinted in the light from inside. Yet although this room was a second-story one, there was a screen inside, a beautiful tall dark zigzag, set with mother-of-pearl and turquoise and silver, concealing the room's occupants from any possible spies.

There was a large old desk with many pigeonholes flanked by bookcases against the wall which also held the works of art. There were several comfortable chairs finished in gleaming thick leather, and little tables with great ashtrays made of black volcanic rock. There was one large table on rock legs and consisting of a single rectangular slab of stone into which had been carved a barbaric representation of the legendary founder of the Incas, Manco Capac, appearing as a boy in golden robes in the cave mouth above Cuzco and proclaiming himself Son of the Sun to his assembled people-to-be. There were dim traces of rubbed-away gold in the areas of stone that were the boy's robes and the dagger-edged sun.

On this table stood a telephone, a bowl of ice cubes, swizzle sticks with elaborately carved "egg-beater" ends, a tall pitcher of *refresco,* some Swedish modern glasses, and several bottles of rum ranging in hue from white through gold to darkest brown.

Professor Talmadge was pacing the room from the screen to the weapon wall, making each time a little jog as he passed the stone table. He was a tall, slender man of about 60, with white-flecked hair and a keen, intelligent face in which the cerebral abstraction of the scholar was oddly mixed with the disciplined watchfulness of the military man. He wore scuffed oxfords, khaki slacks, a soft white shirt, and a pale tan cardigan sweater, unbuttoned. He held in one hand a short glass of white rum on the rocks.

Seated solidly beside the stone table, a rum-"sweetened" *refresco* close at hand, was a short, stocky man about ten years younger than the professor, wearing the uniform of a Brazilian army colonel, though with shirt loosened at the neck, coat hung carelessly by a shoulder on a back corner of his chair, and cap beside his *refresco*. He had a grim, angular face with large, compassionate eyes with brown irises flecked with gold. His name was Carlos Juarez.

He swizzled his *refresco* until it foamed, spinning the stick between his palms, then took a solid swallow of the dark drink and said soothingly, "Please, professor. Perhaps the Cruzeiro is late. Perhaps they encountered a mechanical difficulty with the car."

"No!" Talmadge took a quick sip of his drink without halting his pacing. "Antonio knows how important this is. He would have called."

Juarez smiled, somewhat tiredly. "He would, perhaps, if *you* were running my army…and my irregulars. Won't you ever learn the Latin philosophy of intelligent relaxation, of the true stoicism? You English are chronic worriers. You have ants in your trousers, as the Yankees put it."

"But I *am* worried," Talmadge stated flatly as if it were some basic point of law. He moved a hand to scratch himself, halted it instantly.

Juarez said wryly, "And what good is it doing you to wear your floors out?"

"Are you suggesting that rest will cure my anxiety?" Talmadge demanded, pretending mild rage, the worry still in his eyes. "I've got thick floorboards, I'll have you know—and can walk on them from here to eternity if need be."

"I'm suggesting you sit down, drink off those watery remains, and pour yourself another white stomach burner."

Through several walls, iron chimes clanged faintly.

"They're here!" Talmadge said sharply. "Thank God!"

"There was never any question of that," Juarez said smoothly. "Vinaro doesn't own the cable wires—yet. But don't mistake me, professor, I'm quite anxious to meet this strange jungle superman of yours."

"Superman or not, I just pray he can help. *You* know our problem, colonel."

"Too truly," the other agreed, nodding grimly.

The door they were facing opened. A short man in dark trousers and shirt, with dark gleaming skin and black hair cut in short bangs, said to Talmadge, "There is a...Senhor Tarzan to see you, sir."

"Show him in at once, Huascar."

The servant slipped back. Tarzan was in the doorway, looking no worse for his recent ordeal. Huascar shut the door.

Colonel Juarez studied the newcomer sharply, betraying a little surprise at his pale gray tweeds, black moccasin shoes of thin leather, soft creamy shirt with pale gray tie, and especially at his youthful face and carriage.

Despite his trim, civilized appearance, there was an aura about the newcomer, a sense of depths and powers, a savage electricity, that excited, disturbed, and even frightened one.

"Good to see you, Lionel," Tarzan said quietly. "Though you should have told me your cablegram was loaded."

"Trust you to guess that!" Talmadge said loudly, missing in his relief the somber note in Tarzan's voice. "This is Colonel Carlos Juarez of the Brazilian Army, attached also to the Indian Protective Service—a good Brazilian, for all his Spanish name."

"*Estou muito contente,*" Tarzan said sincerely, yet not as if he were altogether "very glad." He gripped the other's hand.

Juarez did catch the somber note. He said quickly, "Your countryman was concerned about your delay in getting here. But I told him that Antonio is one of my best men."

Tarzan looked him in the eye. "Antonio *was* one of your best men, colonel. *Sinto muito*—though I know being sorry is no help. You will find his body in a copse of pepper trees at the west end of the airport parking lot—*they* may have moved the corpse, but I imagine not."

Juarez took a step forward, pain in his big eyes. "You saw Antonio's dead body? How do you know who it was?"

Tarzan shook his head. "No, I smelled it—no crudity

intended—and made certain deductions. Yet he was well avenged, if that helps any, which it seldom does. The man who killed and impersonated him—and as many as three of his confederates—are lying dead in what I imagine must be the only car-wash in Cuiabá. Along with the corpse of a dead Lincoln. *Your* car—the black Morris?—survived, though it has many bullet holes in it. But it *is* clean. You will, I'm sure, wish to check on these points."

He turned toward Talmadge, who stood staring with jaw dropped just a little. Now he firmly closed it.

"Dear Lionel," Tarzan said, "you've been playing with loaded telegrams again. You've succumbed to the pleasure of teasing me with half information. It won't do. Or else you don't realize that you're up against a very brilliant—possibly uniquely brilliant—criminal madman. I trust you've had more thought for João Ruiz's survival than you've had for mine."

Talmadge flushed, yet, "Carlos!" he said sharply. "*You* said you thought Vinaro had a streak of madness. Tarzan, how do you know?"

"Yes, *por Deus*, how do you know about these matters?" Juarez cried, lunging forward and grasping Tarzan's coat by its lapels.

"Softly, gentlemen," Tarzan said, calmly removing the colonel's hands from his coat. "You're going much too fast. I know nothing about the nature of the mystery which Ruiz is said to have discovered. And just now I heard the name Vinaro for the first time, and it meant nothing to me. However, there are matters which I *do* know, which perhaps I have happened on by merest chance, along with the recent violences here in Cuiabá—and of these I will tell you fully. Let us sit down and speak rationally, though I well know that in matters such as this the irrational often intrudes—and also strong emotions, like yours for poor Antonio."

Juarez and Talmadge complied. The three men sat around the stone table. "*Um refresco?*" Juarez automatically asked Tarzan, raising the pitcher.

"*Sim,*" Tarzan said. "*Obrigado.*"

"With sweetening? A tot of *cachaça*? You must surely need it."

"Not this time," Tarzan said. He drank thirstily, then launched into an account of all that had happened since his arrival at Cuiabá. Within a half minute Juarez had taken up the phone and was making short, harsh-voiced calls, while signing to Tarzan to keep on talking.

Next Tarzan gave a somewhat sketchier account of his movements since receiving the cable from Talmadge at Meseta. His listeners eyed each other sharply when he mentioned the explosion there—and more sharply still when he brought the black silver-trimmed Junkers Geschäfts-Meister into his account. They also showed great interest in the matters Jovanna had told him.

Juarez once interjected bitterly, "All our cable lines run through Vinaro's bedroom, clearly. At some point your cable, professor, must have been unlawfully read."

As Tarzan finished, Talmadge said excitedly, "It must have been Vinaro at Meseta. The Junkers jet proves it."

Juarez nodded. "Indeed, yes. Antonio reported to me that it arrived at sunset here and was promptly hangared. That was why you did not see it, Tarzan, when you arrived here. You shouldn't have seen it at Santos Dumont. Vinaro slipped there."

"But what the devil was Vinaro doing in North America?" Talmadge demanded. He was up and pacing again. "When all our evidence shows that his current efforts are focused in the corner of the Mato Grosso near the undefined boundary with Bolivia."

Juarez said, "A copy of your cable to Tarzan, professor, must have been cabled to Vinaro somewhere near Meseta, though perhaps in the U.S.A. That was why the attacks began in Meseta."

"Not necessarily," Talmadge said, quickening his pacing. "From what Tarzan has told us of the things he did in the bullring, Vinaro might have developed enough hatred of him for that alone to attempt his death. I have always told you, Carlos, that what Vinaro lightly calls his Religion of Death is the key to his character. He venerates the slaughter of the bullring and—"

"Gentlemen, gentlemen," Tarzan protested. "It is high time you began to fill me in on the whole picture here. You can continue your argument afterwards."

"Quite," Talmadge agreed. "I'll begin literally—picture, you said." He took two photographs from a pigeonhole of his desk, handed one to Tarzan.

"That is a blowup," he said, "of the only known picture of Augustus Vinaro."

Tarzan studied the somewhat blurred smiling face. "Yes," he said, "he could be the well-dressed one Jovanna described—and perhaps with 'eyes of command,' if he weren't smiling. Yet the man somehow looks innocent and rather harmless."

The others smiled grimly. Talmadge handed Tarzan the second photo.

"And this is Vinaro's bodyguard. His name is Mr. Train."

"He does bear a striking resemblance to a locomotive," Tarzan said with grim humor. "One-eyed, too, like the locomotives of steel. Yes, you're right, gentlemen—there's now no doubt about it at all—Jovanna mentioned the eye patch and that the man was truly huge, about six feet eight inches, I gathered. These must be the same people who sought to kill or frighten myself and Manolecito at Meseta. I now have a faint memory of seeing the two in a box at the bullring. But who would be the third man Jovanna described?"

"One of Vinaro's Spanish-Indian followers," Juarez said. "Most likely the one named Romulo, who is known to be a skilled pilot, though his Brazilian license was got by forgery or bribery— that's one of the many spots where my inquiries have run up against a stone wall, which will take time and patience to batter down."

"And the blond girl, like a European film star?"

"Sophia Renault, Vinaro's current companion," Juarez answered with a scowl and a shrug. "He picks them up in Rome,

I believe, where they gather around the great film studios like ants, each seeking to become a queen."

"What happens to them?" Tarzan started to ask, but just then Talmadge cut in with, "You mentioned Vinaro's innocent appearance, Tarzan. Believe me, he's one of the most deadly international criminals on the face of the earth. Again and again he has killed to gain his aim or please his will. His favorite target is raw gold and precious gems. We believe that he has fabricatories for expensive jewelry and a worldwide scatter of stores where he sells them at the highest prices—but there again the connections are as yet untraced."

"I believe I can give you one more piece of evidence for his being an international criminal," Tarzan said and told them about the "treasure jet" burned in the Mohave, its bullion and gems filched. "The man may have several crimes running at the same time in different countries," he finished. "Truly international. Oh, yes, and there was a report of a red two-engine jet following the treasure plane. If Vinaro has some swift method of changing the color of his Geschäfts-Meister—"

"Which undoubtedly he has," Juarez put in. "The man patronizes the greatest technicians."

"Yes, he must be the thief in this Mojave case, all right," Talmadge agreed eagerly, "and he'll multiply this latest haul in value by turning it into rings, bracelets, pendants, pectorals, wristwatches, tie pins, fobs, chains. He specializes in producing very heavy solid-gold jewelry, knowing that prosperous frightened individuals everywhere are ravenous for gold and other small-volume wealth, which could survive revolutions and even atom wars. Look how America's decision to stop minting silver coinage resulted at once in the hoarding of miserable dimes and quarters! Vinaro's customers are not allowed by their governments to possess gold coins and bullion, but jewelry they may have in any amount—and they buy it, too, the heavier the better, even though the cost of the gold to them is increased several hundred per cent. In the Mediterranean world and India this gold hunger has long been a fever, but now the fever is spreading in a worldwide pandemic."

"The same ghastly disease that has hardened and embittered Spanish hearts for centuries," Tarzan agreed somberly. "But look here, if you suspect so much about Vinaro's villainies—and if you know he has killed—why can't you at once arrest him, straining the law as much as necessary? For instance, if you can prove two or even one of the men killed at the car-wash tonight—and guilty of the death of Antonio—were his men—"

Talmadge said, shaking his head, "The man has spread protection money everywhere, either as frank bribery or allowable gifts—and not only cruzeiros, but pesos, dollars, pounds, francs, piasters—yes, even rubles and yuans! He has powerful ties with wealthy reactionaries and also with the most merciless revolutionary movements."

Juarez said, "Here in Cuiabá the mayor and governor—for reasons they think innocent—are his friends. The state police wink at his doings. The wealthy and young like him—he is most amiable. The airport only feebly protests his flouting of rules and regulations. A few examples from many, believe me, *senhor*."

Talmadge said, "He makes contributions to charities, political parties, research. He poses like Ivar Kreuger and Samuel Insull as a benefactor of mankind."

Juarez said, "As for arresting him, you overestimate my forces and powers greatly. Besides, where would I find him? Within seconds after his jet landed here, he and his personals—Train, Romulo, the girl—were winging west in a Messerschmitt helicopter to a fortified hideout and—I think—*marshaling point* somewhere near the town of Mato Grosso—a hideout which my agents have not yet discovered. And when I say fortified, I am not talking of popguns! Four nights ago Antonio stole aboard that barge the stewardess Jovanna described to you. Under one of the tarpaulins was a salvaged German Panther tank, equipped with both howitzer and flamethrower—and with knife-edged treads for jungle penetration—a modern version of Assyria's scythe-wheeled chariots. Now that barge has vanished. My troopers, spread along a long frontier, have a few machine guns! There are only a few hundred of them, and I have no authority to move more than a few. Vinaro has a force, concentrated, of forty or fifty men. Recall what Confederate America's General Stonewall Jackson did with a few cavalry men, concentrated, against many, scattered, in the Shenandoah Valley."

"Jovanna," said Tarzan, "judged that at least one hundred hard types, as she called them, have drifted in recently toward the Cuiabá area. Perhaps you should have her in your organization."

"Perhaps I should," Juarez agreed, "though *Serviço Secreto de Gabinête do Ministro*—that's the personal Secret Service of the Ministry of War—does not approve of female operatives. You see, I am frank with you; I am even indiscreet." He poured a tot of the darkest rum into the remains of his *refresco* and drained it.

Tarzan said thoughtfully, "The jungle ranch of João Ruiz is near the town of Mato Grosso. You still have not told me how he comes into this strange secret war that's brewing, but if Vinaro's hideout is at all near his ranch, I have grave fears for him."

Juarez said, "A Brazilian Army helicopter will take us there at dawn—you have my promise."

Tarzan said, "If an immediate night flight is in any way possible—"

"Unfortunately not," Juarez told him. "The ranch of Ruiz is without telephone or telegraph, and my pilot could never locate it in the dark. But at dawn—my promise, truly."

Talmadge cut in. He had gone to his desk and carefully extracted from another pigeonhole a small white gleaming cardboard box ornamented with arabesques of gold. He placed it most gently on the center of the stone table and eased off the top. On a layer of white cotton lay a wristwatch resembling a Rolex Oyster Perpetual Chronometer, but considerably heavier of gold case and flexible gold bracelet.

Talmadge said, "Look at it closely, but pray do not touch it or the table."

Tarzan complied. So did Juarez, with a shrug at Talmadge and with lifted eyebrows.

The face of the watch was labeled under its crystal cover in a tiny gold script which Tarzan's jungle-young eyes read with ease: *"Morte Eterno."* Portuguese for "Eternal Death."

Talmadge said, "Observe that the sweep second hand does not move." Tarzan nodded.

"It has never moved," Talmadge said and poured himself a tot of white rum as carefully as if it were nitroglycerin. "This is a sample of the jewelry Vinaro's fabricators turn out. A very special sample—since the master himself has done the final work on it. Now observe."

He tossed down his rum, set down the glass with exaggerated care, picked up the box again—carrying it in both hands—and knelt in front of the fireplace by the windows.

"Please place yourselves by the door, gentlemen," he said.

Juarez seemed about to say something, then to think better of it. He and Tarzan complied. The latter had an inkling of what was coming. The hairs on his back lifted, and for an instant his lips silently formed themselves in a snarl.

Talmadge wound the watch two careful turns and set it, still in its box, deep in the fireplace. Unhurried, he swished tight across the fireplace its heavy flexible screen of linked iron mail, then rose and walked toward them.

He said, "Normally at this point a man would still be winding the watch or already have it on his wrist. Undoubtedly he would be staring at its face—watching the finest wristwatch he had ever received as a gift, or probably ever seen, for that matter, tick off its first minute. Very likely at this point he would carefully read the *'Morte Eterno'* and puzzle at the sinister strangeness of the name."

Talmadge reached them. He looked at his own wristwatch and said, "Twenty-two seconds have passed since I wound the thing. Twenty-five. At this point the man might get a monstrous inkling.

"Twenty-eight. Twenty-nine. Thir—"

CRAAACK! All three men winced involuntarily at the sharpness of the blast and the simultaneous flare of white light behind the thick-set shielding links. The heavy screen bellied outward sharply, then fell back.

"Come, gentlemen," Talmadge said, taking them back to the fireplace. He knelt and lifted back the screen. There was an acrid reek Tarzan recognized.

"Observe the inside links," said Talmadge. "They are now plated with soft gold. While caught between them are many fine grains of crystal. Such would be the condition of the mangled mask remaining of the face of the man we have been imagining."

He stood up. He said, "You asked, Tarzan, why we do not nail Vinaro for his murders. It is never easy to nail the man who sends poison in the mails. It is still more difficult to nail the man who sends a bomb in that fashion or by some form of special delivery. Consider its enduring gangland popularity. And particularly if the man is wealthy and has for the moment of the explosion a solid alibi, likely attested by some of the highest people in the land.

"That watch was loaded with pure fulminate of mercury, set to go off when the second hand had moved one hundred and eighty degrees. Of course, a sharp jar could set off the fulminate as well, but it is one mark of this sort of murderer that he never cares if the innocent suffer—a servant, a postman, a child."

Talmadge looked straight at Tarzan. "You asked earlier what happens to the girls of whom Vinaro tires. I will tell you what happened to one, a Monica Montressor. Probably sensing the danger of letting Vinaro remain her protector, she caused a young cotton magnate to become infatuated with her to the extent of proposing marriage. She left Vinaro's entourage and established herself in a closely guarded apartment in the best section of Recife—old Pernambuco. On the eve of her marriage a young mulatto woman, dressed as a high-grade servant, visited her, delivering a small package. This woman has never been traced.

Several in nearby apartments heard a knifelike explosion later that evening, but could not locate its source. Next morning Monica Montressor's bridesmaids discovered her dead at her vanity table, the looking glass of which was shattered. Her chin had been blown off and the upper front of her body horribly burned and mangled. Behind her on the floor, as if they had fallen down her back, were the remaining very heavy links of a gold necklace. It had undoubtedly held a huge pendant ruby, or perhaps two or three, for tiny grains of deep red corundum were discovered in her wounds. Along, of course, with the thin spattering of gold. Presumably some of the explosive, at least, had been placed inside the drilled-out jewels. Or the jewel may have been cut cabochon, hollow, or as a hollowed triplet. There may have been a micro-timing device, totally destroyed by the explosion, but more likely it was the sort of explosive which can be set off by the tiniest sharp jarring."

Juarez said, "Some unexplained explosions in the Brazilian postal system would seem to support this view."

Tarzan nodded. "The grains of black diamond I combed from my sleeve..." He did not complete the sentence. He was thinking of a very beautiful girl gazing greedily at herself in a large mirror, lifting her chin and leaning forward the better to admire the huge, heavily gold-mounted, deep red ruby glowing at her throat, and then perhaps remembering something about the cast-off Vinaro, something that frightened her so that she jerked—

It was a picture that sickened Tarzan—to such a degree that he said with deliberate harshness, "It seems that Vinaro desires literally to inflict his *special interests*—his gold and gems—upon his victims, as well as *fear and admiration of him*, at the moments of their deaths. I have met many cruel and maniacal villains in my adventurings, yet I still find it hard to believe in a mind like Vinaro's."

"So did I," Talmadge said grimly. "I had to blow up one wristwatch to convince myself. Another, to convince Colonel Juarez here. Yours was the third. The first two I wound by a remote-control device, but odd as it is, gentlemen, with experience one comes to have a great trust in the absolute perfection and infallible working of Vinaro's murder devices."

Tarzan uttered a snarl of contempt. "He has you hypnotized, Lionel! And perhaps the colonel here, too! How can you know that a surrealist artist like Vinaro, a dadaist of murder, might not arbitrarily alter the time settings and fuse devices of his deadly gifts?" Suddenly his expression changed from anger to suspicion. He advanced upon his friend. "And how comes it that you, Lionel, have had in your possession three of these deadly wristwatches, and known how to operate them? Speak swiftly now! And don't move, on your life! Nor you, colonel!"

CHAPTER 7

A Golden Child, A King of Hearts

L it by moonlight plunging down past the thick high black treetops, by the glow of a small open fire in the center of the great clearing, and by the rich yellow light of kerosene lamps streaming from several windows, the jungle ranch of João Ruiz had an idyllic look. The main house was clinker-built of heavy dark planking. Posts of a jungle wood like locust raised it four feet off the ground. It boasted a long roofed porch, reached by a short stout ladder, not steps.

To one side of the house were ranged some sheds and many cages: some low to the ground and stoutly barred, for animals; others high and of lighter construction, for birds; a few, made of brass and glass, for snakes. Two men were feeding the animals in the two largest cages—a magnificent gold-maned lion and a white jaguar with blue eyes rather than the pink ones of an ordinary albino animal. This beast now growled downwind across the clearing as it tore at its food. Some of the birds, wakened by the noise, trilled, chirruped, and mourned sleepily. From the jungle came the stridulations of insects, the singing of toads, and an occasional hooting call. A large bat dived across the moon.

Seated by the fire was an Indian boy with a gentle, aloof, strangely aristocratic face. He wore primitive sandals, a tunic of pale brown vicuña wool ragged-edged but well-washed, a shoulder cloak of the same material that was like a small poncho, while around his dark hair at forehead level was a double twist of golden wire, on which gleamed beads of fire opal.

Around the entire clearing, close to the huge, dim tree trunks twined with vines, went a rustic fence of posts and saplings, clearly more to satisfy someone's sense of order than for protection or to prevent any creature's escape.

A booted man, portly but not fat, appeared on the porch. The leathery thumb of his left hand was hooked over his serviceable belt, from the other side of which hung a heavy open-holstered Colt .45 long-barreled revolver. His right hand held a pipe, while that thumb tamped down the glowing load. Both his stance and the expression of his face were profoundly tranquil. His eyes might have reminded one of those of Colonel Juarez.

Beside him came elbowing along a chimpanzee with the face of a clown. The chimp raised itself on its long arms at the edge of the porch, swung a foot forward tentatively, and looked up at its master.

"Not tonight, Dinky," João Ruiz said rumblingly in Portuguese. "But tomorrow, if you're good, you may make the inspection rounds with me. Only remember not to mock the jaguar."

The chimp drew back a little at these words and shook his head vigorously.

"Ramel!" Ruiz called quietly. Then, in English, "Time for bed."

The boy arose, smiling, from the fireside and slowly made his way to the house. A woman, perhaps 15 years younger than the man, making her 40, appeared in the doorway, smiling at the boy.

An idyllic scene, surely, yet the man crouching in the bushes beyond the fence, warily downwind from the house and cages, though at the exact point toward which the white jaguar had growled, saw it utterly differently. For him it was a nightmare scene of menace. The house was a huge monster crouched on many legs. It glared at him with its kerosene eyes and then made a snarl at him with the gaping kerosene mouth of its doorway. Ruiz's face in the shadows was the murderous black mask of a fiend. The pipe he held was a second revolver. Ruiz's handsome wife looked like a cunning beaky-nosed witch who smelled intruders and planned to inflict them with vile diseases. The two men feeding the beasts were armed with at least two revolvers apiece stuck in their belts and with long curving knives.

The beasts and birds seemed monstrous slavering, snapping forms to the peering man, but—most strangely—when he clearly saw the bars around them, they all vanished instantly, even the lion. This somehow caused the chimpanzee to vanish for him, too.

But strangest of all, the boy Ramel, who was now mounting the ladder to Ruiz and his wife, had not merely a golden wire around his forehead, but was entirely golden-hued—hair, flesh, clothes and all. He glowed like gold alive.

Perhaps this extreme distortion was caused in part by the strange cameras and microphones of flesh through which the peering man, whose name was Rodriguez, viewed and listened in on life. His skull was swollen, almost as much as a Mongolian idiot's. His left eye was perceptibly larger than his right, likewise his left ear, while the right corner of his mouth was twisted sharply downward. It was as if Rodriguez had been struck by lightning and twisted in his youth.

Between his yellowed teeth, which were bared to the black-edged gums, he held a black whistle, as if it were some insect he had just snapped out of the dark air. In his pale hands he cradled an ancient, well-oiled Thompson submachine gun.

As the boy Ramel disappeared into the house, Rodriguez shut his lips, puffed his twisted cheeks, and blew an ear-piercing blast on the whistle. Then he bounded high in the air and, aiming on his fall, let off two bursts from his Thompson. The two men feeding the animals fell, kicked, and lay still.

Five men broke from the jungle behind Rodriguez, vaulted the fence, and raced toward the house, dark revolvers in their hands.

Rodriguez stayed where he was, menacing in all directions with his submachine gun as if expecting attack by the Devil himself, but all the while keeping up, at the two-second intervals of his breathing, his ear-splitting whistle blasts.

The chimp, unseen by Rodriguez, rolled under the house, scuttled for the center there, and cowered flat.

The charging men split into two groups, three keeping on toward the porch, the other two circling the house, on the side away from the cages.

João Ruiz stayed on the porch, taking two quick steps away from the door as he flung down his pipe and in the same movement unholstered his .45. Without great haste he cocked the gun and drew a bead on the man vaulting the little central fire and squeezed off a shot. The man fell in a rolling tumble and lay flat. Ruiz took another sideways step—no, it had to be three to get him past the lighted window—and recocked the gun and shot at the first man who leaped for the porch. That man fell short and broke his teeth on the edge.

From beyond the fence Rodriguez had seen and calculated. Again he leaped high, aimed, and let off a burst. Ruiz spun. His revolver, flying from his hand, smashed the window beyond him. Then he fell flat with a thud on the heavy boards.

The third attacker from the front leaped to the porch and plunged through the doorway with head low. A machete in a woman's hands chopped down and into his skull, was jerked from her hands by his plunge.

But at that instant there were shots from the rear. The woman let out a scream that ended in a coughing choke. Lights moved and flames flared as the kerosene lamps inside were thrown and burst.

The two who had attacked from the rear came plunging onto the porch, carrying the boy Ramel between them, as if he were a rolled rug.

Rodriguez spat out his whistle like a wad of tobacco and threw wide for them a gate in the rustic fence. As the two others raced through the opening, his pale hand shot out and he touched the boy, who still looked solid gold to him, for good luck.

Then with one look over his shoulder, he made off after the others into the jungle. His look had told him that the hateful house at least would burn entirely. The caged beasts and birds were screaming.

Talmadge said, "Tarzan, I've made mistakes. I never thought you'd come under Vinaro's threat so soon. I didn't think my cable would be intercepted or understood. Yet in it I dared give no hint of what the mystery was that Ruiz had discovered, because it is such an amazing matter—"

"I'm not interested in that now!" Tarzan snarled. "Where did you get those three wristwatches, which are now—perhaps so conveniently—destroyed?"

Talmadge protested, "Colonel Juarez knows the truth about them. He will assure you—"

"I don't care about the colonel. I want the truth from your lips. You've been my friend, Lionel. Nevertheless, speak very swiftly!"

The three men still stood near the door of Talmadge's study, the professor and Juarez both shaken to the core by Tarzan's sudden show of savagery. It made them feel as if the man in gray tweeds were a tiger, briefly given human guise by some jungle sorcerer, and might suddenly lash out with murderous claws.

"It's a longish story," Talmadge began. "If we might sit—"

"No!" Tarzan rapped out. "Now! Standing. And no suspicious moves, either of you."

"Very well," Talmadge said. "Prepare then to travel a strange side trail which will in the end lead us back once more to Vinaro and his villainies. Colonel Juarez has already let slip—wisely, I think—that he is a member of the *Serviço Secreto* of the Brazilian Ministry of War, which concerns itself mostly with possible subversion in the army. Tarzan, from my long work in Brazil, as anthropologist and archaeologist, I have come to love this country deeply—and to value its continuing security and freedom. During World War II, as you know, I worked in the counter-intelligence section of the British Army. Here, though still a British citizen and a busy scholar, I have been for four years an operative of *Serviçe Federal do Informaçoes e Contra-Informaçoes*—the Brazilian Federal Intelligence and Counter-Intelligence Service—which is an operative arm of *Conselho de Segurança Nacional*—the National Security Council."

Tarzan showed impatience. "Very interesting—and possibly commendable. But—the three wristwatches!"

"In good time. The Brazilian Communist Party—*Partido Comunista Brasileiro*—outlawed much of the time, but operating through various fronts, has had a turbulent history since its organization in 1922. Its abiding leader has been Luis Carlos Prestes, who as a junior army officer back in 1924 captured the popular imagination by leading an army revolt and carrying on for three years audacious guerrilla warfare against the government here in the Mato Grosso.

"The important point for us is that in 1961 the Brazilian Communist party split in two. The majority faction, headed by the aging Prestes, favored the Khrushchev policy of peaceful coexistence. The minority faction looked to Mao Tse-tung and Fidel Castro and demanded violence and revolution. Let us call them the minority.

"Now it is our belief—and, I imagine, that of England—though the United States still emphatically disagrees—that the main Communist party, the majority party, presents little threat to Brazil. I have for several years been in close touch with four of its members, whose names I may not reveal, men in university circles, who have dedicated themselves to seeing that the Khrushchev policy of peaceful coexistence be maintained, even if changes should be ordered from Moscow. They seek a Brazilian Communist government, uncontrolled from outside, like Yugoslavia's. They called themselves the Foursquare.

"Now these four men, naturally enough, are anathema to the Minority. Three weeks ago one of them came to me with a horrible story. He had been with one of the others at the time when he—the other—was delivered a gift, from a wealthy aunt, according to the card inside. It was one of those diabolic wristwatches! He watched his friend wind it, admire it—and lose his face, to die a day later in agony! Fortunately the first man was out of range of the blast. Returning home, he found just such a wristwatch awaiting him—again sent as a gift from a wealthy relative. He instantly got in touch with the two remaining members of the Foursquare. They, too, shortly received similar packages."

"Bless the delays in our postal service," Juarez interjected.

"Tarzan," Talmadge went on, "the man realized that this was the act of the Minority, but with a new and particularly vicious element of terrorism—the use of hair-trigger explosives, the heaviness of those golden wristwatches, the sardonic '*Morte Eterno*'—which must be hunted down. He trusted me, and so, at great risk, he brought me the wristwatches.

"I recognized Vinaro's hand at once. I had already suspected him of having ties with certain members of the Minority. Their desire for violence suits him—he may have recruited some of his killers from among them. They get gold from abroad— perhaps from China, through Macao—and Vinaro is forever greedy for that substance, though he expends it so lavishly in his killing devices. He *uses* the Minority, while pretending to support them. There, Tarzan, you have the story of how the watches came into my possession."

Tarzan shook his head thoughtfully. "Any man who tries to make use of or get gold from Communists of the Mao or Castro breed follows a most dangerous course."

"Danger is the air Vinaro breathes," Juarez assured him, "though he rarely risks his own person."

Tarzan said, "Very well, Lionel, you have told me how you got the wristwatches and perhaps why you exploded the first one. It remains for you to tell me why, instead of saving the remaining two watches for possible evidence against Vinaro when you have a real case against him—why, instead of that, you used them to convince the colonel and myself of the threat Vinaro represents and also, I assume, to interest us in the mysterious discovery Ruiz has made—and of which you have as yet told me no word."

"I will," Talmadge assured him, "but can't we now at least sit down?"

"I guess so," Tarzan said, still eying them both warily.

"It's not like you, Tarzan, to bully people so," Talmadge complained as he chose a seat, scooped some ice into a glass, and reached for the white rum.

Tarzan selected a clean glass, inspected it carefully, poured himself some *refresco*, then sniffed and tasted it carefully before he drank deep. "Listen, Lionel," he said, "this is clearly no child's game that's being played here in the Mato Grosso. I was not joking when I suggested Vinaro might have you literally hypnotized. Your behavior in blowing up that wristwatch was suspiciously automatic. As first principle, I must suspect everyone."

"*Por Deus*, I agree!" Juarez said, slapping his knee, then reaching for the *refresco* pitcher and the darkest rum. "This is a man for me!"

"So now, Lionel," Tarzan said, "tell the story behind all this. And," he added in faintly growling tones, as if to remind the other two that the tiger was still inside him, close to the surface, "it had better be a good one."

"It is not merely good," Talmadge said solemnly. "It is to my mind the strangest story out of South America in the twentieth century."

The place called the Castle, where Augustus Vinaro kept his Mato Grosso headquarters, had an interesting history. In 1705 "Midas" Carvajal, a Portuguese Jew, left his declining sugar plantation in Paraíba—one of the great northeastern states of Brazil which had been the world's chief source of sugar during the late 1600s—to join in the great gold rush to the Mato Grosso.

There he struck it very rich. Having always had something of a bee in his bonnet about the Inquisition, due to tortures visited on his great-grandfather, he determined to use his newfound fortune to entrench himself at what seemed then the end of the earth—and from what he considered a Christian tyranny.

Using Indian and Negro labor, he built himself a stone house that was more like a fortress on one of the mile-high forested peaks just west of the tiny settlement called Mato Grosso. Some say he used as foundations of the house the remains of a great Indian fortification of vast, cleanly joined stone blocks showing Incan influence.

It was truly a desolate spot, just on the eastern fringe of what is to this day called "The Land of Mists," sometimes more fully "The Land of Mists and Mirages," an area of constant clouds and weird weather and containing walled mountain valleys into which no aircraft has ever been able to peer. Westward loomed the greater, precipitous heights of the Serra de Huanchaca, today a boundary between Brazil and Bolivia.

South was what would become the area of the "undefined boundary" between the same two countries, a region of swamps and salt marshes, though with sharp hills rising here and there like the half-buried bones of gigantic monsters.

The descendants of Midas expended his fortune in maintaining the expensive, isolated dwelling, though one of them discovered and reopened an artesian well, perhaps first drilled by the Indians, which at least reduced the cost of water supply.

In 1797 the Castle was sold to a very wealthy émigré couple, the De Bailhaches, sole survivors of an aristocratic French family, all of whose other members had perished under the guillotine. They cut windows in the grim walls, laid parquet floors, and lived in grotesque retirement, dressing their *cafuso* servants in a French style—again at the ends of the earth, this time from the French Revolution.

Each generation of the De Bailhaches who remained in the Castle became more eccentric, the last but one consisting of a spinster who lived to the age of 93. She cut off all communications with the outside world, even to the point of having the rude road planted in with trees and all paths barred by hedges. She maintained herself by growing vegetables and raising pigs, with the aid of two devout Indian servants.

Her death might never have been discovered except that the

descendant of one of the De Bailhaches who had left the Castle, a young man named François Frascatti, decided to pay his eccentric aged cousin a visit by helicopter. This harebrained young fellow, who was the sole heir to a great gold and Brazil-nut fortune in Belém, now also fell heir to the Castle. The mysterious Land of Mists caught his imagination. He dreamed of exploring it, collecting Indian legends, discovering its surely many strange secrets, writing a book about it that would make him a Brazilian Sir Richard Burton.

For two years it amused him to refurbish the castle in a half-modern, half-Empire style, airlifting in artists, craftsmen, materials, electric generators and fuel for them, and his huge crew of café-society parasites. After throwing three fabulously expensive "heli-parties" at the Castle, which he called Cloud-Cuckoo-Land, he lost interest and went to live in the French Riviera, where he expended the remains of his fortune in gambling at the casinos, finally forfeiting the Castle to Augustus Vinaro as a result of losing five successive bancos at baccarat.

Thus, by the sort of chance which always followed him, and which he had reason to believe was more than chance, Vinaro came into possession of a fabulous retreat, which was at first simply his most secret hideout and jewelry fabricatory. Then he, too, became interested in the Land of Mists, chiefly because so many of the legends involved lost gold and diamond mines, undiscovered Indian treasures, and forgotten bandit hoards. But unlike the indolent François Frascatti, Vinaro was superbly energetic and systematic, even in his hobbies. He verified to his satisfaction the Incan nature of the foundations and the artesian well—the Castle had indeed once been a small Incan or Incan-influenced fortress like Machu Picchu, a thousand miles to the west and three miles higher. He had lonely-living Indians questioned. He did some exploring on his own. He employed several refugee Nazi and Fascist archaeologists, mineralogists, and anthropologists in the work. He even thought of bringing in Professor Lionel Talmadge, the nearby English authority on the area, until he discovered that the man was an agent of *Serviço Federal do Informaçoes e Contra-Informaçoes.*

He had in no way advertised that the Castle was once more occupied. His lawyers in São Paulo had handled the legal side discreetly. His personnel and materials were airlifted by night, chiefly from Santa Cruz and Concepción in Bolivia.

And now, in part as a result of this study of legends, the Castle had become the headquarters and launching spot for the most promising and exciting expedition of his life, more thrilling even than his tracking down in South Africa, by his great instinct for gems and the aid of a brilliant German mineralogist—who died of a neck injury immediately afterwards—the 4791-carat diamond of which the Cullinan, famed as the world's largest, is only the broken-off lesser fraction. This uncut diamond, weighing about two and one half pounds, was Vinaro's ace in the hole.

His present expedition was going half well, half ill, as he strode from his radio room up the brilliantly waxed mahogany stairs. He went silently on felt slippers. The tappings of his jewelers' hammers in the great basement below, faint as the dancing of mice, now faded altogether. Without knocking, he pushed into the bedroom of Sophia Renault.

She, dressed in turquoise nightgown and negligee, was sipping black velvet and playing the solitaire called Idiot's Delight, while her toy poodle Tiger closely watched the movements of her hands and the cards from the chair opposite, which was upholstered in sea-blue velvet.

"Chéri!" she greeted him. "I am glad your executive labors are over for the night. Tiger is a pleasant companion, but he cannot talk. See his coat! Maria took the best care of him while we were away. When he first saw me, he licked my toes until I giggled!"

Vinaro plucked from its icy bed the champagne, then the Guinness bottle. "Stout!" he said scowlingly. "It advertises its aim!"

"Troubles?" she asked gently, looking at his brow.

"Half-and-half," he said shortly. "Ruiz is dead, and Rodriguez has the boy Ramel. They will join us after the next night. That is the good half. Now we may discover the truth about how he escaped."

"Children are highly suggestible," Sophia remarked. She inspected the eight columns of cards carefully. "I seem to be blocked—"

"On the contrary," Vinaro said, "Ramel is a natural aristocrat, of the stupid sort that always tells the truth. Of course, he may remain silent as he managed to, in part, before. In which case I still dare not use the extremest persuasion on him, since he may be of crucial importance to us in reaching our objective."

Sophia shrugged. "—unless I turn up a red king. About Ramel, you promised me his bracelets—also his necklace to make Tiger a collar."

"I still have need of them," Vinaro said curtly.

"Well, the bad half of the news?" she asked without looking at him.

Vinaro watched her intently. Her chest was motionless. "By some incredible stupidity," he said, "or by some psychological element I have failed to grasp, Tarzan escaped the trap I set for him at Cuiabá. Cabral and the two Italians are dead. Only the Greek escaped to bring Portinari the sorry news."

Sophia shrugged, but Vinaro noticed she had begun to breathe again. She turned the king of hearts. "Oh, look, *chéri*, now I can unblock!" Her hands began to move cards so swiftly that Tiger barked shrilly in excitement. She paused and looked up meltingly at Vinaro. "I am sorry for your sake about Tarzan, *chéri*. But the best-laid plans of mice—"

"So now I am a mouse!" Vinaro said with a harsh grin. "First a pig, a dog, a spider—now a mouse! Well, at the moment I am willing to be a whole menagerie. But first throw that damned poodle out of here! His yapping offends me."

Sophia caught up Tiger. "I will not!" she said fiercely, "I have not seen Tiger for four days."

Vinaro stared at her for a long moment, then he took a

backward step, bowed politely, and smiled most courteously. "Excuse me," he said. "For a moment I forgot the basic feminine nature. Yes, by all means keep the dog. For just now."

He closed the door behind him very softly.

Sophia began to shake. She hugged the poodle to her more closely. The king of hearts stared up at her unhelpfully.

CHAPTER 8

"Die If Necessary..."

With a penknife that had a handle of orbicular jasper like tiny orange eyes staring out of a green forest, Professor Talmadge cut off the tip of a slim black Pôrto Alegre cigar, ignited it with a heavy silver Ronson, and turned it as he inhaled cautiously until it was evenly burning. Colonel Juarez likewise lit up. Tarzan, third around the stone table, sank back in his leather chair, his muscles relaxed completely, his senses receptive.

"It began about three weeks ago," Professor Talmadge said, "in the jungle about fifty miles north of the town of Mato Grosso, which is almost two hundred miles west of here. Near the Galera River, a man of the Indian Protective Service came upon a small Indian boy with his pet, a white jaguar."

"Albino?" Tarzan asked.

Talmadge shook his head. "No, the cat's eyes were blue, not pink, and his fur unusually long, which, although unkempt, showed signs of previous care."

"I never heard of such a breed," Tarzan said.

"Neither had I until I set eyes on it," Talmadge said. "The boy had been ill-used. There were burns on his hands. While the jaguar's back had been creased by a rifle bullet, and the animal was weak with infection and fever.

"The man could not understand the boy's speech, which in any case seemed incoherent, both from fear and a sort of misery or guilt. The man hurried the two—the animal seeming truly tame and in any case made tractable by its illness—to the jungle ranch of João Ruiz, providentially only a few miles distant. It was in any case the proper place to go, since Ruiz is the greatest jungle veterinary of the area and also himself connected with *Serviço de Proteção Aos Indios.* SPI, we call it for short."

"You've probably heard something of that Service, Tarzan," Juarez interjected. "It was established at the beginning of this century by a Brazilian Army major, Cândido Mariano da Silva Rondon, later a great friend of the American president Theodore Roosevelt. The state of Rondônia, larger than all Great Britain, is named for him. He died only in 1958 after a long lifetime spent in making the Service an instrument for the help and pacification of the Indians, without interfering with their way of life and tribal customs. I am proud of my association with it."

Tarzan nodded. "And I know its great motto: 'Die if necessary, but never kill'—a motto several of Rondon's men literally lived up to."

Juarez echoed, *"Morrer se preciso fôr, matar nunca!"*

Talmadge went on, "Ruiz gave all possible medical aid to the animal and the boy, whom his wife nursed. When the boy had rested a day or two and begun to hope he was in friendly hands, Ruiz talked to him gently and discovered that he had two languages, though speaking neither a word of Portuguese nor Spanish. The one language was English, in which he showed considerable proficiency, even understanding without needing explanation—and this may be important—the words, 'Indian Protective Service,' when Ruiz began to explain about himself and the man who had found the boy. Also at this point the boy seemed to become greatly reassured—though with the disappearance of his fear, his other emotion, the misery or guilt, was thrown into greater relief; he shied away from talking about the causes of these latter feelings, and Ruiz did not press him. He did tell his name—Ramel."

Tarzan interrupted, "The more I hear, the more frightened I become—for Ruiz. You are sure there is no—"

Reaching for the phone, Juarez said, "Absolutely not, in

the dark. However, I will order the helicopter and our most knowledgeable pilot to be ready for us at the airport two hours before dawn. That is still three hours off. We'll use the dark to get to the general neighborhood. Meanwhile, professor, keep on with your story to Tarzan."

"The boy's second language was the Indian one, Quechua, though of so peculiar a dialect that Ruiz could hardly understand a quarter of what he said.

"Now that he should speak Quechua, rather than the Tucana or Jibaran of our Brazilian Indians, was not strange, because many of the Bolivian Indians speak Quechua, and the boy was discovered within fifty miles of Bolivia, even if on the wrong side of the mountains.

"But that he should speak a form of Quechua almost unintelligible to Ruiz was very strange, for Ruiz has had many dealings with the Indians of Bolivia and Peru and is familiar with their languages. Quechua, as you likely know, was originally the language of the great, empire of the Incas, which at its greatest glory stretched from Quito in northern Ecuador about four thousand miles south to the Maule River in Chile, a greater distance than that spanned by the U.S.A. or Canada. Only Russia and China today have continuous lands that stretch farther. But I digress…perhaps. The point is that Quechua is still spoken today by the Indians of Peru—the golden center of the old empire—and Bolivia, though in a form that has changed with the centuries.

"Other things about the boy intrigued Ruiz. He had a grave, aristocratic manner unlike the smiling and graceful self-confidence of our best modern Indians. The expensive vicuña wool of his clothing was unusual and clearly woven on a hand loom. Around his fine forehead he wore a few polished fire opals—a beautiful though not very valuable stone—on a double twist of untarnished yellow wire so soft it had to be almost pure gold.

"Furthermore, there were wide bands of slightly lighter skin about each of his little wrists, as if he might have worn bracelets there. Up the side of his left hand was an angry infected tear wound. Ruiz had at first associated it with the burn wounds on the boy's fingers—and signs of thorns driven under his nails and later removed—but now he decided it might have been caused by the jerking of a metal bracelet off his left wrist.

"Finally, another band of lighter skin went around his neck, while on his upper chest was a circular pale patch four inches in diameter."

"As if he had been wearing a medallion on a heavy necklace?" Tarzan suggested. Juarez, still talking on the phone, nodded, and his eyes flashed.

"Precisely," Talmadge said. "At this point the boy would still say little, except to thank Ruiz and his wife for their care, tell them he would depart to his home as soon as he was recovered, and demand that his white jaguar be brought to him in his bedroom. Ruiz at once gathered him up and carried him down to the animal's cage, to show him that his pet was being well cared for and on the way to recovery.

"Then Ruiz sent for me, in part because of my greater command of English, but only in part. He also knew I am something of an expert in Old Quechua and in the history of the Incan Empire and the fate of its peoples after their conquest by the Spanish conquistador Pizarro."

Talmadge chose this point to tap two inches of ash from his cigar, drain the little left of his drink, and assemble himself another with maddening deliberation.

"Pizarro…Vinaro…" Tarzan said musingly. "The names are similar."

"Now *that*," said Juarez, cradling the phone, "is chance."

"Very possibly," Tarzan agreed. "Do you happen to know the name of Vinaro's jet?"

"The *Conquistador*," Juarez answered. Halfway through, his dark eyebrows lifted.

"Very possibly chance, too," Tarzan assured him. "A stirring name for a successful or ruthless man's private vehicle."

Juarez nodded doubtfully; then his face became businesslike as he said swiftly, "Tarzan, my men found three bodies at the car-wash. One bullet-torn and tire-mashed almost beyond identification, but not quite. His name, Cabral—a flier and a crony of Romulo, known to be employed by Vinaro."

"That was the man who impersonated your Antonio," Tarzan said.

Juarez nodded curtly. "The two others arrived a week ago in the same Lincoln that was so cruelly smashed. They came from the direction of Rio Branco. They registered at the Hotel Centro Américano under the names of Luigi and Giovanni Duccio. So, possibly, Italians and brothers. They looked Italian, spoke good Portuguese. One dead of a smashed skull and the other injuries, in the Lincoln. The other looking, my man said, like the victim of the most vicious hit-and-run driving."

"He was," Tarzan said. "But there was a fourth man."

"No sign of one."

"He must have been able to walk away," Tarzan said, "which surprises me. Weapons?"

"None. Though there were bullet marks to be seen on the car-wash and fence, and a few slugs have been found."

"He must have taken the submachine guns with him," Tarzan said. "*Ai*, this Vinaro employs tough *hombres*!"

"*Homens*, we say in Portuguese, but I agree."

"I was thinking of Manolecito," Tarzan said with a faint smile.

"My men also found the body of Antonio at the airport," Juarez said harshly. "It was as you said—three horrible bullet wounds."

"*Sinto muito,*" Tarzan murmured.

"My men next roused the owner of the car-wash," Juarez went on. "They grilled him, but he protests no knowledge of the affair."

"Likely he hasn't any," Tarzan said. "I told you the chain on the gate looked snipped. Who are your men, anyhow?"

"Border troopers and two plain-clothes agents. None knowing the jungle greatly."

"State police?" Tarzan asked.

"One cooperating. But they are too slow—and few.

Gangster-type crime is not their business. A few passion murders, drunken brawls, a little thieving…"

Tarzan nodded.

Talmadge, his cigar and new drink poised in either hand, remarked, "Well, if you're quite through with your chatting…"

"Excuse us, Lionel," Tarzan said, suppressing a smile. "Ruiz, his curiosity about Ramel understandably aroused, had just summoned you."

"Quite. I arrived the day after. By this time the remarkable white jaguar was taking food again, and the boy was much better. I confirmed all of Ruiz's observations about him and was able to make two more about his speech. First, his English had a definite Oxford accent and character. Oh, yes, very cool and la-di-da."

Now Tarzan's eyebrows rose.

"This has a sequel, we think," Juarez put in.

"Second," Talmadge said with a slight frown toward the colonel, "his Quechua was Ancient or Classic Incan, so far as we scholars are able to reconstruct its grammar and pronunciation."

"With the implication that the Incan Empire has survived somewhere?" Tarzan asked. He was thinking of how he had once been thrust into a surviving fragment of the Roman Empire.[*]

"Not that much, necessarily. But that there has been some Incan village or outpost which has had no contact or almost no contact with Spanish-speakers—*or* with other whites or Indians—during the four hundred years since Pizarro's conquest. There are lonely mountain settlements in the eastern United States, for instance, where the inhabitants speak almost pure Elizabethan English—or did until radio and television became universal there."

Tarzan said, "I am not unfamiliar with the survival of ancient things in unexplored—or supposedly unexplored—parts of the world. The dinosaur triceratops, for example. Though the

---

[*] *Tarzan and the Lost Empire* (Tarzan 12).

tail-bearing primitives with opposable toes, whom I discovered at the same time, called them *gryfs*."*

Juarez shook his head. "There are rumors that Vinaro possesses a raw diamond larger than the Cullinan. You have discovered dinosaurs. Frankly, I do not know which of you sounds the more fabulous."

"The killers in the car-wash didn't find me to be a fable," Tarzan answered, a shade sharply. "Nor is it the case with the girls—and men—who receive Vinaro's deadly trinkets."

Talmadge rapped his glass against the table's thick stone top. "The boy, now entirely won over by the loving care of Ruiz and his wife, was willing to talk freely. Ruiz, in fact, made him delay his story until my arrival. Personally, I was much impressed with him. Though his appearance was classically Indian, he seemed at times, because of his speech, more like a British lad of aristocratic background than a noble savage. Do not laugh at me, Tarzan, but I felt a princely aura about him. I believed that he was entirely honest and that whatever he told me would be the truth, or at least the truth as he saw it with his young eyes and understood it with his youthful mind."

"But his story?" Tarzan said.

Talmadge knocked off another length of ash. "Tarzan, he said he came from Tucumai, the City of Gold—yes, he used the English word 'city.' He described to me a vast room filled with golden treasures, and a people—his people—who all wore heavy golden jewelry at their great festivals. His people numbered thousands, he said. He said they were wholly unwarlike, without weapons, protected by natural defenses, and devoted to peace—in fact, peace was their religion. He sketched for me a temple and other buildings. Their architecture bore a marked resemblance to that of Machu Picchu."

"The Incan fortress in the heights above Cuzco," Tarzan said thoughtfully, "the ruins of which Hiram Bingham discovered in 1911."

"Yes. The boy was also familiar with much of the history of

---

* *Tarzan the Terrible* (Tarzan 8).

the Incas and of their conquest by Pizarro. He knew the legends of Manco Capac." Here Talmadge tapped the engraved stone table that lay between them. "But he also said that his own chief was Manco Capac and that he would inherit the same authority in time."

"Where is this Tucumai?" Tarzan asked. "Or did the boy tell you that?"

"He said that it lies toward the setting sun in an oval mountainous valley with rock walls so sheer they cannot be climbed from either side—here you have the natural defenses he mentioned. The only entrance to the place is through a series of caves. He says the air over the valley is misty and turbulent, so that no aircraft ever look down at Tucumai—though he knew a remarkable amount about flying machines, as if he had heard them described by a person of intelligence."

"That's a very baffling part of it," Tarzan said, "along with his command of English."

"Ah, we have made a guess at the explanation of that," Juarez put in eagerly. "Just after World War II a haggard veteran of the British Army named Hugh Malpole came to the Mato Grosso. He was well-educated—at Oxford, in fact. He had a great knowledge of semantics, languages, primitive tongues. Yet he was greatly disillusioned with the world and in particular with war—which he came to hate with a fierceness that at times seemed maniacal. He wanted to get as far away from the world of wars as possible and also to work with and help primitive peoples as yet ignorant of modern conflict. Our Indian Protective Service impressed him greatly—especially the 'never kill' part of its motto, which I think he privately applied to all human relations rather than only to dealings with ignorant savages.

"He pressed to enter the service and after a few months of delay was admitted, despite his nationality and neurotic thought patterns—because of his clear sincerity, his burning idealism, and particularly his great skill with languages: he picked up Tucano and Quechua in a matter of weeks.

"Hugh Malpole was a great success in the service. The Indians came to trust and love him almost as they did Rondon—and Rondon's great successor, Orlando Villas Boas. But then, after only two years of work, he disappeared somewhere in the Mato Grosso. Searches were made, but never a clue uncovered. Tarzan, this man may have discovered Tucumai and, because of its religion of peace, stayed there."

"An attractive story," Tarzan said, "but the evidence is slim."

"We have more than that," Talmadge said. "The boy Ramel told Ruiz and myself that the Englishman, as they called him, arrived at Tucumai about ten years before Ramel's birth, learned their old Quechua, taught them some of his tongue, told them about the new horror weapons of the outside world—the armed airplane, the bomb that kills cities and countries—and urged them to maintain forever their isolation and their religion of peace. He even wanted them to block the caves with great stones, but there Manco Capac would not agree."

"That does sound like your Malpole man," Tarzan admitted.

"You see, you see?" said Juarez, relighting his cigar.

Talmadge continued, "When Ramel was little more than a toddler, the Englishman died. Yet Ramel always remembered the pale blond man with awe and love. He learned more English from the chief he calls Manco Capac, and then when he was a little older, he did exactly the thing Malpole had warned them against."

"Of course," said Tarzan. "He went out into the world. He wanted to see all the wonders—even the terrible ones—with his own eyes. The Englishman's tales had fired his spirit. He headed for adventure. It is the thing I always did as a boy. And still do."

Talmadge nodded, somewhat wryly. "He took his pet jaguar and a supply of food and an old map of the lands round Tucumai—this last he took 'against custom'—they have no word for 'steal,' it seems—and he went through the caves to the outer world."

Tarzan smiled thoughtfully. "He appeared at the mouth of a cave, just like the first Manco Capac here." He touched the deep-cut engraving in the stone table. "Except the Indians of Cuzco weren't there, and he had no golden robes."

Talmadge said bitterly, "He *did* have golden bracelets and head wire, while on his chest was a huge golden medallion—on the back of which the route to Tucumai was engraved, the map he took. And after wandering for a few weeks or even months and becoming weary of his venture and confused in his mind about how the map fitted the territory, he ran into something a lot worse than Indians. He ran into Vinaro.

"It had to be Vinaro. The boy heard him called that name, and there was also the unforgettable Mr. Train of the eye patch, and a beautiful lady with hair like gold—this Sophia Renault, presumably.

"They treated him nicely at first, were all smiles—cat-and-mouse! But then Vinaro began to press him for an exact description of the route to Tucumai. The boy knew thieves when he saw them—even if he didn't know the word! He refused to talk anymore.

"Vinaro tortured him—by such methods as you know by the wounds he suffered. The jaguar tried to defend him, was shot at, fled into the jungle. Ramel's bracelets and medallioned necklace were torn from him. He also lost at this time a golden comb with which he curried his jaguar."

"Now, who, Tarzan," Juarez demanded, "could invent a detail like that? Clearly the boy speaks the truth."

Tarzan nodded impatiently, his eyes on Talmadge.

"Vinaro recognized the engraving on the medallion as a map and continued his cruel questioning of the boy. Yet the woman Sophia seemed to the boy the worst of the three, for he had thought her beautiful and therefore loving, but now she began to taunt him and demand that Vinaro give her Ramel's necklace to make a collar for her dog. She also thrust into her hair the jaguar's comb and danced. Vinaro laughed at these antics, and he and the woman drank together—spirits, evidently, for they grew sleepy. As night fell, the wounded jaguar—or so it sounded—came wailing around the camp. Vinaro sent out

Mr. Train to kill it. Ramel was securely tied. Vinaro pocketed the medallion and fell asleep.

"Then the woman roused from her stupor and came to him like a witch, Ramel said, compelling him to silence, speaking never a word. She had tiny pincers in her hand, and he was very afraid. She took up his poor hands and drew the thorns from under his nails. She untied his bonds, and when they heard Mr. Train call something, she pointed in the opposite direction. Ramel fled. The last he saw of the woman, she had drained the bottle from which she and Vinaro had been drinking and was opening another."

"She plays dangerous games, this Sophia Renault," Juarez commented.

"And brave ones, to judge by this," said Tarzan.

"She was brave on liquor," Juarez said, "of which you don't seem to approve."

Tarzan shrugged. "She used the means at hand. Fortunately for me, my great-ape foster parents knew not how to ferment beer from grain, or distill spirits from beer. Had they known, I might now take my *refrescos* sweetened."

Talmadge continued, "The wounded jaguar scented Ramel and followed him. The boy only tried to put as much distance as he could between them and Vinaro's camp, hiding by day. This went on for two or three nights. Then the *Protecão* man discovered them, with what results you already know. Except this, that in losing his medallion to Vinaro, the boy felt that he had betrayed the secret of Tucumai and its treasure. Hence his misery and guilt."

Talmadge stubbed out his cigar, took a swallow of his drink, in which the ice had all melted, and sat back in his chair.

Juarez looked at Tarzan and said, "Now what do you think of all this?"

Tarzan said, "I think Ruiz is in great danger, and the boy, too. You should at least have given them a few troopers for protection."

"After this night's happenings I agree very much," Juarez

admitted, his eyes unhappy. "But I cannot change night to day. It is still more than two hours until we can start."

Tarzan turned to Talmadge. "I have often run across references to the Lost Treasure of the Incas. Is there such a thing? Could it be in Tucumai?"

Talmadge came coiling out of his chair with remarkable agility for a 60 year-old and went to the biggest map. He pointed to a purplish area, dark with great mountain chains, along the blue Pacific. "Here is Peru," he said, "heartland of the Incan Empire four and a half centuries ago." His finger stabbed a black dot near the top of the purplish area. "Here is Caxamalca, now Cajamarca, where the conquistador Pizarro, with fewer than two hundred Spanish horsemen, took the Inca Atahualpa prisoner by treachery, slaying five thousand of his unarmed followers, one of the most horrible massacres in history. As ransom for himself, Atahualpa agreed to fill with golden orna-ments and objects a room seventeen by twenty-two feet to a point as high as he could reach. Atahualpa must have been as tall as Mr. Train, or the Spaniards greedy beyond sanity, for the red line Pizarro ordered drawn around the walls of the room was nine feet from the floor.

"For months Atahualpa's subjects toiled, bringing gold from as far as Cuzco, six hundred miles to the south—the Spaniards often supervising. Temples to the Incan sun god, with walls and ceilings of gold plate, were despoiled—though it is said much of the golden treasure was spirited away by Incan priests and aris-tocrats yet at large. Half at least of the ransom was gathered—say, five feet of the nine. Pizarro's followers, like the crude pirates they were, could wait no longer—they insisted on a division of the spoils. All that beautiful stuff was melted down—golden birds with opal eyes, great golden bowls with delicate tracery, golden lace, golden faces, all the art of an Empire—so that the followers of Pizzarro, who could himself neither read nor write, might have the crude ingots, easy to pack, which was all they ever understood of gold—the price for lands in Andalusia, or indulgences in Rome, or steel from Toledo, or wenches in Cádiz!"

Talmadge's lips thinned with bitterness. "Atahualpa's power waned a little. He was no more use to Pizarro. The great *conquistador* sent off on a fool's errand the one officer with a shred of decency in him—Hernando de Soto—and speedily brought Atahualpa to trial on charges ranging from polygamy to misuse of national funds—quite in the style of Hitler or Stalin, eh? Atahualpa was convicted by his Spanish judges and—because at the end he agreed to become a Christian—mercifully strangled by a rope tightened with a stick, rather than burned."

Talmadge took a deep breath. "But I am not preaching a sermon against past evils, gentlemen, though they still enrage me. I am simply trying to show you that, if so much gold could have been gathered in mere months solely by imperial order, how much more gold there must have been in an empire far larger than Pizarro himself ever guessed. Several secret hoards were undoubtedly created. Though Pizarro slew his tens of thousands, there were Incan revolts as late as Tupac Amaru's in 1780.

"The Lost Treasure of the Incas? There may have been a half dozen! Some say one was sunk in Lake Titicaca." He pointed to a large blue rectangle 200 miles south of Cuzco, on the boundary between map-purple Peru and orange-edged Bolivia.

Then he eyed both Tarzan and Juarez sharply. "But I assert, gentlemen, that a goodly number of the Incans must early have decided to escape the murderous, steel-and-gun-armed, ship-swift Spaniards in the only direction they really could— *inland*!" His finger traveled east across Bolivia to the green of Brazil. "Only five hundred miles, gentlemen, to the jungles and great hills of the Mato Grosso—the 'Great Underbrush.' Look at it!" His finger swiftly traced a large green circle. "An area twice the size of Texas! A vast hiding place for a nation in retreat! It is a practical certainty to my mind that a goodly number of Incans made this trip, bringing their treasure and culture to safety. There is much evidence of this, which I have slowly collected. At any rate, long before I ever heard Ramel's story, I believed in the existence of Tucumai! Or some such retreat, whatever its name."

He thrust his hands in the pockets of his khaki slacks and stood rocking on his feet, his pale tan cardigan swinging, and stared at Tarzan and Juarez, like a schoolmaster who dares his pupils to contradict him.

Tarzan's imagination was thrilled, wrenched, saddened, and thrilled again. He thought of that tiny band of conquistadors challenging an empire of millions…their horses and firelocks the feeble equivalents of today's tanks, bombers, missiles, atomic bombs…the Spanish drumbeat in narrow mountain defiles miles high…how Pizarro had shod the horses with silver, because the iron gave out…how his lieutenants had been affrighted by earthquakes and weird idols, coming simultaneously…how that murderous old villain, brave as a lion to the last, had, at 65, half armored, stood off alone the 17 fully armored malcontents who had come to assassinate him—and killed three of them before he fell under their swords.

But then he thought of the peaceful and orderly empire of the Incas…the laughing mountaintop villages…the flocks of llamas whiter than the sheep of the Asturias…the rule of one law for 4,000 miles…at times a cruel law, but not a law of genocide…the beautifully calculated irrigation basins and channels which the Spaniards had smashed or neglected as they had those of the Moors…the Dominican Valverde crying out to Pizarro, of Atahualpa, "Why do we waste our breath talking with this dog? Set on, at once! I absolve you!"…and always the sickness, the vile sickness whose germs are as undying as gold is incorruptible, the sickness now threatening the whole world, the horrid sickness of gold lust—to give it a name, the Pizarro-Vinaro syndrome!

But meditation was never Tarzan's way for long. He stood up.

"This Vinaro goes up against Tucumai like Pizarro against Peru. Why does he need a tank?"

"To throw terror into the hearts of the people of Tucumai when he finds them," Juarez said.

"And to slay them to the last child when they have disgorged their gold," Talmadge added fatefully.

Tarzan nodded. "The tank is his horseman armored in steel and armed with shot. He will be Pizarro to the last detail. Also, I think he dreads that the folk of Tucumai may have unsuspected weapons, for there have been legends of the Incans having such, as well as their lost treasure—weapons that are mostly the dreamings of theosophists and such: strange rays, unheard-of poisons, flying saucers, and the like. Still, a man with Vinaro's weird brain might take them into account. Now tell me, why can we not strike at Vinaro at once?"

Juarez's shrug was hopeless. "It shames me, but we do not even know the location of his dwelling here, nor of the spot where his men are gathering—probably have gathered. The barge bearing the tank or tanks we lost touch with two hundred miles down the Paraguay."

Tarzan said, "But if you and Talmadge, with the influence of your secret-service positions, sent word to Brasília that there are a tank and a band of heavily armed men loose in the Mato Grosso—"

"We have," Juarez said, "and we were not believed. It is not exactly the officials' fault—the thing is so incredible. I was asked to send Antonio to report in person about the tank on the barge. Now he is dead. Finally, it is likely that Vinaro's forces are already on the road to Tucumai."

"Do you think he can find the spot? Is the map on the gold medallion that good?"

Talmadge nodded. "Ramel thinks it is. It is only in finding the entrance to the caves that Vinaro will discover difficulty. Also Ramel fears he may have given away other clues without intending."

Tarzan asked, "Can Ramel find Tucumai again without his map?"

"He can try, he says. He will do his best."

Tarzan said, "Ramel can hardly have traveled *very* far before Vinaro caught him. Tucumai can hardly lie more than three- or four-hundred miles from Ruiz's ranch—possibly near the Brazil-Bolivia border to the west."

Talmadge nodded sharply. "I agree. *I* think it lies in the Land of Mists and Mirages."

Juarez smiled. "*If* there is an area really deserving such a name. I've traveled much there. I think the Land of Mists is folklore, though I'll admit to having been caught in a few fogs and a couple of sandstorms from the south."

"I've studied the weather records for a hundred years," Talmadge snapped. "Also there have been unexplained plane crashes."

"What weather records?" Juarez wanted to know.

"Gentlemen!" Tarzan protested. He turned toward Juarez. "It would be best to trail Vinaro, if we could find his expedition, and slowly gather forces against them."

Juarez said, "Tarzan, believe me, I will *try* to find them. I have a plane searching, and promise of another. But the Mato Grosso is vast, and doubtless Vinaro will employ camouflage."

Tarzan paused. His face was grim. "So we must start our hunt for Tucumai from the ranch of Ruiz. I begin to see what you have in mind."

Juarez shifted uncomfortably, but his face was equally grim. "Tarzan, I would not ask this of you if there were any alternative. But we *must* reach Tucumai before Vinaro and prevent the horrible slaughter he intends."

Talmadge nodded curtly.

Juarez went on, "I am assembling a small force of jungle fighters—some of my own troopers, some men of the *Serviço de Protecão ao Indio*, although the latter are unused to guns. They have orders to be at the ranch of Ruiz within two days. They won't be as numerous or well-armed as Vinaro's vest-pocket army, but they will be a force. I want you to take the boy Ramel and lead them to Tucumai ahead of Vinaro. Once we are at Tucumai—well, it sounds like a place easy to defend, while radio reports of it will surely shake Brasília out of her trance."

Tarzan's eyes narrowed thoughtfully. Juarez continued, "I know this is a nearly impossible thing we are asking you to do. In politics we Brazilians have a word called *jeito*—it means the art of doing what seems impossible. So I am asking you to perform a feat of jungle *jeito*. One more small thing—I will go with you. As your second-in-command, but only if you wish that."

"I will go, too," Talmadge asserted.

"Now, professor, we've been into that—" Juarez began.

"So we have," Talmadge snapped. "You told Ruiz he could go. I go, too."

Both men looked at Tarzan. Juarez said, "We know that you, as leader and far most skilled in jungle craft, will have the most dangerous job, and that, realistically, you must expect, very probably, to be dead within the month."

At last Tarzan smiled. "Die if necessary, eh? Though this time, sadly, the 'never kill' proviso will hardly apply. Yes, of course, I'll lead you. And I have just now thought of another motto, from an early British play: 'Like diamonds, we are cut with our own dust.'" He touched the right elbow of his coat. "Perhaps in the end that will be the fate of Vinaro, who kills women and men with the dust of jewels and seeks to corrupt the whole world with gold."

Juarez looked with raised eyebrows at Tarzan. "I didn't think a jungle man like yourself would have the taste, or rather the time, for literature."

"*Amigo*, you'd be surprised the things I've had taste and time for in my life," Tarzan answered with a grin. Then, addressing them both, "And now, *companheiros*, let us set out for the airport—and have a bite of food before we fly. *This* jungle man is famished."

Yellow moonlight, striking in a narrow beam through a chink in the surrounding leaves, fell on the large left eye of Rodriguez. It seemed never to blink, though the pupil and iris, tiny by comparison with the white, constantly crawled about, like a circular black bug with a black center. Beside it occasionally gleamed the blued muzzle of the man's weapon, cradled upright, as Rodriguez rocked it gently. He ceaselessly crooned a melody of only two notes that was softer than the snoring of the other two kidnappers, hidden in the blackness.

The boy Ramel watched, while pretending to sleep, the eye of Rodriguez. Such an eye, he thought, must belong to Cupay, the demon who ruled the wicked dead at the center of the earth. It watched…forever. Of course, he could not escape even if the eye closed—steel handcuffs had been clicked shut about his thin ankles when his captors had made camp here. But if the eye would only close, he himself might be able to sleep.

The evil visage of Cupay recalled to him its opposite: the benign, golden face of the Sun God emblazoned on the western wall of the temple at Tucumai, so placed that the sun would strike it the instant it rose above the sheer mountain-wall to the east. An even greater emblazonment of the Sun God, powdered with emeralds, had stood five centuries ago on the western wall of the original temple at Cuzco—so Manco Capac had told him—ready to smile forth goldenly each day with the first rays of the rising sun…which was strange, in a way, because gold was "the tears wept by the sun." How did tears make smiles?

He wished that the Sun God would glare blindingly now at Rodriguez or tramp dazzlingly into this clearing with his golden arrows and spear. His sister-wife, the Moon, was weak—she could *show*, but she could not *help*.

How he wished he had never left Tucumai! The outer world was as the Englishman had said: There were a few good people, worshiping Peace, but they were outnumbered by the bad, who worshiped War. And the latter had terrible weapons indeed! Now the gentle Ruiz and the motherlike Felicia were dead, and he was in the hands of this Cupay-like brute, who had already spoken the horror name "Vinaro." Which meant that once again it would be demanded of him that he help guide the wicked ones to Tucumai. Sooner than that…! He touched the scars on his fingers. He did not know if he would be brave enough.

He wondered if Xima had survived the blaze. Perhaps the bars of the cage, though wooden, had not caught fire—or had burned just enough for Xima to escape. But more likely…Oh, what a horror it was that flames should be the color of gold! A more terrible puzzle than that of the tears and smiles.

The moonbeam left Rodriguez's eye, faintly silvered a curling leaf, then faded altogether. Although the weird two-note crooning kept on, Ramel at last slumbered.

CHAPTER 9

The Importance of Discipline

Electric light from a dozen ivory-shaded lamps flooded the drawing room of the Castle, but not a photon escaped outside because of closely drawn thick creamy draperies with great black patterns on them like Rorschach inkblots.

Vinaro and Sophia Renault sat in full evening dress across a silver coffee service with plates of cookies and cakes, French pastries and petits fours. On a black cushion at Sophia's feet Tiger sat, formal as if at a dog show. Mr. Train, also in evening dress, stood in the background, beside one of three large, very heavy-looking doors. He gleamed discreetly from his black satin eye patch to his size 17B evening pumps.

Sophia poured. Steam rose from the thin dark stream as it coiled itself into the two tiny white cups.

"You're a martinet, 'Gustus," Sophia complained. "My own mother—damn her dry, pinching fingers—could never have got me up at three-thirty a.m., to be dressed to perfection a half hour later."

Vinaro nodded. "Discipline is important," he said. "Just as time of day—or night—is of no importance whatsoever. I expect punctuality of my men, so I must be punctual myself. Nor do I choose to appear before them bleary-eyed in a bathrobe—or improperly attended."

He waited until she had selected a chocolate cookie almost as thin as a matzoh wafer and reached for the silver pitcher of thick cream. Then, "Besides all that," he said, "black coffee is an excellent antidote to black velvet, with its most fattening

111

components. That diamond looks beautiful at your throat, *chérie.* It twinkles blue-white-blue as you catch your breath."

Sophia took up her demitasse, tossed it down as if it were whiskey, made just that sort of face, and poured herself another. Then, staring quietly at Vinaro, she broke up her chocolate cookie and offered the fragments in her palm to Tiger. The tiny poodle feasted rapidly but elegantly.

"The companion of your slumbers is rewarded," Vinaro said tonelessly.

A clock slowly tolled four. While the last stroke reverberated, there came a single knock at the door beside Mr. Train—a sharp knock made distant by six inches of oak. Mr. Train drew open the door with only the faint hiss of its base against the thick creamy carpet.

Six men strode in, five of them looking like a squad for Mr. Train to lead—six-footers, or more, all. The sixth was Romulo, and what that gorilla-browed *mameluco* lacked in height, he made up in agile-footed burliness.

Only the first of the men made dirty tracks on the carpet—and only he didn't look down to make sure the soles of his boots were clean or stare around covertly at the room's magnificence. This one's blue pants and shirt were frankly sweat-stained. A dark blue, black-visored cap with a hint of silver to it was pushed back on his dark red hair, which, overlong, twisted around his ears. He had the jaw of a Viking and the eyes of a satyr. A pair of Colt automatic .45s hung open-holstered at his hips. Of the six, he looked the only one who might have had half a chance pitted against Mr. Train.

Close behind him stepped another big man in dirty blues, clearly his underling—a man who carried a Garand rifle in the crook of his right arm and looked around him warily—clearly an assassin who would kill at the first stimulus.

The three men with Romulo looked like—and were—two Spaniards and an American.

Vinaro smilingly turned his face toward them, like a lady's silver-plated automatic pistol.

"Ah, Captain Voss. Gentlemen," he said. "I'm pleased to see you're punctual."

The big seaman nodded toward him. "We work…while you play," he said in a voice that sounded deliberately coarse, while in mid-sentence his gaze swung from Vinaro to Sophia.

He stepped toward her, sank on his hams four feet away, and selected the largest and creamiest-looking of the French pastries, broke it open, and offered its whipped-cream interior to Tiger. The poodle appeared almost overwhelmed, then began to sup greedily, with dainty curlings of its narrow, mottled tongue.

The man didn't look at the dog, but at Sophia. She preened herself slightly.

Vinaro said pleasantly, "And just how has your work gone, Captain Voss?"

The seaman grunted. "Just the way I told you it would. My barge delivered all your heavy supplies to the middle of nowhere. And unloaded and camouflaged! Wasn't no easy job, I can tell you—we got in bad trouble twice, but with the Chinese Commies helping, we pulled out—*they're* gonna expect you to blow up Brasília! But anyhow, we got your carts here, and your ammo and gas."

Vinaro looked at Romulo. "And the men?"

Romulo pulled to attention. "Yes, sir! They're with the equipment, guarding and caring for it. Ready to move night or day. Awaiting your orders, Mr. Vinaro."

Voss said to Sophia, thickening his lips and thinning his eyes, "It was sort of romantic, though, Miss, like the old-time pirates of the River Plate. We chugged up the Rio de la Plata with all Montevideo and Buenos Aires—and their radars—looking on and never guessing what we had under our tarps. Then the Paraná—the caimen there snapped at my men's feet and made 'em orderly. After that, the Paraguay and the Paraguai—ow, how those skeeters bit! I met an air hostess at Corumbá—a pretty bit named Jovanna—but she wasn't a patch on you, Miss Renault. Begging your pardon, *Senhor* Vinaro." He eased the automatics on his hips. "After that—well, I think somebody twigged us at Corumbá, but we dodged 'em up the Jauru and the Aguapei. Those are tricky rivers. And so here. A trip that's left me fagged. Are you going on into the jungle, Miss Renault?"

"Non," Sophia answered sharply. "I am the chatelaine of the Castle."

"I feel like a rest myself," Voss said. "I guess you can get along without me the rest of the way, Mr. Vinaro."

"Yes," said Vinaro, very softly, "I believe so." He stood up. "Pardon me, I want to get a cigarette. Oh, Mr. Train, perhaps these gentlemen would care to take coffee. With brandy it might be—say the Napoleon. Or the Marshal Ney, at the very least."

He made toward the door opposite the one through which the six men had entered. It opened, inward, at his touch— another six inches of oak on inch-thick wrought-iron hinges, with bolts to correspond.

Romulo and his three men came haltingly toward the coffee service. Mr. Train strode forward and grasped a dusty bottle. Voss' underling crowded back against the curtain with the "cannibal pot" ink blot, his eyes and rifle roaming. Voss himself looked straight at Sophia as he continued to present the whipped cream to Tiger.

"What do we need with brandy? Eh, Miss Renault?"

Vinaro, swiftly closing the thick door behind him, entered a small room wreathed with the incense of hemp and poppy. The sweet, intoxicating smoke came from the filigreed, bowl-like base of a ghost-green jade idol of Siva, the Hindu master of destruction, set upon a large but cheap, heavily varnished yellow pine desk. There were two matching chairs. Otherwise the room was bare.

He slid open a drawer in the desk and took out two small jade-colored blocks about half the size of a cigarette package. He tucked one in his breast pocket, behind the folded linen handkerchief. The other he placed gently at the base of the jade idol, which faced away from him.

He took from the side pocket of his coat a large, flat gold

case and selected two cigarettes, each marked only with a golden "V" and a thin gold band around its exact middle. He placed them side by side between his lips. Taking from his other side pocket a heavy gold lighter set with amber, he ignited the cigarettes, drawing one long slow breath.

He laid one of the cigarettes on the jade-colored block behind the idol, so that the gold band rested exactly on the edge, the burning end overhanging. Its smoke mingled indistinguishably with that of the incense.

The other cigarette he held lightly between the forefingers of his left hand.

Almost as an afterthought he took a stack of glossy, large photographs from the drawer and dropped them on the end of the desk. Then he went to the door and opened it.

Sophia was chattering animatedly. Voss, drinking in her words, was now feeding Tiger whipped cream off his big fingertips.

Vinaro called, "Captain Voss. I believe I owe you something."

Voss looked over his shoulder. "Yeah, you sure do."

Vinaro said, "I'd like to discuss it with you in private."

Voss said, "Suits me."

With a smiling grimace of excuse to Sophia, he got up and strode toward Vinaro, wiping his hands on the sides of his pants, and, as if by chance, caressing his blued automatics as he did so. Tiger trotted after him hopefully. Sophia made as if to call the poodle, but instead poured herself another demitasse, this time adding brandy from the dark bottle.

Vinaro sat down behind the yellow desk. "Take a pew, Captain Voss," he said. He studied the cigarette in his left hand. It had burned down a quarter of the way to the gold band. So had the other cigarette, but he did not look at that.

Voss complied. "Place smells like an opium den," he observed.

The smoke-wreathed statue of Siva bisected the distance between them.

"We both breathe the same fumes," Vinaro said. "Now then, Captain, what exactly do I owe you?"

"Don't give me none of that, Vinaro," Voss said. "You know as good as I do."

Vinaro said mildly, studying the cigarette he held but never smoked, "Surely you must realize I have more to think about than this one undertaking!"

"Okay," Voss said. "You owe me fifty thousand American dollars over expenses for smuggling all that stuff up the river and into the Mato Grosso. You owe me that now." He waggled a big finger at Vinaro. Tiger, at his side, looked up at it hopefully.

Vinaro said, "Yes."

Voss said, leaning forward a little, "And you owe me twenty per cent of whatever you bring out of the jungle."

"I do?" Vinaro asked like a child.

"Yeah, you do." He ran his right hand down across his gun and pants. Tiger licked it. Voss fondled the dog's neck with a finger without taking his eyes off Vinaro.

Vinaro's eyes grew far away. He said softly, "Twenty per cent actually seems quite fair." He smiled. "You know, I'd even like to do more for you." His cigarette had burned halfway to the narrow gold band.

Voss frowned searchingly, suspiciously. "Don't want nothing more," he said gruffly. "Deal's a deal."

Vinaro said liltingly, "But you've done such a *splendid* job." He slid open the drawer and took out a heavy silver ring set with a large bloodstone carved as a skull. Two of the red patches in the dark green stone burned in the skull's eyes.

Voss eyed the ring as if it were the head of the snake Cascavel, the tropical rattler, *Crotalus terrificus*.

"No, thanks, Vinaro," he said decisively. "I've heard a little about your gifts."

Vinaro laughed like a child. "You don't really think—? Here, let me show you." Using the thumb and two little fingers of the hand holding the cigarette, he slipped the ring on the middle finger of his other hand. Then he suddenly knocked the side of the silver setting hard against the edge of the desk, twice.

He slid open the drawer and took out a heavy silver ring set with a large bloodstone carved as a skull.

Voss' satyrlike lips tightened just a trifle at each impact.

In his peripheral vision, Vinaro noted the second cigarette roll a quarter of an inch sideways…and stop. He thought of a bull's horns slashing past a matador's taut belly, just an inch away.

He said to Voss, "Does that convince you? It's really quite a valuable piece of jewelry. The ancients believed bloodstone was an infallible cure for nosebleed, by the by. They had other curious beliefs, as that wearing a garnet would keep a man sober no matter how much he drank, and that the future could be foreseen in a globe of rock crystal—which is not glass, incidentally, but quartz clear as water."

The ember of his cigarette was now four-fifths of the way to the gold band.

Pulling off the ring, he stood up. "I'll go get your money," he said. He put down the ring near the photographs. "I have still another man-to-man sort of gift in mind for you, but you'll have to guess a bit about that." He walked to the door and quietly let himself out.

Outside, conversation had flagged. Vinaro made no effort to revive it. He accepted a demitasse from Mr. Train. Sophia started to speak to him, but he gave her his "Silence!" look. Romulo and his three had got their demitasses, sweetened with the rare brandy, and were standing about uncomfortably, as if fearing to crush the eggshell cups in their thick paws, yet hesitating to drink, perhaps for fear their teeth might chip an edge. Voss' seaman, rifle straining toward the ready, had backed into the heavy ink-blot draperies and was glancing around suspiciously, even overhead at times, as if he expected a trapdoor to open in the ceiling or a spider to drop down his neck. Mr. Train had melted into the background.

It was all, Vinaro thought, delightfully clownish. A perfect background, by contrast, for the rites.

Inside, Voss reached for the ring, still a little suspicious of it. Then he noticed the stack of photographs. He clamped them with his big hand and lifted them to him.

The top one was of Sophia Renault in a bikini.

The rest were all of Sophia, too, many in evening dress, some in swimming costume and play-suits. Voss thumbed through them greedily. Yet Vinaro had seemed bored with the girl, content that she and Voss stay behind. The seaman scooped up Tiger on his lap, stroking him as he glanced at the last of the pictures.

He put the last one aside, and there was the bloodstone skull, silver-hooded, glaring up at him from his palm.

He looked up at the smoke-streaming jade idol. That junkie stuff sort of made your head swim. Damn it, if Vinaro…

He really looked at Siva for the first time, saw the belt of skulls around his waist, saw the chains of skulls leaping from his neck and shoulders as he postured with grotesque beauty, saw the cruel serene Hindu face and slit-like eyes, all carved in coolest jade.

A big shiver crawled up his spine, faster than any centipede.

In an instant he was poised bent-legged on his feet, crouching over his chair, prepared to spring or fire in any direction, his automatics drawn and menacing. The bloodstone ring had clattered to the floor, looked up at him between his legs. Tiger scuffed to maintain footing on the suddenly hard, angular bifurcated lap. Voss hardly noticed the poodle. He thought, his face barely a foot from the smoking idol, *Whatever way they come, I'm ready for 'em!* Then, suddenly, the afterthought; *But, oh, that clever devil—*

Outside, Vinaro had said suddenly, "Gentlemen, we'll be on our way to the interior in a few minutes." He had turned toward Sophia. "And you, my dear, will come with us, of course."

Sophia had studied his face. Oddly, he was not looking at her but at his cigarette. She had said, "I'd…really rather stay here, Augustus."

"Nonsense," he had told her quietly. "I want you with me at all times."

Faintly embarrassed, she had glanced toward Romulo and the others. "But, Augustus, I…"

"Are you contradicting me?" Vinaro had asked, still looking at his cigarette.

"Of course not," she had said. "It's just that—"

Vinaro put out his cigarette in the nearest silver ashtray with one swift twist.

"Gentlemen!" he said sharply, turning toward the door through which he and Voss had gone. "Watch that room!"

A terrific explosion bellied the thick wall and thick door for an instant, dropping three framed pictures off the wall as if with neat finger flicks. Its roar was like that of a gagged giant. Smoke that was blinding bright for an instant squirted in an even rectangle through the tiny cracks around the door. One could feel its thumb-thick wrought-iron fixtures straining and holding. An air blast slapped gently, almost with the fingers of a ghost. The drapery-guarded glass sang.

Voss' rifleman proved his loyalty and his assassin's instincts by swinging his weapon toward Vinaro while the pictures were still falling.

Mr. Train materialized as if out of the inkblots, seized the Garand with downward swing, bent the barrel of the rifle double, dropped it, and as the man darted past him, brought down the heel of his left hand in a karate chop on the exposed upper spine. The man fell to the floor on his belly, his dead eyes looking upward.

Sophia sprang up and stared at the subsiding, smoking door and screamed, "Tiger! *Tiger!*" Then she dropped back on the sofa, her face twitching, her fingernails digging the fabric.

Mr. Train stood quietly above the man he had killed. Romulo and the others turned shakenly toward Vinaro. Of the four, only the *mameluco* had not dropped his demitasse. This won him an approving nod from Vinaro, as the latter faced the men squarely, drew from his breast pocket the small jade-colored block, and said as sharply as a drillmaster, "Men! That explosion was caused by a packet identical with this. I wanted you to watch—and listen—for two reasons.

"First—to illustrate the power of the explosives we are taking with us. I hope it was an effective demonstration?"

Romulo said timorously, "Mr. Vinaro, sir…what in the name of God is it?"

Thinning his lips, Vinaro replied, "An advanced form of picric acid. A pale, yellow, bitter-smelling, crystalline solid. It undergoes rapid decomposition and expansion, chemically, when exposed to mild heat or sudden, jarring movements."

Romulo and the other three moved uneasily. Mr. Train's face became wooden. Vinaro tossed up the pale green block and deftly caught it. "In layman's terms," he said harshly, "it's one of the most violent explosive compounds known to man. And you must exercise extreme care in handling it. Also, since you men are my lieutenants, my second reason for that little demonstration was to impress on you the importance of discipline."

He paused. "Captain Voss became slightly careless and insubordinate. I could no longer trust him."

He searched them with his eyes. "The heart of the matter is this. If you are disciplined and efficient, each of you stands to become quite wealthy."

His eyes narrowed to slits. "But…if you fall short of what is expected of you, either I or Mr. Train will deal with you… severely."

The last atom of feeling departed from Mr. Train's face. He cleared his throat slightly.

"And now," Vinaro said, easy, smiling, "let's go into the interior."

Backing away for their first steps, Romulo, the two Spaniards, and the American departed. Mr. Train followed them, silently as a tiger.

Vinaro tucked the explosive back in his breast pocket and went about turning off lights.

From the couch, Sophia's faint sobs were more like very long-drawn-out, shuddering breaths.

After a bit they stopped. She said, her mouth barely lifted

from the velvet of the couch, "Couldn't you have let me take Tiger out of that room?"

Vinaro said, "Hmm? That stupid dog? He'd have given the trick away." There was one light left, at the end of the great ink-blot draperies.

Sophia said, "But I *loved* him."

Vinaro, his finger on the last switch, paused.

"So you did, *chérie*, more than me," he sighed strangely. "But be of good cheer—he died in the highest style, accompanying—in a sort of *suttee*—a man who was in some ways quite magnificent. To give only one example, his instant choice of you."

Vinaro's finger moved. The darkness was complete. Through it, his voice sounded softly yet almost liturgically. "At last the Castle is consecrated."

Then there was a long, faintly jangling whir as he pulled the cord that drew apart the thick draperies.

The pale dawn, screened by the wild wall of trees, seeped slowly in.

Slowly Sophia's head rose and looked over the back of the couch. Her face was utterly drained of color, her eyes dark circled, her features as haggard as those of a thin old witch.

Vinaro said musingly, "Leonardo da Vinci jotted in his mirror-written notebooks that a fine flash could be obtained by closely shutting up a room, boiling off a couple dozen gallons of brandy in it, casting resin dust through the air laden with alcohol, and then setting fire to the whole. He added—by knowledge or guess—that the flash would be harmless. But he may have been wrong. Or, if right, the formula could be altered. Someday I would like to do that…"

Then, through the air, it began to come, very, very faintly, almost drowned in the acrid odor of the picric acid combustion products, but not quite: the odor of cooked flesh and burnt hair.

Sophia turned abruptly and vomited over the silver coffee service.

CHAPTER 10

The Sea of Trees and Jewels

Twenty minutes earlier, the helicopter had been thrumming along above a dark, wavering plain faintly lit by the stars. Now, with the swift coming of the jungle dawn, the plain had been transformed into a rippling sea of emerald, of malachite, alexandrite, and amazon-stone green, richly flecked with topaz and amethyst. Talmadge identified those last two colors to Tarzan, who was sitting ahead of him beside the pilot, as the blooms of the cassia and jacaranda trees.

Here and there jewels took flight among the bright green leaves—the red of the parrot, the deep sapphire of the macaw, and the varied colors of the *tuvuyú* or "Gospel Bird"—black head for preacher, red neck for devil, white wings for angel. Once some high-traveling capuchin monkeys, blond as film stars, peered up at the giant "windmill bird."

An irregular gap appeared in the *pantanal*, as the flat jungle is called in the Mato Grosso. The pilot, a wiry middle-aged man in lieutenant's uniform, slanted down, shaving the treetops, and hovered.

There was a slow stream, broadened here to a narrow lagoon reflecting the sky's brilliant blue and the suspended helicopter.

A group of dark golden figures raced out from under the trees. Tarzan, leaning out, saw that they were naked except for their evenly chopped-off black hair, thin black lines painted across their faces and chests, and a white sheath, like a small tusk, concealing the genital organ.

Then he had to lean back, for with surprising rapidity they

fitted arrows to the long bows they carried and sent up a vertical volley of their ancient missiles.

Most of these were turned aside by the helicopter's downdraft, but one flew straight and strong enough to enter the window and affix itself to the aluminum ceiling.

"Good shot!" Tarzan remarked.

As the helicopter lifted and continued swiftly on, Tarzan jerked down the arrow. It was pointed with a long yellowed fang.

"Jaguar's tooth," Juarez guessed, leaning forward.

"The canine of some fairly large feline," Tarzan agreed. "Your local Indians don't seem very pacified."

Juarez shrugged. "The Guaporés are mischievous. Perhaps a troublemaker has come among them. Perhaps someone promised to drop them gifts and then did not, or else dropped gifts of poor quality. My apologies that they should have chosen you for a target."

Tarzan asked, "What is that striking article of adornment they wear?"

"The sheath of the leaf-shoot of the *buriti* palm," Talmadge volunteered. "Most of the Indians are very good at shooting overhead—they desire the feathers of the parrot and macaw for their magnificent headdresses. Though the wiser ones snare them—or bring them down alive with blunted arrows—and keep them to grow crop after crop of plumes. But I'm distressed, Tarzan, that—"

"Not at all," the ape-man cut him off. "That was a good lesson, *companheiros*. You think Vinaro invincible with his tank, aircraft, and heavily armed jungle fighters. Yet just now an Indian might have winged me in the 'copter. The jungle knows how to strike back."

Juarez shook his head. "Vinaro and his men know the *pantanal*. You may be sure they will be ready for such flea bites."

The thin-cheeked pilot chuckled. "I am wondering," he said, "how this Vinaro hopes to keep this famous tank supplied with gas."

"He will supply his jungle column by air if necessary," Juarez said reprovingly. "Keep to your task, Duarte!"

"I got my bearings at the lagoon," the pilot replied with composure. "Ruiz's clearing is the second ahead."

"The one from which the trail of smoke is rising?" Tarzan asked sharply, peering ahead.

"Can you see that?" Juarez demanded, whipping out binoculars.

"And smell it, too," Tarzan told him.

"*Por Deus*, you're right," Juarez said, bringing the instrument into focus. "Here, look, professor." His voice was grave as he handed the binoculars to Talmadge. Then, to the pilot, "*Rapido, tenente!*"

The swift approach was made in silence. Soon they were hovering above the center of the second clearing. They gazed down at the gutted ranch house, of which only black, skeletonized, smoking beams, all fallen together, remained. There were no figures moving. The helicopter sank toward the center of the clearing.

"We could have flown here last night," Tarzan said, unable to keep a note of reproof out of his voice. "There would have been a beacon."

Juarez scowled and pressed his lips together.

"*Ai, sim,*" the pilot agreed soberly.

Tarzan was out of the 'copter as soon as it touched down. His tweed-clad figure looked strangely out of place against the jungle background as he hurried toward the cages, where the lion and jaguar were pacing and snarling, cowing all the other beasts and birds to silence.

The first two sprawled figures were beyond hope. But the third man, burly back propped against the bars of a cage, a woman's figure lying crosswise to him, head in his lap, a galvanized iron pail by his outstretched arm with a blot in the earth by it, where the water it had contained was almost dry—

Tarzan knelt down, noting how the man's clothing all down

his right side was stiff with blood, and the back of the woman's dress, too. The two big caged cats grew silent.

"João Ruiz," Tarzan said softly yet distinctly. *"Amigo."*

The eyes in the scorched face opened. "You...got here... Tarzan."

Tarzan said tenderly, "Your wife, *amigo*?"

The head rocked a little, side to side. "No. She got a bullet... in her lung. I pulled her out, but...it's too late."

Talmadge, hurrying up, said, "We'll fly you to a hospital, Ruiz."

Again the rocking. "Too late...for that, too."

Tarzan said, "The beasts are safe, João. You wet down the cages." Juarez came up silently and stopped by Talmadge.

The hand by the pail moved a fraction. "I...tried." A tiny spasm crossed the burnt face. Then, the voice a shade stronger: "It was...six...of Vinaro's men." A pause. "I shot two. Felícia... killed another...machete." A longer pause. "The other three took the boy...Ramel...into the jungle."

The eyes almost closed. Tarzan laid his hand against the unbloodied shoulder, gently yet firmly.

"Don't worry about that now, *amigo*," he said. "Just hold on. Talmadge is right. We'll fly you to a hospital. And pretty soon you'll be the same old warhorse."

The eyes opened, incredibly managed a twinkle. "Tarzan... friend...you always were...a bad liar. Try...to help...the boy. I wish..."

The eyes closed. The massive maltreated head fell forward. Then Ruiz's whole upper body slowly collapsed upon the shoulders of his dead wife.

Tarzan stood up and faced away, toward the smoking ruins.

Juarez said, his voice almost cold, but his eyes at last furious, "There still may be no proof that will stand up in the courts, but for the first time a witness of repute has survived long enough to speak the name Vinaro. That's enough for me. From now on I'll stretch my authority to the breaking point and beyond."

"What do you mean?" Talmadge asked.

"I promised you and Tarzan twenty men here by day after

tomorrow. I'll double that number, triple it if I can, and have some of them here tomorrow—perhaps even late tonight. I'll have the other heli up from Corumbá—with machine guns and grenades. I'll face the Governor with this evidence and demand that Vinaro's jet be impounded. And—*diablo!*—just *let* him once hint I'm trying to gather a private army for political purposes—I'll devour him! I'll also *make* him back me up in my cables to Brasília and the Army."

Talmadge caught fire. "First a search party can be organized to try to find the men who took Ramel. With good planning, they might get off by noon tomorrow. If we can catch Ramel's kidnappers and rescue the boy, we'll still have a chance of beating Vinaro to Tucumai."

"What do you say, Tarzan?" Juarez asked him.

Tarzan looked toward him briefly. "I say you're too late, just as you were last night. Tonight…tomorrow…perhaps the day after? Once more you'll be too late."

His face a grim, almost cruel mask, he walked straight to the cage against which Ruiz had been leaning while alive. He thrust his right arm through the bars to the shoulder.

It was not until the lion roared that Talmadge and Juarez realized that this was the cage which held that great tawny black-maned 500-pound cat crouching at the back.

Although smarting hotly at Tarzan's rebuke, Juarez had the intuition that he was witnessing a most primitive rite: a man who felt responsible for the death of a friend thrusting his hand into the fire.

Talmadge cried, "Tarzan, watch out!" as the lion sprang.

"Major!" Tarzan called.

The great lion broke his spring, stared at the gray-suited man, sniffed at the offered arm, then rubbed his neck against it.

Tarzan turned back toward Juarez and Talmadge a face that carried a hard, savage smile. "Major and I are old friends," he said. "Ruiz and I caught him in Africa when he was wounded and little more than a cub. Ruiz trained him to hunt like a cheetah—a remarkable feat."

"I always understood he was a man-killer," Talmadge said weakly.

"He is," Tarzan said. "If Ruiz had been able to loose him last night, the story might have had a different ending."

The lion was purring like distant thunder. He licked the hand of Tarzan, who rubbed him twice under the chin, then withdrew his arm.

"It is not well to let even a friendly lion lick you more than once or twice," he explained. "His tongue rasps the skin like a file. And if he tasted blood, even a friend's…" He looked toward the white jaguar, who had been intently watching the interchange between man and feline. "That's the boy's pet, I take it. What did Ramel call him?"

"Xima," Talmadge said.

Tarzan nodded. He gazed around the clearing narrowly, his eyes searching the jungle's edge. Finally he stretched his hand toward a spot thick with the purple blossoms of the bougainvillea vine and called, "Dinky!"

A chimpanzee dropped from the branches there and came shuffling forward, hesitating at the rude fence to stare at the helicopter between him and Tarzan—and at the pilot Duarte, who sat in the machine's door, smoking a cigarette.

Juarez said, "Tarzan, you have rebuked me. In part, I deserved it. I know you share our aims. How can I help? What do you need?"

"At the moment," Tarzan said, "I need my suitcase." He walked to the 'copter and reached in for it past the pilot, who merely leaned to one side and gazed at him curiously.

Then Tarzan called, "Dinky! Come on, you coward," and walked toward the shed beyond the cages. Dinky followed him at last, making a wide circuit of the flying machine. He went around the shed after Tarzan.

"I wonder what Tarzan is up to," Talmadge said.

Juarez shrugged. "He's *your* fellow-countryman. You figure him out."

Ramel stumbled and fell as he did his best to keep pace with his captors through the sun-speckled darkness of the jungle.

He was jerked to his feet by Rodriguez and dragged for a few yards until his feet once more caught the rhythm of the swift tramping.

The three men were making remarkable speed along the twisting trail, despite their burdens. Rodriguez carried only his Thompson and the belt of 20-round box-type magazines for it, but the others in addition to their weapons and ammo had large packs on their backs—a powerful radio sender-receiver and its two batteries.

Nevertheless Rodriguez snarled, "*Rápido! Rápido!* Speed it up, you two mules! *Vinaro* expects us to be near the Rondeau Plateau by nightfall!"

He said "Vinaro" as a fanatic might say "God." Ramel wondered why the Sun God, now looking down from the sky, did not intervene. Perhaps He simply could not see through the great thickness of the leaves, branches, and vines—and the golden specks that filtered through were in truth only his tears.

CHAPTER 11

The Two Armies

The great clearing over which the Messerschmitt helicopter hovered had three great grassy-looking mounds in it, but was otherwise flat and appeared completely empty.

Romulo brought the craft down in the flat area and cut the motors. The vanes slowed, stopped. After a half minute to let the dust settle, passengers and pilot climbed down.

Mr. Train and Vinaro went first. Their garb was stylish, though old-fashioned by modern jungle standards. Each wore heavy boots to the knee, linen suits covering the entire body, gloves, and linen-covered sun helmets. However, the linen fabric was colored a mottled green, so that they melted into their surroundings. Sophia Renault, following them, was similarly clad, except for skirt instead of britches.

Mr. Train strode swiftly toward the three mounds.

Romulo and the other three lieutenants, more lightly clad, yet in a similar mottled green, fanned out to the four points of the compass.

Sophia, standing back with Vinaro by the helicopter, became aware of what was abnormal in their surroundings. The jungle here was silent—no screaming birds, no chattering monkeys, no sound of creatures a-move across dead leaves.

The silence matched the emptiness inside her—the utter absence of feeling, the emotional lassitude, against which she had fought so long—the sense of being a zombi.

Vinaro seemed unaware of her condition, or more likely

pleased by it—in some respects zombis make the perfect audience—for he now began to speak with considerable animation.

"Now, my little one, you have the privilege of watching the operations of a modern conquistador and the launching of a twentieth-century filibuster against a treasure city the world has forgotten."

"Yes, Augustus," she said docilely and wondered why she hadn't said, "*Sim, mestre*,"—"Yes, master."

Vinaro said, "Watch closely, now. It will be like a conjuring trick."

Mr. Train, reaching the center of the clearing, raised a hand.

"*Men!*" he called in a voice like a trumpet.

The circumference of the clearing, empty a moment before, was now filled with men in mottled green, about a quarter of them carrying dark, deadly-looking weapons.

"Almost half of those are British Sten 9 millimeter submachine guns," Vinaro explained. "The rest are BARs—U.S. Browning .30 A1 automatic rifles. The few larger are Russian Degtyarov DP 7.62 millimeter light machine guns."

Sophia was counting automatically, her body wearily swiveling. There must be almost 200 men all told.

Vinaro, noting her occupation, said, "One fourth are heavy-armed soldiers. One fourth are officers, drivers, crewmen, fliers, mechanics, game hunters, other specialists. Another fourth are cooks, servants, and such. The final quarter are light-armed expendables, yet even they are skilled in jungle travel, mountain climbing, and the like."

"Yes, Augustus."

Train trumpeted, "Okay, men! Get those tarps off!"

Contingents raced forward to the mounds, grabbed at the bases of their grassy-looking covers, and trotted forward with them, whipping them up.

Underneath the camouflage were three giant vehicles, all running on double tracks.

The largest was a tank, looking terrifyingly powerful. The other two were Land Rovers. The first of these had a large enclosed cabin up front, with a mountain of supplies and equipment on the storage space in back. The second was three-quarters gas tank, with more supplies racked behind. All three vehicles had radio antennae.

Vinaro said of the tank, "It is a German Panther, but we have reduced its forty-nine tons to forty-two by dispensing with much of the armor. The gun is a two-pounder, such as was used on the British Matildas. The stubbier weapon mounted beside it is a flamethrower. Flanking those are 7.92 millimeter Besa machine guns."

While he was saying this, the tarpaulins had been folded and added to the burden of the Land Rovers.

"Yes, Augustus."

"Aboard!" Train bellowed. "Order of march!"

Crewmen loped to the vehicles, dropped down the tank's turret, leaped to the Land Rovers' cabins. Within seconds the four motors—two for the tank—were roaring, filling the jungle's silence, but not that within Sophia. The vast noise only made her aware of the terrors walling her emotional emptiness.

The tank turned on its great treads, which spurned and threw the soft soil like the hooves of an old cavalry brigade. The Land Rovers swung in behind, the one with the big cabin first, the one with the fuel supply last. Four armed men crouched on the back of the Panther. The others divided themselves into two contingents, half between the two Land Rovers, half a rear guard. Three big chaps came up to Vinaro.

"Aboard, Harris," he told the first with a jerk of his thumb. They bowed around him and climbed into the Messerschmitt. He waited until they were seated, then ordered, "Scout ahead on Pattern Three. Keep in radio touch with the command vehicle, using the scrambler at all times."

Then he walked proudly and swiftly to the first Land Rover. From emotional fatigue and also by an instinct, Sophia walked three paces behind. She climbed the high metal steps and paused in the doorway of the cabin. Behind the driver's seat, now occupied by Romulo, with Mr. Train beside him, were chairs for three more, a couch, a large radio panel, a map board, a fold-out desk, bookshelves, a bar. Everything was dull black trimmed with silver.

"Shut the door!" Vinaro said sharply.

She did and realized one reason: the cabin was air-conditioned.

"Check the tank's armament," Vinaro said.

Mr. Train held up four spread fingers to the man in the turret ahead. The man held up four in reply and bent forward.

There was a sharp blasting roar as the cannon fired. A tall, slender jacaranda tree came down with its wealth of violet blooms and the scarlet flowers of a vine, like an offering for an emperor, but before they touched tank or ground, the flame-thrower WHOOSHED out yellowly, destroying them and shriveling the jungle margin ahead. Into that destruction the machine guns spat loudly but briefly.

"Forward," Vinaro ordered.

Train raised a fist, and ahead of them the tank rumbled toward the scorched jungle and entered it, smashing and crushing everything in its way, moving like an invincible juggernaut. The Land Rovers and the men followed in the road it made, the men moving at a brisk stride to keep up.

An historian would have thought of Pizarro starting off from San Miguel with his slightly smaller army, to storm the two-and-three-mile heights guarding Caxamalca.

Vinaro turned to the map board, to which was affixed, beside the more conventional printings and drawings, Ramel's golden medallion turned front to back, so that the engraved map showed.

Sophia took her hands from her ears and realized that she had a new terror added to the more familiar ones. *What* did Vinaro expect to meet, that he traveled with so great an armament?

The army moved rapidly out of the clearing. The last man noted, high above him, a blond-haired face peering down at him, wide-eyed, around a big branch. He whipped up his Sten and fired a burst. The branch was chopped through, dangled. The capuchin monkey was blown apart.

Out of a hole in the branch a foot from the monkey, a five-inch black scorpion fell, extruding and sheathing its white sting and madly waving its big fore-claws. It fell past the last man, three inches from his open collar, hit the ground, and scuttled under a large leaf.

Wholly unaware of the death that had passed him so closely by, the man grinned widely and tramped on.

Talmadge and Juarez sat on a low outcropping of granite midway between the helicopter and the burnt ranch house. They smoked cigars. The wiry pilot Duarte sat again in the machine's door, smoking another of his cigarettes. They sat in shadow, although the sun was slanting into the clearing now. All three were sweating. Six blanket-wrapped bodies, lined up in an orderly row beside the flying machine, showed what they had been doing.

Juarez said, nodding toward the shed, "Whatever your Tarzan is up to, he's taking his time."

Talmadge said, "I don't know as much about him as you may think. He is an English nobleman. He had an unusual childhood in Africa. Because of somewhat sensationalized accounts of his adventures, he's tried to live in obscurity. From what I know of his dates, he should be an old man, but he looks, acts, *is* young. The chief thing I know about him, to a certainty, is that João Ruiz trusted him like a brother."

The English anthropologist tapped ash to the bare ground. "And Ruiz, who knew more about the jungle than any other man I've ever known, said that he knew only about one ten-thousandth of what Tarzan knows."

Juarez puffed his cigar thoughtfully and gestured with it. "We have more knowledge about him than that now. Your aristocratic ape-man proved last night that he can fend for himself magnificently in so-called civilized society also."

A shadow fell between them from behind. Simultaneously a deep voice said, "I'm leaving now."

Both men jerked around, Juarez snatching at his revolver, a Spanish Llama .38 automatic.

Tarzan stood behind them, wearing only a loincloth of the same bronzed hue as his body. From it hung a scabbarded hunting knife and a coiled lariat. In putting off his clothes he seemed to have become taller and at the same time brawnier and leaner, while his face had grown graver and harder under the short dark hair. Beside him stood his suitcase.

"Excuse me for startling you," he said, without the civilized smile he would have added if he'd been dressed. "As soon as I put on my jungle self, I begin tuning up—in this instance, stalking. It is as automatic with me as drawing breath. I also wanted to locate the point at which the kidnappers left this clearing."

"You don't look like the same man at all," Juarez said wonderingly, slow in dropping his hand from the Llama's checkered walnut grip.

"Even your voice is different," Talmadge said.

"*Rak,*" Tarzan agreed. To the others, this jungle "Yes" sounded like a clearing of the throat.

Juarez said, "But you say you're leaving? Where?"

"Into the Mato Grosso."

"Dressed like *that*?" Talmadge demanded.

Still Tarzan did not smile, though what he answered was, "The outfit is casual—but practical." Without preamble, he walked to the white jaguar's cage. The animal snarled, and Tarzan snarled back, "Xima! *Vando sheeta! Zu-vo sheeta!*"

The weird sounds silenced the words Juarez was about to speak. Tarzan was thinking, *Yes, it must be deeper than what human beings call language, as I've always thought. If a Brazilian—or Incan!—jaguar responds to my telling him in African beast-talk that he is "a good, strong panther," that must be so.*

The beautiful white feline came up and smelled his hand, then rubbed his cheek against Tarzan's wrist, almost as if imitating what he had seen the lion do. The fangs showed like white needles.

"Lionel," Tarzan asked over his shoulder, "do you know if there would be anything about here that the boy Ramel handled? Something that might have been outside the house?"

By now Juarez had found his voice. "But the fighting men to go with us, Tarzan? My troopers, the SPI men, the Indian guides…"

Tarzan said, "I'm grateful for the offer, especially that 'us,' but at this stage the fighting men would just be in the way; they'd slow me down. Even you, colonel, I'm afraid. Here's how it stands. If I leave at once, I *may* be able to catch the kidnappers before they get the boy to Vinaro. That would be a big gain for us."

"But they'll be armed, too. Three heavily armed men."

Tarzan shrugged. "At least they won't have the tank."

Juarez nodded doubtfully. "Then take my gun," he said, starting to unbelt it.

Tarzan shook his head. "Pistols rust," he said. "Also, if you kill one man with a thing like that, you warn the others. Finally, with that in your hand, giving you false security, you can't hear the jungle. Even my senses would be dulled."

Talmadge interrupted with, "Yes, Tarzan, there were some little Carajá figures of animals Ruiz gave the boy. They're statuettes of baked clay made by the Carajá Indians. I remember seeing one when we landed—near a spot in the center of the clearing where someone had made a little fire. There it is!" He began to hurry.

"Don't touch it," Tarzan called. Leaving the cage with a "*Vando*, Xima!" to the jaguar, he went and picked up, by a hind leg, holding it away from his body, the small baked-clay figure of a jaguar, ocelot, or some other jungle cat. It was covered with black squares with dots inside—jaguar, most likely.

The pilot, still chain-smoking, watched Tarzan most curiously.

Juarez asked with a certain professional interest, "You will use it to give the jaguar the scent of his young master and set him trailing?"

Tarzan shook his head. "Xima already knows Ramel's scent," he said. Then, snorting lightly twice to clear and moisten his nasal cavity, Tarzan gravely lifted the toy close to his nostrils, revolving it slowly—rather as Talmadge might have sniffed at a new unlit cigar.

Juarez's eyes widened incredulously. So did those of Talmadge. The cigarette dropped from the pilot's mouth.

Tarzan sniffed once more, a little more deeply, then handed the clay figure to Talmadge. "Keep it if you wish," he said. "I have no further need of it."

Juarez said, "Do you mean to tell me that now you, too, *know* Ramel's scent, as Xima does? That you won't even require the toy for reference?" He did not mention that he still doubted Tarzan's ability to scent like a bloodhound.

"Do you carry a Portuguese dictionary?" Tarzan asked him. "Scent is a language, too—each odor a word—which civilized man has forgotten. It is partly that my ape foster-parents no more smoked tobacco—and taught me the habit—than they brewed beer. It goes deeper than that, but we've no time for discussion. I must be off." He walked toward the cages, calling, "Dinky!" to the chimpanzee, who was wandering beyond the shed.

"If you do recover the boy," Juarez called after him, "you'll return here with him, won't you? Or wait until my force catches up with you? I believe we have red flares in the helicopter. You could set some off in the treetops just before dawn tomorrow or the next day. With some luck, my ground force or the cruising helicopter will spot them. Duarte! Would you please—"

"No!" Tarzan interrupted. "Flares would locate me for Vinaro as much as for you. No, if I find the boy and he is game, I will set out at once for Tucumai, to warn and give aid to its inhabitants. Time is still of the essence, as we decided last night." Then he added, still without a smile, "You have my full permission to follow me with your force if you are able to—employing Indian trackers, jungle-wise veterans, dogs, aircraft, what you will. I am sure your help may be invaluable when the clash comes with Vinaro. I wish you all success—it may save my life...and Ramel's...and the life of Tucumai. But the jungle is a less merciful opponent than even Vinaro. You must seek to defeat her by your own wits, just as I will."

With that he opened the jaguar's cage. Juarez's hand automatically went to the grip of his pistol, as did that of the lieutenant, Duarte, while Talmadge grew very watchful. After all, any jaguar is a mighty feline—smaller than lion or tiger, yet larger and stockier than leopard or panther.

Tarzan ignored them. He crouched by the weirdly white cat, which at some angles looked like a very large sheep or crouching llama, and spoke into its ear, pointing to the spot across the clearing where the kidnappers had fled.

The animal made off in the direction indicated at a steady lope, ignoring the men and the aircraft. Holding its head low to the ground, it quickened its pace as it entered the jungle.

Tarzan had moved to the door of the lion's cage. "This time keep your hands well away from your guns, gentlemen," he warned. "Major has learned about such weapons the hard way. He might ignore my assurances and attack." To Talmadge he added casually, "Look after my suitcase."

With the voice of one making a last appeal, Juarez said, "Tarzan! If you succeed in the first part of this adventure, you'll be going up alone against one of the most formidable groups of modern fighters ever assembled—a small but immensely powerful army!"

"Not quite alone," Tarzan replied. He pointed to where the jaguar had disappeared. "There's my tracker—and advance guard."

He pointed to Dinky, rapidly knuckling his way across the clearing. "There's my scout."

He threw wide the door of Major's cage. "And here's my army!"

The lion roared as he strode out. Tarzan clapped his great maned shoulders and roughed him up in a brief moment of play. "You've gotten fat, Major," he said in English. "We'll run

that off you." Then, pointing after the jaguar, *"Unk!"*—once
more a growling command only faintly resembling that
syllable.

The lion bounded across the clearing. Talmadge and Juarez
sprang out of his way. The pilot scrambled into the helicopter
from one side—and Dinky from the other; evidently the chimpanzee had doubts about his fellow-soldier.

But, "Dinky, *unk!"* Tarzan called, and then, in an astonishing
flash of speed, the ape-man himself was off. Beyond the helicopter he made a great leap which carried him across the crude
fence—he seemed to hang in the air longer than any ballet
dancer doing a *grande jeté*. Landing, he leaped instantly high
into the air, seized a vine, and swung on it out of sight in the
jungle's darkness. The chimpanzee rapidly followed him.

The pilot, staring out of the helicopter after them, said slowly
in Portuguese, "I don't believe it!"

Talmadge said, "Incredible! But what chance can he have,
alone, against Vinaro?"

"None, I'm afraid," Juarez said. "And yet… At all events, we
must seek to follow him with all possible speed as soon as we
have a minimum striking force assembled."

Hours later, the shadows lengthening once more, Talmadge sat
alone in the center of the clearing, waiting for the return of
Juarez and the helicopter—with two or three troopers, at least,
the colonel had hoped, to make up the weight of the dead bodies
they had carried to Cuiabá.

Near at hand were the flares Talmadge would light to mark
the clearing if he heard them coming after dark.

The Englishman's expression was puzzled. With the tape
measure he always carried—along with notebook, magnifier,
compass, maps, small medical kit—he had just measured the
length of Tarzan's leap across the fence and, indirectly, by memory
of a blotch on a tree's bark, the height of his leap to the vine.

The world's record for the running broad jump was still, as
far as he knew, 27 feet 3 ¼th inches—a Russian achievement,

he seemed to recall. While that for the high jump was about 7 ½ feet. But in the high jump the jumper's whole body goes barely higher than the rod he passes over. There was no world's record he knew of for the high leap—the height to which a man can spring into the air and catch hold of something.

However that might be, Tarzan's broad jump had cleared a few inches more than 30 feet, while the vine he had caught hold of had been about 14 feet above the ground.

It gave Talmadge food for thought.

CHAPTER 12

Paper Cuts Rock

Tarzan bounded to the top of the rocky rise abreast of the two big cats, although he carried slung over his shoulder the 40-pound peccary Major had just struck down.

Downhill from them the rest of the drove of South American wild boar went drumming off on their small hooves. Coming with the wind across, Tarzan and his beasts* had encountered the sleeping drove without warning either way. Major had broken the back of the nearest peccary, Tarzan had snatched it up, and then the drove of the dark grizzled beasts with white lips and shining tusks had been after them. They had made good their escape from the angry herd by racing up rock. Which was just as well—angry peccaries have been known to tree jaguars.

Both lion and jaguar were panting, while the ape-man's breathing was hardly disturbed. But Tarzan did not tease the cats about this, even in joking civilized speech of which they could understand only the tone. He knew that felines tire quickly on a long chase, compared to wolves or men. Besides, he had the knack of doing his heavy breathing before and during exertion.

Tarzan was satisfied at the rapport which had developed among the three of them. The lion and the smaller carnivore crouched to either side of him as they recovered their wind.

---

*From his youth, Tarzan worked in close alliance with animals. See *The Beasts of Tarzan* and *Jungle Tales of Tarzan* (Tarzan 3 and 6).

From the nearest tree Dinky began to chatter down at them, now that the peccaries were out of hearing, in a voice that sounded reproachful and also jealous. Evidently the chimpanzee did not altogether approve of Tarzan's close teaming with the two cats, of whom he still showed fear, or of disturbing encounters such as that with the peccaries. Yet the ape had kept up with them, sometimes by ground, sometimes by branches and vines, though he was no more a long-haul beast than the felines.

Tarzan was also developing a very different sort of rapport with the whole jungle around him—a hearing of its myriad voices, from the "I'm not here," of the mouse to the "Don't tread on me," of the surucucu or bushmaster; a mental organizing of the jungle's almost infinite odors, not forgetting the scents of the three kidnappers and Ramel, now become considerably stronger, indicating that the pursuit was gaining.

The checkered light was waning—it was sunset. With swift tuggings and delicate strokes of his knife, Tarzan parted this South American *horta* from his bristly hide. He gave the liver to Xima, but awarded the heart to Major, along with three-fourths of the rest of the carcass. He himself supped lightly off a haunch, knife aiding his strong teeth. This shared meal, besides being needful, should strengthen the already considerable ties between them and increase their potential for cooperation.

Near them Dinky tossed down the husks and spat down the pits of some fruit he'd found—a vegetarian's contempt.

The sunlight was all gone now, yet there had come a fainter checkering of the humus and leaves—that of the risen moon. Tarzan cast about and rediscovered the scent of those they pursued. *"Yud!"* he growled summoningly, and the beasts came after him as he set them a moderate pace that would nevertheless eat up miles during the night.

The kidnappers had made their camp on the edge of the jungle, where the trees gave way to what looked like a long stretch of hilly upland dotted with scrub and rock, which presumably would be the route tomorrow.

Rodriguez was setting up the radio transmitter-receiver. The two other men were eating meat from cans around a small fire.

Ramel lay dazed with a fatigue so obvious that his captors had not yet bothered to chain his ankles. His body ached and burned from bruises and scratches. He held in his hand a chunk of corned beef which his throat still refused. His eyelids were heavy as gold, yet would not close so long as the great Cupay-eye of Rodriguez was open. The second, smaller eye only made it seem the weirder.

Ramel watched the telescoped antenna shoot up into a skinny, barren tree of silver. He knew something of the device from the Englishman and from Ruiz, and now as Rodriguez switched on the scrambler and spoke, "RZ Two to Arrow One," Ramel pictured the message spreading out from the top of the antenna like a huge, invisible, incredibly swift swarm of silver bees.

Two hundred miles away a little red light began to flash on and off angrily in the radio panel of the luxurious cabin of a Land Rover, while measured static sounded loudly from the speaker.

Round about the vehicle lay Vinaro's encampment. Tents were up and fires glowing. Their light gleamed in eerie reflections from the great Panther tank and from the drooping vanes and body of the Messerschmitt helicopter and from the two silvery vehicles. Spaced widely around, a dozen men stood guard. There was the odor of good food cooking. From one large cluster of men came grunts of pain as a doctor gave swift treatment to cases of insect bite and skin eruptions from poisonous plants, and to one man badly clawed by a jaguar which had instantly been shot to pieces.

Beside the command Rover, a large multiple-tent glowed mysteriously with the different lights inside it. Vinaro stepped out, still in his jungle garb, carefully closed the netting behind him, hurried to the vehicle from which the static sounded, and repeated with its door the same quick maneuvers as with the netting. He touched the scrambler and heard, "—row One, R Z Two to Arrow One."

Back at the kidnappers' camp, Ramel heard Rodriguez say that for about the seventh time. Then out of the speaker came softly the words, "Arrow One here. *Informe!*"

Ramel began to shake. The thought of another stream of silver bees carrying *that* voice was almost unbearable. Yet strangely his extreme weariness began to leave him.

The rest of the talk he could not understand at all, because it was in Spanish.

Rodriguez said, "We'll be at the Rondeau Plateau by about ten in the morning, sir. About two hundred fifty miles away from you."

Vinaro said, "Satisfactory. I'll have the helicopter meet you there."

"Yes, sir." Rodriguez's voice, harsh to others, was fawning to Vinaro.

"Guard that boy with your life! We may need his help in finding Tucumai."

"Yes, sir."

Since Ramel did not understand the words, they sounded to the boy like some evil spell—Vinaro chanting from the air, the evil-eyed Rodriguez responding.

Vinaro continued, "And, incidentally, the man named Tarzan was not stopped. Portinari's men seemed to have had an accident."

Rodriguez asked, "Do you know where he is now, sir?"

"I must assume he's searching the remains of Ruiz's home."

Rodriguez chuckled. "Then we can forget him, sir. No human being could follow our trail."

"So? This Tarzan is said to be skilled in jungle matters."

"Sir, we went several times through water and for long stretches on naked rock."

"That sounds sufficient. Incidentally, you of course killed the boy's white jaguar?"

"Yes, sir."

But Vinaro caught the hesitation and pressed Rodriguez with questions.

"The same as killing, sir," the latter finally protested. 'The house was burning. The cages would surely burn, too."

"Inadequate, Rodriguez. But we will speak no more of it. *Keep a strong guard tonight.* Arrow One signing off."

Inside the Land Rover, Vinaro thought, *The Golden Man still loose—not good. The white jaguar loose—no gold about him—yes, the golden comb.* He shook his head.

Yet the expedition was going splendidly. He glanced at the gold medallion gleaming on the map board. All the landscape features he had interpreted from it were turning up as they should. With an effort he stopped himself from dreaming over it. No, it was just that out here in the mucky jungle—or perhaps merely in the confinement of this vehicle—he was beginning to feel a tiny uncertainty in his sense of command of things.

He left the Land Rover, locking the door, and paused in the dark to look out toward his fires and tents. His spine stiffened with pride. So, he thought, must Alexander have felt, and Julius Caesar, and Cesare Borgia in the Romagna, and the great Cortez in Mexico—and Francisco Pizarro, the greatest of them all, conqueror of an empire that stretched almost the length of South America, a golden ribbon of glory down that continent's western coast.

Yet Francisco Pizarro had been a man who could not sign his name—whereas he, Augustus Vinaro (interesting how the names echoed each other), could perfectly forge the signatures of the 200 greatest men in the world, and in at least 40 instances had successfully done so in practice.

He half-closed his eyes and relaxed, and then he began to feel a sense of power streaming out of him to the whole world, to every last being on it—and, even more important, a sense of information coming in to him from the ends of the earth, through the collective unconscious mind of mankind, from every being on earth; to do that he had only to concentrate in a certain precise direction, say the direction of this Tarzan, and there would filter in to him certain and sure knowledge of—

BZZZZ! Some insect swooped past his cheek and ruined his detective reverie. Damn the jungle!—it was a black intrusion into the blackness of the collective unconscious itself.

He deftly slipped past the fine-webbed protective netting into the multiple-roomed command tent. In the duck-walled vestibule, Mr. Train crouched sedately on a tiny-looking camp stool before a tiny-looking table, carefully entering into a note-book with a pen that looked like a black matchstick in his hand precise descriptions of the mineral specimens which Vinaro had ordered gathered today and which lay outspread on the heavy canvas floor—rocks small as a thumb or big as a horse's skull. Mr. Train poised his pen and turned his head respectfully toward Vinaro. His green-mottled eye patch and his sound right eye directed themselves at his leader.

Vinaro said, "Mr. Train. You'll arrange for the helicopter with the crew of three to leave for the Rondeau Plateau at seven in the morning."

"To be sure, sir."

"They'll pick up our men there, with the boy Ramel." Vinaro paused. "Make sure they're extremely well armed. There's a faint possibility of that wild man being in the area."

"Certainly, sir. Wise precaution."

"Wild man?"

It was Sophia Renault who spoke, coming from one of the tent's inner rooms. She was wearing a creamy silk dressing gown. Her blond hair fell straight to her shoulders.

Vinaro looked toward her sardonically. "None other than your Tarzan, *chérie*," he said. "Your bronzed beach boy of the jungle, who capered more nimbly in the bullring at Meseta than any of the other new-wave clown-matadors like El Cordobés, who are turning *tauromachia* into a circus act."

She stamped a slippered foot and, pursing her lovely lips, shook her head, quivering the golden tent of her hair, to deny all this.

Vinaro chuckled. He said to Mr. Train, "Actually, Tarzan is one of those mad Englishmen who rush about the world seeking to astonish mankind with their feats of travel and seemingly audacious exploration—like Sir Richard Burton, Adrian Doyle, Alestair Crowley, or, for that matter, Colonel Percy Fawcett, who, hinting at great discoveries to come, disappeared here in the Mato Grosso back in 1925. It is said—doubtless an invention of press agents—that Tarzan was reared by great apes in the African jungle. It is also said, perhaps with greater credibility, that he is a man of great physical strength." Vinaro smiled thoughtfully. "In a way I almost wish there were some way for him to follow us and catch us up."

"Why? Why, Augustus?" Sophia demanded with another stamp of her foot, her face twitching a little. She seemed to be trying to whip herself into an act of rebellion or at least anger. "Are *you* perhaps trying to astonish mankind—or maybe only yourself—with your ability to snatch success in the face of the strongest imaginable opposition?"

Ignoring this psychological thrust, Vinaro said, "It would be interesting to see how long it would take Mr. Train to kill Tarzan. If he's as physically powerful as they say, he might last several minutes."

Rallying herself, Sophia asked, her voice brittle, "Do you think, Mr. Train, that Tarzan might win even?"

Mr. Train became thoughtful. "There is no doubt, Miss Sophia, of Tarzan's athletic prowess. I watched him in the bullring, and I timed some of his movements there by stopwatch. He is unquestionably one of the finest all-round athletes in the world today, perhaps *the* finest. He has an animal swiftness that is distinctly dangerous. But, as with all other activities in the modern world, killing has become a specialty—as much as nuclear physics, say—requiring years, even decades, of uninterrupted study. In the field of killing, the amateur—the man of mere all-round abilities—can never hope to compete with the expert. So my answer, Miss Sophia, is…no."

"Exactly!" Vinaro applauded. "With his high mentality, great natural talents, and vast physical qualifications, Mr. Train has perfected himself in his chosen profession with admirable dedication. My fortune and my ability to arrange the impossible smoothly have enabled him to take all the important postgraduate courses, we may call them, in the art of killing—at Leningrad, London, Madrid, Washington, and Paris, the world's *savate* capital, and in Japan, Okinawa, Korea, South Africa, and deepest China. He is a profound student of death and of its grand and—yes!—holy rituals. He has devoted his entire life to making his magnificent body into a perfect killing apparatus. How many men, Mr. Train, can kill a man by stabbing him through the abdominal wall with one high velocity finger and drawing forth, at the return, his viscera?"

Sophia controlled a retch.

"Besides myself, sir, only two men in the world can do it cleanly, with a sure knowledge of the location of all the inner organs and folds of gut—both of them Fifth Degree Black Belt *karataka*. There was a third. He gave me this memento—" he indicated his eye patch—"but I was the victor in that particular bout. I screamed at his blow—it is a reflex—but he died. However, if I may say so, sir, the two remaining ones are strictly academy men, while I work in the field."

"They are experts in pure death, eh? While you are master of the applied demise?"

"You might put it that way, sir."

"And what are you, Mr. Train?" Sophia asked acidly. "A Tenth Degree Black Belt holder?"

"No, Miss Sophia, there is no such thing. The Red Belt is the only one higher, and that is almost an emeritus distinction in karate. I am only a Third Degree Black Belt."

Vinaro hissed with irritation. "Actually," he said, "Mr. Train is Fifth Degree, at least, by all technical and scientific standards.

The Orientals have some nonsense about so-called spiritual qualifications for the higher degrees—a man must be at one with himself and the world: he must have inner peace and certainty; when he strikes it must be with the suicidal certainty of a falling tree, and so on. Pah! For that matter, Mr. Train is of almost the utmost spiritual elevation—in my Religion of Death."

"A Black Cardinal, no doubt, to your Black Pope, Augustus," Sophia said. Then in the same artificial, hard voice, she asked, "How many ways can you kill a man, Mr. Train?"

The giant moved his huge hands deprecatingly.

Vinaro said eagerly, "An endless number! Among the more picturesque, he can collapse his foe's windpipe with a strike of the stiffened hand like a hammer flattening a copper tube; this is fatal and quiet, except for the terminal convulsions. With an upward strike of the base of his palm at the nostrils, he can drive a man's nasal bone into his brain. Arming his fist with the extended knuckle of his middle finger, he can strike a man's spine from in front, through the stomach, and break it, snapping the spinal cord—the *karataka* never hits at the surfaces of a man, as a boxer does, but at what lies beneath. Please do not flinch, *chérie;* listen, this is interesting! He can leap six feet in the air and with a downward kick break his opponent's neck. With a strike at the base of the spine he can ruin the brain—transmission of momentum! With a finger strike, as that at the abdomen, he can pluck out an opponent's rib—as good a trick as God did with Adam. With another such, directed at the inner corner of the eye, he can enter and destroy the frontal lobe of the brain as deftly and infinitely more swiftly than the finest lobotomist. I even imagine, though Mr. Train has never admitted this, that with an upward spear-hand strike at the solar plexus, he could pluck out a man's heart!"

"I did not ask you to be an encyclopedia of death, Augustus," Sophia said dryly, though she was exhibiting tremor.

"What a set of volumes *that* would make!" he answered, his eyes glowing.

"You make Mr. Train sound more like a cleaver or a club than a human being," she said. "And all the world a meat block."

"But that is only the simplest truth, *chérie*," Vinaro went on excitedly. "Mr. Train's fingers and hands are deadly weapons. So are his elbows, feet, and knees. And even his head. With any of those, he can deliver a killing blow."

"How admirable! A walking armory! Einstein and Shakespeare too delivered blows with the head, but of a different sort."

Vinaro said softly, "Don't belittle Mr. Train, my dear. Let her see your hands more closely, Mr. Train."

The giant held them out, saying, "As you can see, Miss Sophia, they are edged with callouses tougher and almost as hard as horn, which conceal almost completely the nails. The result of long daily practice against a post wrapped with cable and also of plunging them repeatedly, stiff-fingered, into a barrel of pebbles. Note the great ridge across the knuckles between fingers and palm—there the bones have been broken and re-fused as a result of these exercises, making the hands more potent weapons. Their ability to do fine work is thereby slightly reduced, but the sacrifice has been well worthwhile. Truly, these callosities are nothing compared to the ones I have had to develop around my spirit."

"Show her how your hands work," Vinaro ordered.

Mr. Train picked from the floor a specimen of dark gray rock ten inches through with silvery streaks. He studied it closely for a few seconds, adjusting its position in his left hand. Then, standing up with legs somewhat crouched, he raised his right hand, the four fingers and thumb extended flat and close together. Suddenly that hand descended in a blinding flash; its heel struck the rock, which split in two with a crunching snap. The halves thudded against the hard ground beneath the canvas.

Sophia sucked in a half mouthful of breath and bit her lip.

Vinaro said delightedly, "There is a child's game—which grown men have at times played for great stakes—called Scissors Cut Paper. The two players suddenly and simultaneously put out a hand that is either a fist—rock—or two spread forefingers—scissors—or *four fingers and thumb extended flat and close together*—paper. Scissors win against paper, because they can cut it. Rock defeats scissors, because it would blunt them. While paper bests rock. Why? The schoolboy explanation is that paper wraps around rock. But Mr. Train has just demonstrated the true reason. Paper—*four fingers and thumb extended flat and close together*—CUTS ROCK!"

"Please, Augustus, my eardrums!"

Mr. Train cleared his throat modestly. "Don't be overly impressed, Miss Sophia," he said. "I tricked you slightly. That wasn't entirely brute velocity and inertia. I first studied the grain of the rock, so that I could strike it exactly along its best plane of cleavage."

"Just as a diamond cutter does with a diamond!" Vinaro crowed. "The famed Asscher studied the raw Cullinan for six months before he struck the single crucial blow—fainting dead away when it turned out successful. You seldom take that long, do you, Mr. Train?"

"No, sir, I don't."

"In fact, in action your decisions are made with computerlike velocity. Just as your movements in karate are too fast to be seen by the eye—and your five-yard advance swifter than any sprinter's!"

"I suppose so, sir." And then, as if to take the spotlight off himself, Mr. Train said with one of his rare faint smiles, "Mr. Vinaro, Miss Sophia, is the world's greatest scholar of the Cullinan and, I understand, even larger—"

He broke off because faint frown lines had appeared between Vinaro's eyebrows. Evidently there were some matters he did not care to hear discussed, even in finest flattery and by Mr. Train.

The latter pulled himself to attention and said, "I'll go, sir, and instruct the heli men about their weaponry for tomorrow."

At Vinaro's nod he vanished with a catlike silence and swiftness that was particularly impressive after his display of brute strength. The net curtain hardly seemed to move aside before it was hanging steadily in place again, fully protecting the tent from noxious fliers, crawlers, hoppers, and swingers. Sophia felt a shiver walking in fairy slippers on her spine.

With a feather touch, Vinaro laid his hand on her shoulder. "So, you see, Mr. Train is a good man to have at our side." His voice became slightly animated. "For all his worldliness, he is Death's most devout acolyte—a Galahad of Murder!"

Ruiz's clearing was the scene of a conference. There still glowed on the ground the embers of the three flares that had guided the helicopter to a landing, while some five feet higher glowed three more—the cigars of Talmadge and Juarez and the cigarette of Duarte, the pilot. A little moonlight seeped down from the gunmetal sky.

Not smoking were two border troopers carrying Moisin bolt-action carbines, and two Chavante Indians, Apoena and Ataúl, whose naked skins gleamed darkest bronze.

"—*if* you think you can track them by moonlight," Talmadge finished.

"For all your anthropological knowledge, you underestimate the Chavante," Juarez said coolly, then summarized, "Very well, Ataúl, the troopers and I will take to the trail. You, professor, will follow tomorrow with Apoena to guide you as soon as Captain Lobos arrives with the portable sender-receiver—and you and Lobos feel you have a sufficiency of men. You leave means for the rest to follow *you*. Then the 'copters will maintain liaison as planned."

"I'd like to go with you, Colonel," Duarte said, crushing out his cigarette. "I'm an old jungle hand. While Ricardo here is a better pilot than I."

"Also, I'm no jungle hand at all," the designated trooper admitted.

"Very well, give Duarte your carbine and canteen and pack," Juarez agreed. The whole deal had been made with typical Brazilian casualness.

Then Ataúl, who had got the scent from Tarzan's suitcase and the animal cages, moved ahead in a low swinging crouch, questing this way and that. He was followed by Juarez, now dressed for the trail, the other trooper, and the pilot Duarte. Swiftly they melted into the moon-speckled jungle.

CHAPTER 13

Two-Thirds Feline

Each time a man or beast takes a step, he leaves behind him on ground or grass a few hundred thousand molecules stamped with his name. This is no loss to him, since molecules are incredibly tiny—dump a cup of marked molecules in the sea, stir vigorously, go halfway around the world, scoop up a cup of ocean water, and in it you will find a hundred of the molecules bearing your mark.

Yet the man or beast has left his signature behind.

Every time he exhales, he expels a much larger number of signed molecules. Most of these are scattered by the wind. Yet a fraction drops to the earth, while another fraction finds lodgment on nearby leaves and branches—and if he is going through jungle, this fraction is large.

Such leaves and branches, if he brushes them, take with them their additional hundreds of thousands of submicroscopic clues as to the man's or beast's identity. Still other such clues evaporate from his skin or are teased by the wind from his dry hide, and some of these find lodgment nearby, in the same way as the molecules of his breath.

Of the millions of signed molecules making up a yard of a man's trail, a few dozen are released again each second by wind and heat. If only one of these lodges in a moist sensory trap in another man's or beast's nasal membranes, a nervous circuit is closed as surely as if a switch had been thrown.

This was the means by which Tarzan and Xima trailed Ramel. By dipping their bronzed or black-mottled pink nostrils close to the ground and near likely leaves and tree trunks, they increased their chances of inhaling a few molecules with physiological stamp that was Ramel's and no other creature's in the world. In addition, Tarzan used vision to sight broken twigs, bruised bark, the outlines of sandaled or booted footprints, and other signs of passage. Likewise he used imagination to tell him in what direction a hurrying group of men would next move—much of the time the scent trail followed some long-trampled jungle route.

The fact that the jungle was night-black did not interfere in the least with the ability of wet nasal pocket to identify Ramel-molecule, nor did the millions of other scents, molecules with other signatures—these were inspected and ignored. The slight leavening of filtered moonlight was enough to let Tarzan's dark-adapted eyes see many of the visual clues. And as for Tarzan's imagination, the night only sharpened it—the big, silent, swift-stepping tarmangani was like a hundred delicate yet vastly durable scientific instruments mounted on a pair of lean-muscled legs.

Nocturnal insects droned; an anaconda scraped bark overhead with its great coils; in response a red coati, like a raccoon but longer-snouted, pattered along an escape branch; a sleeping macaw roused and squawked; termites industriously scraped out wood softened by their secretions to make new passageways in their homes deep inside hardwood. Yet none of these sounds, except such as were danger signals, disturbed for an instant the attention of the two trackers—the one human, the other a jaguar with white hair so long it sometimes made Tarzan think of a llama or vicuña; Tarzan wondered if the ancient Incans might not have bred pet jaguars to resemble such wool-bearing cattle for aesthetic reasons. Persian jaguars!

Behind Tarzan and Xima followed Dinky and Major. The chimpanzee, severely rebuked for a burst of chattering, had been silent the past hour. The mighty lion had come to recognize Ramel's scent—and the scents of the three kidnappers—and was operating as a sort of rear-guard tracker, ready to correct the others if they erred.

The scent trail began to grow stronger. Instead of dozens of Ramel-molecules released each second from each yard, there were hundreds, then thousands. Suddenly Xima bounded ahead. Tarzan made a grab at the beast, but it eluded him. The strengthening scent of its master had made it break the easy discipline Tarzan had imposed upon all four of them for the past few hours.

Wasting no time in self-reproach, Tarzan pressed on as swiftly as he dared, cautioning Major and Dinky to keep silent, though there was now little chance of a fully coordinated attack on the kidnappers, or even a surprise one.

From ahead came Xima's hunting wail.

Rodriguez heard the beast's weird cry. He dropped the handcuffs he had been about to put on Ramel and snatched up his beloved Thompson. With greater haste and almost equal speed the men by the fire grabbed their own weapons: a Sten submachine gun and a pair of Colt .45 revolvers.

Again came the strange, hair-raising call.

"*Diablo!* What is it?" asked the man with the Sten, a pale-faced Spaniard. The cooling holes on its outer barrel matched the smallpox pits on his face.

Ramel tried to keep his face expressionless and even pretended to tremble. The bad ones must not suspect that he knew not only what beast, but also which. Inside, his heart exulted, yet chilled with fear for Xima, faced by four guns. If only, when Xima attacked—slowly he began to work himself into a low crouch, facing the nearest man, the Spaniard.

Rodriguez said harshly, "*Tigre!*" for so South Americans name the jaguar, there being none of the larger, striped tigers in that continent. "They never come near a fire."

For a third time the call shivered through the night air. This time it was perceptibly closer.

"What if it's that damned white jag from Ruiz's?" the third man, a dark-visaged North American, asked.

"*Ai!*" the Spaniard responded. "It looked more like a ghost than a beast."

"And *he* didn't shoot it when he had the chanc't," the North American said, jerking a thumb at Rodriguez. "You heard him admit that just now when he talked to *him*."

"*Silêncio!*" Rodriguez hissed. "With *these*—" he shook his Thompson—"we are no more in danger from *o tigre* than from a pussycat!"

The flickering flames cast weird ever-changing highlights on the undersides of their chins, nostrils, and upper eye sockets as they peered constantly about—and overhead, too, where several huge branches arched.

Once more the eerie scream sounded, louder still.

"Sure sounds like a ghost," the North American muttered.

"*Silêncio, cão!*" Rodriguez hissed at the man, who scowled for an instant suspiciously, not knowing *cão* meant "dog," but knowing its meaning must be insulting.

Rodriguez snatched from inside his shirt a golden whistle hanging on a silver chain around his neck. "A gift from *him*," he boasted, his twisted mouth coming as close to a smile as it could—the result a hideous sneering grimace. "It will scare the beast off."

As if the fifelike blast were a summons, Xima shot like a white flash from the jungle. As the guns roared and their nearly half-inch slugs made the dirt leap, Ramel launched himself at the Spaniard's legs. The man's shots went high. He loosed his left hand long enough from his Sten to rip Ramel loose from him with a vicious tug of the boy's black hair, instantly followed by a backhanded blow that sent Ramel sprawling. The jaguar turned course and sprang through a hail of fire from the Thompson and the Colts at the Spaniard's throat and bore him to the earth before he could bring his Sten in play. The two other men danced away, side by side, firing at the big cat without much care for the man under him. Red blood spattered the white fur.

Tarzan dove off the big bough like a human thunderbolt. At that instant Rodriguez turned, so that the straight-armed blow meant for his neck hit his shoulder instead. He smashed into the North American, and they both sprawled on the ground, Rodriguez in the fire. He lay there dazed for several moments, his twisted lips writhing, his mismated eyes almost starting from his head. His shirt caught fire. Ramel, rousing from his daze, saw him and thought, *the god of the inner flames, the volcano god!*

Tarzan hit the ground, rolled over, and came to his feet without an instant's pause. The North American shot at him with the revolver he'd held onto. With a zig and a zag Tarzan was at him. He got off another shot that missed. Then Tarzan had his gun and crashed his skull with it as he drove his knife into the man's heart.

Rodriguez, still afire, was on his feet now and swinging his Thompson toward Tarzan. Then, despite pain, rage, and dread, he was paralyzed in his tracks by a terrific roar behind him. His huge eye looked over his shoulder just as Major struck him, breaking his neck and snapping off the side of his face as he bore him to the soft earth, which put out the fire.

The fight was over.

Major, growling, moved away from Rodriguez. In the growls of beast speech Tarzan commended him for his kill and especially for his bravery in charging at flames.

With difficulty Xima lifted his bloodstained jaws from the Spaniard, who had been doubly killed—by the jaguar and also by two bullets of Rodriguez which had ripped through both animal and man. The jaguar staggered to his feet and moved a few unsteady steps toward Ramel. Then he fell down.

Ramel rushed to his pet and flung his body down beside the red-bedraggled fur.

Xima tried feebly to lick Ramel's face, then the slits in the cat's eyes closed, the blue pupils rolled upward, the noble feline head fell back, and the whole body went slack.

Ramel rose to his knees; tears spurted from the inner corners of his eyes. He pushed his knuckles into them and began to sob.

Tarzan knelt beside him and put an arm around the boy's shoulders. For a long moment they looked down together at the dead jaguar.

Tarzan said softly, "I'm sorry." Then, "But your brave Xima killed one of the men who stole you. Major killed another. They also avenged João Ruiz and Felicia. Those are things to remember."

The boy raised his tearstained face to Tarzan, now using his fists to stifle his sobs.

"You killed...one, too," he finally managed to say. "But the lion killed Cupay."

Tarzan neither nodded nor asked questions, though his mind filed the odd name away. "It's best that you don't stay here," he said gently.

The boy nodded through his tears and stroked his pet from limp ear to hip once more, unmindful of the blood.

Dinky had come with great caution into the clearing a few moments before, staring about with many a lifting of eyebrows and jerking of head. Now he scowled sadly, though the effect of sympathetic grimaces was almost as comic as those of surprise.

Ramel did not see him. Tarzan quietly lifted the boy in his arms and stood looking around. Ramel, leaning back a little, studied the ape-man's face—a small boy measuring the heart and worth of a man and finding it good, despite his sorrow.

Major rumbled restlessly. Dinky hurried to the other side of Tarzan.

The ape-man said, "We'll go on about a mile and make a new camp. The moon will be almost down. There are some things I want to take with us from here. Do you think you can walk it?"

Ramel nodded solemnly.

Fifteen miles behind them, the Chavante tracker Ataúl reached a long stretch of rock, sensed by the untrammeled air above it rather than seen.

"*Difícil também,*" he croaked. "*Não lua. Campo!*"

"Too right it's too difficult!" Juarez agreed, bumping into Ataúl at that moment. "If it's rock, I'd break my neck on it for certain even *with* a moon. And now that *lua* has sunk, camp is the word!"

The pilot Duarte let out a breath of relief. "Fifty-five years is too old for moonlit things," he announced. "Whether serenading *senhoritas* or tracking superathletes, tigers, and lions. Why am I here? I must be an enthusiast!"

"You got here," Juarez told him. "Behold, I am fifty myself."

"Five more years are like five bars of lead," Duarte assured him. "You will discover."

They arranged themselves on the dark rock. The trooper broke out four rations from his pack, and they chewed slowly.

CHAPTER 14

Jungle Jeito

As the paling sky over the western Mato Grosso turned to pink and the sun peered with its golden rim over the eastern horizon, perhaps recalling the old centuries when it had been a god instead of a mere gigantic atomic furnace coasting through space, several things of importance were happening to the seekers of a golden city.

At Ruiz's clearing two parties of four—one of SPI men, one of troopers—had arrived by jungle trails during the night. Now Talmadge had just welcomed down the helicopter piloted by Ricardo and bearing Captain Lobos and the vital radio sender-receiver set, along with a Russian Simonov 14.5 millimeter antitank rifle with ten rounds of ammunition. The Indian Apoena squatted on his heels, a statue of red-gold in the dawn, waiting the moment when he would trail his brother into the jungle.

On the trail Juarez awoke, roused the others, and they drank from their canteens. Then they set out across the rock, Ataúl questing back and forth, his nostrils low to the stone, like a bloodhound's. He picked from a thorn and held up triumphantly a wisp of long white fur—Xima's, surely.

Vinaro, standing on a little hillock beside the command Rover, watched the golden sunlight catch the whirling vanes and an instant later the shimmering body of his helicopter as it mounted above the flowery treetops.

Last night's elaborate camp had been struck. Prodded awake an hour before dawn, his men had packed tents, doused fires,

161

filled in latrines, and now were lined up with the vehicles in order of march.

The helicopter leaned forward and drove out of sight, thrumming like a gigantic wasp.

As Vinaro walked toward the Command Rover, he called to Mr. Train at the door, "The heli's striking power is maximum?"

"Yes, Mr. Vinaro," the giant assured him. "Harris, Benjamin, and Barros—our strongest pilot next to Romulo. Light machine gun, submachine gun, plentiful grenades, anesthetic bombs." When Vinaro frowned at the last, he said, "Under certain circumstances, which are admittedly most unlikely, it might be desirable to immobilize the boy Ramel from the air."

"You are a paragon, Mr. Train," Vinaro said as he mounted past him into the Rover. "You remember everything I tell you, even when it slips my own mind. Ah, Sophia, good day to you. Forward, Mr. Train!"

The latter raised his arm, then pointed it ahead at the jungle as he swung aboard. The four motors roared as one, and the three vehicles rolled forward. The steel teeth, razor-sharp and numerous as a shark's, jutting out from the tank's treads, sliced the jungle's tough stems and lianas as if they were spaghetti. Their sap spattered. Small trees were pressed down, crushed. Insects rose buzzing; birds fled squawking, hurried by a burst of machine gun fire from the tank's Besas.

Vinaro, who had been grimacing at the birds' clamor, smiled. "Now, *that*, *chérie*," he said to Sophia, "is a sound to please the ear and gladden the heart—clean, sharp, male! Only the shrill whiplike crack of high explosive is its superior—just as the heroic trumpet outdoes the brave drum, and the brasses the tympani. Life chatters endlessly and most irritatingly, but Death speaks with soothing simplicity and a majestic finality. While the *1812* overture is at least the equal of Schubert's *Wiegenlied*."

Tarzan had been awake for an hour before dawn, thinking and also inspecting by touch the hardware he had lugged with him from the kidnappers' camp. He had brought the two submachine guns chiefly to keep them from falling into the hands of some possible unkilled enemy. Not too much sense to that, he decided now in the mentally stimulating predawn chill—an additional enemy would have his own weapons. Still these were beautiful pieces, each with a half magazine, or less, unfired—six cartridges for the Thompson, eight for the Sten. He handled the two weapons with sensations of both respect and revulsion. Tarzan admired immensely the good workmanship of the Age of Steel, but he detested the way such guns made people rely on their machines and armies, not on the strength of their own bodies…and on the wit of their own minds. If such guns, and even wickeder ones, were in the hands of their own soldiers, they believed themselves safe—that was all they cared.

He touched his knife and his lariat. Those were better weapons. They kept a man in touch with the things he was doing. He tied two slip knots at the ends of the lariat—there could be times such would be helpful.

The radio was something else. He might be able to use it to annoy and even unnerve Vinaro—bait him a little, as Manolecito did the bulls. Tarzan was skilled in the tactics of harassing a powerful column as it moved through the jungle.* With a heavily modern-armed group like Vinaro's, he could hardly hope to use bow and arrow and then "melt" back into the jungle—a jungle which would be shattered by rapid-fire weapons a few seconds later. Any attack using Major would doubtless meet with a similar reception—the lion might strike down a man or two, but would perish escaping. Perhaps harassment-at-a-distance was indicated, and for that the radio could be excellent. Also, he might be able to use the instrument to contact Juarez and Talmadge.

And certainly it would be an advantage to locate Vinaro's column before they located him.

Despite that, it was more important to reach Tucumai first than to locate or harass Vinaro. And to do that, what guidance Ramel could give him was all-important. In the paling night

---

* See *The Return of Tarzan* (Tarzan 2) and *Tarzan the Untamed* (Tarzan 7).

he looked at the boy, cheeks still stained by tear tracks, sleeping back to back for warmth with the chimpanzee Dinky. It made Tarzan smile that the two anthropoids had slept on the opposite side from the lion Major, who was snoring faintly yet majestically—evidently both boy and chimp were timid about the huge feline.

He dragged toward him his third metallic trophy from the kidnappers' camp—a gunny sack of corned beef tins—and began to twist one of them open. The faint ripping sound of the metal did not disturb any of the three sleepers, but then the odor of the beef, preserved in spices and brine and later desalted and cooked, reached their nostrils. The lion writhed his great lips and opened a slit-pupiled eye, instantly directed at the can Tarzan was opening, as if by some radar of odor. Ramel likewise began to rouse. Only Dinky lifted a long-fingered black hand over his eyes and nose and seemed to try to sink deeper into slumber, clamping the little finger over his nose vents—apparently his claim to being a devout vegetarian was sincere.

Tarzan tossed the cubical contents of the first tin to Major and started to open the second. Major snapped the reddish chunk out of the air and swallowed it entire.

"Chew your food," Tarzan advised. "It's healthier—or at any rate it makes it last longer."

Ramel, his eyes filled with sleep, smiled at that.

The next can had to go to Major, too, but the contents of the third Tarzan quickly divided between Ramel and himself. Thereafter he busied himself with opening more cans for Major—a full half dozen. "Peccary on the hoof is a lot simpler," he remarked.

Ramel, slowly nibbling his chunk of food, smiled dreamily. Dinky rolled away another turn and shut his nostrils tighter against all the meat odor. However, one of his eyes was slitted cunningly.

Meanwhile it had swiftly grown lighter. The fugitive pink of the dawn had upped wave frequency to blue. They were camped in a shallow grassy bowl 50 feet across. A few beetles with copper-colored carapaces climbed lazily over the green. Here and there on the edge were bushes. The jungle behind—and the death camp—were a mile away: the jungle ahead was at least three miles off.

Tarzan happened upon and quickly opened a can of peaches with clean downward strokes of his knife. Dinky caught the smell, roused, came to Tarzan, and accepted the can as if it were a tankard of champagne. He took it away a dozen feet, then dipped out with forefinger and thumb one yellow peach after another, dropping them down his throat as if he were a millionaire eating raw oysters.

Ramel laughed aloud.

Tarzan said, "Life looks a little better this morning, doesn't it?"

"Rather," Ramel said coolly.

Tarzan said, "I guess you learned that word—and the way of saying it—from the Englishman, Hugh… What was his last name?"

"Malpole," Ramel said.

Tarzan said, "I'd also guess it was his stories that brought you adventuring into the outside world from…"

"Tucumai," the boy finished for him. He looked at the ape-man thoughtfully.

Tarzan said, "Don't you think it's about your turn to say something? Or ask?"

The boy looked at Tarzan like a young king viewing an ambassador from another kingdom. "You are…Tarzan," he said at last.

Tarzan nodded. "But how do you know?"

Ramel said, "Mr. Ruiz told me about you. There could be only one—just one of you—in the whole world. He said you were an English nobleman—John Clayton, Lord Greystoke—and that you would take me to *my* land."

"I want to," Tarzan said. "But can you guide me there? Without the map Vinaro took from you?"

For the first time the dark aristocratic face looked doubtful as well as troubled. "I will try. Tucumai lies toward the Sun God's western home, where he returns each night. Around it rise the steepest mountains in the world. I will know them if I see them. But the weather there is strange, with many low-flying clouds and queer changes in things seen, so that sometimes one must wait for the right moment to see them right."

"The Land of Mists and Mirages?" Tarzan asked.

Ramel nodded. "That was what Professor Talmadge called it. But Colonel Juarez and Mr. Ruiz did not believe in it, I think. Yet it *is* there, for I have known it all my life. And how else could a city like Tucumai have stayed hidden so long?"

Tarzan agreed, "That makes sense."

Ramel looked relieved and added hesitantly, "I never told the others this, but the look of the sky and air around Tucumai is controlled by Manco Capac and the other Thinkers of Tucumai. They are able to change the look of things by the power of their minds, especially when they sense the approach of enemies."

"They do this by prayers to the Sun God?" Tarzan asked.

"They make such prayers, too," Ramel said evasively.

Tarzan decided to ask no more direct questions about the matter. Weird and superstitious as it sounded, it was clearly something in which the boy believed, so for the present he must pretend to believe in it, too.

He said, "In that case, won't Manco Capac and the other Thinkers be able to send Vinaro and his little army astray?"

A look of pain crossed Ramel's fine eyes. "You forget Vinaro has the golden map which shows very clearly how you must follow the rivers and ridges to reach the mountains of Tucumai. All it doesn't show is where the caves are that go under the mountains. Vinaro wanted me so he could make me guide him the last part of the trip."

Tarzan asked, "Is the way through the caves narrow?"

Ramel shook his head. "It is so wide that four horsemen could ride through it abreast and pointing their lances upward. Only the outside entrance is a little narrower."

Tarzan looked at Ramel thoughtfully. The boy's last remarks

had made him think of Pizarro and his steel-armed-and-armored cavalry four and a half centuries ago. It finalized Tarzan's belief that here in Ramel he actually faced a princely representative of the Incan Culture, somehow—perhaps miraculously—preserved for almost half a thousand years. A belief which most scientists, Tarzan was sure—except the burningly enthusiastic Talmadge—would scoff at. Yet a belief which, for practical purposes, he must now accept.

Nevertheless it seemed very strange now to Tarzan here in this grassy bowl, with Major rumbling a purr a few yards away and Dinky appreciatively smacking his lips over the last of the peach juice and with the rising sun beginning to strike gleams from the fire opals and golden wire around Ramel's black hair.

"Can you remember the golden map?" he asked, conscious of a new rapport between them since he had accepted Ramel's story of himself.

"I am not sure," the boy replied, his eyes facing those of Tarzan fearlessly, as if he, too, were certain of the link between him and his new savage protector.

"Then we must try to trick Vinaro into leading us to Tucumai," Tarzan said decisively. "Yet it will be a dangerous business."

"I am game," Ramel said stoutly, once again making Tarzan think of the dead Englishman Malpole.

He turned to the two-way radio which he had already set up, its antenna gleaming. He had been careful to keep the dials in the setting in which he had found them.

"Did the men who kidnapped you speak into this?" he asked.

"Their leader did," Ramel answered with a shiver.

"The man Major killed?" Tarzan asked quickly.

Ramel nodded. Memory of last night's horrors, suddenly returning, made it difficult for him to speak.

Tarzan said. "Steady, Ramel. When the man spoke into this, did he say anything first? Before he said anything else."

The memory task helped Ramel control his fears. "*He* said, 'RZ Two to Arrow One.' First he said that, many times, before I heard Vinaro's voice."

Tarzan switched on the set and the scrambler. The power hum came, and Ramel knew the silver bees were speeding through the golden sunlight.

Then Tarzan, coarsening his voice, said, "RZ Two to Arrow One."

Two hundred miles away Vinaro heard the static and saw the red light flashing on the radio panel of the command Rover. It angered him that he must break off the unending, almost narcotic pleasure of watching the knived treads of the tank ahead slashing out a road through the jungle. Even vegetable death had a grandeur in this murky, overblown region—something one missed when witnessing the death of plants on farms. Here lianas and arching roots died like great serpents, and splendid leaves and blooms like birds. It was the pleasure of slashing off flower heads with a cane, magnified a hundredfold.

"Halt the column!" he snapped at Mr. Train. The big vehicle ground to a halt on the chopped greenery. Within three seconds the motors of the other two vehicles had been turned off. In the sudden silence the whine of a wasp became audible as it cruised inside the command Rover between the radio panel and Vinaro's cheek. The latter batted out at it ineffectually and failed altogether to suppress a little gasp of fear. Mr. Train's long arm reached back like a great green snake striking with speed and precision, fingers clapping against palm. He opened them in the direction of Sophia Renault, to show her the crushed yellow-and-black body, smiling at her as he delicately plucked the sting out of his horny cuticle.

Meanwhile Vinaro had switched on the scrambler, got the call, and in a voice of leashed fury said, "Arrow One replying to RZ Two! What's your problem? You're very indistinct!"

At the camp Tarzan improvised, "The radio was dropped. I finally got it working a little."

Vinaro's fury was unleashed. "Idiot! How did that happen?"

Tarzan, who disliked lying even under these circumstances, replied, "The camp was attacked by a wild creature last night. The others are dead. I'm here with the boy."

Vinaro said furiously, "If you let anything happen to that boy—!"

"Believe me, I'll take the best care of him I can," Tarzan answered, perhaps too meaningfully. "But what do you want me to do now?"

"What's wrong with you?" Vinaro demanded, suddenly suspicious. "Meet me as planned, of course."

Tarzan shrugged, as if conceding defeat, yet made his voice halting and apologetic as he replied, "I'm sorry, Mr. Vinaro… but in all the excitement…I've forgotten where we are supposed to meet."

Vinaro's voice became like ice. "You've dropped the radio. You've forgotten the rendezvous. You've also forgotten to speak Spanish in front of the boy! *Cómo se llama usted?*"

Tarzan shrugged again. *What is your name?*—presumably first of a number of questions on which he would surely fail. Yet he must make the effort. Remembering Ramel's words of last night, he said confidently and strongly, *"Yo soy Cupay!"*

The radio was silent for seconds at Vinaro's end. Sophia, Mr. Train, even the sullen Romulo watched their leader with growing fascination. He paled; they could see a shiver and shudder travel up his body: then his eyes brightened and his lips drew back in a thin smile. "I am Cupay!" the strange voice had said, and inwardly Vinaro was filled with terror and delight at having been granted the experience, or at least the illusion, of hearing the voice of one of the Great Lords of Death, whom he truly believed lurked about the collective subconscious mind of mankind—in this case, Cupay, Lord of the Incan Underworld. It was as if he had heard and believed a voice saying, "I am Charon," or, "I am Satan," or, simply, "I am Death."

Then, like a ghost on the airwaves, he heard the voice of the boy Ramel whisper urgently, "Rodriguez!" and the illusion faded almost instantly. Vinaro had his logical mind back again, perhaps the cooler for its momentary plunge into mystical realms, and he guessed where he stood.

"So you are Rodriguez?" he asked smoothly, smilingly.

"Yes, I'm Rodriguez," Tarzan answered roughly, reluctant to continue the pretense, now that it seemed almost certainly blown.

"And how much money do I pay you, Rodriguez, per day?" The voice was oily, gloating.

Tarzan realized that the game was up and any hope gone of getting a line on Vinaro's location. He said harshly, "Not nearly enough, for what happened last night."

"Who are you?" Vinaro demanded.

"A critic of yours," Tarzan said, his voice suddenly cool. "I particularly deplore your taste in wristwatches and necklaces!"

With that Tarzan snapped off the radio and matter-of-factly asked Ramel, "Do you like to run, boy? Do you run well?"

"Yes, Tarzan, I do. Quite well."

"Good! We're going to cross this open space as quickly as we can. I feel we'll be safer in the jungle. Dinky! Major!"

"You're not taking these things?" Ramel asked, pointing at the two machine guns, the remaining tins of food, and the radio.

"Their weight would slow us down," Tarzan said. "Besides, our radio partner seems annoyed with us."

Ramel said guiltily, "I should have told you the man's real name was Rodriguez. But I thought of him as Cupay, our Incan Master of the Dead."

But Tarzan grinned. "So the name Cupay struck Vinaro silent for five seconds. Perhaps we *are* getting under his skin. Come on, now, all of you!"

He loped off easily. Ramel followed, stretching his slim legs. Then came Dinky with his hobbledehoy gait that nevertheless ate up distance. Major bounded along to one side. Their spirits rose with action. Soon their racing through the heat-touched dawn across the grassy plateau seemed the greatest fun.

Vinaro's eyes still glowed as the radio went silent.

"Trouble, sir?" Mr. Train asked sharply. Vinaro's abstraction bothered him.

Vinaro smiled. "I'm not quite certain how he did it, but I have a feeling you may yet, Mr. Train, have a chance to meet this man Tarzan. At the moment he is with the boy Ramel, presumably on the Rondeau Plateau."

Mr. Train said, a touch impatiently, "I'd like to fight him, sir, of course."

Sophia said, with a sudden flare of her old vindictiveness, "Oh, I am sorry for you, *chéri*, that Tarzan is so troublesome. First Cabral and the two Italians at Cuiabá. Now the handsome Rodriguez and the other Spaniard and the North American on the Rondeau Plateau. It is almost alarming."

Mr. Train and Romulo both looked at her angrily. But Vinaro's smile only widened. He glanced at his wristwatch, then rapidly retuned the radio.

"Perhaps you forget, *chérie*," he said, "Barros and the two Britishers. Our heli is due at the Rondeau Plateau in three minutes. I should think that death—or insensibility—coming from the sky like a great hawk might awe even your Tarzan…and generate in him a certain respect for the bone-faced god of gods! There will be beauty in this, *chérie*. Arrow One to Barros! Come in, Barros!"

Tarzan did not waste a second thinking that the helicopter might be that of Juarez. It was coming from the west instead of the south, and it had a different, stronger *thrum*.

They had come a half mile from their night's camp.

The jungle was still a mile away. There was not a spot of cover for a quarter-mile around them except for thorny low bushes and a few outcroppings of sandstone.

"Stop, Ramel!" he cried. "*Dan-do*, Dinky! Major, run—*gom!*"

And now the helicopter was visible, coming like a great swarm of golden bees in the reflected sunlight and growing larger by the moment. Tarzan recognized the typical two counterrevolving set of vanes, the one about two feet above the other, of a Messerschmitt.

He rushed Ramel and Dinky to the nearest, biggest sandstone outcropping that could be reached in the time allowed by the approach of the drumming plane, and huddled them behind it, his own body crouched over that of Ramel.

Major loped on to the north, obedient to Tarzan's command.

The helicopter took no note of the lion, so far as its direction of flight was concerned. It zoomed in, hardly 20 feet above the ground, over the outcropping Tarzan had chosen.

Tarzan expected machine gun fire and pressed his comrades down as hard as he could, Ramel with his body, Dinky with his strong right arm.

Instead, two pale shapes fell, bracketing them 20 feet to either side.

Tarzan expected the whizzing metal of grenade cases exploding and made his mind accept this chance of death—or life.

Instead, a freezing explosion blast slapped his skin, and they were enveloped in clouds of pink gas. Without taking the tiniest breath, Tarzan recognized the fierce aromatic odor of $(C_2H_5)_2O$—ethyl ether, the first of anesthetics and the master drug of imaginative fools. Somehow Vinaro or his technicians had perfected an ether bomb. It must explode by the force of compressed carbon dioxide or some other inert gas, since ether is highly inflammable and would make a great blaze if driven by fiery core-explosives. The pink color would merely be some gaseous additive, to show the bombers their hit.

Ramel and Dinky gasped…and succumbed. Tarzan instantly sprang up from them, left hand clapped to his nostrils and mouth as an additional precaution, eyes slitted against the stinging vapor, and raced back the way they had come—straight toward the camp they had left three or four minutes ago—the camp that was a half mile away.

And I left two machine guns back there, Tarzan thought grimly, beginning to take great rapid breaths as soon as he got outside the pink cloud. *Sometimes I think I ought to become modernized.*

The tiny touch of ether he got seemed to stimulate him, or at least deaden his senses to fatigue.

The world's record, so far as Tarzan recalled, for the 880-yard run, which incidentally is the half-mile, is one minute and 45.1 seconds, set at Christchurch, New Zealand, on February 3, 1962, by the New Zealander Peter Snell—a somewhat amusing name, since *snell* means "swift" in Anglo-Saxon. On this occasion Tarzan probably took at least two minutes to do the same distance, since he changed direction twice and once for a moment dropped flat on his face.

The Messerschmitt had four passes at him, doing figure eights from east to west and back again. Barros was a skilled pilot and zeroed in on the fleeting bronze figure every time.

On the first pass there was a short ravine for Tarzan to run through, crouching low. The machine gun bullets from the two doors of the Messerschmitt exploded dirt from a foot above his shoulders.

On the second pass Tarzan was crossing a flat bare space. He stopped dead, his calloused feet spurning up dry dirt, then sprinted west toward the helicopter. Attacking toward the sun, its gunners' aims would not be of the best.

Bullets made dust fly up pyramidally in great gusts a dozen feet ahead of and then behind him.

On the third pass Tarzan could see from the corner of his eye that the gunners to either side of the pilot were preparing to lob grenades. That was when he dove into the dirt, unmindful of how the gravel scored his chest. The nearest blast was five yards away, and the iron shrapnel screamed inches above him. He was swiftly on his feet again and racing forward, although through an utterly silent world, since the explosions had deafened him.

In the Messerschmitt Benjamin said, "The cove's unkillable! *Come* on, Barros, give us a better angle in."

Barros said, "You shoot, throw better!"

Harris said, "You know, I saw a lion back there. Ain't no lions in South America."

"Save it for your memoirs!" Benjamin yelled. "*You* shoot this time, 'Arris, an' I'll toss a couple. Vinaro says a thousand quid for 'is 'ide! *Come* on, Barros."

Tarzan remembered a low dark rock with a split two feet wide in it. He timed his running to reach it at the same moment as the Messerschmitt's fourth pass—and dove into it, this time not only unmindful of but also insensitive to the scrapes.

Explosions hammered the rock on one side of him. Bullets ricocheted off the rock to the other.

Again he was on his feet and sprinting forward, for now he saw a green bowl ahead and blued steel glinting in the sun.

The next time the Messerschmitt came swooping, he had the Sten in his arms and he fired off its eight rounds.

The whirlybird veered away.

In a sudden blind lust of killing, Tarzan grabbed up the Thompson and shot off its six rounds at the murderous aircraft.

In the Messerschmitt Benjamin dropped his light machine gun out the door, clutched with his left hand at his spurting chest, grabbed at Barros with his right, and screamed, "Elp me, I've 'ad it!"

Barros brushed off his face fragments of glass spattered from the holed windscreen, then fought for control of the machine.

Harris ripped Benjamin's arm away from the pilot's shoulders and gave him a violent shove. "*Get* out, Benjamin, you're done," he yelled, as his fellow-countryman's body dropped out of sight. "*Come* on, Barros! Now you can maneuver."

Tarzan grieved neither for the bullets he had senselessly spent nor for his burst of animal rage. He whipped his lariat from his side, tightened one slipknot around the ten-pound Thompson, the other around the slightly lighter Sten, and began to whirl the gigantic bolo around his head, shifting the grips of his hands with each revolution.

A 35-foot rope, taut with the flashing weights at either end, and singing a hissing song as it spun.

He launched it at the great thrumming vanes of the Messerschmitt as it dove in toward him, not ten feet off the ground, and instantly threw himself to the side in the mighty

He began to whirl the gigantic bolo around his head…

downblast, at least a yard away from the linear blast of machine gun fire that sowed the earth with lead.

The two machine guns crunched into the counter-rotating vanes. There was a moment then while they banged wildly, one crashing down through the windscreen. Then the Messerschmitt went crazy. It swooped around like a blind wounded bird, went pinwheeling off in a great loop through the air, keeling slowly over, and landing on its vanes a hundred yards away.

There were spurts of fire, a great yellow flare as the gas tank went, the SLAMMM! of the explosion, then low clouds of blackest smoke rolling away.

Tarzan struggled to a sitting posture. For a while he only gasped and felt the stingings on his skin, the tremors in his muscles. Then gradually his body grew quiet. Only his ears sang. Then they grew silent, too.

The first sound he heard was the pleasant whine of a tiny copper-colored beetle. The second was of Ramel calling to him.

He waved, a little limply, at Ramel, and looked around. The grassy bowl was empty except for the few tins and the radio. He crawled to the latter and snapped it on.

He tuned the dial until he found static. He turned on the scrambler.

Vinaro's voice sounded out, knifelike and furious. "Barros, come in! *You men in the helicopter, come in!*"

Tarzan, his mouth close to the mike, said flatly, "One of your aircraft is missing," and then stood up and lifted the instrument above his head and smashed it to the ground. Glass valves popped.

Ramel, drawing close, looked at him uncertainly.

Tarzan's glare slowly changed to a grin.

In the command Rover, Sophia Renault murmured liltingly, "And now poor Barros and the two Britishers! Oh, *chéri, chéri, my poor chéri!* This Tarzan becomes too, too troublesome. I agonize for you."

Vinaro spared her one look.

"You will be sorry for that, *little one.*"

Shortly before sunset, Juarez and his little foreguard reached the scattered scene of death at the Rondeau Plateau. They marveled with some horror at the bodies at the camp—all but those of the Spaniard and Xima showing no bullet wounds, only the gaping signatures of fang, knife, claw, and club. From there, the odor of recent burning swiftly led Ataúl to the blackened and broken helicopter with the two charred bodies still in it. A little later, following a blood scent on the northern breeze, the Chavante Indian discovered also the shattered body of Benjamin, pierced by a single bullet, and with a Degtyarov light machine gun lying 50 yards from him.

Juarez and Duarte tried to reconstruct the battle. The latter was in particular fascinated by the downed helicopter. He discovered the blackened Sten submachine gun still jammed between bent and battered vanes, and he pointed out to Juarez and the trooper the gray ash of a rope end still around it. Next he discovered the Thompson several yards from the wreck with the end of Tarzan's lariat—it *looked* the same size and sort of closely braided rope—still tied to it. Their eyes widened, and they looked at each other strangely as they realized what must have happened.

They were so concerned with the helicopter, and Ataúl with tracing the confusion of trails and explosives odors about, that it was left for the trooper to discover the twice-folded square of paper securely affixed to the mast of the smashed radio. Juarez scanned it by the fading light:

"Vinaro's helicopter came from the west, so we have headed in that direction. Will leave signs. Tarzan."

Later that evening Juarez told the story of these various discoveries to Professor Talmadge and Captain Lobos, when they came in by moonlight with a party of 12 troopers and armed SPI men led by Apoena. From the distance could be heard the clink of spades against hard earth.

He ended the tale of the Messerschmitt by saying, "So, incredible as it may seem, there is no question but that Tarzan downed it with a gigantic version of the same sort of bolo the Argentinian herdsmen sometimes use to knock over cattle." He shook his head. "I told Tarzan he would have to walk a perilous tightrope, perform a feat of jungle *jeito*. Behold he has done that. For the first time I begin to believe Vinaro can be vanquished without the aid of another armored column."

Duarte laughed sardonically from the dark. "Thus far all the work we've had is burying the bodies of Vinaro's men! A mortician's column—that's what we are. Though I don't suppose Tarzan will make it so easy all the way."

Talmadge's face showed lined and weary as he drew on his cigar. "And now Tarzan has headed west," he said, "with a boy and an ape and a lion."

Captain Lobos cleared his throat. "I imagine, colonel," he said somewhat hesitantly, "that your wireless message to Cuiabá and your cable to the High Command will bring here the helicopter squadron and jungle fighters we really need for this job—within a day or two at the most."

"Or within a week or never," Juarez replied with a sour laugh. "Helicopters downed by bolos—more mad tales out of the Mato Grosso! Is not this Colonel Juarez mentally disturbed—the high-strung Castilian mentality? Also, what evidence is there that these killed—or murdered—men were employed by the esteemed Augustus Vinaro? No, from now on we use Tarzan's method, too—speed and more speed! Our own helicopter can scout ahead if it finds us here. We will keep radioing our reports home. But at crack of dawn this outfit tramps west, on the trail of Tarzan!"

CHAPTER 15

In the Hoofprints of Pizarro

Four days west now of the Rondeau Plateau, and Tarzan had to admit to himself that this was not only one of the strangest jungle trips he had ever taken, but also one of the strangest jungles he had ever traversed.

He probably would never have attempted such a trip with any other child than Ramel. But this slim-figured boy with his golden wire of fire opals was utterly confident that Tarzan could and would take him home and at the same time desperately anxious that they reach Tucumai in time to save it from Vinaro and keep it secret from the world. It was, in fact, as if ape-man and boy were on a mission to another planet.

So this boy's simpler, purer drive was added to Tarzan's grim desire for vengeance on Vinaro—for the sake of Ruiz and his wife and countless unmet others—with the result that the ape-man thought of little but speeding their trip.

An early crisis came when it became apparent that Ramel's physical resources were not quite up to the pace Tarzan was setting. He proposed that Ramel ride on the back of Major, who was doing a wonderful job for a lion of covering territory. Ramel refused—out of pride, he thought and said, but Tarzan knew that at a deeper level than the boy's own consciousness Ramel still dreaded the great feline. So Tarzan simply picked the boy up in his arms, ignoring his protests, and carried him along at a lope. Within a hundred yards aristocratic courage won out against deep-seated dreads, and the boy was pleading that he be allowed to ride the lion. After some stern injunctions to Major and some advice to Ramel as to where to hold Major's mane and how to keep his heels clamped against the lion's ribs, the arrangement worked out well. Thereafter Ramel made a quarter of each day's march on Major's back.*

That Dinky managed to keep up, too, although unburdened, almost puzzled Tarzan himself at times, for the apes are not notorious long-distance travelers. Perhaps it was that Dinky somewhat shamefacedly gave up his solely vegetarian diet and joined in the feasts of roast meat the ape-man was able to provide each evening. For Tarzan had now fashioned himself a bow and arrow out of native woods, reeds, fangs, sinews, and feathers, and with this weapon he brought down birds, another peccary, and once on the shore of a small lake a web-footed capybara—the world's largest rodent, up to four feet long, though this was a small, tender specimen.

Tarzan couldn't at first think what to call the capybara in African beast speech, which he was trying to teach Ramel, though he doubted that the boy's vocal chords could ever manage certain growls. *Zu-pamba*? No, "big rat" hardly was right. Perhaps *duro-pamba* was better—the creature did have the silhouette of a tiny hippopotamus. At any rate, it tasted delicious.

At other times in the pauses on the march and before sleep, as the sky patches turned from gold to pink to gray, Ramel told Tarzan of Tucumai—its gold-gleaming fortress-temple with walls thick as a house, stone joined to stone so closely a fingernail could not penetrate the crack; its guardian mountains and weird swift clouds; its fields farmed in steep terraces; its reservoirs fed by mountain springs; its girls of the Sun God who heaped sacrifices of flowers on the high gold altar; its hidden treasure rooms; its white-wooled llamas and well-curried vicuñas and equally sleek, longhaired white jaguars; its merry games and manly sports, including what sounded like an effective sort of catch-as-catch-can wrestling; the flower-planted grave of the English-man Hugh Malpole; Tucumai's aged saintly

---

* Tarzan's great ability at training lions and his belief in their high intelligence was earlier demonstrated in *Tarzan and the Golden Lion* (Tarzan 9).

chief, Manco Capac, and his council of Thinkers, who engaged in long meditations and sounded to Tarzan like something halfway between a Permanent Civil Service and a primeval variant on the back-room scientific boys. It was all quite enchanting, quite like a fairy tale, yet Tarzan believed it thoroughly; it fitted so well with what he knew of Incan culture.

Ramel told him that Tucumai numbered about 4,000 persons all told, which sounded like enough to keep a culture going, yet not too many for the resources of a fertile, scientifically farmed mountain valley. Tarzan remembered that the Incans had been noted as mountain farmers, wise in the use of irrigation.

Ramel also told Tarzan the legends of Tucumai—the great trek of its builders from glorious Cuzco across the mountain deserts of present-day Bolivia; the flight from the tall, white-faced men from over the sea with their gleaming steel armor that turned the point of the strongest bronze weapon, their great-chested horses which smote down the strongest, spear-armed infantry; their cunning warped minds which proved that suffering was right and pleasure wrong; the bringing across the Bolivian uplands of the stud vicuñas and llamas...*and* the white jaguars; the transportation of the gold and jewels saved from Pizarro's land pirates; the finding of the empty valley of Tucumai through the caves, as if their first great leader, Manco Capac, who had appeared from a cave, should now find his people refuge in one—in fact, this was why their chief in the trek and all his successors had been named Manco Capac; finally, the building of Tucumai from the great granite quarry of its own valley.

In all of this Tarzan saw the fulfillment of Lionel Talmadge's theories. He also pondered more than once on the strange resemblance of Vinaro's armored column to the original steel-shod (and then silver-shod!) cavalry of Pizarro with their terror-striking primitive firearms. How wonderful it would have been, he once thought, to have lived back in the sixteenth century and somehow foiled the violent old Spaniard's rapacious aims and kept the Incan Empire alive! Well, he had the modern equivalent of that task, it seemed.

Of course there were some parts of Ramel's story not so easy to believe, in particular his claim that Manco Capac and his Thinkers were able to influence the light and the weather around Tucumai to prevent the city's discovery. Still, there certainly was no denying that the weather of *this* jungle that he and Ramel were now traveling was becoming quite strange—and its geography, too. Low, scudding clouds came with increasing frequency, so that sunshine and shadow alternated with bewildering rapidity; winds were forever changing direction, as in squally sea weather, while the landscape alternated between upland jungles and low marshes from which stony ridges and isolated rocky peaks rose abruptly. It did seem they were truly entering the Land of Mists and Mirages, of which Juarez and even Ruiz had been skeptical.

He wondered if Juarez—and the determined old Talmadge!—were following him…and he bent an occasional branch or reed, or slashed the bark of a tree so that it showed a white patch. He seriously thought of sending Dinky back with a message, but the chimp either failed to understand his plan or pretended not to—Tarzan was not quite certain which. Once Tarzan heard a helicopter that sounded like the one in which he had traveled to Ruiz's ranch. He raced to the top of a giant cassia tree and for a moment glimpsed flashing vanes between tatters of clouds, but then the drumming sound faded. Perhaps—Or perhaps Vinaro had a second copter; presumably he had the fortune to bring in a dozen of them if he wanted.

And so the swift yet idyllic westward journey kept on until late on the morning of the fifth day, when a fog descended on the jungle, making its gray tree trunks tall ghosts and its flowers dim pastel lights, and then a little later Tarzan caught from ahead the scent of death.

Major smelled it, too and rumbled ominously. This was no simple scent of death, such as a jungle is a-whiff with everywhere, but the scent of human death, of mass human death.

Ramel paled a little as he caught the feeling of horror from the tall bronzed man and the lion.

Tarzan directed the others to follow him at a distance as he scouted ahead, although the jungle was very silent and the smell of death more than a half day old. Mingled with it now were equally old fuel and machine smells and an odor of chopped vegetation.

A gap appeared in the jungle, and Tarzan found himself traveling along what seemed at first glance a trail recently trampled by elephants. Closer inspection showed the brush methodically slashed, the imprints of the great caterpillar tracks of three vehicles, drops of oil and smears of grease, while a few footprints in the smashed greenery showed the direction that had been taken by what surely must be Vinaro's column.

Tarzan signed to Ramel and Major to stay farther behind as he continued his scouting. The scent of death was stronger than ever and still unexplained. And now there was a burnt odor with it.

The fog grew lighter ahead, and suddenly the trail widened into a natural clearing. Through veils of gray he began to see the outlines of large circular huts. But more than half of these were blackened skeletons and some mashed flat. There had been fire here, fierce and recent.

Then Tarzan began to make out the figures on the ground and realized he had come to the source of the scent of death. He stopped, and as he looked around, horror and pity wrenched at him, to be followed more slowly by the fire of rage.

There were at least a dozen figures, scattered like refuse. Half of them—men, seemingly—were wearing grass skirts and capes which covered their heads as well as their torsos. Alive, they would have looked like two-story straw huts on legs. From the head of each rose a fantastic tall wooden hat painted in bright geometrical patterns and topped with feathers.

But the bright yellow of their grass clothing was spattered with dried blood, and two of the straw regalias had been burnt, like the palm leaves walling and thatching the huts.

The other half of the bodies had yesterday been young Indian women, naked except for loincloths and straw anklets.

Their bodies were painted with strikingly artistic zigzag and maze designs in black and blood-red. Except that now much of the blood-red was not paint, or executed with any artistry at all.

Mercifully the fog dimmed the picture, almost making it seem a hideous colorful painting rather than the hideous reality it was.

A matter-of-fact voice spoke suddenly from close by.

"Mal dia, homen!"

Tarzan whirled around. An elderly Portuguese woman was standing in the doorway of the nearest unburnt hut. She was skinny, somewhat bent, and dressed in long-skirted jungle garb of denim. She carried in her hand a small white tray from which came the odor of antiseptic. From her wrinkled face, her bright eyes looked out dispassionately at life—and now at Tarzan.

And she had said, "Bad day, man."

"Muita mal dia, senhora," Tarzan agreed somberly, drawing his hand away from his knife hilt.

Her gray eyebrows lifted a fraction. "You're English?" Then, "I've seen you before. You were talking with a girl named Jovanna."

"And I you," Tarzan said suddenly. "In a Cruzeiro Heron bound from Goiânia to Cuiabá. John Clayton, at your service."

"And I, Maria Bragança, *médico*, at yours."

"You are of the Indian Protective Service?"

"No, merely *Serviço Especial de Saúde Pública*—The Special Public Health Service. I was making my rounds this morning when I came upon this great crime." She moved toward him, lowering her voice. "There are three badly wounded inside. Two will live, one will die. Are those yours?" Her eyes betrayed no surprise, though what her free thumb gestured toward was Major and Ramel, now a few yards behind Tarzan. They had stolen into the village in Tarzan's footsteps, and now the boy was very pale indeed and leaning against the lion, his arm buried in the mane of the great beast, who was swinging his head slowly and sniffing, his eyes a-gleam. Yards behind them stood Dinky, hand hooding his eyes.

"Yes, they're mine," Tarzan said. Despite the horror, he was having great difficulty accepting this woman, clearly over 70, being on "her rounds" in an area he had come to think of as unexplored jungle, almost outside the world. He asked, "Have the wounded told you anything of—" He gestured at the livid figures around them.

"Nothing that makes much sense. Clearly there were vehicles here and guns—and a flamethrower, I believe. White devils, the Indians might say, and so do I. The people of the village are a distant branch of the Guaporés, I believe. See, the cheeks of each had permanent black dot-centered squares of *genipa* tattoo, whereas the Carajás, say, carry circles. I have only met them most recently. Truly, I am not on my regular rounds, but in a region outside my district, rarely visited. The Land of Mists— you have heard?—some say it is not there. But as I grow older, I have wanderlust."

She looked around her impassively. "Yesterday afternoon these unfortunates must have been preparing for one of their courtship dances, similar to the aruanã dances of the Carajás— the masked youths bound and caper, the girls quiver and step with shy immodesty—when the monsters came upon them. All the survivors who could, have fled into the jungle, I suppose—unless some were carried off by the despoilers."

She shook her head grimly. "Now there will be killing of white men again, and some white men may have to let them- selves be killed to prove to the Indians these monsters were exceptions. But I must look to my patients. Follow me inside and tell the boy to come, too, but keep your cat out." She lowered her voice. "The wounded and even the dying are more welcome to the eyes than these."

Tarzan and Ramel followed her into the hut gloomy with shadow and fog. *"Tand-nala!"* Tarzan ordered Major. The great lion lay down outside the door, head on his paws, looking burningly at the dead. Dinky still stayed far off.

With rather similar expression Dr. Maria Bragança looked out the door at the dead too, as she prepared a hypodermic for the Indian moaning faintly beside her in the indoor dusk. She said softly, "It is almost as bad as in 1788 when the presumably innocent governor of Goiás, Tristan de Cunha Menezes, invited the Chavantes to visit his city. The other whites did not like the idea, or rather took advantage of it. In a mass plot they simultaneously poisoned hundreds of their visitors." She shot the drug home, then shrugged. "Not that the Indians had not killed white men earlier. In 1700 the *bandeirante* Captain do Moto, leading a hunt to the Mato Grosso for gold and gems, established a palisaded camp of two thousand on Rio Manso—the Tranquil River. They exchanged gifts with the Chavantes, adding a few musket shots for good measure. Five thousand Chavantes gathered and killed them all, so it is now called Rio das Mortes—River of the Dead." The Indian under her elbow ceased to moan.

Tarzan heard himself asking, "You were there?" Ramel, crouched by Tarzan's knee, watched the old woman, wide-eyed.

She smiled dryly and tapped her skull. "With *this*, John Clayton," she said. "Still, for the most part, the whites were the aggressors. They treated the South American Indians worse than the white North Americans treated theirs. They enslaved, murdered, tortured, raped. Their rule was 'Catch or kill'—and by 1900 they had killed five out of six." She paused solemnly. "Then Rondon came. Beginning as a simple army lieutenant helping lay a telegraph line across the Mato Grosso, he forbade his men to injure or corrupt the Indians or lead them from their customs. He left the Indians gifts. He founded the SPI. Wounded by an Indian arrow, he said to his comrades, who were seeking vengeance, those words I suppose you know: 'Die if necessary, but never kill!'

"In 1941 his best lieutenant, Genésio Pimentel Barbosa, visited the Chavantes with five white and five Indian SPI men. They were armed, but did not show their weapons. First pretending friendship, the Chavantes attacked them with clubs. Without firing a shot, ten men died—one Indian interpreter escaping. You may see their graves on the Rio das Mortes.

"Rondon, now old and crippled, did some of his hardest work preventing an expedition of vengeance. He succeeded. Slowly the message filtered through Indian skulls. In 1950 peaceful contact was made with the Chavantes."

She moved to another of her patients, taking her pulse. She lifted her eyes to Tarzan. "Why are you here—if I may ask?"

Tarzan's eyes hardened. "I am on the track of the man who commanded this outrage. His name is Augustus Vinaro. I intend to destroy him. Do you believe the 'Never kill' applies to white men, too?"

She nodded. "Yet I cannot judge you. At least you do not seem to have picked an easy victim."

Ramel said defensively, straightening his shoulders, "Tarzan seeks to prevent *my* people suffering the fate of those outside!"

Once more the old woman smiled dryly, her eyes bright. "So you, John Clayton, are Tarzan. I once saw a film of you. I did not believe it—until now." Then she frowned. "Tell me, is this Vinaro merely wealthy, powerful, and cruelly insane? Or does he have a purpose?"

Tarzan laid a warning hand on Ramel's narrow shoulder. "He seeks a city of gold," he said.*

The old woman narrowed her eyes in thought awhile, then nodded. "In 1925 an Englishman, Colonel Percy Fawcett, came to the Mato Grosso, seeking the lost civilization of Atlantis— which would have much gold, one would think. He vanished, yet his wife claimed to receive spirit messages saying he was alive.

"Later it was well established that Fawcett was killed by an Indian chief, who had become bored with the Englishman's demands for guides. Lies were told on both sides—that Fawcett is still in Indian captivity, that Fawcett was brutal to Indians, whereas at most he seems to have been pigheaded. And there still come stories that Fawcett is alive."

She shrugged and began to prepare another injection. "So it seems there are others beside this pitiful, detestable Vinaro who have believed there is a city of gold in the Mato Grosso. I reserve my own judgment. Here in the Land of Mists especially.

---

* Tucumai was not the first such city known to Tarzan. There was also Cathne, ruled by the mad queen Nemone. See *Tarzan and the City of Gold* (Tarzan 16).

Though," she added, looking sharply at Ramel and the red-beaded gold wire around his hair, "one might think of likelier explanations than Atlantis."

Again Tarzan pressed Ramel's shoulder. For a while there was silence. Then Tarzan stood up. "Can we help you?" he asked. "As by burying the unfortunates outside?"

Dr. Maria Bragança shook her head. "If what the boy said is true, you have a more pressing duty."

Tarzan said, "It is possible that in a day or two or three there will come on my trail a party of SPI men and Brazilian border troops led by Colonel Carlos Juarez."

She nodded. "I know him. That would be good."

Tarzan still hesitated.

She said, "Be on your way, man, with your boy and your big cat. To whatever fate or triumph life has in store for you."

Tarzan said, "But if the people of this village, now hating all whites, come back and find you here…"

She shrugged. "They may have other wounded who want help. Yet, if they kill me, they may not kill someone else." She added, *"Morrer se preciso fôr, matar nunca!"*

Tarzan nodded slowly. "Come, Ramel," he said. "Major, *yud*!"

Outside, the sun had at last burned away the fog. Trying not to look, they picked their way between the bodies that were so much more dead for the bright colors on them. Dinky circled widely around them. They reached the mashed, acridly odorous trail. To Tarzan it still seemed a wide green arrow, pointing the way to vengeance. Yet the old woman's last two words echoed weirdly in his skull.

Quite a few miles ahead, Sophia Renault sat at the portable bar in the back of the command Rover, as far as she could from Vinaro and from Mr. Train and Romulo, too. She was drinking French 75s that had much more brandy than champagne in them. She had been silent for two hours, looking up from time to time with dread and loathing at the three men who never looked back but only watched the jungle falling down ahead of them, under the weight and caterpillar treads and knives of the great Panther tank.

The odor of slashed vegetation and the stench of petrol came in, faintly, through the vehicle's air-conditioning vents. While the roar of the motors hammered at her brain despite the cabin's soundproofing.

At last came the point when the drink made her reckless. She did not know whether she had been dreading it or longing for it. Nevertheless, from her momentary icy elevation, smiling most wickedly, she called out, "Oh, I am happy for you, Augustus! Tarzan has killed nine of your men. But now you have paid him off by killing at least twice that many Indians. Does it not make you proud, Augustus? Are you not satisfied?"

Vinaro looked coldly back at her in a way that would have warned her to silence any other time, and said shortly, "No."

She went on, almost musingly, "Yes, Tarzan has killed nine of your men—though of course you have outdone him in numbers, as usual. And in the beauty of your prey—far more elegant folk than your soldiers, I fear. Each time he has killed them by threes, have you noticed? There must be some omen in that, Augustus, don't you think? You are an expert in omens, of course, yet I wonder if it is wise—or safe!—that you ride three in this cabin. I should think it might disturb Romulo or even your nerveless Mr. Train."

Again Vinaro turned. "Silence, slut!" he hissed.

Nevertheless she went on, though an almost maudlin tone had come into her voice, "And now Tarzan will be discovering what you did to those Indians. It will fill him with rage, it will fire him further to vengeance, do you not think so, Augustus?"

This time he did not turn. Instead he leaned toward Mr. Train and whispered, "You took the precautions I told you when we left the village? You set the traps?"

"Of course, Mr. Vinaro," the giant replied imperturbably—and almost in the tones of, "Did you *have* to ask me, sir?"

Even more miles behind, Colonel Juarez and his band halted

breathless on a ridge, over which low clouds sailed like great gray ships, their keels cutting the treetops.

Professor Talmadge, gaunt-faced now, eyes feverishly bright, was looking at a white slash which the Chavante tracker Ataúl had first pointed out in the golden bark of a *pau-amarelo*. Then he walked a little ahead and gazed all around.

Juarez came up to him. "Sit down, professor. Rest."

Talmadge, his lip twitching a bit, grinned at the Brazilian.

"Are you still so skeptical of the Land of Mists and Mirages?"

"No, *por Deus*, I am not. Tarzan leads us from one strangeness to another. Ataúl and Apoena agree that the scent is strengthening a little. We are gaining on them—I hope at not too much cost to you, my friend."

Captain Lobos, who had been working at the radio, came up. "We at last have one firm answer from Brasília." The two other men looked around at him eagerly. He grinned sardonically and said, "An inspection team is being sent to check on the cause of the crash of the Messerschmitt helicopter."

After a bit he continued, "Santos at Cuiabá tells me that all our newspapers are silent about us. Vinaro's money talks or rather suppresses speech. However, there is a Reuters-UP story making the rounds of the English and North American press: that Colonel Fawcett has been at last discovered in the depths of the Mato Grosso, but that he died, or was seriously injured, in a helicopter crash while being flown out."

Even this failed to arouse a curse or bitter smile from Talmadge or Juarez. The latter said, "Our own helicopter?"

Lobos answered, "It is still engaged in ferrying a petrol supply to the Rondeau Plateau."

Juarez said wearily, "Let us go on."

So they took up the trail again, first Juarez and the naked red Indian brothers, then four men armed with submachine guns, then three bearing the seven-foot antitank rifle and its bipod firing support, then more men with rifles, finally the radio, Duarte, Talmadge, and Captain Lobos—19 men in all.

CHAPTER 16

The Religion of Death

Tarzan's heart was a tiny red sun of revenge burning under his ribs as he left the ravaged village of the Guaporés. For a quarter of a mile he marched like a soldier going at the double down the middle of the broad green sap-stained trail left by Vinaro's column, which here went straight as a ruler through the jungle. Ramel and Major and Dinky tramped a few yards behind him. Dinky, most sober-faced, was ahead of the others, as if eager to escape the horror spot behind.

Gradually Tarzan's pace slowed. Then he came to a halt, his skin quivering, almost shuddering. Sweat started from his brow as reason and full awareness returned to his brain.

It may have been that he noted a slight disturbance—a raked-over look—in the slashed vegetation ten yards ahead. Or his acute sense of smell may have held up to his churning mind a report which it refused to read, yet could not wholly disregard. Or it may simply have been that the savage emotions aroused in him by the sight of the slain Indians and by the quiet heroism of Dr. Maria Bragança had finally worn themselves out.

At any rate, he realized he was behaving like a fool. Here he was, following in conspicuous view an enemy, right along the trail that enemy had made. True, the trail smelled at least 12 hours old, but what was there to prevent Vinaro leaving an ambush behind? He could detail off men to post themselves in tree crotches or other blinds for so many hours, shoot down any pursuer, and then rejoin the column by night. Tarzan would

191

have to be lucky indeed to scent them in time, because of the many conflicting odors of men and machines—especially at a moment like this, when the air was hardly moving.

Also he was a fool to be traveling a road where the sour resinous stench of the mangled vegetation almost completely blanketed out all other odors. He was reducing the power of Nature's radar by fully 90 per cent. He—and Ramel and Major—ought to be traveling a few yards or a few dozen yards downwind from the trail, along a route parallel to it. True, it would slow them up—the trail was *so* inviting in its promise of speed—but it would make them safe.

Already he was crouching watchfully and had waved back a hand behind him twice—to signal Ramel that he and Dinky and Major were to retreat to a point where Tarzan looked twice as small as he did now.

Carefully he removed his bow from where it hung over his shoulder and around his chest, and tightened its string of sinew. Then he drew an arrow from the crude quiver at his side and set it to the bowstring and held the weapon, thus "loaded," in his left hand. At the same time touch assured him that his knife was loose in its scabbard and that the lariat of green hide with which he had replaced the one lost downing the helicopter was hanging in smooth loops by his quiver.

All this time his ears were attuning themselves again to catch the faintest false note from the jungle, his nostrils were busy sorting out more pertinent odors from those of sap and bruised leafage, while his eyes were scanning every surface and pocket of space ahead, above, below, and to either side.

He had the growing feeling that he was not alone.

He saw a straight black thorn sticking up between the leaves a bare yard ahead and almost masked by them.

Now, Nature and art both abhor a straight line, though they occasionally use them—and this is as true in the jungle as in the Parisian atelier or British art school.

Still watchful ahead, Tarzan reached for the seeming thorn with his right hand, assured himself by the gentlest tiltings that the thorn was not attached to anything, and lifted it toward him.

Already the sensation of weight told him it was not wood, even the hardest, but some metal, probably iron or steel. He stole time from his watching forward to look at it.

It consisted of four needle-sharp spikes four inches long, welded together so that they thrust out at equal distances from each other, as if toward the apexes of a tetrahedron. This meant that whatever way it was dropped, three of the spikes would become its base—and the fourth point directly upward.

It was a caltrop, one of the simplest of old weapons against cavalry, intended to be dropped in quantity in the path of a charging brigade and stab into the pounding hoofs of the horses.

How much more easily would it transfix the naked foot of a tramping man or any but perhaps the most stoutly soled boot!

But this caltrop was also smeared with a black tarry substance—the heart-paralyzing curare, most likely, in the thick form to which it is boiled down by the Brazilian Indians, especially those of the Amazon…or perhaps some deadlier poison created by Vinaro's chemists. Tarzan carefully set it aside on a jutting root.

Yet this immediate area of trail did not seem raked over like the one ten yards ahead. Could it be that there was a whole blanket of caltrops up there? Or—?

Tarzan's acute senses saved him at that instant, for not even an Indian of the Mato Grosso, trained in archery as soon as he can scamper, can draw a bow in absolute silence. He sprang backward as three arrows hissed out of the jungle to his left. He felt impact and sting in his right side. He took another backward leap, calling out, "Into the jungle, Ramel! To your right! Major, Dinky, *Ian!*"

Three Indians red as new-scrubbed copper sprang from the jungle to his left, setting new arrows to their bows. They were naked except for leather cords around their waists and the white palm-shoot sheath guarding their genitals. Under their bowl-like manes of cropped black hair, their handsome faces were filled with righteous anger, while on their cheeks the black squares of *genipa* tattoo, each holding a single large dot, indicated that they were jungle-fled survivors of the massacre back at the village.

Tarzan withheld his arrow fire and sprang into the right-hand jungle himself.

Then, as instantly as it had begun, the skirmish was over.

Ten yards ahead a fourth Indian leaped from the jungle onto the center of the trail where it was raked over. Instantly there was a blinding flash, a CRAACK! almost to split the eardrums, and the buffet of an explosion front over each square inch of skin, like a lash with 10,000 tails.

When Tarzan peered out from behind the great tree bole behind which he had sought shelter, there was a steaming crater in the trail ahead where the raked-over section had been, while liquefied vegetation, pulverized soil, and less pleasant materials were drizzling down.

From the other side of the trail he heard the diminishing sounds of feet scuffling leaves and thudding the earth below, as his three nearer assailants fled as swiftly, but not as silently as they had attacked.

Tarzan's first thought was the wry one that the Indians would inevitably blame him for the explosion which had disintegrated one of them. Commanding the same sort of weapons, he must be the same sort of man, or even an agent of the arch-criminal. Truly, there was no end to the misunderstandings to which a villainy like Vinaro's gave rise!

He looked down at his side, where the arrow barely underlay the skin, broke it in two and carefully withdrew it, lightly biting his lip.

Then he called out reassuringly to Ramel and Major and told them to advance and join him without showing themselves on the streetlike trail Vinaro's vehicles left behind. It was good that, unlike poor Xima, they had learned in the past few days to follow directions.

Next he moved forward again to the tree on whose root he

had left the poisoned caltrop. It had been blasted off, but scooping gingerly through the dark fallen leaves he recovered it.

Next he swiftly slashed a two-foot square of bark off the tree and rapidly wrote with his knife-point in the glistening white wood: BEWARE OF (here, instead of a word, he thrust the caltrop into the tree) AND LAND MINES. Then, suddenly uneasy and moved to greater haste, he signed the message with two quick strokes that made "T" and stepped back to judge the effect.

With a *whang* a bullet underlined BEWARE. Tiny splinters flew. After no more lapse of time than the tick of a wristwatch there came the *crack* of the shot.

The next shot came only two seconds later, but by then Tarzan was in the jungle.

He found Ramel and Major and the shivering Dinky a few yards in, led them to a spot ahead but farther from the trail, then scouted for the ambusher—who should, he judged, be about 350 yards down the trail unless he had shifted his post.

Tarzan found him quite quickly. He was just across the trail, seated in a comfortable triple crotch about 15 feet off the ground. His camouflage suit was quite good, though it did little to thwart the eye and nothing to thwart the nostrils of the ape-man.

The man had slung his rifle on the stub of a broken branch and was staring about uneasily with a Colt .45 in his hand. Twice he consulted his wristwatch, likely because he must hold his post until a definite hour.

Tarzan spent considerable time unsuccessfully hunting for a second ambusher near about. Two men made more sense on a job like this, it seemed to him, if only because they would keep check on each other.

Then stationing himself beside a tree with a four-foot bole, he carefully drew aim and loosed an arrow.

It lodged in the tree trunk a few inches above the ambusher's head. Frowning sharply, Tarzan slipped behind the giant bole. The ambusher fired off the whole clip of his automatic, two of the shots striking the tree behind which the ape-man was hidden.

Another arrow set to his bow, Tarzan stepped out just as the man was grabbing for his rifle. He had thought it would be that rather than a new clip for the automatic. Again he loosed—and again frowned, as the arrow *thunked* into the trunk an inch from the man's face.

But this time the ambusher's nerve broke. He half slid, half dropped to the trail and, still clutching his rifle, ran off down it.

Tarzan followed him for 200 yards without showing himself. A half dozen times he had the man covered, but withheld his shot. He noticed that the man kept as close as he could to the side of the trail. That might mean he feared there were other booby traps of which he hadn't been told. Also, in spite of his panicky haste and frequent glances over his shoulder, he looked at his wristwatch once more. Evidently, as one would expect, Vinaro was a harsh taskmaster and greatly feared by his men.

As Tarzan hurried back to his comrades to take up their pursuit parallel to the trail, he frowned once more, though this time from thought rather than surprise. Had he missed the man because Dr. Maria Bragança's exaggerated SPI attitude of *matar nunca!* had somehow taken hold of his mind? Had the brave old woman's philosophy shaken his will to kill in what he—and Talmadge and Juarez—thoroughly believed was a just cause? A desperately just cause!

Or had he missed the ambusher in order to see how he would behave in flight—and also with the idea that letting a frightened man escape might spread the panic to many of Vinaro's men, and so do more damage than killing one?

It would be easy to tell himself that of course he had done it for the second two reasons. Yet the ape-man was no self-deceiver. He knew he had had all three ideas in his mind, and which had made him miss he did not know. And that bothered Tarzan deeply.

When he had been a young man and, after his youth among the mangani or great apes, first come into his great inheritance at Chamston-Hedding, England had been a nation which had struck out instantly and with deadly force at whatever had threatened her power and her sense of rightness—in India, South Africa, Belgium, and elsewhere. Now England, even under her Lioness Queen, had shown herself capable of staying and even withdrawing her mighty hand—as at Suez in 1956— and had worked for peace among the great new powers of the world, in particular North America and Russia and China. Was he, Tarzan, now changing, too?

But surely there was no question of the evil of a monster like Vinaro, with all his misused power, and of the need to crush him utterly!

Or was there?

Tarzan shrugged off the problem for the time being. Certainly his comrades must sense no wavering in him; they were out to save Tucumai and that was that!

And in any case, he had relearned one old lesson: that when the desire for vengeance possesses you, you lose your jungle wisdom. Fury might be good in a hand-to-hand fight, but bad on the long haul.

Vinaro's camp had the same sharp military look as the first one he had made. Guards had been posted, tents set up, recently doused cook fires steamed, there was the usual queue-up at the medical tent, while the same lights glowed mysteriously inside the multi-roomed command tent by the command Rover.

But tonight things were busier and somewhat noisier. Bright lights shone over the fuel Rover and the Panther tank, and there were metallic clinks and whirs as mechanics worked to repair failed parts in the motors and running gear of those two vehicles. A gasoline motor throbbed and its electrical generator hummed, providing power for these operations. Huge moths dipped in and out of the light.

Augustus Vinaro sat in the vestibule of the command tent. On the table where Mr. Train had five nights earlier made entries about rock specimens, there lay unopened a sizable attaché case covered with gleaming black leather and adorned with sparkling silver fittings. On the other side of the table were two unoccupied canvas chairs.

Beside him, on a stout tripod like an artist's easel, stood the map board from the command Rover, with Ramel's golden medallion and all the other charts fixed to it.

From Sophia Renault's room in the tent came a soft moaning and stirring, then the faint creaking of a cot, then the even fainter gurgling of a bottle.

Outwardly Vinaro looked calm, even tranquil, as he gazed at the unopened case, but behind his smooth brow, his mind was consumed by fury.

His sense of intuitive contact with the great world beyond the jungle—the world that would someday be his empire—had blacked out. Apparently the jungle had something in it antagonistic to the transmission of clear mental pictures. In addition, there was a peculiarly black mental wall ahead of him, in the direction of Tucumai, and another behind him, almost as black, where that detestable Tarzan—and probably others—were in pursuit. When they caught up with him, he would crush them like flies. But until then—Oh, if only they would hurry!

He looked searchingly all around the canvas room, dissecting the shadows, for some malign influence—say, some jungle insect—that was disturbing his mind.

He spotted nothing.

Well, if he vented his fury, his vision might return. You had to pay a price for everything. Sophia was lovely, but…this afternoon she had been too outspoken.

There had been no sound, no sensory disturbance at all, but Mr. Train was standing inside the door, the netting motionless and widespread behind him. His green-mottled topee noiselessly touched the upward-slanting canvas of the tent's roof. His green-mottled eye patch was directed at Vinaro, while his right eye looked over Vinaro's shoulder.

"Yes?" Vinaro asked.

"The guard is set, sir," the giant said softly. "Repairs to the vehicles should be completed within an hour."

"Good," said Vinaro. "Sit down, Mr. Train. Tell me, do we have any more reports on the activities of *Tarzan*?" He deliberately emphasized the last word and was gratified when he heard the cot in Sophia Renault's room creak sharply.

"No, sir," Mr. Train replied evenly. By contrast, the chair in which he seated himself did not creak at all, he gave it his 243 pounds so gently.

"What about the man we left at the booby trap by the village?" Vinaro went on. "He might be able to give us a report of *Tarzan making a tremendous leap into the air…and simultaneously disintegrating.* An unusual athletic feat."

"According to the schedule you gave him, the ambusher isn't due back for three hours," the giant said softly and a shade reproachfully. "With all respect, sir, two men would have been better than one. Also, I would like to talk to you about our gasoline supply."

But Vinaro had heard footsteps—uneven footsteps—which was what he wanted.

He said, "Mr. Train, if my men do not fear me when they are alone with themselves and God—the God of Death—then I have…miscalculated. Ah, Sophia! Come in here, dear."

Sophia was still in her jungle outfit; her cheeks were feverish, and her eyes were bleary.

"'Scuse me, 'Gustus," she said, attempting a smile. "I drank too much this afternoon."

"And now you are trying to cure it with more drinking, eh? An uncertain method. Still, one sometimes must fight fire with fire—or with high explosives! Charles II fought the Great Fire of London in 1666 by blowing up houses with gunpowder, while the great torch of a petroleum gusher is regularly blown out by a carefully placed charge of nitroglycerin. You need diversions rather than brandy. Come, sit across from me."

By staring intently at the empty chair, Sophia managed to walk to it without weaving. As she carefully seated herself,

Vinaro clicked open the silver locks of the black attaché case. Instantly her wobbly eyes focused sharply on the case, pallor replaced the flush, and her knuckles went white around the arm rests of her chair as she started to struggle up from it again.

"Sit still, Sophia," Vinaro directed her.

"'Scuse me, 'Gustus, but I'm…I'm very tired," she said, looking at the attaché case with barely controlled fear. "I shouldn't have come in."

Vinaro said mildly, "You wouldn't desert me when I'm obviously upset, would you, dear? I cannot concentrate all my intuitive mind on discovering Tucumai"—he gestured at the map board—"because that Tarzan person whom you fancy is still presumably on our trail. He will be filled with rage when he sees those Indians I sacrificed in an impromptu ceremonial. You suggested as much. He may even *explode*…with rage…or something."

His remarks were lost on Sophia, who had eyes only for that case. She wet her lips and said unevenly, "You know that…that *those things* make me nervous."

Vinaro said, "I'm sorry, but I've had a most trying day, my dear. And what else are a man's hobbies for but relaxation? Besides, your presence when I'm engaged in my hobby is proof of your loyalty—for of course I count your fancy for Tarzan as simply a female whim, less than skin deep. At bone level, are you less loyal than Mr. Train?"

"No…" Sophia breathed, almost as one hypnotized.

Vinaro nodded. "I was sure you had a noble skeleton. My dear, I am uneasy, and it will calm me to prepare for the retaliations I intend to make for the losses Tarzan has inflicted on us. I don't know who the recipients of these gifts will be…as yet…but I'll find out."

He softly opened the attaché case. His eyes gleamed. Sophia seemed to collapse into herself. Mr. Train looked impassive—and just a shade bored.

The case was lined with foam rubber covered with yellow velvet. Every object in it had its tiny luxurious jar-proof womb.

About one-third of the compartments were filled with tiny glass jars of oily fluids or with blocks colored rose, lemon, violet, and jade—such as the one that had disposed of Captain Voss. Other compartments held hypodermic needles and tiny plastic units—pygmy batteries and sparking devices, infinitesimal radio receivers. But fully half the compartments, including the larger ones and all the lower tray, held elegant jewelry in barbaric, highly artistic, uniformly heavy gold settings.

With a movement swift yet steady, Vinaro picked up the heaviest of the gold bracelets, one set with emeralds.

"The emerald was Cleopatra's favorite gem," he said. "The diamond was unvalued in those days—none had the skill to cleave or polish it, to release the beauty sleeping in the recalcitrant milky pebble. But to me the emeralds never mean as much as the gold. Shall I tell you why? Yes, I shall. When I was a child, I won a tennis tournament—I shall not tell you where except that the surface was the clay the French call *en tout cas*, meaning 'in any case,' since it dries quickly after rains. For this victory I was awarded a small silver cup. I didn't mind that it was small, because—I told myself—it was solid silver, cousin to the first Athenian drachma ever minted. And it was lined with gold! I slept with it.

"After two months—perhaps because I slept with it next to my skin and the acids of my sweat did their work—a blemish appeared on my cup which no rubbing could cure. In that fashion I learned that the silver plating on my iron cup was no thicker than paper—while as for the gold wash inside, it peeled off thin as tissue paper, thinner than the translucent skin we lose when we sunburn.

"Today such trophies have not even the film of silver and gold on them. They are coated with gold-seeming and silver-seeming alloys which the acids in the air eat through even faster than the genuine rice-paper-thin article. *Nothing in the world is as cheap as trophies*—they cost far less than the price of engraving a name and date and competition on them. Once men got real gold medals for saving a life or winning a prizefight or a track-and-field event—real gold which they could hug to themselves and pawn or sell in an evil hour. Now…trash! Nothing but trash! Governments hoard gold. It is the darling stuff of bureaucrats. Scientists plate satellites with it and line chemical tubing with silver—too good for the private citizen!"

Vinaro's hand holding the heavy golden bracelet set with emeralds began to shake with the sincerity of his anger. Mr. Train's eyebrows lifted. Vinaro nodded to him gratefully, and his hand became once more still as marble.

"I was furious about my treacherous little tennis cup," he went on, smiling wryly. "Then and there I determined to devote my life to *real* gold and *real* silver—and to real gems, too, though they're never as important, since they aren't malleable and so have no deep appeal to a male. Jewels are women's baubles—their flinty hardness reflecting the female heart.

"In dedicating myself to the heavy metals of rarity and beauty, I discovered that I had allied my career to man's deepest longing—that for enduring possessions, free from rust, tarnish, and even planned obsolescence. As a natural result I became a multimillionaire, which is quite beside the point."

Sophia had begun to nod at the end of every sentence—and to blink a little, too. To wake her up, Vinaro extended the bracelet toward her, letting it swing—a pendulum.

He said, "I so love gold I have even made it my hangman—given it that honor. How we delight in receiving baubles, in possessing them! How often our lives are molded by them! An Italian duchess was shot to death with pearls—did you know that?" He paused. "And how surprised the person who receives this bracelet will be when she puts it on." He smiled as the swings shortened. "The cyclonite in it is so unstable."

Sophia seemed to shrivel up—her face was the hag face it had been in the Castle when he had opened the draperies on the gray morning—her features began to twitch as they had on the *Conquistador* when he had thrown the licorice ball at her.

He let down the bracelet, with a tiny clinking, into its glowing yellow compartment.

Mr. Train said with infinite smoothness, "Yours is the matador's courage, sir—to let the horns come a fractional inch closer on each pass. If you had dropped that a shade harder, it would have blown. You are the Manolecito—no, the Manolete, of dear Barbara, patron saint of those who deal in high explosives. Or perhaps, with slightly greater precision, you are the racing car driver—the Carraciola, the Nuvolari, the Moss—deciding whether another fraction of a mile per hour—at well over the hundred mark—will make your vehicle skid rather than drift. Though of course an explosion is a remarkably violent skid of molecules, or a remarkably violent hook by *Señor Toro*."

Vinaro smiled appreciatively.

"However," Mr. Train went on, "such explosives as cyclonite are so unstable that they might be set off by a cosmic-ray burst, coming by chance from outer space, or by a moderately hot beam of sunlight."

Vinaro nodded solemnly. "We are all in the Hands of Death."

Sophia, unable to restrain herself, stood up. "Augustus, I'm very tired and nervous. It would be best if I—"

"Sit down, my dear," he said. "Mr. Train, would you be so good as to fetch Miss Renault her brandy? It seems she needs fortification for a session of this sort."

The giant moved with alacrity, possibly even relief—at least from boredom.

"Death is my god," Vinaro said thoughtfully to Sophia as they sat alone. "It is my intention to build him a great chapel, holding the bodies of all the women I have ever known—some of whose mortal remains will be recovered only with difficulty—and also perhaps the remains of a few great heroes, such as Mr. Train, who have served me well. And there may be a few skulls of worthy enemies. There I will worship my god—his finality, his honesty, his lack of pretense, his frank, rude, fleshless face. The creator gods are dubious in their claims, but none can question the destroyers. This chapel will be fitted with silver and gold and platinum—the metals of immortal beauty—incorruptible, undying. Ah, Mr. Train! Serve Miss Renault her Dutch courage. Take a good drink, my dear."

He picked up a heavy gold necklace, of the sort called a choker, to be worn at the base of the throat. From it hung a huge blue diamond.

"This stone is something of a cheat, *chérie*," he said. "It is a triplet, being made of three layers of diamonds cemented together. The middle and largest layer is hollow, but it has a diamond plug which screws in and out, and which I will now remove with this delicate plastic tool, as you can plainly see."

He laid down the tiny opalescent screwdriver with its glittering tip, took up a hypodermic syringe, filled it with an oily transparent fluid from one of the cushioned bottles, and injected it drop by drop, delicately, into the jewel's hollow core. Then he screwed in the plug again and dangled the necklace toward Sophia.

"For the lady who will wear this proudly between her breasts—" he said, "—fifteen cubic centimeters of trinitro-toluene. How that will *burn* when it explodes."

At that instant a jet-black spider scuttled rapidly up over Vinaro's shoulder and down his arm holding the jewel. Vinaro's eyes opened so that the whites showed all the way around the irises, and the arm began to shake. Mr. Train reached forward casually and caught the vermin between finger and thumb as it reached Vinaro's cuff and crushed it. He flashed toward Sophia its gleaming underside with the red hourglass mark of the black widow.

With a supreme effort, Vinaro restrained himself from shaking the necklace in her face.

"*You* let that creature in here with your drunken carelessness!"

Sophia shrank back from him, unconcerned with the spider, her eyes only on the blue diamond.

"*Please*, Augustus!" she begged. "I'm *scared* of those things. *Please* let me go!"

With another effort, Vinaro put the necklace down gently. "Well, now, you have said it, *chérie*," he said. "You have been the first to say it. Frankly, I have been thinking of letting you go for some time—ever since the boy Ramel first escaped."

"Then *do* it," she begged. "Turn me out! Leave me in the jungle."

"Now you have said that, too," he told her. He shook his head sadly. "It is really too bad. With your—shall we say checkered past?—I thought you might be stronger, more fitting as my companion, perhaps even as my High Priestess, my Kali, than the other poor homeless girls I've selected."

"Selected?" Sophia said furiously, holding out her brandy goblet to Mr. Train, who filled it. "*Kidnapped* is more like it."

Dreamily scanning his attaché case, Vinaro said, "To recover most of those girls now would require a grave-digging operation rather than a snatch. Fully furnishing my chapel will require much work of an…archaeological sort, one might call it. But you and I, my dear—to think that after only four months, it's come to this. A shame. When first I found you starving in Rome, dear girl, and showered you with gifts, you came with me quite willingly. A poor Parisian acrobat, a contortionist from Montmartre, who made her centimes by walking on her hands and doing tumbling acts for her supper."

Sophia drained her goblet and thrust it out again to Mr. Train. "You told me that if I ever wanted to, I could leave you!" she raved. "You didn't tell me that half your gifts have cores of dynamite! And you've kept me a prisoner!"

"How ungrateful you are," Vinaro observed. "Quite hysterical. Drink some more brandy. You need it."

Sophia cried out, "If you're going to kill me, *do* it! But stop torturing me!"

And without more warning than that, she hurled herself at the attaché case.

Judging from the speed with which he moved, Mr. Train could have stopped her before she was halfway. Yet somehow her flailing arms were inches from the velvet-lined chest when his left arm went around her waist and his right arm around her shoulders, depositing her back in her chair as if she were an unruly infant.

Now she collapsed indeed, shaking and jerking. Mr. Train knelt by her side and courteously eased more brandy between her chattering teeth, which clicked against the crystal. He seemed to tower over her.

Vinaro peered like a weasel over his attaché case. He was white to the hairline, but his expression was gay. "My dear," he said, "I am disappointed in such a show of desperation and disloyalty. But *kill* you? Well, that is your suggestion. On top of trying to kill all three of us. It's a pity you aren't as strong as I."

Her eyes glazing with Mr. Train's ministrations of strong drink, Sophia rallied to gasp out, "It's not a question of strength. It's a question of sanity."

Vinaro frowned sharply. "That's a hard word, my dear," he said.

Mr. Train touched Sophia's shoulder, reassuringly, and then fed her some more brandy.

There was a flurry of noise outside, growing louder. First pattering distant footsteps. Then a guard demanding the countersign. Then the countersign gasped. Somewhere outside, a motor switched off. Then more footsteps, those of two men at least, pounding across hard earth.

Romulo thrust his simian face past the netting.

"It's Folsom, sir, Mr. Vinaro, come to report on the ambush at the village."

"Let him enter, Romulo," Vinaro called. "But gently." Then he added in a softer voice, "Mr. Train, stand by me. Sophia's bolt is shot. She needs no further attention."

Romulo and a man who looked as desperate as an indigestion advertisement entered the tent.

The latter gasped out, "I watched like you told me, sir. This Tarzan came, with the lion and the boy and the ape. But he held back from the mine. Then some Indians attacked, sir, dozens of 'em, and one of them blew himself up with the mine. I shot at Tarzan, and he fell into the jungle. Then the Indians came up at me with their arrows, sir—dozens of 'em—and I got out."

Vinaro stood up. He said, "That 'Tarzan fell into the jungle'—it could, I suppose, have been 'Tarzan dodged into the jungle'?"

Folsom looked uneasily at Vinaro. "I don't think so, sir. I think I got him. In fact, I'm sure I did."

"Ah, surely he got Tarzan. Did you hear that, Sophia? He got Tarzan." Vinaro looked into his attaché case. "And so, Folsom, you came back two hours ahead of schedule to tell me about destroying Tarzan and to warn me of this attack by dozens of Indians? Dangerous Indians of the Mato Grosso?"

Folsom hesitated a moment. Then, "Yessir," he said rapidly.

Vinaro plucked out of his attaché case a golden round with a black triangular ribbon fitted above it and a golden bar fitted above that. "Good, Folsom," he said. "You must be rewarded. You must receive a medal. Here, let me pin it to your chest… over your heart."

"Yessir," Folsom repeated as Vinaro advanced and swiftly stitched the needle on the bar to the flap of his left breast pocket and clicked it to its catch.

"Over your heart," Vinaro repeated, stepping back.

"Yessir, sir. Thank you, sir," Folsom said rapidly, saluting. He could not see the medal was a blank, without engraving or description of any sort, and that the bar was a blank, too.

"Mr. Train," Vinaro said sharply, "escort the fortunate Folsom out of the tent. Romulo, stand back."

One moment Mr. Train was pressing a glass of brandy into Sophia's hand. The next he was standing beside Folsom. He took two steps with him, then suddenly with his left foot kicked Folsom's legs back from under him, while with his left hand he clapped him hard on the back, so that his chest would be the first portion of his anatomy to hit the ground.

There was the fierce CRAACK! of an explosion. Everywhere the white tenting bellowed outward. Smoke shot from under Folsom in every direction. His body lifted 12 inches, then settled.

Vinaro said, "Pride goeth before a fall."

Mr. Train bent over Folsom like a most concerned doctor or intern.

Romulo said, "Ow, Mr. Vinaro, sir, that burnt my ankles, sir!"

Vinaro, gazing at Mr. Train's smoking boots, said softly, "A good execution, Mr. Ketch…I mean Train. Romulo, lug the corpse outside. Explain to the others—they will be excited by the noise—that Folsom failed to stay at his post of duty. By two hours…though two minutes would have qualified him for the same medal. Which infallibly destroys the heart without blowing through the back. A fine calculation. Sophia, darling, what do you think of this?"

Romulo hastened to obey orders. Vinaro glanced with distaste at the trail of blood and at the smoking hole, a foot and a half across, in the heavy canvas floor.

Mr. Train said, "The blast will surely have killed all insects and arachnids under the tent within a range of five feet minimum…and discouraged the rest."

Vinaro looked at him. "My comforter. Romulo—see that the netting on the door is carefully left in place! And summon someone with a patch who knows how to sew canvas closely."

Outside, there was the footbeat of men pounding up—and then the voice of Romulo raised in explanation.

Inside, Vinaro and Mr. Train looked at each other. The latter said, "Sir, if you persist in setting off explosions within fifteen feet of your attaché case, it is only a matter of time before you—and all near you—are blown to bits."

Vinaro said, "But not this time! Sophia?"

They looked at the beautiful blond girl. She was using both of her shaking hands to tilt the last of her brandy down her throat. Then she reeled her upper body erect in her chair. With great difficulty she opened her left eye and said slurredly, "He din't kill Tarzan or you wun't ha' killed him." Then she fell backward in the canvas chair, so that her beautiful throat was exposed.

Vinaro said, "She tricked me once by getting drunk after-wards—when Ramel escaped. But not again." He pointed at her throat and said, "There is a job of gold soldering to be done. Heat the iron."

"The necklace, sir? Around her neck?" Mr. Train asked.

"Of course," Vinaro said. "And then we carry her into the jungle. To await the morning light—or whatever comes in the night. I imagine the brandy you administered is sufficient. But a hypodermic of morphine will make sure. I would not have her tossing in her sleep. She must be as quiet as death until the instant she wakes."

"Very well, Mr. Vinaro," the giant said. "I will help you in one more act of private revenge. But after this will we devote ourselves to holding this expedition together, to eliminating Tarzan, to reaching Tucumai?"

"Do you doubt me, Mr. Train?" Vinaro demanded, his eyes wide.

"No, sir. Merely, on occasion, your judgment," the giant replied. But it was with an obvious reluctance that he lifted Sophia in her chair and shifted her around so that her shut eyes and slowly pulsing neck were near the attaché case.

CHAPTER 17

The Frozen Princess

Dawn found Juarez, Talmadge, Duarte, and three of the SPI men tramping into the ravaged village of the Guaporés. They carried no guns, except for Juarez, who had his .38 Llama concealed inside his pants and was rather beginning to regret it. All their other weapons were back with the remaining 13 of their party, a mile outside the village.

On either side of them stepped naked Indian braves with arrows nocked to their bows and dot-centered squares showing on their cheeks. Their leader—Urubuena, he called himself—had a most sinister, almost gloating look.

When the dead bodies of the slain Indians came within sight—and within smell, too—Duarte said, "Well, it seems there is more grave-digging for us to do—if we are allowed to survive so long. Though this does not seem to be Tarzan's work."

Talmadge said quietly—because a harsh voice might have touched off an arrow, "We have been traveling in Vinaro's track since our parley with these Indians."

"That is utterly clear," Juarez put in. "Only a civilized savage like Vinaro does such things as we see now."

It was another foggy morning. So they were close to Dr. Maria Bragança before they saw her tied by her thin old arms to the door of the hut in which she had nursed Vinaro's victims. Her wrinkled face had a sallow pallor, but her little eyes still glinted brightly. An Indian to either side of her menaced her with hardwood sticks, the ends of which were jet black and pointed sharp in fire.

"Greetings, Carlos Juarez," she croaked. "It is some time since I taught you first aid at Belo Horizonte. Still you seem to have learned your lesson well. Urubuena—you old monster—set me free now. At once! Did not these brave men come as I told you they would?"

The Indian leader hesitated. After all, he had at his mercy a fraction of the white race which had the day before yesterday twice decimated his tribe. He looked at the old woman uncertainly, holding up a thin length of stainless steel that gleamed in the gray gloomy dawn light—her scalpel.

"I will cut you free if you give me this," he bargained, speaking purest Aymara.

"And you are welcome to it!" she replied. "Unless you choose to return it to me so that I may lance one of your boils."

The tough, braided grasses were cut. Juarez and Talmadge stepped forward and supported the old woman by either elbow.

Juarez said, "Will he grant passage to the rest of our party now?"

There was a quick interchange between the old woman and the Indian leader.

"Yes," she told Juarez, "provided you bury these unfortunates. There is one more inside this hut."

"I told you there would be more grave-digging," Duarte said. "Yet at this heroine's instruction, I would seek to perform any act."

"You are a romantic," Dr. Bragança told him.

Dawn intruded only 15 seconds later beneath Sophia Renault's eyelids in prickles and shoots of light in the small clearing. There was no mist. With the light came a macaw's screams, which for a few moments seemed to her the chiming of bells in her native Normandy. Then she became aware of dead wood and of leaf mold under her body, with all its implications of the jungle's infinite life—creeping, crawling, wriggling, oozing.

She had the impulse to struggle to her feet, but simultaneously there came, killing that impulse, an awareness of *weight* on her neck and *weight* on her chest, just under her throat. Glancing down, she saw a cruel glitter of blue below her blurred nose and edges of cheek and lip. She remembered Vinaro injecting the oily fluid into the hollowed diamond triplet—and suddenly the weight of the gold was like that of hands poised to strangle, while the pressure of the diamond was like that of the foot of the shaft of Death's scythe.

She studied the expanse of branches and leaves around her as they changed from pale gray to shades of green and brown. High in the branches, living on blown and sifted dirt in a crotch, was a violet orchid splotched with red.

I could pretend I'm in a flower shop, she thought. *Except there would be blue flags, blue irises, chrysanthemums blue from the iron filings around their roots...and blue diamonds.*

The newly awakened drinker's urges to writhe and jerk and toss—all the agonizing urges of hangover—were on her. Yet she could no more have moved than if she had been injected with curare.

A tiny spider, gray and white, like an infinitesimal death's-head, came climbing down one of her golden hairs, so close she could barely keep its image from blurring. Something crawled on her leg, something stirred under her back.

Yet all these tiny threats were infinitely counterpoised by the weight of the blue diamond on her chest. All the months she had known of Vinaro's explosives, the fear had been growing. The blue gem would blossom into flames with the tiniest jar, the slightest sudden movement, she was absolutely convinced. Even a moderately hot beam of sunlight, Mr. Train had said. The jungle was lanced with them. Looking down her cheeks, she saw the diamond palely and bluely a-dazzle. The vision swam and blurred—salt stung her eyes—not tears but sweat pouring down her forehead.

Then she began to shake—from animal fear beyond reason's control or weeks of too much brandy. By doing the multiplication tables she managed to control it, but she had to keep reminding herself not to speak the numbers aloud.

At last she nerved herself for an effort. Bracing her upper body on the back of her head—and praying the dead wood she could not see would not break—she lifted her hands an inch at a time to a point behind her neck and felt with slippery fingers for the choker's clasp. She found it—and touched irregular blobs of metal on the links. They had been welded.

Low leaves a dozen yards away parted, and a hideous face stared at her—that of a large ape. Yet as it continued to stare at her with little frownings, she realized it was not hideous to her but a mask in which she saw only a fundamental kinship with humanity. She wished she could call, "Run away, dear monkey. Keep yourself safe. Sophia Renault has nothing she can share with you but death."

Suddenly the ape glanced sharply sideways. Despite the sunlight, a black shadow was advancing from the clearing's end, turning the leaves and branches and dark brown humus to deepest black.

There was a very faint, low general rustling and tiniest crackling.

The ape turned and fled.

The black shadow was alive.

Army ants!

Tarzan, with Ramel riding Major, emerged on a sunlit hilltop. A breakfast of fire-roasted fish sat comfortably inside them. Dinky was scouting through the jungle below, nearer the trail of Vinaro's column.

The weather was weird, as always lately. Behind, the sun peered over a sea of fog, turning it gold. Ahead, ragged pink clouds seethed and churned as if the sky were an ocean. Through ever-changing gaps in them, a rocky horizon lifted in jagged points, like a rock palisade.

Ramel jumped off Major, his eyes widening with thrilled excitement, and he threw out his arm.

"Tarzan! I know those mountains!"

He almost danced in his excitement at being close to home, and he impulsively hugged Major.

"The Valley of Tucumai is on the other side of them! We're almost there."

Tarzan asked, "Can you find the caves again?"

"Yes, I *know* I can! The caves are under the three high pinnacles—the Three Brothers."

"Then we'll head straight there. Come on!"

As they bounded down the opposite slope, Dinky came hurrying out of the jungle. On seeing them, he chattered shrilly.

"Ramel, stop!" Tarzan ordered. "Major, *dan-do* Dinky, *gogo Mangani!*"

At this command to "talk ape," the chimp cried, *"Tarmangani! Mu! Kando! Ho ho Kando!"*

"A white woman. Many, many ants," Tarzan translated for Ramel almost simultaneously. "Stay here with Major and Dinky."

Tarzan bounded past Dinky and, following the ape's scent trail, was in Sophia's clearing in five seconds. He saw the supine girl with the golden hair and the blue-golden gleam at her throat, he saw the black ant army advancing only yards from her—first the thin lines of scouts, then the black quivering mass of the foragers—he knew from their African cousins how they devoured everything living in their path.

"Keep away!" she screamed faintly.

He would have grabbed her up regardless, but the blue gem at her throat sounded a danger signal to him.

"I won't hurt you," he said rapidly. "We've got to get out of the way of those ants. You need help."

"No one can help me," she whimpered. "Please, *please*, don't come close, Tarzan. You may be killed!"

"You know my name? How killed?" He ripped off a nearby branch and swept back the first columns of ants with it. A name shot into his mind—Monica Montressor. Of course! The ruby necklace of which Talmadge had told him.

At the same time the girl on the ground said, "This thing on my neck—it may explode at any minute—the slightest jar—I'm afraid to talk—"

"Vinaro? And you're Sophia Renault?"

"Yes…No, don't come closer. You can't get it off. It's welded."

"Do as you're told!" he said to her harshly. Suddenly he hated the blue gem at her throat worse than any spider or scorpion whose life he had ever crushed out. "For now, keep holding still. What ants get through will sting. Don't jerk."

With another great sweep of his broom at the advancing black army, he stepped around her and knelt behind her. Then his right hand moved around her neck and smoothly prisoned the blue gem between finger and thumb. The other three fingers of that hand went under the choker, as did all the fingers of his right hand. His hands were little finger to little finger.

"I may seem to be strangling you for a moment," he warned.

"The ants are stinging," she said.

Tarzan felt a red-hot needle in his own ankle. "Bear it," he told her. His knuckles levered together hard; there was resistance; he strained; he saw the soft gold links lengthening and thinning just in time to avoid letting his right hand jerk when the links finally parted.

With infinite gentleness, holding all the necklace in his right hand now, finger and thumb holding the blue gem snugly, he thrust it out nearly to arm's length.

Then, keeping that hand absolutely still, as if he had hold of the air at that point, he stooped and with his other hand grabbed Sophia by coat and shoulder and dragged her to her feet. He began slowly half-dragging her, half-walking her away from the ants.

"Can you walk by yourself?" he demanded, keeping up the dream-slow gliding movement.

"Yes."

"Then walk ahead," he told her, letting go of her only when he saw she was able to step without falling. "Keep on now. Up that hill ahead. Brush the ants off you."

She turned. "Tarzan!" she said, her eyes widening at the sight of what he was still holding. "Throw that thing away!"

"Shut up and obey orders! I will dispose of this thing in my own fashion. If you really wish to do something for me, brush the ants off my legs. There, that feels better. Don't be alarmed at the blood here and there—and on your own legs. Evidently some of the butcher ants got at us also—the ones equipped by nature to saw up carcasses after the stingers have been at them. Now do as I ordered and go up that hill and join my three companions! One is a lion, another a chimpanzee. Do not show fear."

Sophia Renault did as commanded, feeling almost delirious with relief and fatigue. On her face was a wild smile, which widened as she saw Major's great ominous mask. At this moment, she knew, she could have gone up and hugged and kissed that lion affectionately and without the faintest feeling of fright. An ant bit her on the thigh. Without great haste, she found it through the fabric and crushed it between finger and thumb.

Tarzan deposited his dreadful burden at the base of a small tree. Even from the hilltop the others could see the diamond glittering blue. He slowly walked up to them, selecting on his way a round stone about as big as a baseball.

"Your poor legs," Sophia said.

Tarzan wrinkled his nose at her and grinned.

Ramel said, "Oh, Tarzan, I'm so glad we found the lady." His boyish hand clutched hers. The two hands were the same size.

"You know her?" Tarzan asked.

"Oh, yes. She's the one who let me get away from Vinaro."

Tarzan nodded. Then glancing at the ground about him, he wound up and pitched the rock hard downhill. If Sophia had been a sports fan or if Malpole had told Ramel of baseball or even cricket, they might have remarked on his delivery.

The stone sped true to the foot of the tree. There was a bright flash, a stilettolike, high CRAAACK!—and the small tree toppled.

Major crouched back with a snarl; Dinky covered his ears and jabbered reproachfully.

"But why didn't you throw the thing away?" Sophia asked. "Why did you make that terrible walk with it?"

"Yes, Tarzan," Ramel demanded. "Why didn't you throw it among those horrible ants?"

"The wrist snap of my throw would certainly have set it off," Tarzan told Sophia. "I did not choose to lose a hand, or more. While as for you, young man," he said to Ramel, "the ants are a far older civilization than the Incans.* Even if these ants, like the Spartans or the Mongols, are addicted to war and consider us their prey, we should respect them. I believe your mentor Malpole and your poor protector Ruiz would have said, *Matar nunca!*"

"You throw like a rifle," Sophia said admiringly

"Only about as accurately as a well-made smoothbore musket," he told her realistically. "How far ahead is Vinaro?"

"He abandoned me last night, while I was drugged with brandy—and perhaps more, if this mark on my arm is not an insect bite. His camp lay just ahead. How far he has gone depends on how early he started. You are *after* him?"

She added that last with a fierce, hopeful smile.

Tarzan nodded. "We'd best find an astringent herb for these cuts, and others to poultice the stings. Then on to Tucumai!"

Miles ahead, in the faintly roaring cabin of the command Rover, Mr. Train said thoughtfully, "Well, sir, you have now given Tarzan another sight to whet his ire, and there are still just *the three* of us in this cabin, more than yesterday. Or do you suppose that Tarzan may have found Miss Renault in time to free her of the necklace?"

"That's impossible!" Vinaro reported, his voice cold and knife-like. "No one could have done that without special vise, special cutting tools, perfect planning, and luck."

"*I* could have, sir," Mr. Train said mildly, flexing his huge, horn-edged fingers.

"Are you questioning my judgment, my authority?" Vinaro demanded, bristling.

"Oh, no, sir. *Keep your eyes on the driving, Romulo!*" he added

---

* *Tarzan and the Ant-Men* (Tarzan 10)

icily as the simian-faced man looked around, as if expecting from his master the command to kill. "Oh, not at all, sir. I was first, sir, only speculating, if you'll excuse it, why you never wait to watch your victims perish, even when you're in a good position to do so. I might, myself, I think."

"Pah!" Vinaro retorted. "You are always the empirical one, the practical scientist, the engineer, the mechanic! I am the artist. When my plans are complete and fully set in motion, I *know* the outcome. My imagination compasses reality. I know when and how the lady died as surely as I knew the fashion and instant of the death of Captain Voss. I would no more wait around to see such a death than a great author would rush out to read the first printed copy of his book."

Mr. Train nodded. "Thank you, sir. Second, sir, I was speculating that it might be wise to mount a full-scale action against Tarzan at once."

"Never! When I have my target, I drive at it without a second wasted. Such was ever the way of Caesar, of Napoleon, of Pizarro! The Germans lost the First Battle of the Marne and World War I because they diverted divisions to foil a falsely reported British landing in force on the Belgian coast, instead of striking with every man at Paris."

Mr. Train answered quietly, "And they lost World War II because they failed to foresee Normandy and strike at the landing there with all their forces. This Tarzan is no D-day, perhaps, but as yet we have prepared for him only footling ambushes. Twice your helicopter has spotted and lost him and his beasts in these strange mists. Right now the wind is east, the terrain favorable. If you could give me forty men—"

"No!"

"Or twenty, sir, the helicopter cooperating—"

"Shut up!"

For fully five minutes the three men in the cabin were silent. Once Romulo started to edge a look back, but instantly desisted.

"Well?" Vinaro demanded at last, a shade hoarsely, of the giant.

"Yes, sir," said Mr. Train with only the faintest hint of a smile.

CHAPTER 18

"Because It's There!"

Juarez read aloud the terse message Tarzan had carved into the white window in the bark.

"The underlining appears to have been done by a bullet," he added.

Three of the SPI men were already infiltrating the jungle ahead to either side of the trail, hunting for ambushers.

"While that crater ahead provides a potent exclamation point!" Talmadge quipped, his voice high and nervous. "Look, the leaves are blown off the trees for ten yards around."

Captain Lobos reported, "Ataúl and Apoena agree that Tarzan's and the boy's trail and those of the animals definitely head off into the jungle here."

"And this is the thickest jungle we've seen yet," Juarez commented, shaking his head.

They all looked down the avenue cut by the tank. It was edged with torn vines, overhung here and there with branches, and floored with a welter of mashed greenery.

But it was temptingly wide and straight.

Dark shadows and golden glows seemed to walk down it in wildly swift alternation as the low clouds racing overhead cut off and let through the noonday sun.

Duarte finally spoke, "Colonel Juarez, according to Dr. Bragança, we are now a full day behind Tarzan. In the jungle we will fall still farther behind.

"As a youth I fought in World War II and came to have the

job of clearing mine fields. I know something of that work—the signs to look for—and I am also jungle-trained.

"Now is our great chance to catch up with Tarzan—and Vinaro—by this straight, easy avenue.

"Let me foot it ahead! I do not think any land mine planted by Vinaro's gangster-soldiers will fool me. As for such as those—" He pointed at the caltrop. "Well, our boots are thick, and we have eyes. If any one or two jungle-trained characters should care to tramp it beside me, so much the better."

Before Juarez could respond, "I will take my turn!" Talmadge cried out like a schoolboy, an eager light in his feverish, dark-circled eyes. A couple of troopers crowded forward, nodding.

Juarez looked around at them grimly. "This is a dangerous course," he said. "I will excuse any man who prefers to wait for us back at the village with Dr. Bragança. But we are well into this Land of Mists and Mirages—yes, professor, I believe in it now—and I myself feel we are nearing Tucumai and that the moment of truth with Vinaro approaches. And—how did Tarzan put it?—time is more than ever of the essence. So come, Duarte, I will march beside you. The rest, leaving a gap of twenty yards, fall in behind."

With no more than that, the 19 men began their rapid march down what could be called without any poetry at all the Avenue of Death.

Tarzan and his party were moving due west through grass thigh-high up a gentle slope ending less than a mile ahead in an irregular gray wall that shot up vertically a thousand feet. At that height, mists brimming over from out of the west, as if out of a pot, half concealed the jagged pinnacles. On this side of the cliffs, the mists dissipated swiftly, though here and there white tendrils came twisting down like snakes.

As far as they could see to north and south, the same condition existed: gray palisades topped by mist with gently fluted valleys and ridges of grass leading up to them from the jungle behind. To the north, the palisades were higher.

Sophia Renault was riding Major. After she had seen how easily Ramel managed, she had been persuaded to. It was a necessity. The girl was in no shape for tramping. Weeks of terror and brandy had taken their toll of her youthful physique and basically steely character. Even now she was holding on grimly, fighting down nervous exhaustion with an effort. When opportunity afforded, she tried to speak gaily to Tarzan. Sight of that great bronzed man smiling replenished her store of courage.

Ramel was in a transport of delight that they should be reaching the mountain wall guarding Tucumai with such dreamlike swiftness. He chattered to Sophia and to Tarzan, too, until the latter had to remind him that he was for the present a young soldier.

Tarzan was as badly puzzled as he'd ever been in his life and now also filled with a mounting uneasiness, though he concealed this from the others.

This morning, when he and Ramel had first glimpsed the mountain barrier, he would have sworn it was two miles high and four or five days' journey away—and here they had reached it in not twice that many hours, for the sun had slid only halfway down the west and was still visible above the mists, giving them a golden gleam.

He had seen many mirages in his life, many eerie weather effects,* but never had his senses been deceived so completely as on this occasion. Of course, it was easier to credit the secret survival of Tucumai if it was a small valley, guarded by small though precipitous mountains. A range of 10,000 feet or more could hardly go unnoticed in the Mato Grosso.

Also, he had the uncomfortable feeling that they were straying closer to Vinaro's track than he'd intended. It should be several miles south, by Tarzan's calculation, but now he was not sure. He had *tried* to keep his party headed straight for the pinnacles Ramel called the Three Brothers, but those had been visible only on four brief occasions, and now he was wondering if he hadn't veered off-course during the longer overclouded periods. Once he had had the strong illusion of the mountains

---

* The strangest were in Pellucidar. *Tarzan at the Earth's Core* (Tarzan 13).

themselves moving north, slyly, against the intervening jungle—
and he had dispelled this illusion only with difficulty.

He began seriously to wonder if there mightn't be some truth
in Ramel's stories about Manco Capac and his Thinkers being
able to influence the weather and create visual illusions about
Tucumai, so that near seemed far, and far near, and even Tarzan's
jungle-tested inner compass began to swing and veer wildly,
like a magnetic compass in a lightning storm. The ape-man
thoroughly disliked the superstitious mood roused in him by
these speculations, yet found it hard to cast off.

They were a half mile from the wall with clear, grassy valley
around them for that distance in every direction, when a huge,
booming voice that seemed to come from the sky said calmly,
"ALL RIGHT, I SEE YOU NOW. STOP WHERE YOU
ARE."

The voice came as such a shattering surprise that even Tarzan,
in his present mood, had the primeval feeling that a god had
spoken from the heavens, or perhaps from over the misty top
of the cliffs ahead. He realized he was searching for giant eyes
and a terrible brow peering sternly or inscrutably over the crags.

Major growled balefully. Dinky clapped his long hands over
his ears.

But the reaction of the others was more startling, for Sophia
gasped, "Vinaro!" and Ramel said, "Yes, it is he!"

For one more instant the beast-half of Tarzan's brain—his
primitive core—controlled him entirely, making him imagine
that the villain he was trailing had expanded into a gigantic
God of Evil, who might pick him up in one great hand and
dash him to the earth.

Then the civilized half of his brain began to play its proper
part, too.

"Lie down," he called sharply to his party. "Major, Dinky,
tand-nala!"

As the four others became indentations in the high grass,
which bent over them concealingly with the wind from the
west, Tarzan raced up the ridge to the south, keeping his body

low. He wriggled the last few yards through the grass, then parted it cautiously to see what lay on the other side.

This grassy valley leading up to the cliffs was twice as wide as the one up which his party had been traveling. Over the next ridge to the south came slanting in the track of Vinaro's column—a 15-foot width of grass mashed flat by the treads of three vehicles and the feet of about 150 men.

The column itself was drawn up 50 yards back from the foot of the cliffs—first two vehicles which Tarzan identified as Land Rovers, one with a large fuel tank, he noted, the other with a horn that must be three feet across its mouth mounted on the cabin.

Behind them was a tank—yes, it was a Panther, all right, and it made Tarzan think of the dinosaur triceratops with its hunched blocky build, though knowledge of its striking power recalled to him *Tyrannosaurus.* Atop it he could see three men sitting around the open turret hatch—its crew, he presumed.

Around about, Vinaro's foot soldiers lounged, watching the cliffs. Tarzan noted the rifles and submachine guns and light machine guns. It startled him, the more he thought about it, that they had no flank guards out. There ought to be men on this ridge and even much farther out. A good thing for Tarzan and his party, of course. Still…Vinaro must think of his force as a battering ram or thunderbolt, for one powerful forward stroke only.

He wondered if Pizarro had been such a single-minded and foolhardy tactician when he had struck at Caxamalca. The resemblance was striking—the compact steel and fire power, even though this steel was painted or blued or browned, rather than shining or rust-touched.

Tarzan still did not understand the giant voice, though he was beginning to get ideas. There was the residual fear that Vinaro had somehow seen him and the others. One thing was sure: he *had* strayed south of his course toward the Three Brothers.

He began to study in detail these men tinier than toy soldiers, but sharp to his keen, youthful vision. Three stood by the Rover with the horn mounted on it. Of these, one was very tall—the formidable Mr. Train, perhaps. Another, scarce by two-thirds the tall one's height, but burly, held a rifle. The third was equally short but slim and held binoculars to his eyes. All three were looking sharply upward.

Tarzan followed their gaze and saw, about 600 feet up the cliff, two men clinging to holds entirely invisible at this distance. Evidently Vinaro, coming to the end of his golden map, was trying to force a way straight over the cliffs. Perhaps he didn't know about the caves—Ramel was uncertain whether or not he had revealed anything about them under torture. And even if Vinaro had a second helicopter, the mist would foil it.

Then the slim, short man handed his binoculars to the giant and lifted a hand to his mouth.

Suddenly the huge voice boomed out again—this time, since there were no echoes to confuse, clearly from the horn on the Rover, "YOUR BEST ROUTE IS TO YOUR LEFT."

Apparently what the slim, short man had lifted to his lips was a microphone and—just as obviously—he was Vinaro. Tarzan wriggled back through the grass and ran crouching to his obedient party of four, still invisible in the wind-pressed, swordlike greenery.

They must turn north and search swiftly for the caves.

But what a megalomaniac Vinaro was, to want a voice like God's!

Vinaro said, without benefit of his microphone, "What are they doing, Mr. Train?"

The giant said from under the binoculars, "They're moving left very slowly, sir…Clark is driving in a piton…They're lengthening rope between them…They're trying it upward again… It looks a very difficult pitch…They're hesitating…Now they've stopped again…"

Vinaro lifted his microphone.

"DON'T GIVE UP, GENTLEMEN. YOU CAN DO IT. *I* AM WATCHING YOU."

To those near the huge bullhorn, the sound was almost deafening. Mr. Train winced, very slightly. The more distant men made faces, careful that Vinaro did not see. Only Romulo, cradling a rifle with telescopic sights, grinned broadly—as if a trumpet blown in his ear was his idea of bliss.

Mr. Train said, "Now they're edging down, sir."

Vinaro said into the mike, "DON'T GIVE UP. THIS MUST BE A MAXIMUM EFFORT. *I* WILL WATCH AND APPLAUD YOUR TRIUMPH."

Mr. Train said, "They've stopped…They're still coming down…"

Vinaro remarked, "Some English fool, one of the Tarzan breed, when asked why he climbed a mountain, replied only, 'Because it's there!' I know of a more cogent and persuasive reason for attempting the impossible in mountaineering—the same reason that drives common soldiers into battle: that they fear their officers, and particularly their general, more than they fear the enemy. Romulo!"

With a long smile, the low-browed man nestled his rifle against broad cheek, raised it almost to the vertical, bending backward on his wide-braced legs, drew a breath, let it out, became motionless as a statue.

CRAACK!

Mr. Train reported, "A good shot. It struck only ten feet below Clark. He's lost his footing and holding by his hands… Now he's regained his footing… Now they've started upward once more, sir."

Smiling broadly, Vinaro said into the mike, "THAT'S RIGHT, GENTLEMEN, KEEP TRYING."

Mr. Train said, "They're ten feet above their previous highest… Now fifteen… Ten feet more and they'll reach a ledge. Petucci has lost his footing! He's clinging by a hand… He's falling, sir! Clark is being dragged off by the rope."

The two bodies came down, growing in size, the rope taut between them and they swinging slowly, as if they were a giant bolo. A few men edged farther from the cliff. The bodies struck with great thuds, rebounded a little, were still.

Vinaro turned his back on them and spoke into the mike. "ALL RIGHT, MEN, WE'LL EXPLORE FARTHER NORTH."

Mr. Train remarked lightly, "Well, the mountain *was* there, wasn't it, sir? I expect we'd best hunt those caves about which Ramel let slip a word."

Vinaro said sharply, "Mr. Train! The most gold-rich part of Tucumai is exactly opposite where the men climbed. I *know*. I strike *directly* at my target."

Mr. Train said, "But lifting the tank over the palisades would have been something of a problem. Tomorrow Helicopter Two should be here with the gas supply. They can scout for you, even across the palisades."

Vinaro said, "Tomorrow! I do everything today. Then I consider whether anything is left over to do. As for Helicopter Two, it has already once missed contact with us in this meteorologically insane region, where clouds seem imbued with purpose and even the gyroscope compass goes wrong. As for scouting Tucumai from the air, the same mist cover will be over it as today. I *know*. I sense dark, disturbing mental forces working against us, limiting even my own extrasensory perception. But not a word of this to the men."

"Yes, sir. I respect your judgment there, sir."

The two men were standing alone by the door to the Command Rover. Romulo had already climbed into the cabin. The rest of the column was in order of march.

Vinaro scanned it quickly. "There seem fewer than there should be." He lifted the mike. "WHEN YOU GET THE WORD, MEN, MOVE NORTH ALONG THE WALL." He mounted into the cabin.

As Mr. Train deftly jackknifed his body through the door, he said, "I sent north an advance guard of five, sir. Normal precaution."

"You should have consulted me," Vinaro expostulated as they seated themselves. "Surprise is essential in my attack. We are up against dark, supernatural forces, Mr. Train." The air-conditioning blew chill around them. "Your advance guard could give it away." He spoke into the mike, which Mr. Train had shifted from outside to inside jack. In the soundproofed cabin the booming voice was only like muted thunder: "ALL RIGHT, MEN. ADVANCE!"

"Yes, sir," Mr. Train apologized. He said nothing of how a voice that could be heard for two miles gave warning ahead to any enemy. He did say, "However, sir, as regards even dark, supernatural forces, it is my belief that there is nothing in this universe a karate strike can't crack."

Vinaro answered, almost affectionately, "How right you are, Mr. Train—so long as you get your enemy at close quarters."

"I have a very long *ma*, sir," Mr. Train responded, referring to the "killing range" of a *karataka*.

Colonel Juarez and Captain Lobos spoke together quietly, a little apart from the rest. They sat on a huge fallen trunk beside the trail of the Panther, which at this point passed through the edge of a large clearing. The rest of the 19 were scattered back along the trail. Talmadge and Duarte knelt beside a trooper resting supine on a blanket. He was snoring. One of his boots had been removed, and that foot, its instep bandaged, rested across the ankle of his other leg. He had stepped on one of the poisoned caltrops, and within a few minutes he had shown signs of paralysis typical of curare poisoning, and his breathing had stopped. Fifteen minutes of artificial respiration had got it going strongly again. Talmadge had administered a dose of chloral from his medical kit, whereupon the trooper had fallen into a deep sleep.

Captain Lobos said, "I finally made contact with our helicopter at Rondeau Plateau, though the static in this magnetically distorted area is on the verge of blotting out all speech. Lieutenant Fontoura had just returned from an unsuccessful attempt to locate us this morning. He says he found fog everywhere with extreme turbulence above. Also, something disordered his compass so that he missed the Rondeau Plateau by twenty miles on his return."

Colonel Juarez shook his head. "This Land of…Impossibilities."

Lobos continued, "However, he will make another attempt tomorrow at dawn."

Juarez said, "Suggest to him the possibility of starting by starlight, if he knows celestial navigation. The stars might be better guides than this mirage-breeding sun. Emphasize to him that the trail of Vinaro's tank should be a sharp landscape feature."

He lowered his voice. "Also order him that, if he finds Vinaro's track, he should land at the village of the Guaporés, pick up Dr. Bragança, and bring her to this clearing. I will tell the man we leave with the wounded one to mark it with their shirts. The victim should get expert medical attention as soon as possible. There might be elements in Vinaro's poison worse than curare. And I am not certain Talmadge did best in giving him chloral."

"I'll attend to that at once," said Lobos, standing up.

A little later Juarez ordered the march resumed. The 17 men pressed on.

CHAPTER 19

The Glittering Daggers

A s Tarzan and his party entered the fourth fluted valley to the north, the mist lifted from the crags, like a great white hand momentarily withdrawn, and showed the outlines of three pinnacles which looked like those of the Three Brothers.

Ramel pointed excitedly at a copse of bushy trees and tall yellow reeds growing at the foot of the palisades.

"The entrance to the caves is behind them," he cried.

"Silence!" Tarzan warned as they raced forward.

Sophia clung desperately to Major's mane and ribs, like a jockey at the end of a battering steeplechase.

Very faintly, like the most distant thunder, there came the amplified voice of Vinaro echoing along the rocky wall: "…ALL RIGHT, MEN…ADVANCE…"

Ramel hurried through the copse and into an irregularly arched opening 12 feet tall and six feet wide.

"Come on!" he called from a few feet inside. "Come on before they see us! Tarzan, what are you doing?"

The ape-man had laid aside his strung bow with an arrow beside it, drawn his knife, and was slashing down handfuls of the tall, dry reeds.

"We'll need torches to light our way. You had one, didn't you, when you came through?"

"You're right, Tarzan," Ramel agreed shamefacedly. "I forgot."

"But get inside, all the rest of you," Tarzan said. "Major, Dinky, *zor!*" He handed most of the reeds to Sophia, then began searching

229

for the dry, downy stuff and fine, dry grass that makes good tinder. All the while he kept alert for the approach of an enemy. He was on the north side of the copse, but facing south, whence Vinaro's column would come. He still couldn't hear motors.

"Oh, hurry, Tarzan!" Ramel couldn't help saying.

They made a striking picture in the dark cave mouth: the slim dark boy with his gold-wired fire opals, the gaunt, blond young woman in her mottled green, the wary-looking ape, and crouched in front of them protectively the great lion.

Tarzan grinned as he gathered together his tinder in a neat nest. He said, "I'm glad, Ramel, that the entrance to the caves is so narrow. I thought you told me they were wide enough for six horsemen to ride abreast." He was thinking, of course, of Vinaro's vehicles.

"The caves *are* that wide, Tarzan," Ramel protested innocently. "This doorway is only a shell."

Drawing a flint from a fold in his loincloth, Tarzan struck a shower of sparks off his knife, then knelt to nurse the tiny charring spots inside the tinder nest. One glowed and grew, then flickered into flame. Tarzan fed the flames until it was enough to set fire to the first yard-long tight bundle of reeds.

All this while Tarzan had kept careful watch, but the wind was at his back and the copse intervened, so it is not to be wondered that he missed the cautious silent approach along the rock wall of two men in mottled green and did not see the first until he himself had been spotted.

But Major, having no fire-building task to distract him, was ahead of Tarzan for once. He launched himself in a silent leap that bore to earth with a sickening thud the first attacker just as he was lifting his submachine gun.

By the time the second attacker had mastered his momentary shock at the suddenness of the beast's onset and at the vast unlikeliness of a lion in Brazil, and was preparing to chop Major down with his rapid-fire weapon, Tarzan had snatched up his bow and arrow and sent the latter winging into the man's brain through his left eye. A nasty kill, but Tarzan did not trust the penetrating power of his arrowheads.

Calling Major back from his prey with a *"Rand! Zor!"* Tarzan grabbed up the flaming torch, stamped out the first fire, and plunged into the cave after Major—and just in time, for a spray of bullets smashed through the copse from the crest of the southern ridge, sending leaves, dirt, and splinters of wood and rock flying.

Wasting no time in blaming himself for having stayed to build the fire outside the caves, Tarzan surveyed at a glance the green-shot limestone chamber in which he found himself, and seeing that it was the beginning of a wide, gently winding corridor, he set out at once at a trot, calling on the others to follow him close and holding his torch high, so that his own shadow would not confuse their footing.

He added to Ramel, "Speak only if I start to go wrong. We must move fast if those scouts decide to follow us at once."

Sophia, no longer riding Major, said, "Vinaro tells his men to wait for *him* if something new appears."

Very soon the dwindling arch of daylight behind them had moved sideways out of sight.

The rocky surfaces revealed by the torch became more irregular. Stalactites hung from the ceiling, stalagmites rose from the floor—none of the latter looking big enough to impede a tank, Tarzan judged. There were small side passages and wells going downward—whatever underground stream that flowed through this cave had sought a new channel.

The torch burned low. Tarzan took a new one and thrust the burning stump of the old down into its top. "Mustn't leave so obvious a clue as a burned-out torch," he explained.

A variety of minerals began to show in the drab walls—glittering yellow pyrites, silvery speckled granite, inset with jewels of rose and green and violet quartz.

Suddenly the great corridor debouched into a still vaster one leading downward at a slight incline. Here and there clustered boulders washed by immemorable floods, but still leaving enough clear space for the passage of vehicles.

But one hardly noticed the floor because of the grandeur of the roof. From it hung rank on rank of glittering, slim stalactites thick as a shark's teeth. They hung like overlapping bands of golden and silvery fringe on a dancer's dress, and they stretched on as far as the light of the torch would show. Here and there on the stony floor were glints where one had fallen.

Sophia caught her breath. Tarzan picked up one of the fallen shards. It was two feet long, sharp-edged as volcanic glass, and surprisingly heavy. Tarzan could no more identify the mineral than he could explain the weird rock formation from which it had fallen. Surely Nature could have devised no more suitable canopy for an avenue leading to a city of gold. There was something hypnotic about that endless, serrated overhead glitter...

"Tarzan! Sophia!" Ramel was saying. "That is *not* the way. See, here, to the left, we almost turn back on ourselves, but then the path straightens again."

Sure enough, just inside the entry to the huge, dagger-roofed corridor, there was a drab yet large level passageway leading off. One tended not to see it, because of the fascination of the other.

"But where does the big one go?" Tarzan asked.

Ramel answered, "Some say to the realms of Cupay at the center of the earth, where the wicked dead live. Once *I* followed it for...I do not know...a mile perhaps...and it only went down. I will tell you *one* thing, though. Three hundred of my paces down that great tunnel—two hundred of yours, I guess—there is in the left wall a narrow tunnel, good only for crawling, which slants up to rejoin the right path."

"How do you know?" Tarzan asked.

"Because I crawled through it! Xima and I explored these caves many times before we ventured into the outside world. But come now, Tarzan, please, we must get to Tucumai."

Almost reluctantly they turned aside into the drab passageway. The wonder of that glimmering ceiling enchanted the memory.

Sophia said, with a tiny laugh, "Do you know something?

I am deathly afraid of tunnels, basements, subways, caves! I had forgotten that until now. And now I am afraid no longer." She smiled at Tarzan gratefully and with the beginnings of adoration.

But his mind was grappling with an idea, a plot, that had not quite yet come clear.

Ramel said enthusiastically, "Tarzan has taught me courage, too, Sophia! To ride on the lion, to observe death without flinching, to shelter from the bullet without running. But you must be braver than I, Sophia, for you were able to ride Major without Tarzan carrying you first."

She answered, "I was an acrobatic performer—not a very good one—in a small circus. So I knew lions a little."

Tarzan said, almost absently, "You each have your share of courage. Perhaps I helped you learn how courage about one thing can become courage about all things."

The burnt-down second torch had to be thrust into the top of a third. Tarzan noted with fleeting satisfaction that there were numerous big boulders—and many smaller ones like cannonballs—in this passageway. Not enough to stop a tank for good—but time would be demanded in levering or blasting them out of the way.

Ramel said, "Now we're almost there! No more chance of losing our way."

There was a dim explosion behind, felt as much as heard. Tarzan stopped. The sound was repeated.

"What is it?" Ramel asked.

"I'm not certain," Tarzan answered. But he was, almost. He handed the torch to Ramel and the remaining spare to Sophia. "You two go ahead to warn Tucumai. Take the beasts with you."

"You're not going back?" Sophia asked. "What good can you do?"

"Maybe slow them down, at least see what they're up to. Ramel, that crawling tunnel you told me about—would it be big enough for me, all the way?"

Ramel looked thoughtfully at the ape-man's broad shoulders.

"Yes, Tarzan," he replied with a decisive nod. "And look—there is the hole where it reenters this tunnel." He was pointing ahead to an opening scarcely more than two feet in diameter that was in the right wall of the corridor about four feet above the boulder-strewn floor.

The ape-man nodded. "Good-bye then," he said. "I will rejoin you in Tucumai by sunset. Forward now, all of you!"

Major started to turn back with Tarzan, but a "Major, *unk!*" sent the lion pacing after the others.

The dim distant explosions continued at regular intervals.

As Tarzan loped back into the darkness, Sophia called after him, "But how will you see, without a torch?"

"I have an inner light," Tarzan called back with a heartening laugh.

Figuratively, this was quite true. Tarzan had a well-nigh perfect judgment of distance and of three-dimensional configurations. He also had a photographic memory, which worked as well for touch and odor as for sight. So he had only now, as it were, to reverse in his brain the memory-tape of their trip through the caves, and he could lope through the utter darkness with complete confidence about each stony footing-place.

The Panther tank faced the mouth of the cave and, at point-blank range, was blasting the entrance wider with shots from its cannon, under Mr. Train's direction. Already the opening was ten feet wide, with a great cloud of rock dust around it.

The other vehicles and most of Vinaro's foot soldiers watched the process from a respectful distance.

Romulo said to Mr. Train, "Our master shows great personal courage to scout ahead with only twenty men. He is matchless."

Even in Vinaro's absence, the *mameluco's* tones as he talked about him were fawning.

Mr. Train was tempted to answer, "Yes, when Mr. Vinaro finds anything like a rat hole, he is in his element." The giant's patience with his master was wearing a little thin, now that he was showing so many more signs than usual of mental aberration.

What he did say was, "Most true, Mr. Romulo. And now would you be so kind as to break out the gas masks? There are enough for the officers and drivers—and we shall surely need them going through a cave poisoned by the exhausts of three large vehicles."

Then he began to call directions to the man in the Panther's turret as to the next placement of shots. The job pleased him, although he knew it could have been done more efficiently by a couple of well-placed charges—it was like battering down the wall of a medieval city with primitive artillery. And Vinaro *had* ordered that it could be done this way. Just as Pizarro would have.

When Tarzan reached the big corridor with the glittering roof, he found that he no longer entirely needed his "inner light." A powerful narrow-beam searchlight from the other entrance was questing among the big boulders and—dazzlingly—among the countless pendant golden and silvery daggers. The dim distant explosions had ceased.

As the searchlight swung the other way, Tarzan darted into the big corridor and concealed himself behind the nearest group of boulders.

The searchlight swung back, then away again. Tarzan made use of this interval to run crouching to the next group of boulders—*down* the great fabulously ceilinged corridor, in the direction Ramel had said might well lead to the realm of Cupay.

Tarzan repeated this maneuver twice. Behind him he heard Vinaro's voice, unamplified but resonant, order, "All right, men, that's enough gawking. Advance!"

But Tarzan suddenly smelled tarmangani close at hand. Yes, there he was, momentarily revealed in the swinging searchlight beam, a big fellow cautiously footing it along with a Sten submachine gun. For once Vinaro had sent a scout ahead of him.

The man turned as Tarzan sprang at him. Two shots from his

Sten, thunderous in the cavern, screamed off the walls before Tarzan's knife buried itself in his heart and Tarzan's other hand jerked the weapon from him. He snatched a clip of ammunition from the man's belt as he fell, then raced for the next cluster of boulders—a large one. The searchlight pinpointed him just as he dived behind that cover. The next moment rifle and submarine gun fire was harmlessly, though deafeningly, pounding the great rocks guarding him, which were also outlined on every side by the searchlight's glow.

"Cease fire, men!" Vinaro ordered. "But keep the searchlight on those boulders! And turn on the other two."

In the sudden silence, amid the ghostly echoes of the fusillade, came three sharp clashes—single stalactites detached from the glittering roof by the vibrations.

The light playing on the boulder redoubled.

Tarzan, gripping the captured Sten and the spare clip, glanced intently behind him. He was well-protected here, but there was no farther group of boulders to which he could retreat without exposing himself to the searchlights. And certainly he couldn't spring up and shoot it out with what sounded like at least a dozen rapid-fire weapons.

He had accomplished his purpose of leading Vinaro off the right track, but he had trapped himself in the process.

As if echoing this thought, there came Vinaro's ghostly cry, "Tarzan! You may as well give up! You're hopelessly pinned down!"

Tarzan pondered the wisdom of leaping up and shooting down Vinaro with a single burst. His ears were becoming so well attuned to this particular cavern that he could pinpoint the exact location of the source of each sound. He already knew the exact position in the cave of Vinaro's main group and the three lights.

Unfortunately, the quality of Vinaro's voice had shown that he was hiding behind some rocky defense like Tarzan's.

At least the searchlights had helped Tarzan in one way. Playing along the left wall of the corridor, they had revealed a single black narrow gap about a hundred yards beyond him.

Since he had already come about 100 yards, that should be the return-tunnel Ramel had mentioned. But reaching it was another matter.

Now there came, very faintly, a pulsing whine and roar.

Vinaro called, "You're a fool if you don't come out while you can. My heavy armament is coming up."

Almost immediately Vinaro ordered, "All right, men, half of you—Prestes' group—cover him. The rest move forward."

They didn't make a great deal of noise, but Tarzan knew the exact location of each group—and then suddenly he knew what to do.

He raised the Sten and fired three bursts at the roof—one exactly above the advancing group, one above the Prestes' group, the third and longest—shooting out the clip—above the lights. He would have fired over Vinaro, except that he seemed to be in a shallow grotto.

The glittering huge daggers fell by the dozens and scores. There were crashes and screams and thuds. Best of all, one light went out while the other two angled up crazily.

Tarzan sprang up and ran at top speed the 100-yard course he had memorized while the searchlights were on. Behind him he heard continuing orders, curses, screamings. Undoubtedly some of the men had been badly hurt by the deadly chandeliers—which likely meant some killed, too.

He had finished 75 of the 100 yards when the two remaining searchlights spotted him again. Instantly he dodged behind the nearest boulders, shoved the other clip into the Sten, and repeated his first maneuver.

Again he got the searchlights.

Dropping the Sten, he raced for the return tunnel. And just in time, for a shower of the knife-edged strange stalactites clattered down a second later in his hiding place. Someone had learned fast.

As he swung into the return tunnel, which required an upward vault, he saw two other searchlights, side by side like a monster's eyes, join the others.

He was barely inside when heavy machine gun fire swept the corridor, coupled with the still heavier single bark of a cannon.

The tunnel began with a diameter of four feet, which rapidly narrowed to three. It led upward at an angle which varied between 15 and 20 degrees.

Bringing fully into play his bat-keen sense of echo and of air currents' messages as they rebounded from invisible obstacles, Tarzan crawled up into the blackness as rapidly as if he had been using elbows and knees for locomotion all his life. His head ducked away from this and that projection. Sometimes, though rarely, he stretched forward a feeling hand—without ceasing to hump along.

For fully 60 elbow-steps, the tunnel was straight as an arrow. Then his inner compass told him it was turning right, to his immense relief.

One other thing warmed his heart. His nostrils picked up, just on the threshold of sensibility, the months-old scent of Ramel…and Xima! It was like having ghosts of stouthearted friends at his side.

He could not hope the enemy had not seen him enter this tunnel. He could only hope they would think he had darted into it blindly, to escape their fire, and that Vinaro would send his main column down the huge, glittering-ceilinged corridor—to Cupay, or whatever.

But they would certainly not neglect him—as was instantly demonstrated when a searchlight flooded the tunnel behind him, light reflecting around the curve.

The reflected light showed him that the tunnel began a leftward curve just ahead, reversing the rightward trend.

There was a soft *zing* past his head, followed instantly by the *craaack* of a rifle behind him and the *snick* and *snack* of the bullet's ricochets behind and ahead of him. Thank the Higher Powers that the first man at the tunnel's mouth below didn't have a rapid-fire weapon! Tarzan scraped and slithered around the second turn faster than he had thought possible.

Then there came the whip-cracking of rapid fire behind him.

He raised the Sten and fired three bursts at the roof....

One spent slug stung his foot. Another dropped on his back. He shook it off—it was blisteringly hot. A few more kneesteps and he was beyond any ricochet range.

The shots behind him stopped altogether.

He inhaled deeply in the cave—sweet air, untainted here as yet by the carbon monoxide of Vinaro's guns and vehicles.

The tunnel narrowed to a diameter of two feet, so that he could no longer crawl, but had to progress by a series of movements midway between snakelike undulations and flopping heaves, aided by flipperlike clawings of fingers and toes. Tarzan thought of superior ways of constructing the human body, mostly involving tentacles and suckerlike gripping pads. Oh, to be a fly or an amphibious octopus! But the Xima-and-Ramel scent stayed with him, encouraging him.

A tiny round of pale light glowed ahead. At first he thought it was just in his brain or his eye. Then, slowly, it began to grow. It might be the end of this gutlike tunnel or...

But he did not slack off in his effort. Unmindful of damage to epidermis, he kept humping and scrabbling ahead. He did not like it that this stretch of tunnel was straight. Any straight stretch meant someone could aim at him from behind.

The pale round ahead grew large as a shield. The tunnel widened. He crawled rapidly the last few yards and dove over the edge of the hole at the end with only the quickest glance to tell him he wasn't diving into a downward infinity.

And just in time! A small swarm of bullets—perhaps eight—*ziinged* out of the tunnel just behind him and *craacked* against the rock wall opposite the hole and 20 feet away from it.

He was in the tunnel to Tucumai at the point where he had left Ramel and the rest.

A torch of reeds was slowly burning out on the mineral floor. Sophia or Ramel must have lighted it and left it there, with the idea that it might help him. Once more—friends with him!

Meanwhile it was clear that Vinaro must have expert speleologists among his following as well as mountain-climbers. One, at least, of them had followed him rapidly along the tunnel, bringing a gun with him, and fired along the last straight stretch. And would now be rapidly climbing toward him in the tunnel, gun ready.

He sought for a solution to this problem. It was easy. By the last flickerings of the torch, he began to pick up small boulders—the cannonball-size ones—and toss them into the tunnel. Their rumbling as they rolled down it rather delighted him. He tossed in more and more. There was another burst of fire, but only two bullets came out at this end that he noticed. There was a faint gasping cry. He threw in more of the bigger boulders, more and more of them, ending with three a foot thick. He could hear them rumble down and come to crashing stops.

That, with whatever man's body was being crushed or driven back at the other end, should block the return tunnel adequately.

He puzzled for a moment at his strong compulsion never to kill directly with a gun or any other modern weapon involving explosives—despite the fact that he knew guns well; in fact, they were one of his many secondary hobbies. It made him a kind of natural anti-Vinaro, who seemed to delight in explosives before everything else. He *could* have used the false Antonio's gun back at the car-wash; he could have accepted Juarez's offer of his Llama, or equipped himself with one of the weapons at Rodriguez's camp. It was a strange quirk. Mankind had invented the gun—and the neutron bomb!—and would clearly have to live with them. Was he—Tarzan—some sort of romantic, a jungle reactionary? Or *was* it important to keep demonstrating to men that they did not need to use guns on each other or to live in fear of them? To demonstrate the naked-handed man's power of defense and offense. To demonstrate the oneness of all the mangani.

He shrugged. It had occurred to him that he had used a gun directly against the Messerschmitt helicopter—and killed a man that way, too. So he couldn't boast of being a purist—or to put it another way, his anti-gun compulsion was not yet crippling.

The torch had gone out. Through the blackness he followed the scents of Ramel, Sophia, and the others toward Tucumai.

The Panther and the two Land Rovers were lined up, their motors idling, in the corridor with the glittering shark-tooth roof, many of the shards of which now littered the floor. The three vehicles pointed toward the depths. Great searchlights shot fantastically through bluish fumes. Eyes were already watering and blinking, and men were rubbing them. Mr. Train was reporting to Vinaro, gently expostulating with him, and trying to put a gas mask on him all at once.

"There are three dead and six badly wounded, sir," the giant was saying. "No, sir, no word yet from the man sent into Tarzan's rat hole. Another's been sent up after him. I think, sir, it would be wisest to shut off the motors and send strong reconnoitering parties in all directions from this point, until we are completely certain of the route to Tucumai. Please, sir, if you'd hold your head still—"

"No!" Vinaro snarled, jerking away and glaring with bloodshot eyes. "This must be the route to Tucumai—the golden ceiling is an infallible omen! If we delay, we give them time to prepare a defense. We've trapped Tarzan and must take advantage of it. As for the wounded, set up a hospital for them here—did you know that Mammoth Cave in North America was once used as a tuberculosis sanitarium? So, into the Land Rover with me and then *forward*! Its air-conditioning functions below ground as well as above. No, keep that mask away from me! Wear your own pig's snout if you must, Mr. Train—it goes well with your eye patch. But as for me, I live and breath machinery!"

CHAPTER 20

The City of Gold

Tarzan saw a faint golden glow ahead of him. As he strode toward it through the dark of the cave, it took the form of a long oval lying on its side. Then a tiny line of pale yellow sky appeared at its top, the cave widened, and he found himself faced by a great semicircle of steps, as if he stood on the stage of an ancient Greek theater.

As he slowly climbed straight ahead up to them, into the outer air, he noted the bloody stains on his elbows and knees—mementos of his trip through the return tunnel—and immediately became aware that he was bruised and aching in almost every part. Even his shoulders and head had got bumps he hadn't noticed at the time. Well, perhaps his battered appearance would help convince the folk of Tucumai of their peril.

At the same time he became aware of a combination of odors that he hadn't encountered since leaving Chamston-Hedding for his flight to Meseta: moist, well-tilled farmland, sweet pasture and flower beds.

He reached the topmost tier and halted, blinking at the last sliver of deep orange sun as it disappeared behind a jagged-topped rocky wall almost two miles ahead of him. Then the blinding sliver was gone, a great yellow afterglow reflected from high clouds filled the sky and the air, and he was able to survey the hidden valley of Tucumai.

It was, he judged, five miles long and two miles wide, from his north to his south or his right to his left, everywhere surrounded by a 1,000-foot palisade of rock fully as steep as that on the outside. It had the shape of a bottle with the gently narrowing neck toward the north. In that direction the ground rose sharply until it was a full 2,000 feet above the spot where he stood and the rest of the valley. The rock wall rose with it. That would be the valley's head and the source of the streams watering its vegetation. This deduction was supported when he noted, two miles away and about a mile from the bottle's mouth, a towering semicircle of stone looking as if placed by man rather than Nature. That could be a fort, but Ramel had emphasized the peacefulness of his people, and in any case it was much more logical that it be the wall of a reservoir husbanding the valley's water.

Fitting with this, there were broad terraces coming down from the reservoir, each filled in orderly fashion with greenery. Tarzan recognized the opulent pagodalike forms of the Indian corn plant. Along each terrace, he was sure, led irrigation channels.

Nearer at hand, the terraces of crops gave way to eight or ten terraces of houses. Tarzan could not determine whether they were built of stained pale stone or stained stucco or adobe, but they were colored with the same soothing pastel tints that Manolecito had pointed out to him in a Mexican graveyard in Meseta—pale green, rose, blue, and violet. They looked thick-roofed, cool and cheerful. Each terrace was fronted by a walk and a wall, and stood about 20 feet above the one below it.

There were many people standing on the sidewalks behind the walls, but save that they were dark and as gaily clad as their homes, Tarzan could tell little about them.

That was north. To the south—the bottle's foot—was rolling pasture land. Tarzan made out several white flocks, two looking longer-haired. Those would be vicuña, he supposed, the others llamas. From nearer at hand came a half-familiar squealing. Pigs? Or had these folks domesticated the peccary?

Straight ahead—west—in the half-distance, was a small oval lake with an island in its midst, holding four great sculptured figures. Around the pool were flower beds. Beyond the pool an avenue stretched west straight as a spear between a ribbon of tall trees—hardwoods?—to the north and a ribbon of squat trees—fruit orchard?—to the south. At the end of the avenue there appeared to be a building of some sort, backed up against the opposite palisade. But since it was two miles away and in shadow, he could distinguish no details and hardly be sure it was there.

Reluctantly his eyes focused closer—the broad fields of civilization are a welcome sight after jungle and cave.

From the semicircular parapet on which he stood, larger semicircles of steps led down to a great flat earthen plaza, flagged here and there with stone, 30 feet below him.

The plaza was surrounded, very irregularly, by some six or more stone buildings. Each was square or rectangular, straight-walled, flat-roofed, and footed on all sides by a dozen or so steps, like the beginning of a pyramid. They gave a tremendous impression of strength and imperishability. The biggest by far stood to the south, facing the terraced homes across the plaza and backed by the fruit trees and the llama pasturage. At the top of a score of steps, it had a square doorway wide as the cave mouth from which Tarzan had just emerged. Its great size perfectly balanced the ribbonlike stand of tall hardwoods to the north, making all of Tucumai a perfect picture.

It was ten times the size of the building—temple?—close to Tarzan on the north, between him and the terraces of pastel homes. From the roof of this close one there lifted the stone shoulders and squatty neckless stone head of a demoniac shape that stared straight at the cave mouth with the black, bottomless eyes of a fiend—just circular borings in the stone, but most impressive. The other temples—or buildings—seemed to have undecorated roofs.

During all this relatively swift scanning, Tarzan was aware of one jarringly modern note, which now at last he identified. On the earth of the plaza, about 100 feet from the foot of the semicircular steps and a little to the south, lay a blackened skeletal shape like a cross about 70 feet long each way, with a smaller cross at the tail. Its shape was carefully outlined with ribbons of bone-white stones set in the earth. From another of his secondary hobbies, Tarzan knew that shape well—it was undoubtedly the crashed and burned wreck of a Curtiss-Wright Condor twin-motored transport, last of the great biplanes.

And now, in a large rectangular area of the terrace planted with flowers and lying a little to the north in front of the pastel homes, he could see similar ribbons of white stone outlining the black, slightly mounded "graves" of a Douglas DC-4 and, unbelievably tiny beside it, a Santos-Dumont Demoiselle monoplane.

Off in the terraced cornfields and the meadows he could make out three or four other white-pricked blackened shapes of airplanes. One was a Stinson four-passenger monoplane, he was almost sure, another a twin rotored Sikorsky helicopter.

Everything else he had looked at had given him a feeling of the *glory* of Tucumai, but those wrecks suggested that there was a *power* with the glory—a mysterious power. That a half dozen or more aircraft should have crashed in this tiny valley in the 70 years of aviation's history seemed beyond the workings of chance. Santos-Dumont had been a Brazilian, though living much in France. The only known Demoiselle had been the first powered aircraft to fly—back in 1898. Tarzan shivered a little at the shadowy implications. Now, too, it was no longer surprising Ramel had known so much about aircraft.

Then he began slowly to descend the wide stone steps before him and inspect the assembly of persons approaching him with grace and assurance across the plaza from the direction of the biggest building.

They were copper-dark in complexion and of moderate height, the men smoothly muscular, the women slender. Most of them were clad in gaily colored tunics of fine wool—llama or vicuña, he supposed—and modestly decked with ornaments of silver and gold. Their features had the grave classical cast of Peruvian Indians, though most of them were smiling. Brushing against their knees, there advanced with them several long-haired white jaguars like Xima.

In their midst walked four men in black tunics, wearing no jewelry. Their faces were unsmiling, preoccupied—their brows furrowed, their heads shaven. Tarzan wondered, *the Thinkers?*

Ahead of them walked an old man in a long robe of undyed wool and with long silvery hair silver-banded. On either side of him, holding his hands, stepped Ramel and Sophia. She looked worried; Ramel looked proud and happy, yet worried, too.

"Tarzan!" the boy greeted. "This is Manco Capac, our chief."

The old man reached out his hands and firmly pressed those of Tarzan, holding them while he courteously looked Tarzan up and down, noting the barely scabbed gouges and dried bloodstains and the friendly yet somber expression on the bronze face.

With a warning pressure he let go Tarzan's hands and said in remarkably pure English, "You are welcome in Tucumai, my son. We know you have risked your life many times to bring our prince home and to try, in your fashion, to guard us. We—my Thinkers"—he indicated the impassive black-tunicked men—"my people, myself—are very grateful."

There were soft, smiling comments from all around in a tongue unfamiliar to Tarzan. Evidently Manco Capac's thanks were being repeated in ancient Quechua.

"You are wounded, my son," the old man next remarked. "Let me summon nurses and a litter."

Tarzan shook his head sharply. "Those can wait," he said. The old man nodded politely. "Then if you will come, my son," the slim old patriarch said, holding out an arm and beginning to turn.

"Wait!" Tarzan had not moved a muscle. He said tautly, "Ramel has told you what's going to happen—almost certainly?"

Manco Capac paused in his turn. "He has, my son."

"Good!" Tarzan rapped out, with a fierce nod of approval at Ramel. "What preparations have you made to stand off Vinaro?"

Manco Capac's brown, wrinkle-edged eyes looked straight into Tarzan's. "None," he said.

Sophia burst out, "Tarzan, they don't believe a man like Vinaro can exist!"

"No, we believe that," Manco Capac said with a faint smile. "Our forefathers were harried and cut down by Francisco Pizarro, and since then greed and lust have often sniffed around our valley and flown over our heads. But come, my son. Be gracious. We may discourse and even argue as we walk."

Tarzan yielded. They all moved slowly across the plaza, between the blackened Condor outlined by its huge white beads and the corner of the great rectangle of flowers. The white jaguars paced sleekly with them.

Manco Capac continued, "Also, there has been a man here from the outside world during my lifetime. His skin was fair, his hair had been gold, yet inwardly he was one of us."

"Hugh Malpole?" Tarzan asked.

Manco Capac nodded. He pointed to the flowers around the stony white dots outlining the butterfly wings of the Santos-Dumont. Tarzan noted small pale stones half-hidden by the blooms. "His grave lies there," Manco Capac said, "among those of our greatest. He taught many of us your language—and he taught us much of the changing world beyond Tucumai and the new modern evils."

Tarzan said, "Then you must know you've got to do *something*. Either get ready to fight—or run away! You seem to be magnificent engineers—there may be time to block the cave mouth with stone, or build a vast fire there and keep feeding it. A force of men above the cave mouth, armed with spears and boulders, could cause Vinaro's column much damage. There may even be time to dig tank traps and disguise them!"

Manco Capac shook his head. "My people would never approve such disfigurations of Tucumai."

Tarzan said, "Believe me, they're nothing to the disfigurations Vinaro will inflict on your city and valley!"

Manco Capac said, stepping along evenly, "We've lived here for four hundred years in peace. We're not going to stop living here—or stop living in peace."

Tarzan said harshly, "If you leave it up to those men, you'll just stop living!"

The black-tunicked men seemed to take note of Tarzan at last. They eyed him with distant disapproval. There was a quick murmuring in Quechua among the gayer-clad folk, some sounding alarmed, others reassuring them.

Tarzan ignored all three groups. Despite the sharp interchange, he had been unable to keep his eyes from roving around the city and valley, spying new details while the yellow afterglow lasted. He made out gaps in the walls to the far north that looked like quarries. He traced the road down from them. It led beside a stream running down the terraces in a series of gentle waterfalls, feeding the irrigation ditches and eventually the large pool or small lake with the island in it, and then going on to replenish the pasture land.

Manco Capac said, "Besides maize, we grow the potato, the cassava—for manioc—and the quinoa, which yields us a sort of rice. Some of the corn goes to fatten the llamas and peccaries. Among the fruit trees ahead, to the left of the pool, the banana and pineapple are paramount. You may also see there coca shrubs, which yield a drug that is invigorating when used in moderation and with periods of abstinence. Now there"—he pointed to some sheds on the edge of the pasture, beyond the big building which they were preparing to pass to their left— "are our workshops for weaving, stonework, carpentry, metalwork...our smithies—"

"—which should be turning out spearheads and arrowheads to resist Vinaro!" Tarzan put in bitterly. "Pardon me, Manco Capac, but I believe your people had something to do—perhaps only by psychological means—with the wrecking of the aircraft I see buried around us. Weren't there people in them? Wasn't that killing? Then why do you refuse to defend yourself against naked attack?"

Manco Capac raised a hand. He said softly, "We never gave aircraft permission to fly over our valley. If their pilots became confused and crashed, that is no affair of ours. We honored the ships' graves." The black-tunicked men looked quite complacent, smiled faintly. Manco Capac frowned at Tarzan, seemingly with genuine sympathy for his inward struggle, and laid a thin hand on the ape-man's upper arm. "My son, I know that you and this young lady and Ramel, momentarily accepting your warlike philosophy because you are his hero, are trying to help us. But try to understand—"

"It's you who's got to understand," Tarzan shot back. "Those men are coming here with weapons you have never heard of!"

"We have heard of the atomic bomb," the silver-haired old man answered seriously. "Hugh Malpole told us all about it. Just one would destroy all Tucumai. It would be as if the Sun peered too closely at us. Should we provoke such a war?"

With all respect to the dead, Tarzan was becoming heartily sick of hearing about Hugh Malpole. Whatever residual warlikeness the Tucumaians may have had, that madcap soldier-turned-pacifist had obliterated it.

They were passing a strange circular stockade occupying a considerable area of the plaza. It consisted of light posts seven feet high set five feet apart. A similarly "fenced" avenue six feet wide led off to the pastures. It struck Tarzan as a singularly useless structure, at least in its present form.

Manco Capac noticed and said, "Therein our llamas show off their skills under the orders of their herdsmen. The animals treat the posts as if they were a solid fence, though they could easily go between them. This is a symbol of the way the civilized man masters his barbarian impulses."

"I would say it shows just that llamas are sheep," Tarzan retorted. "Stupid mindless creatures!"

"Ramel tells me you are able to talk with beasts," Manco Capac remarked innocently.

"With lions, apes, elephants, even bulls!" Tarzan retorted. "But not with sheep! Not with animals unable to take thought for their own safety, that run between walls that aren't there into a pit! Manco Capac, Vinaro has at least one hundred forty men armed with rapid-fire weapons and bombs. He has one of the mightiest armored vehicles of the last world war—it breathes flame! Almost certainly he will be here within a few hours. He would probably be here now, except—" and without false modesty Tarzan explained how he had decoyed Vinaro's column into the wrong passageway in the caves.

Ramel beamed with pride at his hero; Sophia's eyes glowed.

When Tarzan's account was done, Manco Capac nodded with interest and approval. "Brilliant! You are wiser than I gave you credit for," he said. "You did not kill; you simply misled. It is not your fault if they follow the wrong passageway, which indeed does lead to a pit. And even with the gun, you did not shoot at any man, but only at the glittering daggers. It is not your fault that Vinaro's men chose to stand under them. Most ingenious! Without knowing it, you are like our Thinkers, who never kill, but do not blame themselves if men insist on going to their deaths."

Tarzan snorted impolitely at what seemed to him the merest hairsplitting and logic-chopping. Also he had the uncomfortable feeling that Dr. Bragança's "Matar nunca!" injunction was still with him. He said testily, "I misled rather than fought solely because I was one man against one hundred fifty—and also have some love of my own hide! And if your Thinkers are so good at that job, why haven't they misled Vinaro?"

Manco Capac shook his head sadly. "Vinaro had the golden map," he said. "No, Ramel, it was not your fault," he said swiftly, as the boy's eyes filled with tears. "You could not have foreseen it."

"But I should have!" the boy protested, mastering his sobs. Tarzan thought that the boy showed more spirit at that moment than all the rest of Tucumai. Or was it only that Ramel had rubbed against the outside world?

One of the black-clad Thinkers said softly, in English almost as good as Manco Capac's, "We've been bending our thoughts all day to mislead Vinaro in the caves—and we are still at it. But we thank you for your assistance, Man from Outside."

Tarzan stifled the obvious retort about any witch doctor being able to claim credit for anything, once someone else had done it, and said instead, "Very well, Manco Capac. But at least have your people set about blocking the mouth of the cave. That is not killing."

Manco Capac nodded. "I will consider it. But this evening is one of religious observance. We commemorate Cupay, the Lord of Death."

Tarzan said, "Vinaro is Death himself, Cupay incarnate, Pizarro come again!"

For the first time Manco Capac lifted a hand to Tarzan for silence, then extended it toward the small island in the rippling pool they were approaching.

"We live always with Death, my son," he said. "Look!"

They were near enough now so that, between the fading afterglow and the strong moonlight beginning to pour from behind them, the four great stone figures on the island came clear. They were thick and blocky in the Incan style, yet beautifully proportioned and—such as were human—instinct with humanity. Tarzan caught his breath in admiration of the simple magnificence of their artistry and concept.

The tall figure in the rear clearly represented the Sun, for his face was surrounded with an aureole of short thick outward-pointing spokes. Within the aureole, the serene face gazed straight ahead, wide-eyed. In front of the Sun and a little to the right a man stood straight, one foot advanced as if taking a step. His left hand rested on the shoulder of a woman, whose body arched with the promise of a child.

Off to the left, tall as the Sun, loomed a figure whose head was a stone skull. His empty eyes glared at the man and woman. The woman looked over her shoulder at the man. The man glared back at Death.

After a dozen heartbeats, Tarzan said, "That man would fight. Manco Capac, this is great art. Vinaro will probably use it for target practice for his tank, sparing perhaps the figure of Death. I do not believe I have misled him for long. Nor, with due respect to them, do I believe your Thinkers can. He will be here within a few hours!"

"A few hours," Manco Capac said. A calculating look came

into his eyes. "Then will you give me less than one hour to show you Tucumai?"

Tarzan did not like the look. "Every minute wasted will cost you lives!" he rapped out.

For the first time Manco Capac's voice grew stern. "We have argued long enough, my son. Tucumai is grateful for your services. I seek to be a good host. Be you a good guest."

There was a general murmur of agreement at this. Smiles were still directed at Tarzan, but they were tentative now. Even Ramel pleaded with his eyes.

With a gracious inclination of his head, Tarzan bowed to the unavoidable—with the inward proviso that he would seize the first good chance to rouse the fighting spirit of Tucumai, if it held any. So long as he received no cooperation, so long as these people persisted in their dream of invulnerability, the best thing he could do was learn all he could about Tucumai's resources.

As if Tarzan's nod had been a signal, the twilit plaza burst into life. Youths of Ramel's age came running with newly lit torches down from the terraced homes and from two small temples at either side of the pool—the one a temple of the Sun, judging from the round serrate plate of gold above its doorway; the other a temple of the Moon, from its similarly placed crescent of silver.

Smiling women came to Tarzan with silver bowls and soft towels and gently bathed his bloodstained limbs. Others relieved him of his weapons: bow, arrows, lariat, knife. Manco Capac said it was taboo to wear them at a festival. They would be returned to him, he was assured. Another woman offered him a large silver cup of pale yellow liquid.

"It is *sora*," Manco Capac told him, "a mild beer made from fermented maize."

Tarzan tested it, judged that its alcoholic content was slight, and drank enough to satisfy his thirst. Then he hungrily crunched a buttered corn cake. *Llama milk butter—and excellent*, he thought. And no taste like corn!—the New World's greatest gift to humanity. Better than Russian wheat, German rye, Egyptian sesame, Chinese rice, Scottish oats, or even British barley!

Suddenly two brawny, brown young men in loincloths were wrestling in front of them. Tarzan admired the strength and swiftness of their grips, trips, and slips. Both laughed as one of them fell. The loser was instantly helped up by the winner, whom Manco Capac presented to Tarzan.

"This is Herdin, our champion. You understand, of course, that if anyone is hurt in a bout, the fighting immediately stops."

Tarzan casually shook hands—and suddenly had to exert most of his strength to keep his fingers from being crushed. Certainly these Tucumaians weren't muscular weaklings! Yet Herdin's grin seemed wholly admiring.

"Good meet Ramel's bringer," he said. "English poor."

"Much better than my Quechua," Tarzan assured him.

Sophia pinched Tarzan's forearm with her right hand. Her other held a goblet of *sora* and a small sandwich of cornbread and peccary loin. She grinned up to him. "This is like a circus," she said. "You know I once was in one. Truly it is better than Mardi Gras or Fasching! Most like Fasching, maybe—I never can understand German."

Her mood did not match Tarzan's, but rather reminded him of how ephemeral this gaiety was—dancing on the edge of the abyss, as before World War I. Yet he managed to wrinkle his nose and grin back at her. And then his mood did begin to change. He found himself melancholy, yet somewhat happy and not overly worried about Vinaro.

Unseen musicians struck up a lilting yet eerie music of low-whistling pipes, like recorders, and dry seeds rattling rhythmically in dry gourds. The boys with torches retreated toward the pool. The crowd became not exactly silent but less noisy. Then from a low stone building between the Temple of the Moon and the terraced homes there filed in slow graceful dance steps a procession of figures bearing great bundles of cut flowers. Moonlight was the chief light now, so it was a few moments before it became clear that they were long-haired young women wearing lacy robes of filigreed gold and silver. They moved sensuously, yet smiling, from side to side in a fashion more friendly than challenging. Each paused and dropped her pale, perfumed burden in a round black hole about five feet across, which Tarzan now noticed for the first time 20 feet ahead in a flagstoned section of the plaza.

"Maidens of the Moon," Manco Capac explained quietly to Tarzan, "wed for a season to the Sun and giving pleasure to Tucumai. Only our most beautiful and lively girls are granted this honor."

Tarzan nodded politely, forbearing to mention what bait they would be for Vinaro's men.

"Tonight they cast flowers into the Outer Well of Cupay, or the Well of the Maidens, as it is sometimes called," the old man went on. "They seek to cajole the old dragon Cupay down below. Someday, when he has smelled enough flowers, he may mend his destructive ways."

"How deep is the well?" Tarzan asked.

Manco Capac shrugged. "You drop a stone and hear no echo."

"I should think with your safety-mindedness you would fence it around," Tarzan remarked conversationally.

Manco Capac smiled. "Not needed. Remember the llamas and the stockade. Also, although we forebear to inflict death or hurt, we do not banish risk. But come, you and the young lady. It is time you saw another sight." He spoke an order in Quechua. As the last of the Moon Maidens danced back beyond the temple with the silver crescent, the boys with torches ran from the pool-side and formed themselves into two lines, making a path between Manco Capac and the biggest building of them all, from the huge door of which yellow light now shone.

"What sight?" Tarzan asked, going on the silver-haired chief's right side, as Sophia went on his left, with Ramel beside her.

Stepping forward along the torchlit path, Manco Capac said, "The treasure of Tucumai."

Inferno described the scene. The three crazily angled pairs of headlights showed the air still thick with blue fumes, although the motors had been switched off. They struck weird jutting and bulbous rock formations that looked like the snarling masks of monsters. Those of the Panther tank glared down at an angle into an endless blackness ahead. Its treads were on the edge of an abyss. One of its crewmen sprawled unconscious halfway out the turret hatch.

Fully a third of Vinaro's men lay about on the rocks like damned souls, felled by carbon monoxide from their own vehicles, breathing snoringly. Others staggered about as if drunk through the shadows and smoky light, or were doubling up and retching. The few wearing gas masks went about trying to give relief, but looking like snout-nosed fiends of the pit.

Two of these were Mr. Train and Romulo, who knelt by Vinaro, who was stretched out on a narrow mattress outside the cabin of the Command Rover. His face was an unnatural red. Romulo held a flashlight. Mr. Train was administering oxygen to Vinaro through a cuplike face-mask.

As he carefully turned the cock that released the life-giving gas, he said thoughtfully, "I wonder if I am doing the right thing, Romulo?"

The other bobbed his head. "Oh, I am sure you are. Oxygen must be right."

Mr. Train smiled very faintly, narrowing his eyes, as he gave a slight nod, too. Then with a little shrug, he said, "We have probably lost a few dead. As soon as the rest are recovered sufficiently, march them back to the beginning of the corridor with the metallic-appearing stalactites. I believe it was there we missed a turning. But watch out for another ambush! Mr. Vinaro had best go by stretcher. I will bring up the vehicles, though no nearer than two hundred yards from the men. All drivers and others with me must have masks."

"We will hope Mr. Vinaro is recovered by then," Romulo said. "He put a great strain on himself, leading us here."

"He surely did," said Mr. Train.

"He hung on until the last moment."

"Until the last possible moment," Mr. Train agreed, glancing toward the abyss.

Colonel Juarez's troop was finishing a largely cold supper in thin jungle by the light of the rising moon. Professor Talmadge ate little, drank two cups of coffee, and still sagged. Yet what he said to Juarez was, "I feel certain we should press on by moonlight. That last skyline the sunset showed was exactly the way Ramel described the mountains guarding Tucumai. And they can hardly be more than five miles off. The jungle's getting so we can walk to one side of Vinaro's trail."

Juarez said, "I, too, have that feeling of climax close at hand. But I do not think you are up to it, old friend."

"Give me five minutes," Talmadge said doggedly.

As soon as the colonel went to talk to the others by turns, Talmadge surreptitiously took a white pill from his kit, crushed it for quicker assimilation, and washed it down with the rest of the coffee.

When Juarez spoke to Duarte, the latter laughed. "I was sure we would go forward tonight. This old nose already sniffs corpses demanding burial."

As soon as Juarez had made his rounds, Talmadge came up to him springily. The professor's eyes were bright by moonlight in their black circles.

"Well, what's delaying us?" he demanded.

"You have taken benzedrine, professor," Juarez said reproachfully.

"And if I have?" Talmadge demanded fiercely.

The other shrugged. "To be sure, it is your heart, Lionel, to do with as you wish. *Desculpe.*"

CHAPTER 21

"...Matar Nunca!"

Manco Capac led the way up the dozen steps and through the great stone doorway, 20 feet high and wide, of the largest building in Tucumai. Behind them the torches held by the boys grew dim, the happy noise of the plaza began to fade. Tarzan walked at his right hand, Sophia and Ramel at his left. Behind them came the champion wrestler Herdin, his brawny defeated opponent Tegno, and also the four black-clad Thinkers. These last faced around, evenly spaced, before the doorway, as if to insure against intrusion.

Tarzan noted that the walls were ten feet thick, yet he could detect no signs of joints and crevices in the dark rock. Either the stone-fitting was of a higher order of precision even than that at Machu Picchu, or else some mighty blocks indeed had been dragged down from the quarries to the north. Tarzan's imagination boggled at the thought of the ramps and rollers, vast dragropes, and other physical labor involved.

They entered a stone room 30 feet across—ahead of them—which stretched out 40 feet at either side of the doorway in two great wings. Flames lighted it from spherical stone bowls set about the floor—graceful, primitive oil lamps.

Since the room was only as high as the doorway—20 feet—and since the building had appeared 80 feet high from the outside, not counting the steps, Tarzan calculated that there was room for a second floor 40 feet high, allowing ten feet each for ceiling above and roof above that. There would even be room for a third story.

258

In answer to a question from Sophia, Manco Capac said, "No, it is not a temple. It is our Treasury—and in a fashion our museum. Yet the gods guard it." He waved a hand first to the right, then to the left.

In the right wing was a yellow stone figure of the Sun, rather like that on the island in the lake. The left hand of the Sun clasped the upraised right hand of a somewhat shorter green-stone figure of a woman, whose serene, forward-peering face was framed by two crescents turned inward—evidently the Moon, the Sun's sister-bride by Incan custom. To the right of them, at the Sun's pedestal feet, done in white stone, crouched a splendid youth, whose tentlike hair reached to the floor and who gazed up over his shoulder adoringly at the Sun.

"The white one is the planet Venus," Manco Capac explained, "whom we view not as a woman, as you Europeans do, but as a youth who is page to the Sun and always stays close to him, whether as the Morning or Evening Star."

In the left wing, spanning it from wall to wall, crouched two squat, dark, stone demons—the one with mouth open so wide to bellow that it was all of his face, the other fierce-eyed, sharp-nosed, and poising at shoulder level a short, thick, jagged spear.

"Illapa," Manco Capac said. "Thunder and lightning."

There seemed to be no door out of this narrow room except the one by which they had entered. In fact, there was no decoration on the walls except for a series of flush handholds in the gray wall opposite the entrance doorway. There were 48 of them in four rows of 12 each—the lowest 12 at the level of a man's knee, the highest above his head. Forty-seven were colored gray like the wall, while one, toward the center, was black.

Tarzan's keen eyes noticed two tiny vertical crevices 20 feet apart, running from floor to ceiling and enclosing the handholds.

Manco Capac said, "We stand in the antechamber."

Sophia murmured, frowning, "I'd hate to figure out how to get to the chamber." She grinned, still happy from the plaza. "Secret panel?"

The old man heard and smiled. "Like all mysteries, it is simple once you know the rule. Herdin! Tegno! Tarzan, my son, do as they do, if you please—it will speed matters."

The two young wrestlers strode forward and each grasped a shoulder-high gray handhold in the wall with both hands. Tarzan imitated them, noting at close range that each handhold was centered in a finely lined square a little more than a foot wide. Tarzan expected them to heave upward, but instead each gave a strong backward jerk and drew gratingly out of the wall a stubby pyramid of rock, not quite a cube, and carried it with some difficulty to one side. Tarzan did the same, stiffening his wrists at the sudden weight. No wonder it was difficult!—the block must weigh close to 300 pounds. His muscles strained as he lugged the thing. The three gaps left looked like broken teeth.

Herdin and Tegno came back quickly and seized another handhold. This time Tarzan reached experimentally for the black one.

"Stop, my son!" Manco Capac called quickly. "As *they* do, I said, meaning exactly."

Tarzan tugged out and carried to one side another gray-handled block.

There were six gray teeth lacking now in the wall—six square pits.

"Stand back, my sons," Manco Capac directed.

Slowly the wall in front of them began to rise—that is, the section of it between lines 20 feet apart. A slit of darkness 20 feet long and an inch wide appeared below it and rather swiftly widened. Herdin and Tegno crouched like runners preparing to run a dash. Tarzan imitated them. He noted, crouching low and peering ahead, that the rising section of wall was fully ten feet thick, equal to the outer wall of the building.

As soon as the door before them was four feet high, Herdin and Tegno raced crouching under it. Tarzan did the same. They were in a great shadowy room like the first, except that it held a glamorous golden glow on either side. They sprinted across it through a second door 20 feet high into a third even more shadowy room. In a 20-foot-wide stone-backed recess in the wall ahead of them, there was descending a stone mass identical to the one that was rising behind them—even to having the 48 handholds, including one black one.

Reaching high and working fast, Herdin and Tegno dragged two blocks apiece from it, Tarzan imitating. The second huge stone mass slowed in its descent. Then Herdin, raising his palms to Tego and Tarzan to desist, dragged out a seventh block. The second stone mass slowed still further. The black slit beneath it narrowed to an inch, a half inch, a hair, and the whole vast thing came to rest with never a sound.

Herdin, Tegno, and Tarzan carried the seven blocks to the side. Herdin gave Tarzan a comradely, comically wincing grin at their shared straining. Then they turned back into the second of the rooms.

The solemn Thinkers bore in four lamps from the antechamber, set two in either wing of the first of the two new rooms that had been revealed, then stationed themselves across the doorway under which Tarzan and the two wrestlers had just sprinted.

Manco Capac, Ramel, and Sophia entered between the Thinkers.

The old man shook an admonitory finger at Tarzan. "Had you tugged at the black handhold," he said, "that door would have shot up and perhaps never come down again. While if you jerked at the black handhold which is now in the far wall behind you, the newly risen door behind us would fall in the space of seven heartbeats and we would all be imprisoned forever, between walls the thickness of twice the height of a man. But all's well that ends well."

He smiled. "As you may have guessed, Tarzan, the two great stone masses are of equal weight and hang at the ends of a lever of stone at least as thick as the doors are wide and which rides by a central groove on the jewel-dusted knife-edge of a stone prism. That great lever occupies all the attic of this building. Removing six stones from the door lightened it so that it was pulled upward by the counterbalancing mass in the far wall behind you. Removing *seven* blocks from that second mass restored the balance. Now the second mass is lighter than the first by some 300 pounds, but friction holds it down—if I have remembered aright the physical terms Hugh Malpole taught me."

Tarzan asked, "What do you do when the blocks are all gone from the door and the counterweight, from repeated openings and closings?"

Manco Capac smiled again. "Into the attic above us leads a secret way, whereby we can carry up the blocks removed and fit them into whichever mass is overhead, thereby restoring the situation as you first saw it. Hugh Malpole always wanted me to let him into the attic. He said he could not understand such a lever, that it was impossible. But that was one favor I would not grant him."

"Nor me either, I suppose?" Tarzan asked.

"Certainly not, my son," Manco Capac agreed. "You and Hugh Malpole have both served Tucumai well, but not to the point where all her secrets can be revealed to you. I myself think the builders of this place and in particular this strange door were somewhat mad—those were the Manco Capacs of the first two centuries of Tucumai. Concealing and even fortifying gold had become almost an insanity with them. Also, perhaps, they had to find difficult and arduous work for the inhabitants of this valley, to keep them here and to keep them disciplined. But we have changed with the years and found other values. I am not the Inca. If I were, I would decorate my dress with gold and wear the scarlet, many folded, tasseled turban called *llautu* and bearing two feathers of the bird corequenque. I would maintain absolute authority over my subjects, punishing what displeased me with death. But the Inca is no more. We have learned reason and mercy, Nature's laws, the *true* laws of the Sun."

He smiled. "Now, however, let us take pleasure in looking around us at Tucumai's gold and gems—as if they were so many flowers."

"The treasure?" Sophia asked breathlessly.

Manco Capac shook his head.

Yet the gleaming sight, in the two wings of the central room, was breathtaking. In the forefront, on either side, were opulently swelling vases of gold, luxuriously embossed with the figures of jaguars, serpents, scorpions, locusts, men, women, and other animals. Behind these were life-size golden figures of llamas, vicuñas, and peccaries. Behind those in turn were life-size golden figures of women, while on either side of them, from hooks on the walls, hung golden dresses made entirely of golden beads, presumably strung on wires of the same substance. They hummed faintly when Sophia touched them. Here and there were scepters, crowns, breast-cups, medallions, loin-pieces, and other emblems and also ornaments made of gold and set with emeralds.

Tarzan recalled how the Dominican monk Pedraza had told Pizarro's followers that the test of a genuine emerald was that it was unbreakable, whereupon many of Pizarro's loutish though formidable soldiers had "tested" their emeralds by smashing one or two of them, up to the size of a pigeon's egg. Deciding they were only green glass, they had given the residue to "Brother" Reginaldo de Pedraza, who profited greatly thereby. Restitution had never been made, to Tarzan's knowledge, either to the soldiers' heirs or to those of the Indians.

The sheer amount of gold was overwhelming, like two thick strands of golden shrubbery, yet the artistry with which the imperishable element was fashioned was even more impressive.

Sophia said, "This is grander than Tiffany's or Cartier's, or the Metropolitan Museum in New York, or the Leningrad, or the Tower of London!"

Tarzan nodded. He was impressed by the quantity of openly displayed gold, that delightful substance 19 times heavier than water which the governments of almost all nations of the world have locked away, unwilling to entrust it to their theoretically trustworthy citizens. Yet Tarzan, knowing how this metal had warped history, could see both horror and beauty in it—golden flowers and golden fungus.

Tarzan said, "No wonder they haven't found much gold in

Lake Titicaca—or anywhere else in the Andes. What Pizarro didn't get came here."

Manco Capac looked from side to side contemptuously. "Yet all this gold…is not worth one human life." His eyes glittered at Tarzan. "*Now*…having feasted your eyes on this lusted-after, pleasingly robust stuff…would you care to see the treasure of Tucumai?"

Tarzan and Sophia looked at each other, then nodded. Even Ramel seemed surprised.

Manco Capac led them into the innermost room, where the counterweight, with its seven gray handholds missing, stared them in the face.

The four Thinkers brought four more spherical lamps from the antechamber, to show them the contents of this innermost room.

Heaped in the wings, these contents were not gleaming but dark. Knives of stone, of greenly corroded copper and bronze, but all of them broken. Broken bows, arrows and spears—the heads of these last broken like the knives. There were also three Spanish cannon, light fieldpieces, their touch-holes gaping and ringed with red, as if once spiked with iron, their muzzles ripped apart by charges of gunpowder set off there, finally the whole of them beaten flat, as if by stones used as hammers. And there were some revolvers and rifles of the past hundred years which had been somewhat similarly dented and made useless.

Manco Capac said, "*This!* This is the treasure. Gold and silver are stuff—to buy steel from Toledo or Krupp's or television sets, as Hugh Malpole told us is your current rage. Broken weapons are a hero's guerdon! Four hundred years ago, in this valley, every weapon designed to maim and kill men was broken and put here, in this treasury, forever. From time to time we have added to it—even Hugh Malpole had a revolver. Would we had an atomic bomb, broken into two halves! Would we had *all* the atomic bombs, similarly nullified!"

Sophia said softly and sympathetically, "I'm beginning to understand how you feel. After all, the French armies started a mutiny in World War I that, if it had been successful, might have changed the history of the whole world, but—"

Tarzan said, "I think Mr. Vinaro would prefer the middle room with the gold in it," though he said it without his earlier fierce conviction. He was beginning to feel overpoweringly tired. He wondered if there could have been a slow-acting drug in the *sora* or if the Thinkers behind him were able to control the tides of sleep like those of the weather. But what the deuce, today's exertions—especially in that devilish return tunnel— were enough to explain his sleepiness.

Manco Capac caught eagerly at his remark, however, and said quickly, "That's exactly my point. I'm sure Mr. Vinaro would prefer the contents of the room of gold. And he can have it! We won't exchange one single life for it."

Tarzan yawned, forcing himself awake, and said, "Vinaro will simply grab this gold and ask for an equal amount in addition—your people's adornments, the insignia on your temples, your maiden's clothing, all! And he will still be unsatisfied! In the end he will worry about witnesses, he will remember that dead men tell no tales, and he will kill every inhabitant of Tucumai. So-called civilized men have slaughtered every passenger in a great airplane to dispose of just one person. You will be a second Atahualpa, Manco Capac, forced to fill one room after another with gold, to satisfy someone who is insatiable—Vinaro, who would like to eat gold for breakfast!"

"You believe so?" Manco Capac said. "I will consider it. You sound overwrought. Perhaps you are worried about your animal friends, Major and Dinky. Perhaps you would like to see them."

Ramel said eagerly, "Yes, Tarzan, Manco Capac is taking very good care of them. They could not be let out with the white jaguars. Come on, I'll show you."

Tarzan hesitated in the Room of Broken Weapons. He mastered his weariness and said, "Manco Capac! These men coming here like weapons that *work*. And they like to *use* them."

Manco Capac shrugged. "But we do not intend to give

Vinaro the broken weapons. We intend to give him the gold. The gold-for-breakfast man! Come, let us see your Major, who though the color of gold, has better eating habits. And Dinky, too."

"Yes, let's do that!" Ramel echoed. Sophia smiled encouragingly.

Tarzan pointed at a dark opening, about four feet across, which he had spotted in the floor at the end of the western wing of the Room of Broken Weapons. "What's that?" he demanded, a little groggily.

"The Inner Well of Cupay," Manco Capac answered. "If the old dragon cares to come up and steal our gold—or even our broken weapons—he is welcome to them."

"So," Tarzan said critically, realizing his mind was not functioning as cleverly as it should, "you guard your gold with walls and doors ten feet or more thick, yet leave the cellar door open!"

Manco Capac said evenly, "If someone human can climb up that slick-sided well for hundreds of feet, he can have the gold, too. Come, my combative and suspicious friend!"

Tarzan shrugged and fell in beside the old, silver-haired chief, the golden-haired Sophia, and the black-haired Ramel. The two wrestlers, Herdin and Tegno, and the four black-clad Thinkers followed behind.

The plaza was empty now, although there were gay lively lights and sounds coming from the terraced homes and also from the low, long House of the Maidens behind the Temple of the Moon. Moonlight shone brightly from the silver crescent of that fane and from the emblem of the golden sun, four feet in diameter, over the door to the matching small Temple of the Sun on the other side of the pool. The moonlight also flooded the plaza and made walking sure.

Manco Capac said as they left the Treasury, "We'll leave the door open, so that Vinaro—when and if he comes to Tucumai—can see his objective at once. If there's no reason to kill, there'll be no killing."

Tarzan noted that, now that the door to the golden room was

raised into the ceiling, there seemed to be no doors at all to the Treasury or to the Room of Broken Weapons—just straight square arches.

He shrugged. Letting Vinaro get gold at once might at least delay his urge to kill.

They walked between the posts of the strange unfenced stockade. The Thinkers spread out so each could have a space to himself.

They approached the white stones outlining the grave of the Condor. But then Manco Capac turned sharply right into a small, four-stepped building lighted with one of the nearly spherical lamps outside the door.

"This was Hugh Malpole's dwelling for a time," he said.

This building had a square door, too, but barely head-high. The ceiling inside, however, rose to a peak. The room inside, occupying the whole building, was divided into two halves by wrist-thick bronze bars set about five inches apart, which traveled from side to side, horizontally, instead of from top to bottom. In the center was a door of heavier bars. Major and Dinky were sleeping on mats in the dimness by the far wall. There were other furnishings in the barred room. Manco Capac pointed out bowls of water, milk, fruit, and cooked flesh.

"They've had the food and drink suited to their natures," he said.

Three of the Thinkers sprang up lightly, grasped a lever parallel to the slanting ceiling, and brought the lever down by their weight to the horizontal. The door of bars opened, silently at first but with a final clank. Manco Capac confidently led the way inside, Ramel's hand in his. Tarzan and Sophia followed.

Major roused with a fierce growl, which made Dinky come awake chattering—exactly as if he'd been having a nightmare.

Tarzan strode forward quickly, placing himself between Manco Capac and the lion, to whom he spoke sharply.

At the same instant, moving much faster than he had at any other time in the evening, Manco Capac stepped out of the cage, drawing Ramel with him. The instant they were out, the Thinkers thrust up the lever and the door of bars closed.

Tarzan turned back with a word of reassurance and saw how he and Sophia had been trapped. He came to the door and gripped it, but made no effort to shake it—there was enough light to show him the bars were probably beyond his strength.

Manco Capac, the silver of his hair and head bands glinting from the single light behind him, his face in shadow, said somberly, "I am sorry it was necessary to deceive you. But you have the heart of a warrior—and we must treat with Vinaro in our own fashion. There must be no bloodshed."

"But there *will* be!" Tarzan said. "And it will be *yours*! Ramel's too—and any number of your people!"

"Forgive me, please," the old chief said. "But you mustn't be free to start any violence when those men come to meet us."

"Free!" Tarzan said bitterly. "You will be handing over myself and this young lady to a man who hates us bitterly."

"Rather than that, I would die."

"Manco Capac, you very well may."

Up until this moment Ramel had seemed paralyzed by the hand of age and authority on his wrist. Now his chest began to quake and he burst out sobbing with, "Father of us all, you've got to let Tarzan go! He is wise, too—I know!—and he brought me home."

"We will, later, my son. Believe me, this is best."

The boy broke away and rushed to the lever. Neither Manco Capac nor the four Thinkers attempted to stop him. He sprang for it at the only point where he could reach it—near the wall. Hanging from it, he jerked at it, to no effect. Battling the lever almost as if it were an animate foe, he swung his way to the end, which was four feet at that point from the slanting ceiling. Then he swung back and pressed with his feet against the wall as he tugged. All to no effect—the lever did not budge a fraction. He dropped down, panting and still sobbing, now with rage.

"It is beyond your weight and strength, my son," Manco Capac said calmly, "as this whole problem is beyond you and Tarzan."

He signaled to one of his Thinkers, who firmly yet unmaliciously took Ramel by shoulder and wrist and led him from the room.

The boy looked back wildly over his shoulder. "I didn't *know*, Tarzan!"

"I understand, Ramel," Tarzan called after him. Then turning his eyes burningly on Manco Capac, he said, "*You* think you understand Vinaro. You believe he is open to reason. But *I* know he is a madman. It will be Pizarro at Caxamalca all over again. The old Spanish villain killed five thousand there in one massacre—more than the entire population of Tucumai. Yet Pizarro was at least a Christian, though of a miserable sort and badly advised. But Vinaro's god is Death!—as this young lady can tell you. He will be worse than Pizarro. And you will be a second Atahualpa."

Manco Capac's answer came calmly from the dark of his face. "We know these things about Vinaro, Tarzan. In the four centuries since Pizarro, we have sought to develop the means of dealing with them. Now comes the time of testing. We do not believe Vinaro is open to reason, but we do believe he is open to other powers of the mind, which we have spent four centuries learning."

Tarzan shrugged. "Was it part of your deception when you said Hugh Malpole lived in this cell?"

Manco Capac shook his head. "No, we had to confine him here when he suffered *his* sort of madness about Tucumai—that he should go forth and tell the world about us and take some of our Thinkers with him and teach our secrets of peace to the world—*when we have not yet even tested them.* After a few weeks of confinement he came to understand our point of view, and it was possible to let him go free again. We were always infinitely grateful to him for bringing us the great message from the outer world."

"Which was?" Tarzan asked.

Manco Capac moved toward the door, two of the Thinkers

falling in behind him, while one sat himself below the lever and stared steadily at Tarzan and Sophia.

In the door the old Incan turned, so that the lamplight gleamed for a moment on his eyeballs before he turned them back toward Tarzan.

"Die if necessary, but never kill," he said strongly. "The motto of the SPI. It applies as much to Vinaro as it does to the lowliest savage. You will pardon me, my civilized friend, if I claim a civilization superior to yours. Malpole thought it so important that he even taught it to us in the other languages: *Morrer se preciso for, matar nunca!*"

For a moment Tarzan had the weird feeling that he could not be sure whose black silhouette he faced—that of the aged, silver-haired Manco Capac or that of the equally aged Dr. Maria Bragança.

Then the doorway was empty. Tarzan turned back from the bars, shaking his head.

"What now?" Sophia asked.

Tarzan shrugged. "All we can do is sleep—with the beasts. Perhaps a plan will come upon waking."

It was a quiet night, yet the two words *"…Matar nunca!"* seemed to hang on the air, until Tarzan wondered if he was cursed by their sound.

In the caves Augustus Vinaro planned his attack.

"Mr. Train!" he said. "Finish the clearing of the boulders from the final passageway. Then a half hour before dawn, march *all* the men without masks to the stairs leading up to Tucumai. I am satisfied that Romulo's scouting report is correct. But do not move beyond that point until you hear the vehicles."

"Yes, sir," Mr. Train replied. "But do you mean all the men literally, sir? I sent five back to post themselves at the mouth of the tunnel, in case we are followed."

"Then recall them!" Vinaro ordered sharply, his bloodshot eyes glaring. "*All* our forces will be required for the stroke at Tucumai. You did well, perhaps, in saving us from the abyss, though I still believe an entrance could have been forced in that direction. However, since my consciousness failed there, my genius could not operate. But do not make the mistake of dividing our forces!"

"Yes, sir," Mr. Train said woodenly. "I will recall the men at the cave mouth."

A little later Romulo remarked to Mr. Train, "Our general is a great strategist. He always sees the advantage of striking with maximum power."

"He is certainly an exceptional strategist," Mr. Train agreed.

Beyond the caves, Juarez's 16 men came to the point where Vinaro had tackled the palisades. The roped bodies of the two men who had perished in that attempt glared up white-eyed in the strong moonlight.

"I protest," Duarte said softly. "That we should stop to bury these is asking too much."

"For now, yes, I agree," Juarez said, "though they are a miserable sight, *por Deus*. But now speed is all. Ataúl and Apoena agree that Vinaro is not ten hours ahead. If the caves Ramel spoke of exist and if we find them, we might take his tank at disadvantage, unable to turn."

"Though what madman would send a tank into a cave..." Captain Lobos began, shaking his shoulders.

"We are dealing with a homicidal maniac," Juarez said simply, waving a hand toward the two moonlit corpses as his party started on again.

Talmadge was fumbling open his medical kit. Juarez laid a hand on his shoulder.

"No more benzedrine, professor," he ordered. "Here is cold coffee in my canteen. And take my arm."

CHAPTER 22

Pizarro Come Back

There are battles that are won or lost by a single charge—Cromwell's Ironsides at Naseby bursting the lines of Charles and Prince Rupert, the French knights plunging to defeat feathered by English arrows at Agincourt, Pickett's men mown down by the Northern guns at Gettysburg. But never was a stranger charge, or one that came closer to absolute success, than that at Tucumai.

It began a little after dawn, when the sun peeped over the mountains to the east.

Vinaro's men had gathered in the cave mouth. Now, at the sound of the vehicles behind them, they came crowding up to either side, their rapid-fire weapons ready.

They left a wide avenue between them. Up this the tank rumbled, roaring like a monster, making 20 miles an hour up the steps. The man in its turret jolted in the hatch to which he clung. It swung to the right and drew up beside the Temple of Cupay, from the roof of which the stone monster stared down at it as empty-eyed as the Panther's cannon and flamethrower.

The two Land Rovers followed the tank at a more sedate pace, since their motors hadn't that much power. They drew up parallel to the Panther, the Fuel Rover in the center, the Command Rover to the left, its treads crushing the white stones outlining the grave of the Condor.

Vinaro and Romulo stepped out of the Command Rover. Romulo cradled in his arms a Thompson submachine gun. Vinaro had his microphone—the same with which he had blared directions to his mountain climbers. This time he shouted into it so loudly that all that came out of the loudspeaker atop the cabin was a blare of grating static—a dragon's roar. Mr. Train came walking up from the foot soldiers to the left. Romulo nervously motioned Vinaro to move the microphone farther from his face. He did so, and the thunderous shout came out intelligibly:

"I DEMAND THE UNCONDITIONAL SURRENDER OF TUCUMAI!"

Opposed to these attackers was the entire population of Tucumai, ranged about the great pool, between the small Temples of the Sun and Moon. In front of the latter the Moon Maidens stood, the white jaguars among them; in front of the former, Herdin and the young men of the valley—muscular, arms folded across their chests, nearly naked. Among these was Ramel. The balance of the people were gaily clad and smiling.

The first rank consisted of eight of Manco Capac's black-clad Thinkers with the old chief himself on their right in his silver and undyed robe.

They looked thoughtfully at Vinaro's men and at his three vehicles.

Then the nine of the first rank began to walk forward.

They walked at a steady pace. Their faces were impassive, but their eyes seemed to grow in size. Their people behind them smiled.

Other Thinkers watched them from their dormitory between Tarzan's prison and the cliffs.

Tarzan and Sophia watched them through the bronze bars of the prison.

They simply strode forward, a rank of nine men, obviously unarmed. But with them, from the massed Tucumaians behind them, and from the whole valley, went a beauty, an acceptance, a friendliness, a love that was a power real as a wind. A power that could penetrate the knotholes in the frightened, greedy, gold-hungry, selfish minds of Vinaro's men and their lieutenants and bring coolness and peace.

Deadly weapons drooped in the hands of their holders. All three crewmen climbed out of the tank, staring. Mr. Train, walking forward to join Vinaro, returned the automatic he held to its holster and gazed forward very thoughtfully, as if at a phenomenon whose existence he had no more suspected than Galileo suspected nuclear physics. Romulo's Thompson pointed at the ground.

Hard to tell what mistake Manco Capac made, if there was a mistake. Perhaps his rank marched too swiftly or too slowly. Perhaps the sight of the nearly naked Moon Maidens aroused desires that were vicious rather than loving. Perhaps there was too much gold in sight—especially when it winked in the first sun rays from the larger Temple of the Sun at the end of the two-mile avenue leading west from behind the pool. Perhaps the black tunics of the Thinkers suggested the black robes of priests and so awoke varying sorts of resentment.

Or perhaps it was simply that Manco Capac overlooked that Vinaro was psychotic.

Sophia said to Tarzan, "I think they're going to make it."

The first of the Thinkers to the left had already disarmed the foremost of Vinaro's men on that side, gently taking from him his Sten, his revolver, his knife.

The ranks of the other Tucumaians began to move forward, too, in particular, Herdin and his young athletes.

Suddenly Vinaro snatched Romulo's Thompson from him.

A little afterward he boasted to Mr. Train that it was the most difficult thing he ever did in his life, like conquering paralysis.

He pressed the trigger and whipped the dirty black weapon almost drunkenly from right to left, shooting off its clip of 20.

Some slugs ricocheted from the flagstones; others buried themselves in the graveyard of the human beings and airplanes. Vinaro himself jerked with the recoil.

But five of the Thinkers were felled, blood spurting from their black tunics, while Manco Capac was knocked down by the impact of a crease-wound in his left arm.

Two other Thinkers fled toward their dormitory.

Sophia pressed her hands to her eyes. Tarzan watched impassively.

Fog began to form instantly in the plaza. There was a faint blurring of all figures and buildings, while the palisades walling the valley grew dim. Tarzan, imprisoned, remembered his arrival at the village of the Guaporés.

Vinaro's men, shocked at the shots, stared at each other groggily, fumbled at their weapons.

The Thinker who had disarmed one of them jammed the muzzle of the Sten he was holding into the dirt of the Graveyard, then faded back.

From in front of the Temple of the Moon, the white jaguars—two score of them—raced screeching toward Vinaro's right wing, where the tank was. In the thickening mist they looked weird and deadly.

From in front of the Temple of the Sun, Herdin and his youthful horde sprinted forward, too. Their expressions were strange, as if they did not know whether they were going to fight or simply render aid to Manco Capac and the fallen Thinkers. Ramel raced with them.

The white jaguars leaped at the gangsters. This touched off shooting. Also, one of the crew members had leaped back into the tank, which suddenly fired yellow roaring flame with a great WHOOSH into the midst of the animals. Long white hair burst into flame.

Sophia, beside Tarzan, screamed, *"Tiger!"*

Yet a dozen of Vinaro's men were fiercely mauled, clawed, and bitten before the remaining jaguars tore off through the Graveyard.

On the right wing, Herdin and his youths were met with clubbed weapons. Here Vinaro's men, still somewhat dazed by the power that Tucumai had put forth, had not regained the will to kill, at least with bullets. Yet mere clubbed steel could do damage to bodies unarmed even with sticks. The youths fled in the fog. Herdin and Tegno, racing toward Vinaro, were subdued by three adversaries apiece. Two more grabbed Ramel.

The other Tucumaians fled to their homes up the terraces. They dashed inside. Somewhat belatedly, at Vinaro's order, the Panther swiveled around and shot at the pastel homes with the cannon and the two Besas. But most of the Tucumaians had dropped down the "dry wells" in their homes—truly, primitive atomic shelters—and were safe. The walls battered away by the cannon shot showed only empty rooms behind them.

A flock of vicuña came up to the fence in the south. Vinaro's nearest men let off a volley at them, thinking them more white jaguars. A dozen died. The rest trotted off squealing.

Despite the fog, Vinaro followed up his victory swiftly. The two Land Rovers drove up to the wooden stockade. Technicians clad in mottled green swiftly ran heavy copper wires around the wooden posts, eight inches apart, making a spiraling wall of wires from eight inches above the ground to a height of seven feet. The ends of this wire were attached to the generator of the Fuel Rover.

The captives—Manco Capac, shocked more than wounded; the struggling Herdin and Tegno; Ramel; five of the civilian inhabitants of Tucumai who had been slow in their escape; and seven of the Moon Maidens who had chased after the jaguars— were hustled into the stockade. The motor of the Fuel Rover began to chug. Vinaro demonstrated to the prisoners the killing power of the electrified fence with a sword cane which he unsheathed with a smiling flourish, then plunged into the earth against the bottom copper wire. There was a small spark when he did that. He held it there for five seconds by its dry wooden handle, then withdrew it and offered its blade, between the copper wires, to the nearest of the Moon Maidens. She touched it and screamed. It was almost red-hot. Vinaro smiled.

"Manco Capac!" he said softly. "I have come for your gold."

The old Incan, crouching in the center of the stockade, looked clear-eyed at Vinaro. He said, "The open door to your rear, white barbarian! Take it all and go!"

"I can promise the first, but not the second," Vinaro said suavely, strolling off toward the Treasury, surrounded by a dozen heavily armed attendants. With all the mottled green about, the plaza of Tucamai looked as if it had been invaded by bushes covered with fungus.

Tarzan had Sophia unweaving the mats on which they and the animals had slept and plaiting rope from the fibers. Undoubtedly it would take an extremely strong rope—probably much stronger than they could weave—to pull down at an angle after he had lassoed with its end the lever which had moved only at the weight of three Thinkers, perhaps 450 pounds. At the best angle he could manage, a pull at least twice that would be necessary. Still, it was a good idea to keep Sophia busy, and prisoners should always try to escape.

The Thinker-guard had fled when the first shots had come from the plaza.

Tarzan himself had been testing the strength of the thick horizontal bronze bars that were the front wall of their prison. He would grip a higher one, step on a lower one, and push with all his might. Finally he found a pair that seemed to give a trifle. After careful instruction, Dinky was persuaded to add his efforts to those of the ape-man. Closely side by side, they pushed fiercely, Dinky somewhat making up in length of arm what he lacked in torso and leg. Tarzan wished Major had hands and fingers instead of paws and claws. Perhaps…

The bars gave about a quarter of an inch each, then began to resist more strongly.

Soldiers of Vinaro entered the room, arranging themselves to either side of the door and aiming their submachine guns at the spaces between the bars. When a dozen had entered, Romulo came in, almost capering, cradling in his left arm a bundle of golden ornaments and in his right the Thompson. Vinaro followed him at a majestic pace, holding in his right hand a golden scepter topped by a spiked image of the Sun.

He smiled curiously at the bronze-barred cage. "So we find all the beasts together—the lion, the ape, the ape-man and the monkey-girl from the circus. They surely have a sense of fitness in Tucumai. Tell me, *chérie*, have you been diverting Tarzan by walking on your hands? Perhaps a competition between you and the chimp? And how in the world, dear, did you ever get out of that charming necklace I made for you?"

Sophia glared at him. "Tarzan with his bare hands ripped apart your puny gold, holding your explosive from jarring between his finger and thumb, with less fear of being burned than if it had been a cigarette butt."

Vinaro shook his head thoughtfully. "That hardly seems possibly, though Mr. Train did suggest a similar method. Never mind, I'll find out the truth—my intuitive powers have been wonderfully restored ever since I left that damnable jungle and arrived in Tucumai. Gold is a wondrous medicine, there is no doubt, and the closer one is to it, the greater its curative powers— did you know that one of the things the alchemists searched for was *aurum potabile*, drinkable gold? Next time I'll make you a more suitable necklace, dear, perhaps from stainless steel or wrought iron, which both resemble gold in resisting rust—they are an inferior metal's attempts at grandeur. But come now, Romulo—convey these two new prisoners to the stockade. I have certain divertisements in mind. I fancy two or three of you pulling on that lever over our heads will open the door."

He walked to one side, gently swinging the golden scepter as if it were a stem of goldenrod.

"Okay," Romulo said, "you three jump for the lever when I tell you. You others cover 'em all in the cage. Now, Tarzan, Sophia—you two come out when the door opens. And *just* you two. If the lion or chimp make a move for the door, they'll be cut in half—and you two! Ready now!"

In that fashion Tarzan and Sophia were conducted down to the copper-wired stockade. There were never less than three guns at Tarzan's back and always several men between him and Vinaro.

The plaza was still eerie with fog, though now some of the heat of midday struck through it. The nearer buildings—the prison, the Treasury, the small Temple of the Sun—showed quite clearly, but the farther ones—the Dormitory of the Thinkers, the Temple of Cupay, the Temple of the Moon—were only dim shapes; likewise the great statues on the island in the pool, and the terraced homes, some of them now broken-fronted. Here and there were greenish knots of Vinaro's men. The 16 prisoners stood or sat on the ground toward the center of the wired stockade.

Almost the only sound was the chug of the Fuel Rover's motor putting electricity through the wires. A faint stench of exhaust fumes mingled with the fog.

Vinaro walked up to the stockade, switching his golden mace close to the copper wires. "Old man," he called to Manco Capac, "I am happy to tell you your offer is adequate. That is a pretty roomful of golden trinkets." He gestured negligently with the mace toward the Treasury, the gold hardly an inch from the copper. "It will preserve your life for twelve hours. In fact," he added, all the greed in the world on his face, "*it will do for a beginning*, old man."

"A beginning?" Manco Capac asked, his old face haggard. Herdin, Tegno, and Ramel stood strongly around him. "Oh, you told me, Tarzan—Atahualpa!"

Vinaro nodded, bowed, and smiled malignantly. "An apt parallel, *Senhor* Beast-man," he said to Tarzan. Then, to Manco Capac, "Yes, old man, now I want to know where *all* of your gold is!"

Manco Capac said, touching his bandaged wound, "But the gold in the big building which you have just inspected is *all of it*—except the fraction we use for religious purposes. We were ready to *give* it to you."

Vinaro bowed neatly, his head almost brushing the copper wires. "Thank you for your generosity," he said, "but your accounting is incomplete. I have my own Domesday Book. We also desire not only the gold on your temples, but also the gold on your people, who seem to have hidden themselves in holes under their homes, along with your remaining temple girls and those black-clad ones who are such troublemakers. We require the gold on all of them within six hours—in other words, by sunset. By the same time I want a beginning made on stripping the gold from your temples."

He turned toward Sophia. "Meanwhile, we have another prisoner to join the sheep. No, Romulo, don't bother to turn off the current, just throw her in—she is an acrobat. Ah, here comes Mr. Train—belatedly—to help you!"

"Yes, sir," said the giant, looming out of the mist. "But may I first place a strong detachment at and above the cave-mouth and also send a large squad to hunt down the remaining black-dressed persons who may somehow be abetting this fog?"

"You may not, Mr. Train," Vinaro said. "Division of forces—remember? See, we have caught Tarzan here without giving you any detachment of forty men plus a helicopter. Also, I have a rather special sort of work for you this afternoon. But first, the girl."

While three submachine guns and a pistol menaced Tarzan's back, Sophia was brought forward in her mottled-green garb. Tarzan kept watching covertly for his chance. If he could kick Vinaro against the copper wires he flirted with— If he could grab any weapon and throw it against the bottom wire to short it— But there were too many guns, too many of Vinaro's men. No, he must watch this insane scene play itself out, always awaiting the unexpected, always awaiting opportunity.

Romulo with grinning pleasure kicked Sophia's legs from under her and snatched them by the booted ankles. Simultaneously Mr. Train strongly grasped her wrists. They swung her twice, then tossed her over the copper wire—by her colors, a lunar moth. Herdin and Tegno caught her, as if it were, weirdly, some rehearsed adagio act.

Vinaro grinned very broadly for once, showing his china-white dentures, inset in gold with the letters of his name. "Neatly done," he said. "Once a circus performer, always a circus performer, eh, *chérie*? Now we shall occupy the afternoon with somewhat more serious athletic exhibitions. There is a tedium in life now I have reached Tucumai. I desire strong diversions.

Mr. Train!" He turned toward the giant. "I have not seen you kill a man for two months." He listlessly waved his spiky golden scepter and sat himself in a canvas chair, facing the pool—a chair which Romulo abruptly produced for him.

Tarzan thought—how like the Roman emperors: Tiberius, Caligula, Nero, even Sublatus.*

Vinaro looked up at Mr. Train. "Dear servant," he said, "it is my pleasure that—in preparation for the main event of the afternoon—you warm up on these two natives." He motioned toward Herdin and Tegno.

Herdin and Tegno, getting the meaning, glared.

Tarzan tensed himself.

Vinaro said, "Keep a very close watch on the ape-man during this match."

Mr. Train looked at Tegno and Herdin, his glance troubled, and then back at Vinaro. "Excuse me, sir," he said, "but they seem very poor sport. And there is work to be done."

"Your work is to serve me! Always—as you promised when I procured your release from the cells of Franco!"

"You also promised at that time, sir, that you would never mention the last matter."

"I have been forced to this afternoon."

"Very well, sir, I will serve you this afternoon."

Staring impassively at Herdin and Tegno, like one of their own Thinkers, Mr. Train removed his hat, coat, and shirt, revealing his almost incredibly huge, powerful, hairless body. Captain Voss would have been reminded of the jade idol of Siva he stared at before he was blasted. The giant removed his boots and stripped to his calf-length jungle pants. Tarzan was impressed. Here was no muscle-bound strong man's body, but a great lithe machine for killing. Tarzan knew the karate physique well enough, having once interviewed its greatest Japanese master to further his own knowledge of karate and also of ákido—the higher art by which the momentum of a fighter's blows are used to lead him to his undoing, as when

---

* Whom Tarzan encountered in *Tarzan and the Lost Empire* (Tarzan 12).

a deadly punch is transformed by a "pull along" into a fall deadly to the striker. Was there something in ákido of *Matar nunca*, he wondered, irritated that the idea should be so obsessive.

Vinaro snapped out, "Romulo! Shut off the electricity! A dozen guns on the stockade—never forgetting to cover Tarzan—while those two savage wrestlers crawl out between the copper wires! Now, Mr. Train, are you ready to compete with these two men? I am told that they are the strongest in the Valley of Tucumai."

"I am ready," Train answered, flexing his thick, long muscles.

"Which would you care to fight first?" Vinaro asked.

"If it's all right with you, sir," Mr. Train answered, "both of them. Though even that does not make it a fight."

"Both it shall be," Vinaro decreed harshly. "Don't be so dull, Mr. Train. I expect entertainment."

Herdin raised a hand toward Manco Capac. "Do you allow us to fight him, Lord? Fight him truly?"

The old Incan nodded his head. "It is permissible, so long as you use no weapons."

Mr. Train glanced down at the edges of his hands and smiled faintly. "I would agree to that, too, oh, Manco Capac," he called, "except that, as it happens, I *am* a weapon."

"Enough!" Vinaro ordered. "Electricity in the fence! Guns on Tarzan! Ten soldiers before the pool! Ten soldiers before the Graveyard! Shoot down either Indian who tries to pass you! Begin!"

Colonel Juarez peered most cautiously over the green ridge at the blasted and trampled group of thorn trees before the jagged-edged cave mouth showing the marks of two dozen cannon shots.

"The entrance to the caves," he whispered to Captain Lobos on his right. "See, the vehicle tracks go no farther."

"*Mãe de Deus*, you are right," the captain replied. "They all go into the caves."

"It is like the tale of *Ali Baba*," Duarte murmured from Juarez's left, "except that Vinaro has nearer one hundred and forty than forty thieves."

"It is my judgment," Captain Lobos whispered, a shade severely, "that Vinaro will have left a rear guard here, if anywhere, or at least liberally dug the area before the doorway with land mines."

"So do you suppose we should say, 'Please don't open, sesame,' as we advance?" Duarte asked.

Juarez looked at the older man coldly. "You are not only a romantic, as Dr. Bragança said, but a comic romantic, such as is rather out of place so far from the opera stage. Captain Lobos, have we any who can lob grenades as far as the cave mouth?"

"I can," that one replied.

"Then lay a pattern of six. We can hardly spare more of our twoscore."

The blasting-off of the grenades awakened Lionel Talmadge, who had been snoring on the hillside a few feet behind Juarez, who had laid him down there.

"Tucumai?" he demanded, jackknifing up. "Vinaro?"

"Not quite yet, professor," Juarez told him. "But we *are* testing out the mouth of Ramel's caves."

The fragments dropped and the dust settled from the grenade blasts. There was no sign of action ahead.

Juarez said, "Very well, with you six covering us to the cave mouth"—he indicated the men—"let the rest of us advance."

Duarte added, "Our blasts having given warning to any ambush party well inside the cave."

"Romantic optimist!" Juarez reprimanded him.

CHAPTER 23

Karate versus Tarzan

Mr. Train spread his great legs in a karate stance with legs and thighs nearly at right angles to one another, the left leg and foot directed toward Herdin and Tegno.

Mr. Train seemed, in assuming the stance, to be sitting in mid-air, almost as if there were some rigid support beneath his buttocks, so straight and stiff was his torso.

He also seemed to have put off absolutely the feelings of uncertainty and troubledness Tarzan had felt weighed on him.

He thrust his huge arms into attacking position, the left thrust forward, fully extended, the right slung back, cocked against his ribs. His hands balled into fists, the second joint of the middle finger pointing from each.

"At your service, gentlemen!" he called to Herdin and Tegno who were standing perhaps 20 feet away, looking at him puzzledly and with the beginnings of apprehension.

"Gentlemen, we mustn't keep Mr. Vinaro waiting," announced Mr. Train. "It seems hardly my duty to attack, since I am outnumbered. Also, it would be admitting that you were fit sport for me. Attack!"

Tegno and Herdin flashed looks of uncertainty at each other. This great pale-skinned giant in his alien, slightly absurd pose seemed so confident, so certain of an easy victory. And this was not the sort of combat the Incans were used to. This was not wrestling, where one gripped and tugged, using all the skills of leverage. This was like fighting with swords or clubs—so solid and threatening did those huge bunched fists seem—and even clubs involved skills of which they had no knowledge.

Also, fighting to the death was something they had been trained against since infancy.

"Come, gentlemen, do your worst!" Train went on more sharply. "If you have hidden weapons, produce them! If you can find rocks, throw them! All's fair in free-style karate. Only gather your courage, if you have any, and attack!"

The Incans still hesitated.

Mr. Train inched forward, flat-footed, his large, squarish calloused toes gripping the ground to fix his balance.

"Cowards!" shrieked Mr. Train, and at the same time, stomped the ground with his left foot.

Almost in the same motion, Herdin and Tegno lunged forward, Herdin seeking to grapple with Train's arms and Tegno tackling below.

But Mr. Train had anticipated their rush. Almost negligently, yet with blinding speed, he shifted laterally left, and kicked upward his long right leg along a powerful arc, catching Tegno across the chest and flinging him into Herdin, who was slightly above and behind him. The Incans, like a team of acrobatic clowns, were flipped over onto their backs by the force of the blow.

"Bravo, Mr. Train," said Vinaro, more flushed with victory than Train himself. "Truly, Tarzan, is he not a wonderfully efficient fighting machine?"

Tarzan gazed calmly at Vinaro. "And more than that," he said, "he has a sense of humor. That was a very witty maneuver."

"*Touché*, Tarzan! But on to the kill, Mr. Train."

As Herdin, then Tegno rose dazedly to their feet, Mr. Train turned his back to them in order to face Vinaro directly.

"Sir, this is a sorry exhibition at best. These boys can be slaughtered in dozens of ways. I have just thought of a method which is perhaps the most dramatically pleasing, sir. With your permission—"

Mr. Train swiftly approached Vinaro and with delicately-poised thumb and forefinger, lifted Vinaro's handkerchief from the breast pocket of his coat. He then strode to the center of the circle of soldiers, paused, and without glancing at Herdin and Tegno bound the handkerchief around his head, directly over his eye patch and his good eye.

"Perhaps, gentlemen, this will slightly reduce the odds," announced Mr. Train. "At any rate, it may summon up more courage on your part."

At this, something began to stir within Tarzan, the beginnings of a raging passion to humiliate this man who was so disgracing his newfound friends.

"Gentlemen," called out Mr. Train in an imperious tone, "I cannot see. Come and kill me!"

Squatting low, he again assumed his fencerlike stance, his long left arm, around which corded veins wound like snakes, thrust before him like a muscular shaft, and his right hand clenched at his waist.

This time Tegno and Herdin positioned themselves to either side of the giant and slowly, almost without a sound, began to close in upon the immobile figure.

Suddenly, sensing that the Incans were within striking range, Mr. Train began a whirling, twisting series of movements—cutting the air with heavy blows from fists, forearms, and elbows. As he spun around nearly full-circle, he also swatted outward with lightninglike kicks. In addition, he made what Tarzan discerned were defensive maneuvers, as when Train for an instant crouched almost double, his massive forearms shielding his face and his knees protecting his crotch. So quick were his movements that they melted into a blur into which Herdin and Tegno sprang headlong.

A sickening thud, a *woomph*, and another thud were perceived by the waiting groups of soldiers outside the circle and Vinaro. Only Tarzan, whose alert eyes had never left Mr. Train, saw clearly what had occurred through the growing mist.

Tegno had been rendered senseless by a kick, Train's heel having caught him squarely in the forehead. Herdin had first been doubled over by a tremendous "focus" punch to his abdomen from Train's right fist, then received a mighty jolt on his jaw as the giant followed through and over with a swinging elbow. Both Incans lay supine and motionless on the ground, their faces frozen into expressions of wrought agony.

Then, almost imperceptibly, Herdin's left hand flinched and his stomach muscles fluttered ever so slightly—or so it seemed to Tarzan. Perhaps Mr. Train had "pulled" his punches and kicks by the merest fraction, had softened the impact ever so little, but enough to spare the boys' lives. Why? Could there be such a thing as pity in Train's character, he wondered. Or had Tucumai and its Thinkers undermined the drives of even this murder machine?

On the other hand, Vinaro's men, even Romulo, guffawed at the sight of sudden death, delivered as if to stockyard cattle. While the people in the stockade, saddened and sickened by the brutality, turned away. The Moon Maidens, and Sophia, too, covered their eyes.

Vinaro, however, rose from his canvas-backed chair, which was so like that of a movie director, and said, "Excellent! Superb! Mr. Train, that Death should be as blind as justice is a grand concept, providing sublime entertainment. I forgive you your surliness. Romulo, get rid of those!" He pointed at the bodies of Herdin and Tegno.

Mr. Train, who had removed the handkerchief from his brow, raised an arm in protest. "Pardon me, sir," he said, "but I will attend to that."

Stepping swiftly, he went first to Herdin, then to Tegno, lifted each up under an arm, and walked to the edge of the Graveyard. The submachine-gun-armed, green-mottled soldiers parted before him. The giant let the two bodies down among the flowers.

"Come, come, Mr. Train," Vinaro, impatient, ordered in short staccato bursts. "You have served us an hors d'oeuvre— now the entrée!" He settled back languidly into his chair, and Mr. Train, returning from the Graveyard, stood at an attentive pose before him.

"Your demonstration of the *kata* maneuver has surely warmed you up." The tone of Vinaro's voice was almost mocking. "Now it is the fabled Tarzan's turn—and keep your guns on him, you guards! Tell me, Tarzan, before you face Mr. Train and die, what fate befell my lovely Lincoln and my most expensive Messerschmitt helicopter. I'm truly curious about that."

Tarzan shrugged and smiled disarmingly. "You only made the mistake of hiring slightly inexpert drivers," he said. "Unluckily, one of them encountered a rhinoceros, the other a couple of big birds that got themselves entangled."

Vinaro grinned. "You Nordics always fall back into fantasies. Birds—the giant roc, I suppose—and a rhinoceros! Well, if those are bad luck, your own good luck has run out. My command to you is to seek to kill Mr. Train. But please, do not die easily. I enjoy the sight of a lingering death. Kill him slowly, Mr. Train—*slowly!* Romulo, place five more of your men on either side, and five before the Temple of the Moon—the fog is growing thicker."

As the soldiers took new positions, the giant nodded to Vinaro and gave exactly the same curt, decisive nod to Tarzan. If Train had felt any compunctions during the first bout, they were gone now, the ape-man knew.

He also knew that he was about to engage in the most dangerous hand-to-hand combat of his entire career. If anything could match animal instinct, it would be the years-long training in speed and reflexive suddenness of the *karataka*. And Mr. Train seemed to be that rarity—a big man who has not relied on his size, but rather sought to make himself the equal of small men in agility, balance, and velocity.

Mr. Train on his part had measured Tarzan's abilities. There would be no question of prolonging this bout—whatever Vinaro, in his growing megalomania, demanded. He must kill as quickly and perfectly as possible this talking being who was not only a man, but also, in some fashion, an animal.

They faced each other five yards apart—the bronzed, muscular, rangy, black-haired figure in the loincloth and the huge, pale-skinned bald man in the close-fitting, green-mottled, calf-length pants, almost a head taller than Tarzan and outweighing him by more than 50 pounds.

The fog was indeed getting thicker, so that the soldiers completing the square were blurred and the figures inside the stockade dim ghosts.

As if to make his nod crystal-clear, Mr. Train said softly, "I've wanted to kill you ever since I started on this expedition. You have been a tactical thorn in our side, but more than that, you've presented a technical challenge to me ever since I watched you in the ring at Meseta: the challenge the naturally gifted amateur presents to the trained and educated professional."

Tarzan noted the tall, sleek column of muscle beneath Train's arms extending from armpits to waist, the *latissimi dorsi*, flutter. They were the true source of strength of the trained *karataka*, he remembered. The ape-man hissed, "You cannot defeat me, Train!"

"Ah, you are defeated already, Tarzan!" Mr. Train announced succinctly. As if to emphasize his words, he took a squatting crouch and looked Tarzan straight in the eyes. Suddenly his single great amber eye became wider, gave forth an almost luminous, malignant light. Tarzan, against his will, felt himself retreat an inch, then another.

At that moment Tarzan recalled a conversation with Matsu Hirokoshi, the oldest living *karataka*, the master whom Tarzan had visited in Japan many years before.

"You have come here to learn, my son," the wizened tough proud-looking ancient had said, as he sat with legs crossed upon a woven mat in his modest home. "That is good. But perhaps it is I who should call you Master, since you could teach me much of the jungle and the ways of its inhabitants. The mastery of my art requires much training, great patience, and long dedication. It is the study of a lifetime. For karate involves not only training the muscles, but learning to discipline the mind as well."

Tarzan had said nothing. He had been interested in the

Eastern forms of hand-to-hand combat, and this rare audience with the acknowledged master of karate had cost him greatly in time, money, and inconvenience.

"There are the true *karataka* and there are those outriders of the cult who practice it for their own material gain and personal ennoblement," Hirokoshi had continued. "The self-styled professionals! We hate them intensely because they demean the very central ideas and intents of our search."

Tarzan had noticed that Hirokoshi's soft brown eyes had suddenly been charged with an eerie light. The Master's voice had hung like gently tinkling crystal in the fresh breeze that coursed through an open window.

"Remember, my son, when attacking, to consider yourself as an old tree. An old tree in the forest about to fall and die. Remember, as the old tree knows, that death is the only certainty and that it is not to be feared. Proceed with a glad heart. Your house, your innermost being, is in order. Your conscience is cleared of all offending thoughts, all evil desires and passions."

Hirokoshi had paused and gazed at Tarzan intensely.

"You are intelligent, my son, but in some ways as innocent and naïve as a child. I trust you not to use any knowledge you have gained here for bad reasons, for *professional* purposes! Ah, with your spirit and character, you could become the greatest fighter of this age…but I caution you, once more, to use this knowledge only in the most extreme crisis, for men are never the same after they have become aware of their powers, and sometimes it corrupts…"

All these things were recalled to Tarzan as he faced Mr. Train's single, glittering amber eye.

"Professional!" Tarzan cried. "Your mind is full of the dry-rot of corruption. YOU CANNOT WIN!"

As the ape-man bent swiftly to the ground, somewhat obscured by the fog, Mr. Train's eyelid blinked over its fierce orb. The effect was that of a shutter thrown down over a brilliantly lit Coleman lantern.

"This is not a football game, Tarzan!" he said somewhat nervously. "Get up! What are you doing there? Come and fight!"

"I am ready," Tarzan said. "Attack, coward!"

Train crossed the intervening five yards between them with lightning speed, intending to cleave Tarzan in half with a blow to the stomach.

"*Diieee!*" Train screamed, expelling all his breath with the tremendous punch.

With animal quickness that even the most highly trained *karataka* cannot quite achieve, Tarzan sprang to his left away from the punch. As Train's heavy fist glanced off the ape-man's right ribs, he clutched the giant's head and mashed a handful of dirt into his one eye.

Train scrabbled backward and pawed at his face. He uttered a terrifying scream of mixed rage and frustration.

Tarzan was shaken, almost stunned by the force of Train's glancing blow. From the great ache in his side, little needles of pain worked their way up the length of his back and down again. His ribs felt as if they had been struck with the head of a 14-pound sledgehammer. Nevertheless, he forced himself to close with the staggering, momentarily blinded giant before he could recover.

Quickly, but with terrific force, Tarzan brought his closed fist down upon the bridge of Train's nose. As Train opened his mouth to gasp for air, Tarzan jerked his left knee into the giant's unguarded crotch. Train doubled over, emitting an agonized grunt. Tarzan, coldly wondering how any man could maintain his balance after receiving such punishment, measured Train off and delivered his right fist fully into Train's gaping mouth. The crunchy splintering of teeth seemed only to further arouse the ape-man's blood lust. Yet when Train lurched backward and fell onto his back, Tarzan did not attack him. He was aware that the giant could still deliver killing blows even thus reposed, and he was taking no chances.

What a sight faced Tarzan as the giant, a tottering figure

whose one dirt-smeared eye seemed to sag in its socket, rose slowly to his feet!

His nose—there was no longer a nose but merely a swatch of bruised flesh, blood, and bone splinters smeared over his face.

Train raised his hands in a mock caricature of his former stance and staggered toward Tarzan.

But now Tarzan had maneuvered the fight into the exact part of the plaza he wanted.

"Hey, *toro!*" he yelled. "Certainly, Train, even a sick, corrupt animal like you has an instinct to survive. Come and kill me!"

The giant came at him with a lunging rush, at the last lowering his great bald head to butt, while his horn-edged hands went up like actual horns, defending temples and neck.

Tarzan feinted to his right, then merely stepped swiftly to his left as Train plummeted past him.

The plaza was flagged around that area. There should have been the sound of Train recovering from his plunging thrust.

Instead, Mr. Train had simply disappeared into the thick fog without a sound.

Into the unwalled well that had gradually been forgotten… by all but Tarzan.

Vinaro called the soldiers in, so that they circled Tarzan closely, and he rushed up incredulously himself—after Romulo.

Tarzan said, breathing heavily, "It is a well…that goes down… to unknown…central depths. Ask Manco Capac." He stared steadily at the astonished Vinaro. "Yesterday Moon Maidens… dropped flowers in it. It is the well…of the virgins. But I thought it appropriate…for Mr. Train…because it is also… the Well of Cupay!"

Tarzan saw pallor and a thrill cross Vinaro's face at that last word. The small man's hair, cut *en brosse*, actually lifted. His eyes grew wide and staring, his mouth slack. He peered forward toward the misty depths fearfully, yet thoughtfully.

He murmured, "Mr. Train. Cupay. But Mr. Train! You do not know quite how appropriate, Beast. I have called Mr. Train the Galahad of Murder, and Galahad was a virgin. But Mr. Train!"

Romulo grated, "Shall we kill him, sir?" His submachine gun was leveled across the well at Tarzan.

Vinaro shook his head. "I must think…Take five and conduct the Beast back to his cell with the other animals. Springer, get climbing tackle and De Ville—this well must be explored. For Mr. Train…and Cupay! The rest of you follow me to the stockade."

Solemn horn notes, like the lowing of cattle, but more rhythmic, sounded as Vinaro and his cortege of gunmen reached the stockade and saw beyond the copper wires set eight inches apart the haggard, accusing faces of Manco Capac, Ramel, and Sophia. The horn notes echoed and reechoed over the chugging of the Fuel Rover that was putting electricity into the wires.

Vinaro stared about, seeking their source. He finally faced the flowery Graveyard and, beyond it, the homes of Tucumai, only the first two terraces of which could be distinguished in the fog.

"What is that sound?" he demanded.

From behind him the voice of Manco Capac came effortfully, faintly, yet distinctly. "The bronze horns of my people. They would parley with you."

"Tank!" Vinaro commanded. "Train your guns on the terraces!"

A motor of the Panther kicked into life long enough for it to take a swinging step with its treads, facing its cannon and its Besas the way Vinaro wanted.

Tarzan was marched close past the stockade by his guards to the small prison building. He was thinking of how brutally he had defaced Mr. Train—an end to all *"Matar nunca!"* precepts. Yet he had let the battered man fall to his death, rather than kill him.

Sophia and Ramel watched the ape-man. Ramel moved forward, almost blindly. Sophia caught him by the shoulders. "Don't touch those wires," she reminded softly.

Ramel said, "He is brave. He killed the giant. They are locking him up."

Sophia whispered, "It may be we can release him. If we lie by the wires, pretending to sleep, and scrape the dirt away gently…"

Ramel whispered back, "Even the two of us together could not work the lever."

Sophia answered as softly, "Let us first escape, then find the answer to the next problem. That would be Tarzan's way. Your Tarzan."

From the fog where the horns had sounded came a voice calling in strange syllables like swift-flying exotic birds.

"What does he say?" Vinaro demanded.

Behind him, Manco Capac translated, "He says that if you don't release us and go away, taking if you will the gold in the Treasury, our people will attack tonight."

Vinaro gave a short laugh. "Attack with what?"

Manco Capac answered sadly yet proudly, "With their bare hands if they have to—as Atahualpa's knights defended him to the death at Caxamalca."

Vinaro said, "Cold steel and hot lead have always been a sufficient answer to bare hands. Don't worry, old man, I'll arrange a suitable welcome for your people. In fact, I shall unroll a welcome carpet, if you understand my idiom."

In the caves, Juarez and his group followed the false track down the corridor roofed with glittering stalactites that now showed so many gashes and rips, while the rocky floor was strewn with their fragments like glass.

Professor Talmadge, holding onto the shoulder of a trooper as he tottered along, looked up at the tattered, silvery-golden ceiling and said, "It is as one dreams of the entrance to Tucumai. Almost too perfect."

Duarte looked with wrinkle-nosed distaste at the scattered corpses of Vinaro's men, slain by monoxide and stalactite fall.

"What an untidy, unhygienic fellow this Augustus is," he remarked. "Well, there's no digging graves in rock with spades."

"Or time for attempting it, my dear undertaker," Juarez told him. "I fancy we are about, at long last, to run ahead of his leavings and catch up with Death himself."

Sunlight had drained out of the thinning fog and night was seeping into it as Herdin awoke among the flowers, his head ringing from the great blow that had put him out. He did not move a muscle until his mind was fully aware of what had happened up to the moment of unconsciousness and until he had guessed where he lay. He had for some minutes been aware of Tegno's heavy breathing beside him. Now his fellow Tucumaian began to stir and groan. Herdin gently clamped a hand over his mouth and whispered into his ear, until Tegno understood the situation and was able to move. Then very slowly they began to worm their way through the flowers toward the terraces.

Through a gap between two stones bordering the wings of the A-20, Herdin looked back at the weird dimming scene on the plaza he had known as the world's center during his whole life.

A great white light was suspended on a tripod ten feet above the Outer Well of Cupay and glared down it, as if it wanted to shine to the center of the world. Ropes seemed to go down into it, too, and a man at the mouth was calling down the shaft.

The stockade was unlit. He could make out people in it, but not well enough to tell if Manco Capac, Ramel, and the stranger woman were still among them.

He saw no sign anywhere of the giant who had felled Tegno and himself.

The Cupay-Beast squatted darkly on its endless, knife-nailed paws in front of the stockade, pointing its mismated empty eyes straight at him, he thought.

Cupay's Fat Wife, also looking his way, still crouched by the stockade in front of the prison. And she was still muttering in the stenchful fashion that meant she was letting flow the killing milk that flowed through the wires around the stockade.

Cupay's Other Wife crouched near the Well of Cupay. She muttered, too. In a flash of intuition, Herdin wondered if she was making the light that went down the well.

The small evil one who had brought all this horror to Tucumai was standing in front of the open door to the Treasury, outlined by the lights inside, as if he were Manco Capac himself dispensing justice. Most of his men stood in front of him. He seemed to be giving them orders. With a final loud phrase he pointed at the Graveyard—or, for all Herdin knew, at himself. The men began to move this way, some taking things from the back of Cupay's Other Wife.

Herdin watched no longer. He whispered tersely to Tegno, and they crawled swiftly toward the terraces.

CHAPTER 24

Electricity and Land Mines

Nightfall brought a complete change in the weather. The fog had gone, but low clouds that ran in frighteningly symmetrical ribbons from north to south were steadily moving in from the west. The moonlight striking between them striped the Valley of Tucumai, giving that ovoid expanse the appearance of a sleeping silver tiger.

Entering the small, barred window of Tarzan's cell, the moonlight illuminated the mask of the lion Major, making him, too, a silver beast. His head rested upon his paws, but his eyes were open and roving.

Tarzan stood at the bars of his cell, his forearms lightly resting on one. His face was in gloom, his features barely perceptible to the one observer.

The one observer was Vinaro, who stood inside the doorway to the building, having just ordered out the guard who had been watching Tarzan to make sure he made no further attempts to bend the great bronze bars or to escape in other ways—such as somehow lassoing the bronze lever that slanted upward, out of the wall four feet below the slanting roof.

Vinaro was silent. Tarzan matched him. Finally Vinaro said, "Today you cost me the best man I ever had. They're three hundred feet down in the Well of Cupay and still haven't found bottom, not even a handhold. Strange, eh?"

Tarzan shrugged. "If Mr. Train was your idea of a best man, I must criticize your taste, though my ribs still feel like stone from the jolt he gave them. He had a little warped honor, I believe, and some sanity, but he was fundamentally nothing but a paid murderer."

"You do not understand these things," Vinaro said patiently. "Mr. Train stood at the top in the great profession of killing. Of all the great assassins, spies, and counterspies—"

"Your attitude disgusts me!" Tarzan interrupted. "Informing, spying, counterspying, and assassinating are *not* professions, no matter for whom they're done! They do not deserve the dignity of that designation. They are things a man may sometimes stoop to, if he must, but never be proud of afterwards. They corrupt more than power does, because they are nothing but *secret power*."

Vinaro shook his head. "A strange attitude for someone who has killed as often as you surely have."

"Never but by necessity!" Tarzan answered. "Never but as the lesser of two evils!"

"Strange for a beast-man, also," Vinaro continued in the same mild tones. "Beasts have murder built in."

"Beasts kill for food or to avoid becoming food! There are also battles for shes. But killing for power is man's special insanity."

There was a pause. A ribbon cloud passed over, and the place grew dark. Vinaro said quietly, "I am unhappy in this place. My remaining lieutenants are stupid, however skilled and efficient. As always, my victory has proved trifling. The gold, such as it is, has given me back some of my insight, yet…"

His voice trailed off. It came to Tarzan, without great surprise, that Vinaro had come to him for sympathy, for understanding. The fiend was lonely!

This was borne out when Vinaro said softly, ingratiatingly, "You, Tarzan, could be a far greater Mr. Train. You have tasted all of life, I believe. But I could open to you the Second Horizon. I could show you the true beauties of Death, the majesty, the wonder—"

"No!" Tarzan snarled out without pausing to consider

whether it mightn't help to play along. "You and I are enemies forever. And as for your Religion of Death, I spit on it!"

Major growled faintly.

Vinaro let out a great sigh, then drew himself up and said snappingly, "Very well! But you will nevertheless soon have to witness one of its rites. Your savage friends have promised to attack us tonight to try to free the old man. My men are preparing a surprise for them. They are sowing that flower-grown Graveyard with land mines. Look, you can see them at work now! When your friends come rushing across it with the rocks or sticks—or whatever it is that they intend to drive me off with—I have seen their ridiculous Room of Broken Weapons—then they'll blow themselves to pieces! The bones and memorials of the dead will rise up to destroy the living! It will be beautiful to watch!" His voice rose hysterically. "It will quell my melancholy and inspire me to devise *your* fate!"

He turned on his heel and strode out. Tarzan realized that the man was not only a homicidal maniac, but was growing more deranged by the minute, now that he had reached his goal and lost his mental companions…and perhaps the Thinkers of Tucumai were playing some obscure part, not to mention how the philosophy of this city must grate against Vinaro. Passive resistance…a kind of äkido, one could hope.

Yet out there, true enough, were more than half of Vinaro's men, sweatingly busy with lights and shovels. How Vinaro could think the Tucumaians were so stupid as not to suspect a trap!—and in any case it was like trying to kill flies with a sledgehammer. Yes, this was perhaps like äkido—Vinaro drawn to expend his power in sprawling thrusts.

Vinaro ordered the guard back inside. The man obeyed somewhat surlily, sitting down, his back against the wall, with a grunt of fatigue and laying his Browning automatic rifle beside him.

Outside the other guard was saying, "But, Mr. Vinaro, you've had me on duty thirty-six hours."

Vinaro snapped, "I am on duty eternally. Not a sparrow falls, except because I strike it down. Do not anger me with your womanish weakness, Gabin!" Then he strode off.

Tarzan considered the inside guard. The ape-man had finished braiding into a respectable lasso the rope Sophia had started. But if this guard persisted in sitting with his head against the wall, he could hardly toss a lasso over it. And this man could not be drawn into conversation or movement—Tarzan had learned that earlier.

Then he remembered the flint in his loincloth. It weighed four ounces or a bit more. As the ribbon-cloud passed and the moonlight came again, he sat back in the dark corner of the cell and began braiding the end of the lariat around the flint.

In the stockade Sophia and Ramel lay by the depression they had gradually scraped out in the earth below the lowest wire. Some of the Tucumaians stood around them concealingly.

"It's deep enough now," Sophia said, her whisper blanketed by the chug of the Fuel Rover. "I'm going to go when the next cloud comes."

With a small bronze knife carried by one of the Tucumaians, she had chopped her hair short and slit her skirt front and back, pinning it around each of her legs, so that in her mottled green garb she might at least have a chance of passing as one of Vinaro's men. She had, however, taken off her boots and was barefoot.

She lay on her back with her head toward the wire. Straining her eyes upward, she could see its deadly moonlit glint a little beyond the narrow blurred gleam of her eyebrows. She remembered how she had looked down at death on her chest in the jungle. But this new risk she was running of her own free will.

"Let two or three of us go with you," Ramel whispered. "It takes the weight of three men to work the lever."

"Any of you would be noticed at once outside the stockade," she whispered back. "Dressed as I am, I can get through. And I can work the lever alone—you must trust me. As soon as

Tarzan is loose and the wires are safe—*he* will know how to do that—lead Manco Capac and the other prisoners swiftly out behind the Treasury. Here comes another shadow. Take my feet now and *push*!" She helped with her elbows.

Her breasts cleared the copper wire by two inches, her pelvis by one. Two seconds later she was on her feet and moving through the darkness.

Tarzan had his weapon ready now and was waiting for the right moment to use it. He could see the outside guard slouched a dozen feet beyond the door, his back turned, silhouetted by the lights of the men planting mines in the Graveyard. And although the darkness would have seemed to most men absolute, he could also see the inside guard, still open-eyed and watchful, his hand on his Browning, sitting with his back to the wall.

Then he caught the scent of Sophia. A second later a slender shape appeared silently in the doorway, having moved along the outer wall without attracting the attention of the outside guard.

Tarzan's right arm made a long, swift, backhanded sweep. The braided lariat flew silently between two of the horizontal bars, and the flint tied at its end struck the skull of the sitting guard like the thong of a cracked whip, but with only a hollow *thunk*, and then returned silently with the lariat between the bars as Tarzan swept his arm back. He caught the flint in his free hand. The entire stroke had been calculated to an inch and even the force of the blow predetermined—enough to bring unconsciousness, but not the convulsions of a serious brain injury.

Sophia slipped inside. The outside guard straightened, looked around, waited a few moments, then shrugged and resumed his original position.

Without a glance toward Tarzan, Sophia walked to the wall under the lever and sprang up and grasped it as gently as if her hands were two moths alighting. The bronze lever remained motionless, and there was not a sound from the mechanism it worked. She chinned herself, got a knee over the thick bronze, and with a sudden effort thrust herself upward, straightening her arms. Still no sound or motion from the lever. On her hands, she walked out on the upslanting lever for a few feet from the wall, then began to swing her legs from side to side in greater and greater arcs. Suddenly they flipped all the way, she dropped her body until her chin was an inch from the lever to compensate, her bare feet found the rough stone at the ceiling with the faintest brush and stayed there.

She was now standing on her hands, arms bent, on the bronze lever, while her feet pressed against the ceiling.

Still the lever stayed motionless, nor did its mechanism make a sound.

Tarzan watched her from beside the door to his cell. The moonlight came again. Major roused and padded up to the door itself, but in utter silence, so that Tarzan's barely breathed *"Tand-panda!"* was not needed. Dinky's face—ape-fearful—appeared in the barred parallelogram of moonlight Major had just quitted.

Handgrips changing by six inches at a time, Sophia walked out along the bar to its end. There, keeping her feet firmly against the ceiling, she straightened her arms and bent her legs. Then with her arms stiff, using her stronger leg muscles, she pressed with all her might against the ceiling.

Coming from her diaphragm, her breath sighed forcefully through her nostrils. Her upended head pounded with its load of blood. Nevertheless she focused her muscular effort and pushed steadily.

The bronze lever moved down a fraction of an inch, then a larger fraction. Her legs straightened as it began to move more swiftly. Tarzan noted the locking bars of the cell door ascending into the ceiling and descending into the floor. Sophia gave a final shove against the ceiling and then dropped limp, at the last moment doubling her arms and putting all her weight and downward momentum into a final jerk on the descending lever.

The locking bars vanished. The door opened…with a clank.

The outside guard turned and came toward them with startled, stiff-legged strides.

"Major, *bundolo!*" Tarzan commanded.

In a huge, bounding leap the lion hit the guard as his gun loosed three ricocheting shots against the stone floor. Instantly following the *cracks*, there was a crunch as Major's teeth met in Gabin's face.

Tarzan raced past Sophia, still clinging to the lever, and Major worrying at Gabin, with only this message to the former: "Lead the prisoners toward the pastures as soon as I break the connections!"

The ape-man dashed down the steps, sprang into the empty cabin of the chugging Fuel Rover, put it in gear, and started it crawling toward the Graveyard, its treads moving faster and faster.

From the men still planting land mines among the flowers there came cries of, "What's he doing?" "He better keep away from here!" "Hey, keep off! Turn off!" and finally, "Run! He's coming straight through!"

The cables between the Fuel Rover and the copper-wire fence parted.

Tarzan set the throttle a notch higher. A dozen yards short of the Graveyard, he sprang from the cabin. Hitting the ground at a run, he slowed and turned himself in four steps and headed back toward the stockade.

Vinaro raced out of the Treasury where he had been brooding over the gold, took in the situation with all his old quick grasp, and bellowed, "Tank! About face and kill the prisoners in the stockade! Flamethrower!" The man on watch in the turret relayed the orders, and the Panther's motors roared into action. It began to swivel around, kicking earth.

Urged by Ramel and Sophia, the Tucumaians were crawling between the now harmless copper wires.

The Panther had turned almost halfway when there were flashes of gunfire at the cave mouth and a score of slugs *zinged* off its armor. Juarez's party had at last got through the caves. But with the slugs went, from the Simonov antitank rifle, a most lucky 14.5 mm shell which exploded in the viewslit, killing the Panther's driver, though leaving the two other crew members uninjured. The man in the turret dropped down it, to escape the unexpected shots.

In the flowery Graveyard the careening Fuel Rover hit the first of the land mines. In the blinding flash, the driverless vehicle bucked and changed course. Three more mines went up. Concussion felled running men. Others, running away, trod on the mines they had just dug in and were blown up by them. The slowing, crippled Fuel Rover hit two more mines. Then its gas tank split in a deafening roar and with a great gust of flame that illuminated the whole plaza brighter than day.

CHAPTER 25

To Kill a Panther

Vinaro raced down the steps of the Treasury toward his stricken tank. A quarter of his force destroyed in the Graveyard, his Fuel Rover gone, the prisoners escaping from the stockade, a new hostile force appearing at the cave mouth, Tarzan and his lion on the loose, the Panther paralyzed—all these things released the master criminal from the intolerable burden of his victory and set his genius afire once more. He scampered as recklessly and happily as if he were a boy again, determined to return an impossible lob on the tennis court.

He whipped out his Smith and Wesson .38 and took potshots as he ran—more to fix in his mind the elements of the situation than in hope of hitting anything. He fired at Major, still worrying Gabin on the prison steps; at the prisoners slipping through the wires of the stockade—he killed a Moon Maiden dressed in lacy silver; at Tarzan, racing like a bronze flash toward the stockade; at the gunfire flashes at the cave mouth; even at stupid Romulo, who stood gawking beside the Well of Cupay—that shot happened to shatter the searchlight going down the well.

Slugs from the cave mouth zinged close past him. Then the tank was between him and that particular source of death. He raced toward its beloved silhouette, scrambled up its side, and dove down its turret amid another harmless volley from the cave mouth.

The cabin of the Panther was full of fumes and defeat. The dead body of the driver was still slumped on the saddle.

305

Vinaro jerked him off and settled himself on the blood-covered leather. His fingers brushed the controls as if they were the beloved parts of a woman. His eyes grew larger as they scanned through the view slit. He screeched at the twittering, explosion-shocked crew members, "Jackson, the Besas! Girodeaux, the flamethrower! First we destroy the lion. Aim at the prison."

The tank began to caterpillar in that direction.

Vinaro was thinking, *Did not William Blake say that the tiger's brain and sinews and heart were forged and born of furnace, not of female? Does not the iron cat always best the fleshy feline?*

Duarte, a .38 slug in his chest, laid down his Moisin carbine on the parapet of the cave mouth, settled himself as comfortably as he could, and remarked with some difficulty to Colonel Juarez on his right, "*Aii*, Carlos, this hurts! Now someone will have to dig *my* grave." The big blast of the Simonox on his left prevented speech for a moment. The trooper who had taken the antitank rifle's recoil grunted. "*Maldição!*" he said. The one who steadied the rifle's bipod support held out to him another shell. Colonel Juarez ducked down to put another clip in his Llama. "How goes it, Duarte?" he asked.

"Carlos," the other answered, "I am an aging man. Aging *very* rapidly at this moment, I fear. Yet I have seen more wonders in this little trip than in the past ten years before. One thing let me tell you: blood spurting from the pierced heart feels like high fever. Women and wine and laughter. A warm vanishment." His eyes closed.

Tarzan shouted to Major, "*Numa, gom!*"

The great golden lion let go of Gabin and loped off just before the Besas pocked and the flamethrower blackened the facade of the prison.

The prisoners—Manco Capac, Ramel, Sophia, and the rest—were escaping around the Treasury, toward the west.

Tarzan deliberately stayed at the back corner of the prison, his only escape route to the east.

"Hai, Katze!" he screamed at the tank and made faces at its two terrible eyes, the one with the filament of the flamethrower glowing red-hot in it. At this moment the beast-half of his mind was sufficiently in control so that it seemed quite proper for him to scream at a German tank in German.

Then he dodged behind the prison just as the Besas began to bark and the flamethrower growl thunderingly, belching a mist of burning napalm in the space where he had been. He meant for the tank to pursue him rather than the slower-moving prisoners hurrying behind the Treasury along with Major. As he paused at the next corner of the prison, preparing to lead the Panther back to the plaza between it and the Dormitory of the Thinkers, he noted six black-tunicked figures crouching on the roof edge of the latter building and facing northwest toward the smoldering flaming Graveyard.

The ribbon clouds had broken up, and the atmosphere over Tucumai was a confusion of low churning vapors lit on the underside by the flames and with a great hole in them over the plaza where the hot trapped gases had burst upward.

Vinaro delighted in the power and speed of the Panther—the way it snapped the posts of the stockade like twigs and slashed the copper wire with its knife-edged treads. He had driven the tank before, but only for recreation—this was real! As he rounded the prison, he saw the figures on the roof and commanded, "Jackson, elevate the Besas!" and he had the satisfaction of seeing three of them fall before he saw Tarzan again, mocking his vehicle.

"Depress the Besas! Flamethrower!" he cried and took up again the chase of the ape-man. The passage between the Dormitory and the prison was barely wide enough for the Panther. As his great metal beast emerged into the plaza, he had a momentary impulse to crush the party in the cave mouth, but instead he turned left after Tarzan, his primary target. *Crush the enemy leadership,* he told himself. His view slit swung past the dark Temple of Cupay and the long stretch of terraced homes, their pastel hues fitfully lit by the dying flames in the Graveyard. Ah, there was Tarzan, once more darting around the prison. The Besas smote dust and rock chips from the plaza a couple of yards from the ape-man's feet. Vinaro accelerated the vehicle close to its top of 30 miles per hour. Once more there was the pleasure of snapping off stockade posts. He had the momentary impulse to order the cannon fired at the statues on the island in the lake. But there was Tarzan again, this time darting up to the stairs to the Treasury. Now he had him! Once the beast-man went under that great square arch, there was no escape—except down the Inner Well of Cupay, as sheer a shaft as that of the outer. How fitting if Tarzan shared Train's fate! He ordered the flamethrower. Girodeaux's response was instant, and the great gush of orange flame showed the ape-man dashing under the huge archway and almost licked his heels.

With delight Vinaro sent the Panther lumbering rapidly up the steep steps after him, unmindful of the couple of little high-explosive shells which burst against the back of the Panther from the Simonov rifle, though both Girodeaux and Jackson winced at the shell's jolts and cursed frightenedly.

With the Panther's nose in the antechamber of the Treasury, Vinaro ground the vehicle to a halt. Now *he* felt himself an animal, a dinosaur, *Tyrannosaurus Rex*, determined to gobble this Tarzan. He peered carefully to either side. No, the human beast did not seem to be hiding behind either group of statuary, neither the Sun-Moon-Venus Trinity nor the Thunder-and-Lightning demons. Two quick *whooshes* of the flamethrower made sure. *Ah, I breathe like a dragon,* Vinaro thought.

Then he advanced with a grinding of treads into the second chamber, the one containing the golden treasures. Here he let the flamethrower roar to either side for a longer period—until the surfaces of the golden objects began to melt and run, and the lighter of them leaped up like leaves in the blasts. Too bad to destroy such art, but Tarzan might be hiding behind them.

Then he turned toward the huge door leading into the Room of Broken Weapons.

Tarzan, who had been hiding in that last room all this while, breathing air that grew hotter and more acridly stenchful every moment, now jerked out of the counterweight the block with the black handhold and sprinted past the Panther on its blind side, the one toward which it was turning.

A solid stream of cold molten silver gushed out of the square hole the block had plugged—it was mercury, quicksilver, a stuff 13½ times as heavy as water, spurting out in a shining, thick rectangular rod that went straight for six feet before it began to curve toward the floor, and decreasing the mass of the counterweight by hundreds of pounds a second.

The Panther automatically fired at it. The quicksilver splattered in silvery sheets and spray; it vaporized in the breath of the flamethrower.

Then the entire counterweight began to move upward more and more rapidly. With it, the mercury stream went out of range of the guns and flamethrower. It deluged the tank with silver which splashed off in a profusion of gleaming beads.

Meanwhile the outer door was descending from the ceiling as swiftly as the counterweight was rising. Tarzan had to dive under it into the antechamber, like a baseball player barely getting home without being tagged out. Two seconds later the ten-foot-thick rock door came down with a stony *CRAAASH* that shook the whole Treasury.

Tarzan staggered to his feet, then reeled into the wing of the antechamber holding the statues of the Incan Trinity.

And just in time!—for a burst of small-arms fire came from outside, pocking the newly fallen door that sealed in the Panther.

Tarzan sought refuge under the statues. They might be some protection if the whole roof caved in.

There still sounded, dully through ten feet or more of rock, the explosions of cannon and machine gun fire. Evidently Vinaro was still madly firing off the Panther's guns, possibly in an effort to break down the walls.

Suddenly those same walls rocked. Vibration transmitted through the stone stung Tarzan. From the hairline cracks, ten feet deep, around the door there came a brilliant, thin, rectangular flash of light, 20 feet by 200.

If Sophia had been there, she would have thought of the death of Captain Voss in *his* locked room. From where she now crouched, in the pasture land by Ramel, it only seemed that the Treasury grew infinitesimally larger for an instant before there came the sound of the blast.

Almost certainly the Panther, struck by a ricochet of one of its own shells, or by a throwing back of its flame, had been blown up by its own fuel tanks and ammunition.

Probably if the explosion had not had the Inner Well of Cupay down which to vent itself, the mighty building would have been blown open.

But as it was, it stood firm, a Panther's tomb.

Romulo, though momentarily stupefied by the sudden turn of events, had come to his senses quickly enough—no physical shock could stun that *mameluco*'s brain for long—and taken charge of Vinaro's remaining shaken forces with speed and rough authority. By the time the Panther was trapped he had 60-odd men gathered near the Temple of the Moon—the survivors of the Graveyard mine explosions and men on other duties. Half of them were well-armed and there were heavy machine guns near at hand on the Command Rover. It was easily a large enough force to take over Tucumai despite Colonel Juarez's 15 soldiers.

It was this group which had fired at Tarzan.

Romulo was giving orders for the taking of Tarzan and the attack on the newcomers now ranged around the Temple of Cupay as well as in the cave mouth, when a cook named Piresi pointed east and screamed.

The weather had changed again.

Coming across the moonlit plaza from the direction of the Dormitory of the Thinkers were scudding low compact clouds having the shape of huge jaguars, spiders, serpents, and centipedes—not perfectly formed illusions, which might have seemed ridiculous, but ragged and irregular, as if indwelling animal spirits were forcing the clouds to take their shape.

An automatic burst of fire at these clouds did not break them up, but only illuminated them more frighteningly. Many in Romulo's group shot out the clips or loads of their guns. Some ran; others huddled wildly, clubbing their weapons at the sky.

At the same time there came a silent-footed, well-disciplined rush of 200 male Tucumaians from behind the House of the Maidens and out of the orchards, led by Herdin and Tegno. They fell upon Romulo's soldiers, tackling and butting, before any of them could sound a warning. A half dozen Tucumaians fell to gunfire, a couple more were clubbed in the hand-to-hand struggling, and then Romulo's force had been disarmed and overpowered. Herdin had the personal satisfaction of wrestling Romulo to the ground with such force that the fall knocked out the *mameluco*'s breath and left him writhing.

The battle of Tucumai was over.

CHAPTER 26

The Legend of Tucumai

Late next morning the visitors to Tucumai were finishing dining at tables set in a horseshoe before the Temple of the Moon. They had feasted copiously on roast peccary, llama chops and leg of llama, tortillas, thicker corn bread, potatoes, puddings of manioc and of guinoa rice, bananas, pineapples, and other fruits, all washed down with *sora*, *maté*, and llama milk.

A report had just been brought to Manco Capac that the walls of the Treasury, abnormally hot to the touch at dawn, were at last growing cooler.

"It will be some trouble, I should think, raising the Treasury door again," Tarzan commented conversationally to the slim old patriarch, who looked as if he had completely shed last night's events, despite his bandaged arm. "That quicksilver surprised me as much as I imagine it did Vinaro. I just pulled the black-handed block and hoped."

"My dear chap, quicksilver always goes with gold and silver," Professor Talmadge put in talkatively. "It's the stuff the Spaniards used to dissolve silver and gold out of their rock mixtures. Makes an amalgam with the noble metals—teeth fillings, remember?— and then you press out or boil off the mercury." The old Britisher looked gaunter and his eyes blacker-circled than ever, but he was grinning toothily. He had breakfasted mostly on *sora*.

Manco Capac said, "I do not think we will try to raise the door, while I have a say about it. Those alluring and deceiving metals are best shut up, until all men can look on them as no more than flowers."

"Yet they are so very beautiful," Sophia said wistfully.

"And so gracious to the hand of the craftsman," Juarez seconded her.

"Also, it's a shame that your Museum of Broken Weapons shouldn't be open to the public, Manco Capac," Talmadge rattled on. "That Panther tank is a notable acquisition!"

Manco Capac frowned slightly. "I believe we have agreed, have we not, that the only public involved will be the inhabitants of Tucumai?"

All around the table nodded quickly and earnestly. At a more solemn meeting before the meal it had been decided that every attempt must be made to keep the existence of Tucumai a secret from the rest of the world.

Relenting, the old Incan chief said graciously to Talmadge, "It grieves me, professor, that you will not be able to stay on and study my people as an anthropologist. I can understand the blow to you as a scholar."

"Think nothing of it, old chap," Talmadge assured him glibly. "It will be my pleasure to know that the culture of Tucumai is maturing as it should—in complete isolation from the corrupt outer world. From time to time I will look at my maps—at a certain unmarked spot in the Land of Mists and Mirages—and say to myself, 'There's something, now!'"

Captain Lobos waved a hand out across the plaza, saying, "I wonder, however, how *those* can be kept from talking about Tucumai…and also plotting to return."

In the stockade, most of its posts snapped off now, there sat dispiritedly the remains of Vinaro's army—about 70 men. Around them were ranged eight of Juarez's force. A heavy machine gun was trained on them to emphasize the futility of any attempt at escape.

Colonel Juarez said, "After their imprisonment or deportation, they can talk as much as they want. Who will believe them?

Remember, we are all pledged to tell even Brasília that Tucumai is a myth."

Tarzan said, "I doubt if any of us will find it easy to return to Tucumai once we are away—especially now that the city has back its map." He looked at the beaming Ramel, who wore proudly on his chest the golden medallion which had been discovered in the Command Rover. "Vinaro's trail will be overgrown in a matter of weeks. Besides, Manco Capac and I have decided on one further device for the protection of Tucumai. No, I cannot tell you yet what it is."

Herdin said, frowning as he chose his words, "Too bad you cannot stay in Tucumai, who served city so good."

Tarzan smiled. "Major and Dinky may stay here—that is, if Manco permits."

"Tarzan, that will be wonderful!" Ramel burst out.

"It is permitted, my son," the old Incan confirmed.

The lion and the ape, who were both stretched out, well-fed, near the tables, seemed to grin, as if understanding.

Colonel Juarez said solemnly, "There is *one* who will stay here in any case."

Other faces grew grave and there were nods. All had heard the story of Duarte's death.

Manco Capac said, "He shall be buried beside Hugh Malpole—one more outlander who served Tucumai better than most of her sons."

The silence that followed was broken by a high drumming. Golden vanes flashed in the still air, and there descended from the sky the first airplane ever to land safely in Tucumai—a helicopter. It came to rest not far from the tables, its vanes slowed, and before Lieutenant Fontoura could leave the controls to help her, a small, bent figure in denim jungle garb stepped spryly out.

As Dr. Maria Bragança hobbled briskly toward them, she looked about her saying, "So this is fabled Tucumai! One gets to see strange places in one's old age if one has wanderlust. One hopes still stranger places remain. Colonel Juarez! Your man is safely recovering from his curare poisoning—and from your dose of chloral, Professor Talmadge! Ah, colonel, *obrigado!*"

She sat down in the place Juarez had vacated and made herself acquainted with Sophia. Soon the two women were talking quietly yet animatedly together. Tarzan noted that the lady physician's silver hair exactly matched that of Manco Capac and that also there was a marked facial resemblance between the two. He decided there were many more mysteries to Tucumai than those he had solved.

Lieutenant Fontoura walked up to Tarzan and handed him his suitcase. "See, *senhor*, we have kept it safe for you all this while. Professor Talmadge was most particular in his instructions."

To Tarzan that neat gray case, breathing Bond Street, looked the most incongruous object imaginable.

"I trust," he said, a shade embarrassed, "I will be forgiven if I don't at once put on my tweeds."

"Lieutenant, I fear you may have given our benefactor a false impression," Juarez said hurriedly. "I am sure we all agree that Tarzan is welcome to stay in Brazil forever!"

"Hear, hear!" Talmadge approved, rapping a golden goblet with a silver spoon.

"Or in Tucumai, my son," Manco Capac assured the ape-man. "You have served the city immeasurably and given me much food for thought. Our Thinkers will have to reexamine the whole question of fighting." He shook his head sadly. "Sometimes, perhaps, one has to use violence."

"I'm not so sure of that," Tarzan told him, "at least for Tucumai. You almost defeated Vinaro without a physical wound given or taken. And—"

Talmadge interrupted, "And whatever mental illusion or feat of psycho…psychokinesis your Thinker chaps managed with those clouds last night, it was brilliant! Utterly unbelievable— don't believe it myself—but brilliant!"

"Vinaro's men believed it," Juarez put in dryly.

Tarzan went on to Manco, "And considering Vinaro's mania and the weapons he had, remarkably few lives were lost."

"You are kind, my son, and tactful," Manco Capac answered. "I sometimes think that the oldest civilization is that of the beasts. If the felines are not civilized, by their facial appearance, who is?"

Tarzan said seriously, "I could have done little for you, Manco Capac, had not good friends given me heroic aid. The Panther would have shot and flamed you dead had not Colonel Juarez, Professor Talmadge, Captain Lobos, and their men labored every moment for days to bring that Simonov antitank rifle to the point where they did at the first possible moment—which was also almost the last possible moment."

"*De nada,*" Juarez muttered, while Talmadge rambled, "Oh, come now, Tarzan, that's rot, perfect rot. We just wandered around in the jungle like a pack of bloody idiots…"

"I beg your pardon, *Mestre*—" Captain Lobos began with an edge on his voice.

"*Also,*" Tarzan interrupted loudly to stifle this dispute, "I could never have reached Tucumai except for the help of my young friend Ramel." The boy beamed. "Nor," he went on, "do I believe that the party of Colonel Juarez could possibly have followed my trail so swiftly except for the keenness and dedication of the two Chavante Indian guides, Apoena and Ataúl!" He extended his arm to the full across the tables to where those two naked savages, rosy as newly scrubbed copper, sat grinning with Herdin and Tegno.

"Finally," Tarzan said, and here he grew a shade abashed, "I could never have escaped from my prison and played any part at all in the battle of Tucumai except that a certain young lady"… he looked toward Sophia without meeting her eyes—"under constant threat of gunfire and in depleted physical condition, performed the grandest feat of acrobatics I have ever seen a woman manage in my life!"

Sophia was ahead of the applause. And she was laughing, "I have done the same feat for *lire* and less in Naples!" she said.

"My, we are all modest here!" Dr. Bragança observed loudly. Then in an undertone she remarked to Sophia, "You're in love with him, aren't you?"

"Yes," Sophia responded quietly, "but he has a wife in England, you know."

With her spidery hand, Maria pressed the girl's.

Lieutenant Fontoura went on to Colonel Juarez, "Brasília is sending three helicopters tomorrow to the village of the Guaporés. They will bring in guards for the prisoners and help us evacuate the wounded. They seem to have no clear idea of what's been going on here, but they are eager to be helpful. You *are* planning, aren't you, sir, to march back toward the Guaporés village this afternoon?"

"*Por Deus,* yes," Colonel Juarez told him. "With the prisoners, too—every last soul."

Professor Talmadge grumbled, "I think it's a mistake, letting the government forces get so close to Tucumai."

"Lionel," Juarez said patiently, "we can tell Brasília that Tucumai is a city in Tasmania, and I am sure the bureaucrats will believe us absolutely—and be much relieved!"

"One more matter," Lieutenant Fontoura said, crossing once more to Tarzan. "I have a cable for you, sent to Cuiabá."

Tarzan read it aloud: "'*Amigo,* I was just awarded a tail and 10,000 boos in Cuidad Mexico. Have you cut any ears in the Mato Grosso? Manolecito.'"

Tarzan laughed. "I will have quite a story to tell that *hombre* someday," he said.

Three hours later Tarzan sat beside Colonel Juarez as that worthy drove the Command Rover at a steady clip through the caves leading out of Tucumai.

Lieutenant Fontoura had evacuated by heli four seriously wounded persons direct to Cuiabá. Among these was Professor Talmadge, asleep from an injection of morphine after Dr. Bragança had diagnosed his case as acute exhaustion complicated by too much *sora.*

The prisoners had been marched through the caves an hour before, guarded by Juarez's group under the command of Captain

Lobos. With them went liberal rations of food from the people of Tucumai.

Tarzan, still in his leather loincloth, the beautifully tooled gray leather suitcase leaning against his knee, was making in his mind a preliminary summing-up of his adventure and his reactions to it.

Certainly he had gained some great new friends in Brazil and Tucumai: Ramel, Manco Capac, Herdin and Tegno, Jovanna (mustn't forget her), Duarte (too bad he had barely met him), Juarez at his side, and the two others sitting behind. Even Mr. Train, in a very crooked way. And he had become acquainted with a great country and a great hidden culture. He would have a great deal to tell Jane and his children…as well as Manolecito!

He had had demonstrated to him once more the truth of the platitude that money is the root of all evil. At least when it took the form of gold. Pizarro or Vinaro—the viciousness was evident.

He had also learned, more fully than ever before, that to kill for gain, whether privately or corporately, whether in peace or war, was pure evil. Matsu Hirokoshi, Manco Capac, the SPI were all together there.

Matar nunca!—that was a tougher problem. Certainly he had killed enough men this trip: Cabral and the Duccio brothers at the car-wash, the nameless American at the camp of Rodriguez, the three men in Vinaro's Messerschmitt helicopter, and Mr. Train. And that didn't include the three men Major and Xima had killed, more or less at his order, nor did it count Vinaro and whoever had been with him in the Panther. Though Vinaro and his tank crew had certainly done themselves in—it was ridiculous to blame himself there.

The others he had killed in self-defense, or in defense of Tucumai or Ramel. His conscience was clear there, or pretty clear.

Somehow Mr. Train bothered him the most. There had been elements of greatness in that man—he had deliberately spared Herdin and Tegno. Yet there was no question that he had intended to destroy Tarzan with his stomach punch…or that

Tarzan had given him a chance of life by letting him fall into the Well of Cupay.

Morrer se preciso fôr, matar nunca! A great motto! But how many men could live up to it? And how many villains might not try to take advantage of it? A most knotty problem.

Suddenly Tarzan began to chuckle. Here he was, a mortal man, albeit a long-lived one, thinking he could solve the riddles of the universe. What egotism!

Under cover of that long chuckle, Dr. Maria Bragança, sitting behind Tarzan in the cabin of the Command Rover, said to Sophia Renault, "Do you plan to return to Europe?"

The slim blond girl shrugged. "I don't know. I have jewels enough from Vinaro, concealed here and there, to go three times around the world. But I don't have a strong impulse."

The older woman said, "Then why not stay in Brazil? It's the biggest country there is. I know a girl named Jovanna who could certainly get you a job with the airlines."

"I'll think about it," Sophia replied.

Dr. Maria Bragança pressed her hand.

The Command Rover debouched from the caves into the grassland and went a hundred yards.

Tarzan said, "Carlos, stop awhile. I'll be back in twenty minutes."

The ape-man lifted from a compartment in the Command Rover a black leather attaché case edged with silver.

Sophia Renault sloped away from it in horror.

"It's the last time you'll see it," Tarzan assured her, carrying it with him out of the vehicle very carefully.

He was back in 15 minutes or less.

"Obrigado," he said to Juarez. "Let's move on."

There was a CRAASHING explosion from behind them that shook the Command Rover, sound-conditioned as it was.

Tarzan, half-turning in his seat, explained, "I collapsed the entrance to the caves of Tucumai. Maybe, if they're not found for a long time, the rest of the world will be able to catch up with them."

Juarez said, "I bet you Ramel will climb the inner walls of the Valley of Tucumai within ten years."

"Maybe that will be time enough," Tarzan responded.

About Edgar Rice Burroughs

The creator of the immortal characters Tarzan of the Apes and John Carter of Mars, Edgar Rice Burroughs is one of the world's most popular authors. Mr. Burroughs' timeless tales of heroes and heroines transport readers from the jungles of Africa and the dead sea bottoms of Barsoom to the miles-high forests of Amtor and the savage inner world of Pellucidar, and even to alien civilizations beyond the farthest star. Mr. Burroughs' books are estimated to have sold hundreds of millions of copies, and they have spawned 60 films and 250 television episodes.

About Edgar Rice Burroughs, Inc.

Founded in 1923 by Edgar Rice Burroughs, one of the first authors to incorporate himself, Edgar Rice Burroughs, Inc., holds numerous trademarks and the rights to all literary works of the author still protected by copyright, including stories of Tarzan of the Apes and John Carter of Mars. The company oversees authorized adaptations of his literary works in film, television, radio, publishing, theatrical stage productions, licensing, and merchandising. Edgar Rice Burroughs, Inc., continues to manage and license the vast archive of Mr. Burroughs' literary works, fictional characters, and corresponding artworks that have grown for over a century. The company continues to be owned by the Burroughs family and remains headquartered in Tarzana, California, the town named after the Tarzana Ranch Mr. Burroughs purchased there in 1919 that led to the town's future development.

In 2015, under the leadership of President James Sullos, Jr., the company relaunched its publishing division, which was founded by Mr. Burroughs himself in 1931, continuing a long tradition of bringing tales of wonder and imagination featuring the Master of Adventure's many iconic characters and exotic worlds to an eager reading public.

www.edgarriceburroughs.com
www.tarzan.com

PELLUCIDAR

Sci-Fi

BOOK SERIES #5

A Soldier of Poloda

By Lee Strong

FURTHER ADVENTURES
BEYOND THE FARTHEST STAR

Worlds at War! American intelligence officer Thomas Randolph is teleported from the World War II battlefields of Normandy into the belly of the evil Kapar empire on the planet Poloda. The Kapar's only passion is to conquer and destroy the outnumbered Unis forces who had been engaged in a century-long struggle to survive. Rechristened Tomas Ran, the Earthman now understands that the same fierce determination to defeat Hitler must now be used as a weapon to defeat the fascist Kapars – a merciless foe bent on global domination.

Available at www.ERBurroughs.com/Store

CPSIA information can be obtained
at www.ICGtesting.com
Printed in the USA
BVHW071428181220
595416BV00012B/199/J